"You can tell me,"

Daniella pulled away. "Tell you what?"

"Why you're so afraid."

He thought she was going to leave the hospital room without replying until she said, "I just hate bombs, that's all. They're so indiscriminate. So lethal."

Isaac nodded. "This one wasn't much, if that helps any."

The heartrending look in her emerald green eyes penetrated his defenses despite his strong resolve. It had been a long time since he'd seen that much poignancy and sorrow in a person's gaze.

This shy, quiet woman had given his heart a twist without saying a word.

Why is she so afraid?

Valerie Hansen
and
New York Times Bestselling Author
Lenora Worth

Keeping Guard

Previously published as *Detecting Danger* and *Proof of Innocence*

HARLEQUIN® LOVE INSPIRED®CLASSICS

 LOVE INSPIRED BOOKS

Recycling programs for this product may not exist in your area.

ISBN-13: 978-1-335-08185-8

Keeping Guard

Copyright © 2018 by Harlequin Books S.A.

First published as Detecting Danger by Harlequin Books in 2015 and Proof of Innocence by Harlequin Books in 2015.

The publisher acknowledges the copyright holder of the individual works as follows:

Detecting Danger
Copyright © 2015 by Harlequin Books S.A.

Proof of Innocence
Copyright © 2015 by Harlequin Books S.A.

Special thanks and acknowledgment are given to Valerie Hansen and Lenora Worth for their contribution to the Capitol K-9 Unit miniseries.

www.Harlequin.com

Printed in U.S.A.

CONTENTS

Valerie Hansen was thirty when she awoke to the presence of the Lord in her life and turned to Jesus. She now lives in a renovated farmhouse in the breathtakingly beautiful Ozark Mountains of Arkansas and is privileged to share her personal faith by telling the stories of her heart for Love Inspired. Life doesn't get much better than that!

DETECTING DANGER

Valerie Hansen

Fear not for I am with you;
be not dismayed for I am your God.
I will strengthen you, yes, I will help you.
I will uphold you with my righteous right hand.
—*Isaiah* 41:10

To my Joe, who is with me in spirit, looking over my shoulder and offering moral support as I write. He always will be.

ONE

"Capitol K-9 Unit Five, safety check at Washington Monument complete," Isaac Black radioed via the comlink he wore. "DC police are also on scene for crowd control."

"Copy," echoed back into his earpiece. "Stand by."

Isaac turned his attention to Detective David Delvecchio of the DC Metro squad and smiled. "You look like something's bugging you. What's the matter?"

"I'm just not fond of congressmen who throw their weight around and cause unnecessary overtime." He eyed the gaggle of news vans and cameramen surrounding Harland Jeffries. "If he wants to grandstand he should do it on his own turf."

"And preferably during office hours," Isaac added. He glanced down at Abby, his brown-and-white bomb-detecting beagle. She had stretched out on the grassy verge skirting the Washington Monument, panting and cooling off after the excitement of doing her job. "At least one of us is happy to be working tonight."

"Yeah. I'm sure glad we have you and the rest of the K-9 team on call. My men didn't have time to do a proper sweep of this area. By the time we got the word about the congressman's impromptu press conference, we only had an hour to deploy."

Isaac nodded. "Not to worry. If Abby says there's no bomb on the grounds, it's safe. You can trust her."

"I do," Delvecchio replied.

Curious tourists were gathering outside the police line, milling around and straining to get a peek at whoever was the center of attention. Politicians and their aides in dark business suits stood out against the colorful garb of the bystanders as Secret Service agents would have at a three-ring circus performance.

Isaac was about to withdraw to his SUV and wait to be released when he noticed his dog stiffen and ease to her feet. Since he had not given the command, her independent actions drew his attention.

"Abby?" He crouched, following the beagle's line of sight. She was clearly focused on the small group nearest to the congressman. "What is it, girl?"

Instead of relaxing, the dog froze in place, her hackles bristling. Her nose quivered. Her tail was half-raised and still. If they had not just completed a search of the premises Isaac would think…

He stood and grabbed the detective's sleeve. "Pull everybody back. Clear the area. Now!" Isaac's commanding tone left no doubt of his seriousness.

"Why? What do you see?"

"Nothing," Isaac said. "But Abby senses something's wrong and that's good enough for me."

Delvecchio was already shouting into his radio. Patrol officers immediately began to shoo bystanders farther away from the monument.

Isaac moved forward with Abby. "Seek it, girl. Seek it."

They didn't have far to go. The little beagle cut straight across the inner circle, zeroed in on a briefcase leaning against the base of one of the concrete benches that ringed the obelisk and plunked down into a sit.

"I have a suspicious object on the west side, at about two o'clock from the police staging area," Isaac reported via the com-link.

His new orders followed in moments. "Secure the area and pull back to a safe distance. Bomb squad is on its way."

"Copy."

He scooped up his dog, checked to make sure no one else remained nearby and would be in danger, then began to jog away.

As he ran, time seemed to slow unnaturally. His feet weighed a ton, making him feel as if he were slogging through cold molasses.

Tension grew with every step, pressing against him and making his heart pound.

Abby was trembling as though she sensed impending doom.

Suddenly, a concussion rocked the atmosphere. Isaac saw the flash through his closed eyelids an instant before he heard the blast.

Instinct made him hunch over his dog's body to protect her as he was knocked to his knees by the force of the explosion.

Most of the debris it created fell like fistfuls of tossed pebbles, but a few chunks of concrete were heavy enough, large and jagged enough, to do damage.

One piece grazed his shoulder. Another hit the back of his lower leg. Both stunned him rather than caused immediate pain.

How could this have happened? Abby is never wrong.

Which meant that the bomb had to have been placed there *after* he and the dog had made their rounds. That fact should narrow the list of suspects considerably.

Propping himself on one elbow with the other arm gripping his wiggling partner, Isaac tried to blink the grit from his watering eyes. Gray, cloudy residue filled the air. People coughed and wheezed. Many were in full flight while a few others had paused with cell phones to take macabre pictures of the chaos.

Isaac rolled into a sitting position and brushed himself off. He first checked to make sure Abby was all right, then peered back toward the source of the blast to check for casualties.

"Please, God," he prayed, "let my warning have been in time."

He rubbed his smarting eyes on the sleeve of his uniform jacket. It looked as if there were some injuries but the apparent victims were all on their feet. A few were reeling and being assisted by police and friends. Others appeared merely stunned. A cacophony of horns and sirens filled the night.

Ears ringing, head spinning, Isaac knew what he must do. There was no time to waste. Where there was one bomb there could easily be another. And another.

He wanted to lie back on the cool grass, close his eyes and wait for full recovery of his senses, but that was not how he and his fellow K-9 officers operated. The public came first. He'd tend his wounds later. As long as Abby was all right, they'd keep doing their job.

Isaac tightened up on the leash, struggled to his feet and took a step forward. His calf muscles knotted.

Intense pain radiated from his boot to his hip and dropped him where he stood.

The flow of patients through the ER at DC General Hospital had been surprisingly sparse for a balmy spring evening. Daniella Dunne stifled a yawn and smiled at a fellow RN who was also battling to stay alert.

"Every time we have a slow night I wonder why I like this shift so much," Daniella remarked.

"Because you crave adrenaline just like the rest of us," the older woman replied. "When this place starts to really hop we all feel a lot more alive."

"I suppose you're right." As far as Daniella was concerned, staying awake half the night was profoundly better than working days when so many more reporters and photographers were liable to be on the job. The last thing she needed was to become an unwilling star of some viral video. She'd matured and changed her hair color from blond to brunette, long to shorter, but that didn't mean she wouldn't be recognized by the same criminal element that had caused her to enter witness protection in the first place.

"Prepare for casualties," someone shouted. "There's just been an incident at the Washington Monument!"

Daniella froze for a heartbeat, then jumped to her feet and hurried down the hallway to the ambulance receiving area, where the majority of the night shift was gathering around a police scanner.

"Was it an accident?" one of the young orderlies asked.

"Doesn't sound like it. The first responders pegged it as a bomb," someone else answered.

Daniella clenched her fists. Her stomach churned. She suddenly saw herself as a frightened teenager again and pictured her father being arrested for the bombing death of her mother. Ten long years had passed since then, yet those terrible memories were as vivid as if everything had just happened.

Her initial disbelief about her mother's fate had quickly been supplanted with righteous anger, especially when she'd heard her estranged father begin to laugh. *Laugh!* And so she had done the only thing she could. She had mustered her courage and agreed to testify against him in court.

While most of the ER staff remained gathered around the scanner, Daniella eased away and headed for the hospital chapel.

Until the victims of this current attack arrived for treatment, the best thing she could do was pray. Fervently. The way she had prayed for her mother—even though she'd known in her deepest heart that Mama's survival was impossible.

Being incapacitated made Isaac frustrated and angry. He'd repeatedly waved off paramedics, sending them to tend to others. As the area was systematically cleared, however, he realized he was eventually going to have to let the medics look at his throbbing leg.

Detective Delvecchio approached. "I wondered where you'd gotten to. Is Abby all right?"

"Yes." Isaac tried to rise and was stopped by the other man's hand on his shoulder. "Relax, man."

"I can't. There's work to do. What if there's a second bomb?"

"If there is, your team will find it. Some of them are sweeping the area now. So far, so good."

Isaac heaved a sigh. "Thank God—literally."

"I have been. Particularly since there don't seem to be any life-threatening injuries."

"That's a relief."

"Yeah, and a surprise. So, are you ready to go to the hospital?"

The detective offered a hand and Isaac took it, grimacing as he rose. Standing wasn't too painful as long as he kept weight off his injured leg by leaning on David's shoulder.

"If you can make it to my car I'll drive you to the ER."

"That's against protocol."

"Your choice," Delvecchio said, arching a brow. "All the ambulances are busy. I consider this an extenuating circumstance, but it's up to you. Do you want to wait?"

"No." Isaac leaned slightly to glance at his calf. Blood had stuck the dark fabric of his uniform to his lower leg but seemed to have stopped flowing for the present.

"Why don't you help me to my car so I don't get yours dirty?"

"That's what plastic sheets are for," the detective said with a slight smile. "There's no way I'm letting you drive in your condition. I saw you send the medics to other victims and I figured it was high time you got some TLC yourself."

Isaac managed a smile. "No offense, buddy, but I'd rather have a pretty nurse taking care of me than a bossy cop like you."

Chuckling, Delvecchio slipped his arm around Isaac's waist for added support and started to move toward his unmarked car. "I'll see what I can do about finding the right nurse when we get to the hospital. What about Abby?"

"I'll handle my dog. You just get me to a doctor who can sew me up so I can go back to work."

"You're pushing it again."

Isaac sobered, glancing over his shoulder. "I know. But I feel responsible for what happened tonight and I intend to catch whoever did this."

"I've already ordered every news crew to give me copies of their raw footage. My men are also collecting the shots taken by bystanders so we can run facial recognition on anyone we don't know."

Pausing, Isaac gave the man a serious look. "Don't just concentrate on strangers. Watch the politicians, too, particularly Harland Jeffries and his staff. Considering his long-standing reputation in dirty politics, I wouldn't put it past him to try to create sympathy by pretending to be exposed to possible injury. It wouldn't be the first lie he'd ever told."

Isaac got a sinking feeling when David shook his head. "I strongly doubt that's what took place tonight," the detective said.

"Why? Was he hurt in the blast?"

"No. He may be a master manipulator but he was complaining of chest pains when they hauled him away. If this bomb scare was supposed to boost his chances of getting his new crime bill passed and it caused him to have a heart attack instead, he badly miscalculated."

Daniella had been working behind the scenes while one of the on-call doctors did triage on the victims. None seemed badly hurt and outside of a little first aid, a few stitches and a tranquilizer here and there, they had been easy to treat.

She was cleaning up one of the exam cubicles and hoping she could avoid the reporters who were still milling around the lobby when the head nurse separated a gap in the heavy curtains.

"I've got another victim here—brought in by private vehicle. All the doctors are busy and we're out of wheelchairs. Take care of him for me, will you?"

"Of course."

Daniella relieved the other nurse and slipped her arm around the uniformed officer's waist, starting to guide him. She was careful to avert her face for the brief moments when she was exposed to the public, hoping no cameras would capture her image. That was when she noted the leash in the patient's hand. "I'm terribly sorry. You can't bring a dog into the hospital."

"This isn't a dog."

"Sure looks like one."

"Nope. This is officer Abby of the Capitol K-9 Unit. See her vest?"

"She's still a dog."

"I beg to differ. You permit service dogs, don't you?"

"Yes, of course, but…"

"Then you have to allow Abby in. Besides, I'm injured and she's my partner. She goes where I go."

"Do you promise to take the flak if the hospital administration finds out and pitches a fit?"

"No problem. I'm already wearing a flak vest under my jacket." He glanced toward the foyer, where Delvecchio was speaking to additional reporters. "Don't I have to fill out paperwork?"

The direct answer was yes. Daniella chose to handle it another way in order to keep her distance from the news crews. "I can help you with those details while you hold your dog—I mean your partner."

She helped him lie down and lifted his boots to rest on the narrow exam table. When she picked up a PDA and began poking its screen with a stylus, she wished her hands would stop shaking. "Your name, please?"

"Isaac Black. How long have you worked in ER?" he asked, frowning.

When his fascinating, dark gaze locked with her green eyes she could barely force herself to look away. "Seven years. Why?"

"Because you're acting awfully nervous. You aren't afraid of dogs, are you?"

"Don't be silly. I love animals."

"Then what's wrong? If you had already examined my leg I'd think I was hurt worse than I'd imagined."

"I'm sure you'll be fine, Mr.—I mean Officer—Black."

"May as well call me Isaac. It solves lots of problems."

"Fine. Can you put the dog on a chair long enough for you to be treated?"

"Of course. If I'd been able to drive myself over here I'd have left her at headquarters. Unfortunately, I was overruled."

"A wise decision," Daniella said. She laid the tablet aside while her patient pointed to a chair and the beagle obediently jumped into it.

"I'm impressed," she said. "My cat barely comes when I call him for supper."

"Not surprising. Cats have devious minds."

If he hadn't been smiling at her, Daniella might have thought he was serious. "That's debatable."

The resulting twinkle in his dark eyes was so appealing she had to force herself to look away. He was taller than most of the men she knew, and far more muscular.

His smile was amiable enough, yet there was an aura about him that made her think of danger. Either that or she was simply being influenced by the disquieting thoughts that had begun the moment she'd heard the news of an explosion.

Once she had recorded Isaac's necessary preliminary information, she slit the leg of his uniform pants the rest of the way to his knee, folded back the fabric and carefully removed his boot.

"Well? How bad is it?" he asked.

"The doctor will make that assessment when he gets here."

"Let me put it this way." Isaac reached for her wrist and clasped it, gently but firmly, sending another shiver zinging up her spine. "If I just bandage it up and go back to work, will I be sorry?"

"I would certainly think so."

He heaved a telling sigh. "That's what I was afraid of."

"You got hurt at the monument, like the others, right?"

"Right. Abby and I were there to do a safety inspection of the area. She couldn't have missed detecting the bomb. It had to be placed there *after* we made our sweep. There's no other possible explanation."

Her brain absorbed very little more after he said *bomb*. That word had been a trigger for a surge of negative emotions for many years, and this instance was no different. Latent fear gripped her heart, stilled her movements and turned her fingers to stone. It wasn't until she felt his warm touch on her forearm that she snapped out of it. Sort of.

"You okay?" The dark, dancing eyes had narrowed and he was studying her as if she were a specimen under a microscope.

"I'm fine."

"You keep telling me that but every now and then I see something else."

"Must be your imagination," Daniella assured him.

The expression on the police officer's face was clear. He didn't believe her. And little wonder since she was anything but fine. Matter of fact, at this moment, all she wanted to do was run out the door, disappear into the night, leave everything behind and never look back.

TWO

Isaac had been visited by a physician and was sporting twenty-three stitches by the time his boss, Captain Gavin McCord, arrived at the hospital and began berating him.

"You broke at least two rules tonight. You should have cleared that area the instant your dog alerted and waited for an ambulance instead of hitching a ride," McCord said with a scowl. "Care to tell me what happened?"

"I did clear it. The problem wasn't because of me or Abby." Isaac had been enjoying the pretty nurse's company as she'd begun to bandage his calf and he smiled in her direction.

McCord eyed her, too. "Could you finish that later? I'd like to talk to my team member privately."

"Of course." She stripped off her latex gloves.

In spite of her quick, compliant reply, Isaac could tell she was hesitant to leave him. Why? They hardly knew each other.

Given no personal background on her he was in the dark, but if he'd had to guess he'd have concluded that she was either normally high-strung or suffering from serious guilt. He hoped it was not the latter.

Isaac and his captain watched her edge away, then

disappear through a gap in the curtains surrounding the exam area. Their eyes met.

"Was she that uptight when you got here, or have you done something to upset her?" Gavin asked.

"Hey, don't look at me." Isaac raised both hands. "If anything, she's acting a little better than she did at first. Her jitters were so noticeable when I walked in, I asked her if she was new on the job."

"And?"

"And, she said she wasn't."

"Curious. You'd think an experienced trauma nurse would have steadier nerves." His brow knit. "I think I'll run a background check on her, just in case."

"She can't have been responsible for the incident tonight. She was working here, right on schedule, when it went down."

"That doesn't mean some of her friends weren't involved." McCord studied Isaac's leg. "You sure you guided Abby to every bench?"

"Yeah. The area was clean when we'd finished our sweep. She didn't alert until after the press conference had started."

"Okay. We'll concentrate on looking for newcomers to the scene when we get a chance to review the videos. Want me to hang around to give you a lift home?"

Isaac shook his head. "You don't have to bother. Culpeper's not that far. I can call my brother or sister to come get me."

"And miss my big chance to grill you all the way to your place? No way. I want to hear every detail."

"Do you have any info on the device yet?" Isaac asked.

"Other than the fact it was an amateur job, not really. We'll be sending the remnants to Quantico for analysis."

"I guess that's better than deciding it was made by an expert."

Isaac's gaze drifted aimlessly as he mulled over his own observations at the blast scene. Movement caught his attention. He froze, nudged the captain and pointed at the feet and ankles visible on the opposite side of the cubicle's curtain.

Gavin McCord moved silently, swiftly, to yank away the cloth barrier. A woman gasped. Covered her mouth with her hands. The nervous nurse had been eavesdropping on their discussion!

Both officers stared at her, not speaking.

"I—I was just waiting to finish that bandage," she said, hurrying to Isaac's side and pulling on a fresh pair of gloves. "I take it you're through talking."

"For now," Isaac said, turning to his boss. "I'll meet you outside when I'm done here, Gavin. Will you take care of Abby for me?"

"Sure. No problem. I'll get your boot, too."

Isaac tried a slight smile to see if it would relax his nurse. "Is it still a madhouse of reporters out there?"

She nodded, yet didn't meet his gaze directly.

"That reminds me of another thing that struck me as odd," Isaac told his captain in parting. He knew McCord was friendly with Jeffries but he just had to ask. "What made Congressman Jeffries decide to call a press conference so late?"

"He says he decided to go public because his pet anticrime bill was coming up for a vote in the morning."

"He couldn't have waited until tomorrow?"

"Apparently not. He was allegedly proving to his constituency how much that bill is needed to keep DC safe." McCord touched the brim of his cap and picked up the beagle. "Take your time in here. I'll be waiting outside, asking questions and listening to rumors."

Isaac lay back and let Daniella work on his leg, noting her unsteady fingers. As soon as she stripped off her gloves again, he reached for one of her hands.

"You can tell me," he said tenderly.

She pulled away. "Tell you what?"

"Why you're so afraid."

He thought she was going to leave the room without replying until she said, "I just hate bombs, that's all. They're so indiscriminate. So lethal."

"This one wasn't much, if that helps any."

"People were still hurt." After a barely perceptible shiver she continued. "The doctor has released you. You should see your family physician for a follow-up in a few days. Watch for redness, swelling or discharge from the wound and keep it clean and dry."

"Yes, ma'am. Can I walk without crutches?"

"Your leg will hurt more in a few days than it does now but walking won't do any more damage, if that's what you're asking. The injection we gave you will get you home tonight. After that you can take one of the pills in this envelope every four to six hours or switch to over-the-counter painkillers. Just don't double up."

"Anything else?"

"I would say, 'Get a different job,' but I can tell that's not an option for a man like you."

"A man like me? What kind would that be?"

"One who's strong-willed and sure of himself, a person who never wastes time rehashing the past and thinks he's invincible."

"Maybe I really *am*," Isaac teased.

The heartrending look in her emerald-green eyes penetrated his defenses despite his strong resolve. It had been a long time since he'd seen that much poignancy and sorrow in a person's gaze.

This shy, quiet woman had given his heart a twist without saying a word.

Daniella was in no hurry to return to the hospital's common areas, where she could be spotted. Yes, her father's promised vendetta might have vanished with the passage of years but she wasn't willing to take that chance. As her US marshal handlers had warned, leaving the witness protection program was not optional. Once you were in, you stayed. Period.

"Which is the whole point," she murmured. "Having a long and happy life." It was only at times like tonight, when violence brought her past peril to mind, that she fretted so uncontrollably.

Hurrying through the halls, she had almost gained sanctuary when she was paged to go back and assist another doctor. The way she saw her predicament, all she had to do was reach that particular private exam room without passing any nosy reporters or photographers who might inadvertently broadcast her picture and cause untold damage by revealing her hidden identity. Under normal circumstances it would not have been difficult to dodge them. Given the presence of the congressman and his entourage, plus the press corps, moving around in the ER could prove tricky.

Daniella grabbed an extra clipboard, held it beside her cheek to mask her features and hurried toward her new assignment. She was looking ahead so intently she missed noticing a dark-haired figure to her blinded left.

She and the muscular man came together with a thump and he grabbed her.

It was all she could do to keep from screaming.

"Hey, settle down," he said. "It's me, Isaac. Are you okay?"

His voice sent tingles racing from the arm he was holding all the way to her toes. Regaining her balance, she helped steady him in return.

"Sorry. I hope I didn't hurt you. I thought you'd already left," Daniella said.

"I was trying to catch up to you and thank you."

"You're quite welcome. Just doing my job."

Before the K-9 cop could reply, she was blinded by an intense flash of light and someone shoved a microphone in her face. "Are you working on the congressman?" a reporter demanded. "Did he really have a heart attack? What's his prognosis? How soon can we see him?"

Isaac's immediate intervention—his arms outstretched and his badge in hand—sent the crowd back a few steps, providing an escape route for Daniella. She held the clipboard between herself and the others and ducked in the exam room door, slamming it behind her.

Her back pressed against the door. She fought to see through the orbs of color that danced in her vision after the camera flashes.

"Over here, Dunne," the doctor said. "I want you to prepare Congressman Jeffries for an X-ray of his shoulder and an EKG, just in case his pain is the result of strain on his heart. I'll send a tech down to take him to radiology. Stay with him until then."

"Yes, Doctor."

"And pull yourself together," he whispered behind his

hand in passing. "The last thing our patients need is to hear you shrieking."

"What? When?"

"Just before you opened the door."

"I—I didn't scream. Did I?"

"You made enough noise for me to hear you in here," he said, shooting her a look of disdain. "See that it doesn't happen again. Understood?"

"Yes, sir."

Tall, gray-haired Harland Jeffries was removing his dress shirt and carefully folding the sleeves together before laying the garment aside atop his expensively tailored suit jacket and silk tie.

"You'll need to wear one of our gowns for your tests," Daniella said. "Would you like me to assist you in removing your T-shirt?"

"Fine."

Jeffries's reply was gruff but she wasn't offended. Illness or injury often brought out the worst in patients. *Except for the K-9 cop*, she added. It was really nice of Isaac to step up and physically defend her the way he had. Instead of him thanking *her*, she should be the one dishing out thanks. She owed him. Big-time.

Gently easing the stretchy, white cotton shirt over the congressman's head, she glanced at his back. One side showed a nasty scar from the time he was shot several months ago, sadly at the same time his son, Michael, was murdered.

The opposite shoulder bore an interesting café au lait mark near the scapula. Judging by its odd shape, she guessed it to have been present from conception and birth rather than being another scar or a discoloration caused by trauma.

Daniella fitted the gown around her patient and stepped back. "All right, Congressman, you're ready. I'll wait here with you, as the doctor said, until they come to escort you to radiology."

"Whatever."

His off-putting attitude was nothing like his public persona. If he had behaved this way toward the press, he'd have killed his chances for reelection long ago.

Thoughts of people who were not trustworthy and genuine reminded her of her childhood. That was all it took to bring back images of the deadly explosion her father had orchestrated.

Yellow billowing fire had leaped and curled back on itself while black smoke roiled. Pieces of metal had rained down. She flinched, wanting to throw her arms over her head and duck just as she had that fateful day her mother had been brutally murdered.

Thankfully, the radiology tech appeared at the door with a wheelchair and distracted both Daniella and her patient.

"Ready, sir?" the tech asked.

"I suppose so." Settling himself in the chair, the congressman pasted a resigned expression on his face, raised his chin and visibly prepared to meet his public. "All right. Let's go."

Daniella waited until the hall was empty before she slipped out. She didn't have to be a licensed physician to suspect that Jeffries was either faking or at least making more of his condition than was warranted. There was no way that man was having heart trouble the way he'd indicated.

Then again, she was very good at spotting falsehoods. After all, she'd grown up in a household where her father's lies were the norm. He was no businessman in the sense he'd implied. His business was crime and his methods for controlling his family were violent. She should know. When he'd tired of abusing her poor mother, he'd graduated to trying to keep Mama in line by hitting Daniella.

That was what had eventually caused her mother to call it quits and file for divorce. And that was also what had inevitably led to her murder.

To this day, Daniella wondered. If she had been courageous enough to run away when she was younger, would her mother still be alive? Was it all her fault?

Logic said no. Guilt had a different opinion.

Isaac was already beginning to feel the effects of his injury and the pain medication as Gavin drove him out of downtown DC, proving that the decision to let someone chauffeur him home was a wise one. Abby lay on the second seat, content to nap during the short trip.

"It's a good thing your brother and sister live with you," the captain said.

Isaac nodded and stifled a yawn. "Yeah, that's us. The Three Musketeers, 'One for all and all for one.'"

"Must be interesting deciding who's in charge. Do you do it by age or former military rank?"

Chuckling, Isaac shook his head. "We tried both after we inherited the place from our great aunt, but it didn't work very well. We each have our strong and weak points. Jake is a great manager so we leave the running of the farm to him. Becky got into real estate when we were selling off some small lots to help with back taxes and repairs. It suited her so that's what she's doing now."

"And you're the only one in law enforcement."

"Right. Me and Abs." He glanced over his shoulder at his napping partner. "She's a real treasure."

"You need to find somebody like my Cassie."

"Uh-uh. Women are too complicated. Besides, I have Abby and my job."

"That's not enough."

"You underestimate the positive influence of a happy beagle," Isaac replied. "She gives great kisses, too."

McCord rolled his eyes and chuckled. "Sometimes, Black, you really worry me."

Groggy from the pain meds, Isaac yawned again. "Yeah. Sometimes I worry about myself, too."

He closed his eyes, intending to rest, and was surprised to visualize the face of the pretty nurse he'd just met. There was something about her that called out to him; that spoke to his inner man the same way wounded warriors in the VA hospital did. She was haunted, but by what? Or whom?

Isaac blinked and forced himself awake to ask, "Are you still planning on investigating my nurse's background like you said earlier?"

"I think I should, don't you?"

"Yes." There was no way Isaac could make himself doubt Daniella's apparently good character, yet he was curious about what was frightening her. She was plainly scared to death. And judging by the way she'd tried to keep from being photographed, he assumed she was hiding from something. Something that had cut to the core and left her shell-shocked.

Whatever her problem was, or had been, he was determined to learn enough to help her. That kind of thing wasn't in his official job description, at least not for the K-9 unit. It was, however, part of his Christian faith and upbringing. If a neighbor needed assistance, it was his duty to render it to the best of his ability.

Turning his back on the problem was not an option. The good Lord had brought Daniella Dunne into his life for a reason. Now all he had to do was figure out what that reason was and decide whether or not he could do anything for her.

A lot would depend upon what they learned from the background search. After that, he'd pray about it and make his final decision.

Truth to tell, Isaac thought, smiling as he dozed off, he wasn't going to mind becoming involved in the nurse's troubles. Not one bit.

THREE

The rising sun was painting the sky in streaks of pink and gold before Daniella felt calm again. She had volunteered to stay past the end of her regular shift, just in case there were more bombs or other emergencies, but had ended up idle for most of the rest of the night.

She had considered sleeping at the hospital and not going home at all. If it hadn't been for the needs of Puddy, her black Persian tomcat, she might have opted to stay there indefinitely.

Bone weary, she yearned for solace and privacy and for the quiet companionship of her feline roommate. Her senses were already dulling and she knew that lack of adequate sleep would affect her more and more as the hours passed. She owed her patients her best. The only sensible choice was to give up and go home.

She'd picked up her Windbreaker and purse when someone shouted from the break room. "Hey, everybody! Come here. Look. We're famous."

Daniella joined the rush to peer at the TV screen. A rapid progression of scenes with smoke and a booming sound were followed by pictures of an ambulance, then the inside of the very ER where they all worked.

"There I am." One of the ambulance attendants cheered. "That should prove to my girlfriend that I really was working last night."

Daniella held her breath. The camera panned. She recognized other staff members. There had been more than one news group present so this airing was no guarantee that she had escaped being photographed. Nevertheless, not seeing herself was a good start. If the other major stations were running pooled footage, all the better.

Just as she started to turn away, someone tapped her arm. "Wow! Look at our Daniella acting like a pop diva."

"What?" Her jaw dropped. Not only had she been caught facing the camera, but the white paper on the clipboard next to her cheek highlighted her features. Even someone who barely knew her would recognize her in that shot.

She sagged against a wall. Moving to a big city was supposed to help her blend in. She liked living in DC. Loved her job and her apartment and the people at work, even the sourpusses. Acceptance of others had accompanied thankfulness for survival and the realization that she was getting a second chance.

Was she going to have to give it all up? Did she dare stay; stand her ground? What were the chances that her father or one of his former cohorts would recognize her on TV and track her down? She'd changed a lot from the gangly teen she'd been back then, but would it be enough?

Wresting the remote from the hand of another nurse, she paused the picture and backed up the scene. There she was, all right. In all her brunette glory. Thank goodness she was still putting a dark rinse on her honey-blond hair.

Daniella ignored murmured protests as she moved the scene forward, then back, then forward again until she was sure of the seriousness of the slipup. In one of the shots her hospital ID badge was visible. It was impossible to read her name as she'd hurried past the reporters, but anyone who had the capabilities to freeze those few frames and enhance the image would also know her false identity.

She clenched her empty stomach and dropped the remote. With one hand clamped over her mouth and the other clutching the strap of her purse, she wheeled and ran from the room.

At his murder trial, ten years ago, her own father had threatened to kill her. Even though he was still in prison, she figured he could hire an assassin. She had done nothing wrong and yet she was serving a longer sentence than he was. She was going to have to keep running and hiding for the rest of her life.

It wasn't fair. She was one of the good guys. This nightmare was *not* supposed to be haunting her.

Isaac didn't remember much about his ride home with Gavin at the wheel and he was asleep minutes after his head hit the pillow. When his phone rang midmorning he was surprised to note how long he had slept.

He answered, "Black."

"How's the leg?" his captain asked.

"Now that you mention it, it hurts. The pain meds I took last night must have worn off."

"Good. You may want to drive and you'll need a clear head."

"I can't drive to work. You carjacked me. Remember?"

"I had your unit delivered to you this morning."

"Are you serious? You really want me to come in today?"

"I have something I think you'll want to see. Of course, I could email the file to you."

"Wanna give me a clue? I'd hate to get dressed and drive all the way into the city for nothing."

"It's about your girlfriend."

"My *what*?" Isaac was sitting on the edge of the bed by now, running his fingers through his hair and taking mental stock of his injury.

"The nurse you wanted me to check on."

"Okay. Go ahead."

"She has a spotless record at the hospital and graduated from nursing school at the top of her class."

"So? That doesn't sound bad."

"Her career is not the most interesting part of her past," McCord said. "Prior to entering college ten years ago, Daniella Dunne didn't exist."

"That's impossible."

"It is if she's on the up-and-up. I don't know who she was before or where she came from. All I know is she's not who she implies she is."

There had been a time when Daniella had tried to keep close tabs on her jailed father. Then, as the years had passed, she had slowly stopped worrying about him and had gone on with her life, content to have a purposeful career and to be a truly new person.

Now, however, she felt it was vital that she know more about the man, if only to set her mind and heart at ease. There was no sense panicking and going on the run if it wasn't necessary. For all she knew, he might have died in prison.

One phone call would tell her everything. The question was, if she did contact the emergency number her original US marshal contact had provided, would she be opening Pandora's box?

She hesitated, her cell phone gripped tightly. Then, before she could make up her mind whether or not to call for information, the phone rang. Caller ID was no help. All it showed was Unknown.

Could it be the marshal's office taking care in case the call was being monitored? Logically, that might be possible, particularly if she were at work. There was only one way to find out.

She clicked the green button and pressed the phone to her ear. "Hello?"

A low menacing chuckle was followed by, "Well, well. Remember how I always taught you to finish what you started?"

She knew instantly who was on the line. Her father had tracked her down. "How—how did you get this number?"

"I have friends in many places." He laughed again. "I'll see you soon, girl."

Daniella was speechless. That awful voice! Not only did he have her cell number, he probably also knew her address!

Staring at the tiny screen, she noted that he'd ended the call.

Her hands shook and her legs were close to collapse. Every sense insisted that she flee. Immediately. She glanced around at her cozy home. The mere thought of leaving all this behind made her sick to her stomach. Not only would she be in limbo once more, she'd have to give up her friends and career and maybe even her pet, since Puddy was microchipped and might be traceable via his former veterinarian.

She sank into the closest chair and cradled her head

in her hands. Although she would have welcomed the release brought by tears, there were none. Numbness and disbelief filled her to overflowing, leaving room for nothing else.

Her first change of identity, when she'd fled Florida as a teen, had been easy compared with what she was facing now. She had often tried to imagine what it would be like to have to abandon nursing and relocate again, but nothing had prepared her for the chilling reality she now acknowledged.

Her murderous father had tracked her down. Life as she'd known it was over. Period.

Isaac was driving himself toward headquarters when his captain radioed Daniella's home address.

"That's right on my way," he replied. "Okay if Abby and I make a stop there, first?"

"Officially?"

"Not exactly. Our mysterious woman may be more willing to fill in some information gaps if I approach her casually."

"It's worth a try. I've already checked with the hospital. She stayed on duty all night so she should be at home now. Just keep us posted. I don't want you going off the grid."

"Who? Me?"

McCord laughed. "Yes, you. Remember that case last fall when you forgot to radio your position and almost got yourself killed before backup could reach you?"

"That was an exception. Getting hurt at the scene last night was not my fault, either," Isaac insisted, noting the dull throbbing in his injured calf. "I followed all the rules precisely. Somebody obviously breached the police security lines after Abby and I checked. If she hadn't acted funny we might have ended up with a lot more casualties."

"You'll get no argument from me on that score," his captain said.

"Good. Listen. I'm almost to the nurse's. I'll have my cell and Abby with me but I'm leaving the rest of my gear in the unit."

"You sure that's wise?"

"Hey, you didn't find any connection between her and terrorists, did you?"

"Not in the last ten years, no."

"Then I'm not taking much of a chance." *Besides, I kind of like her,* he added silently. If there had been anything nefarious about her he figured he would have sensed it—and if he hadn't, Abby would have. Of all the partners he'd ever had, human or otherwise, it was the little beagle he trusted the most. People could be swayed by appearances. Dogs looked beyond the obvious and into a person's true heart.

Slowing as his GPS led him to the address, Isaac pulled into the driveway of an apartment complex. Mc-Cord had told him Daniella Dunne lived on the first floor. A mailbox check showed names posted for the other occupants but not for her. That, alone, would have struck him as strange. Coupled with the information he'd gotten from headquarters, it stood out like a red flag.

Her apartment sat at the end of a long interior corridor, next to the rear exit door. Isaac called Abby to heel and limped toward it, mentally preparing an opening line to relax the nurse.

He'd paused at her door when he heard a voice inside. Good. The woman was home. If she failed to respond to his knock he'd have further proof that there was something odd about her.

Isaac raised his fist.

At his side, Abby edged backward.

He was frowning and looking down at his dog when the door was yanked open and Daniella barreled into him so hard he almost lost his balance.

His arms flew out to steady them both. All he managed to say was "Hey..." when she let out a screech that could have made her the star of a horror movie!

"Whoa," Isaac said, grabbing hold of her upper arms while Abby's leash went flying. "Take it easy. I didn't mean to scare you."

The emerald eyes that were staring into his dark gaze reflected so much raw fear he was taken aback. Her scream had become a whimper and tears were beginning to slide down her flushed cheeks.

As unexpectedly as she'd crashed into him, she flung both arms around his neck and held on as if he were her only lifeline from a sinking ship.

Astounded, he nevertheless embraced her gently. "Easy. I've got you. What's wrong?"

All the answer he got was the sound of her gasping for breath, so he turned to place himself between her and the open apartment door. "Is there somebody else inside?"

Daniella shook her head emphatically, then seemed to come to her senses. "I—I have to get out of here."

"What's the hurry?" he asked, holding her away by cupping her shoulders.

She blinked rapidly and swiveled her head to look up and down the hallway before she said, "Because he's coming."

"Who is?"

"That doesn't matter."

"Whoa. Slow down and start from the beginning. Why are you so scared?"

"He—he threatened to kill me."

"When? Why?"

"A long time ago. I put him in jail."

That was enough information for Isaac to make a sensible decision. He slipped an arm around her shoulders and held her protectively. "Okay. Where do you want to go?"

"Away. Anywhere he can't find me."

"I'll drive."

Daniella twisted out of his grip. "No. I need my own transportation, at least until I can get something untraceable."

"Then Abby and I will follow you," he insisted. "Where are you parked?"

"In the back. The blue car right there." She pointed through the heavy glass of the outside door.

Isaac scooped up the dog's leash. "All right. We'll go first and make sure there's nobody lying in wait. You stay here until I give the okay."

Surveying the parking area until he was satisfied it was deserted, he pulled his smaller holdout gun from the ankle holster he always wore and started toward the parked cars. If Daniella was telling the truth, it was his duty to protect her. If she was making up stories in order to evade law enforcement, his job was to keep track of her. Either way, she was not getting out of his sight.

Isaac cautiously drew closer to Daniella's vehicle.

He felt a tug on Abby's leash.

When he looked back and saw the determined little dog firmly planted in a sitting position and staring straight at the blue sedan, he realized his canine partner had just saved at least two lives: his and the frightened woman's.

Abby was *never* wrong. There was no doubt. Someone had planted an explosive device in the nurse's car.

Waiting at the door, Daniella saw the officer returning rapidly and interpreted his closed, somber expression as either anger or angst. In a smooth motion, he encircled her with one arm and had her back inside her apartment without time for discussion, let alone argument.

"I want you to stay put for right now, understand?"

"No. I told you. I have to leave."

"Not in that car, you don't." He hooked a thumb over his shoulder to indicate her sedan. "I've notified local police. I'm going back outside with my dog to guard the scene until the regular officers relieve me. After that, we can go wherever you want."

"Police? What are they for? I already told you…"

"I don't care what you did or who's after you, lady. Pull yourself together and listen to me. My dog sensed a problem in or around your car, and nobody is going to touch it until the bomb squad has had a chance to look it over. Am I clear?"

She wanted to answer verbally but her body refused to cooperate. There was no breathable air in the apartment. The walls were closing in on her.

She staggered back until she felt her legs contact the front edge of the sofa cushions, then plopped down on them with a whoosh. Her jaw hung slack. Her eyes refused to focus properly. This was even worse than she'd imagined. If Isaac Black had not arrived at just the right moment, she'd have gotten into her car, just as her mother had, and then…

Tears gathered in Daniella's eyes and spilled silently down her cheeks. Her voice was thready. "Are—are you sure?"

"No. But Abby is and that's good enough for me. Now, stay put and let me take care of everything." He drew the living room blinds while his sweet-tempered dog wagged her tail and licked Daniella's fingers.

When he returned and gathered up the leash, he paused with one hand on the doorknob. "Lock this after me."

Her "Okay" was little more than a weak whisper, but at the moment she couldn't manage anything more forceful.

"It'll be all right," Isaac assured her. "Just sit tight and don't move."

"Can I pack a few things?"

"No!" was almost a shout. "Listen carefully. We know that couch is safe because Abby didn't react to it, but I don't want you wandering around in here until I've had a chance to let her explore every room."

"You—you think there's a bomb in here, too?"

"Probably not. But are you willing to take the chance?"

"No. Of course not." She whisked away her tears with the back of her hand.

"Good. Now you're being sensible."

The door closed quietly behind the K-9 officer. Daniella twisted the dead bolt, listening to its click for added assurance. She was safe, at least for the present.

The fortuitous arrival of Isaac and his remarkable dog still amazed her. Could God have somehow spurred him to make this impromptu visit?

She shook her head, clenching her jaw tightly. *No.* God might protect innocent people, but she was far from naive. Her lack of initiative had gotten her mother killed, and her foolish choices afterward had sent her into perpetual hiding.

Although she had no trouble praying for others, she'd long ago given up asking the Lord to watch over or guide her.

Ella Fagan, aka Daniella Dunne, didn't deserve God's love or his forgiveness. The most she could hope for was the wisdom to once more escape her father's vendetta.

Her whirling thoughts would not, could not, carry her further than that.

For all she knew, there would be no life beyond the next few days.

FOUR

With local police waiting outside for the bomb squad, Isaac returned to the apartment. When there was no response to his light knock, he rapped harder.

"Who is it?"

"Isaac Black and Abby."

The moment Daniella opened the door, he smiled. "Good job. I'm glad you're being so careful."

"Careful?" She made a wry face. "I'm scared to even breathe, thanks to you. Do you really think there's another bomb in here?"

"No, I don't. But letting me and Abby check the apartment while you sit on the couch and stay out of trouble is the smartest choice."

She shrugged. "Okay."

His attention now fully on Daniella, Isaac noted that she was wearing jeans and a T-shirt instead of her hospital scrubs. He scowled. "You changed clothes since your shift?"

"Yes, after I got home this morning and showered. Since I was so wide-awake I was planning to run a few errands before taking a nap. I'm almost out of cat food."

"You've already been in the bedroom?"

"Yes." He saw her blanch as reality grew.

"All right. How many cats do you have?"

"Just one. Puddy is black with long hair." She eyed Abby. "Don't let your dog scare him. He doesn't have all his claws."

"I'll keep Abs on a leash." Isaac started for the closest room, the kitchen, noting that it led to a hallway. "This will only take a few minutes. If she doesn't react we'll be right back."

"What if she does?"

"If she does, then we'll both go out the front door and I'll have the bomb squad come in here, too."

"Terrific." Daniella made a silly face.

Isaac had to smile again. "It's good to see that your sarcastic side is still operational."

"It's a coping mechanism a lot of nurses have, I guess."

"So do cops. Civilians don't usually understand how much it helps us when we have to deal with crime and loss so often."

It was clear from the expression on her face that Daniella understood perfectly. Whatever her full background was, she was a sensible and, he hoped, a reasonably stable person. Why that should be important to him was somewhat of a puzzle. Logically, however, she needed a temporary safe house, and he had plenty of extra room on the old farm. Unless Captain McCord came up with some heinous crimes in her past, there should be no reason why he couldn't take her home with him, at least for now. His sister might even have some clothes that would fit her and perhaps change her image enough that she'd be less easily spotted by whoever was menacing her.

His plans were almost fully formed by the time Isaac returned to the living room. "All clear," he said. "I'm satisfied that there's no danger in this apartment right now. You can go pack but don't take too long. The sooner we get out of here, the better."

"*We?* Where did that come from?"

"I'm taking you home with me—unless you have a better idea."

"I can't go with you. Not just like that."

"Why not?"

"Because you don't really know me."

Isaac smiled wryly. "If I did, should I be afraid of you?"

"Of course not, but..."

"Then it's settled. I'll go put Abby in the SUV, tell the local police what we're doing and be back in a flash. I'll expect you to be ready to leave by then."

"You're *ordering* me to go with you?"

His smile widened. "No. I'm offering a lifeline to a drowning citizen. You can always swim off into shark-infested waters by yourself if you choose."

"I see your point. All right," Daniella said, "but we have to take Puddy. I'm not abandoning him."

"Do you have a carrier?"

"Yes."

"Then put him in it and I'll take him, too."

She began to call, "Puddy? Here kitty, kitty." There was no response. Not even a faint meow.

The stricken look on her face touched Isaac. "I didn't see him when I searched. Maybe he hid when he spotted Abby. I'll take her outside. Keep calling to him while you're packing. Just try not to sound overly anxious. Okay?"

"Okay."

Isaac waited until he heard the door lock click into

place before heading down the hall. Getting Daniella to agree to leave her apartment had not been too difficult. Getting her to actually go if she couldn't locate her missing cat might prove far more perplexing. For all they knew, whoever had placed the bomb by the car might have also let the cat out. Anything was possible.

At present, his fondest hope was that the frightened feline would show up.

Daniella was frantic. She faced Isaac, eyes wide, short of breath. "I can't find him. He's not here!"

"Was the door locked when you got home?"

"Of course it was." She frowned. "At least I think so. I was so tired I really didn't pay much attention."

"You weren't scared at that point. So what set you off before I got here?"

Although she hated to answer, she felt she owed him a little more information. "I got a threatening phone call," she said, continuing to search for Puddy while she talked.

Isaac followed her. "Maybe it was a prank."

She shook her head so dramatically her hair brushed against each cheek in turn. "No way. This was for real."

"You know who called?"

"Yes. What I can't figure out is how he managed to get my number so fast. I was only on the news a few hours ago." She explained about seeing herself on TV as part of the coverage about the bombing.

"Maybe he saw you and hacked into the hospital's personnel files."

"I suppose that's possible."

Studying the officer, she could tell he was thinking as various expressions flashed across his face.

"All right," Isaac finally said. "Here's what I know.

There is no record of you before you entered college. No high school or grammar school transcripts. Nothing. That means you're either a criminal on the run or a witness who was given a new identity. My guess would be the witness."

Without giving it much conscious thought, she nodded and lowered her gaze, unwilling to meet his directly.

"So why are you acting guilty?"

"Because my family is involved in the whole mess."

"Criminally?"

"Not my mother. She was an innocent victim. My father murdered her."

She heard him draw a quick breath. "And you saw it happen?"

Another nod. She blinked back unshed tears as she raised her face to look at him, hoping to see neither condemnation nor pity. His expression was more quizzical than anything, so she explained further.

"My dad was doing business with some very bad people, drug dealers and hardened criminals. Mom wanted to leave him, we both did, but I was in my teens and I kept hesitating, hoping there was some spark of good left in him."

"That's understandable. He was your father and you were still a kid. You didn't want him to be evil."

"Exactly." She sniffled and continued while peering behind the sofa for the cat. "It was a sunny Sunday afternoon when everything came to a head. Mom told him we were both going to leave for keeps. She started to get into her car. I should have been with her but Dad sent me back into the house to bring him something. I never dreamed he'd already…"

"He saved your life?"

"Yes. But he took hers. The authorities proved he'd rigged an explosive device under her car. I wasn't allowed in court until it was my turn to testify so I don't know whether it was set to go off when she got behind the wheel or if he set it off remotely."

"You testified against him," Isaac said. It was not a question.

Daniella nodded slowly, purposely. "Yes. I had to. A man like that didn't deserve to walk the streets."

"And now you wonder if he might have been released?"

She shrugged. "I can't believe that's possible. Not yet, anyway. I'd rather think he hired someone to terrorize me in his place—except for the fact I recognized his voice on the phone."

"Let's start by finding out for sure where he is. Keep looking for the cat. I'll be right here," he told her, pulling his cell from his pocket and pushing a preprogrammed number. "Give me his full name."

She barely managed to whisper it.

As she worked her way back into the bedroom to search the closet once more, she heard Isaac say, "I need to check on a convict. Terence R. Fagan. If he's been released we need to locate him. Fast."

Daniella paused for a deep, telling sigh. The urge to pray that God would intervene and save her by somehow eliminating her father was strong. And wrong, she knew, yet the disturbing thoughts continued to whirl through her mind. She should be praying for the faith and strength to forgive him, to show him the kind of pure love Jesus demonstrated.

Truth was, she was a long way from that degree of forgiveness and there was no way she'd be able to pray and ask such a thing, not even if her father came to her on his knees and begged.

Surely God understood, she concluded, realizing almost immediately that she was violating one of the important yet simple instructions in the Lord's Prayer.

To be forgiven she must first forgive.

Clenching her jaw and her fists, Daniella refused. There was no way she was ever going to get over what that terrible man had done.

Her broken, battered heart wouldn't allow it.

The news Isaac received in the ensuing few minutes floored him. Terence Fagan had won early release on a technicality and had been roaming the streets for several years. Whether or not he might have located his daughter before her TV news appearance was a moot point. Circumstances seemed to point to a real, present danger. That was all that mattered. The details would eventually sort themselves out.

"Ms. Dunne," Isaac called as soon as he'd ended his phone conversation. "Come on. We have to go. There's no time to waste."

She poked her head around the corner into the kitchen. "I can't go yet. I'm not leaving without Puddy."

"Yes, you are."

The mist filling her eyes made them glisten like jewels in the rain. "No. Please. I know he's here. He has to be."

"Unless someone let him out while they were trying to break in." Isaac saw little chance of that but persisted. "Why don't you leave dishes of food and water in the usual place in here, then put others in the hallway, just in case? I'll either stop by to check or have members of my team do it. Puddy will show up as soon as he gets hungry enough. The problem is, you can't stay here and wait for that to happen."

She stared at him, her hands trembling.

He approached her slowly, hoping to keep her as calm as possible when he delivered the bad news. Stopping an arm's length from her, he looked deeply into her eyes, willing her to continue to trust him, at least enough to heed his sage advice.

Her eyes widened. "What are you not telling me?"

"That call I just made? It was to our tech support. Terence Fagan has been out of prison for several years."

"That's impossible!"

Isaac lightly cupped her elbow to steady her. "I'm sorry. It's true. His appeal was granted on a technicality."

She swayed as if dizzy, so he continued to hold her arm, just in case. "No. Your information must be wrong."

"Sorry. Our Fiona Fargo is the best computer tech in the business. If she says your father has been released, he has been."

"Why wasn't I told?"

"I don't know. When you get in touch with the marshals' office to arrange to be moved, you can ask them. It was probably an oversight."

"Oversight? This is my *life* we're talking about."

Isaac nodded soberly. "I'm glad you realize that." He let go and opened her cupboards to locate usable dishes. "Will these do for your cat?"

She barely nodded.

"Okay. I'll fill one with water and you put dry food in the other so we can be on our way."

This time she not only didn't argue, she moved to comply as if in a stupor. That state of mind wasn't any better for her than her earlier panic, although it did make his current task easier.

Until they could coordinate with the US Marshals office in DC, his best option would be to take her home with him, as he'd already been planning.

There was more than one good reason for that choice, too. His injured leg was starting to really throb and the sooner he was free to take his prescribed medication the better he'd feel.

Reasoning that a nurse would be sympathetic and therefore more compliant, he decided to tell her. "Listen, I hate to mention this but I'm starting to feel awfully sore. I couldn't chance taking my morning meds and getting behind the wheel of a motor vehicle so I haven't had any painkillers since what you gave me last night."

That snapped her out of her doldrums enough to frown and caution, "You should have kept up with them. It's not just for comfort, you know. Controlling pain will help you heal faster. Plus, one of those scripts was for oral antibiotics."

"Afraid I didn't stop to look," Isaac admitted. "When my captain called me, I didn't question his reasons."

"What was he *thinking*? You're injured."

Isaac chanced a slight smile. "Actually, it was my decision. He told me he was worried because there was no record of your past and wanted to confer with me."

"That's a lame excuse if I've ever heard one," Daniella said. Hoisting a bulging tote bag, she sighed as she started for the door. "I won't be responsible if you develop an infection. Let's go."

Following her out the apartment door and waiting while she carefully relocked it, Isaac couldn't help feeling relieved and more than a little glad. She was finally thinking more clearly. That was a definite plus.

Now all he had to do was take a small enough dose of painkiller to allow his own brain to function properly and they'd be a formidable team.

Visualizing himself and Daniella as a team caught him by surprise. They had little if anything in common, so why was he seeing her as part of his work, let alone his life?

Because the effects of this injury have addled me, he concluded. That aberration would surely pass.

His smile waned. *It had better.* In his line of work, letting a pretty face distract him could be fatal.

Since there was a logo on the door of the SUV that matched the patches on Isaac's uniform shirt, it was easy for Daniella to tell which official vehicle belonged to the K-9 cop. None of the responding agencies had pulled into the apartment driveway. Consequently, the street was blocked both ways.

She looked to him as they walked. "How did you know to park so far away?"

"I didn't. I moved my car for safety when I put Abby inside."

"Oh. I thought for a second…"

"That I was part of the plotting against you?"

"I never considered it seriously," she alibied. "I'm just jumpy."

"That's perfectly understandable."

"What else can you tell me about my father? You're absolutely positive he's out of prison?"

"Yes. His attorney filed an appeal and got his sentence reduced because of some glitch in the gathering of evidence at the crime scene. He pleaded guilty to providing the plans for the explosive device but insisted some of his cronies had actually made, planted and detonated it because they wanted to get rid of *him*, not your mother."

"Then why did he send me into the house at just the right moment to save my life?"

"He claimed it was a coincidence."

That statement gave her pause. Finally, she said, "If that's true, you know what it means, don't you?"

Isaac nodded as he opened and held the passenger door for her. "Yes. If he was being honest about his innocence, he wasn't showing his love, like you thought, by keeping you away from your mother's car."

As she slipped into the seat, she wished there weren't unshed tears threatening to trickle down her cheeks.

Daniella waited until Isaac was behind the wheel before she commented further. "Dad set that bomb. I know he did. The expression on his face wasn't surprise or shock after it went off, it was victory."

She sniffled and swiped at her damp cheeks. "He killed Mom as surely as I'm sitting here." Sighing, she stared out the SUV's window.

"That doesn't really explain why he'd be causing you trouble after all this time," Isaac offered.

"Sure it does. That man never forgave a soul. After I testified against him he swore he'd get even. That's why I agreed to go into witness protection in the first place."

"You believe he meant what he said?"

Daniella huffed and set her jaw. "Oh yeah. Of all the things he ever told me, that's the one promise I know he intends to keep."

"I'm sorry," Isaac said.

She knew she'd start to sob if she saw pity in the officer's eyes, so she kept staring out the window.

The voice on the phone had been unmistakable. Her father was on her trail and closing in. Every moment that passed was one more she had managed to eke out.

And brought her one more breath closer to her last if Terence Fagan had his way.

FIVE

Once they were past the beltway, the country quickly turned to farmland. Isaac waited to give the pastoral scenes a chance to calm his companion. When he finally spoke, it seemed to startle her.

"How're you doing?"

"Oh!" Her head whipped around. "Sorry. I guess I was daydreaming."

"That's better than some of the things you could have been thinking about. We're almost home."

"It's pretty out here. I just have trouble picturing you as a farmer."

He chuckled. "I'm not. My sister, brother and I inherited the place from an aunt and decided to fix it up to sell. That was five years ago and we're still there."

"*We?* You don't live alone?"

Isaac could see her relief. He laughed. "Nope. I'm not inviting you home for disreputable reasons. My sister, Becky, will see to it that Jake and I behave. I can guarantee it."

"Are they older or younger than you?"

"Jake's older. Becky's younger, but not by much. Our

parents had us close together so we'd get along better, and it apparently worked because they're my best friends."

"Except for Abby, you mean."

"Right. Abs and I are best buds."

"How long have you worked with her?"

"A little over two years, counting the training. I was recruited for the K-9 unit by General Margaret Meyer after I left my other government job."

"Which was?"

Her expression was so open and innocent looking he answered without hesitation. "I worked for the CIA."

"You were a *spook*?"

Letting his amusement show, he shook his head. "Actually, I spent most of my time training dogs to be sent into the field, until someone decided I belonged in an office, organizing the whole project."

"No wonder you wanted to get a different job. I couldn't stand being stuck behind a desk, either." She took a deep breath and released it with a whoosh. "What am I going to do? I love being a trauma nurse and working ER."

"So, you tell that to the marshals and insist they find you another similar position."

"What if they won't? Suppose they feel it's too dangerous? I mean, wouldn't that make it easier to trace me?"

"Maybe, maybe not. Don't borrow trouble, Daniella. There's enough of it already around."

"That sounds biblical."

"Probably. My folks were pretty religious."

"Were? Are they gone?"

"Sadly, yes. They were both killed in a traffic accident while all of us were stationed away. Jake was a marine and Becky flew for the air force."

Detecting Danger

"Really? That's impressive. I'm sure you all made your parents proud." Her smile faded and Isaac could see the light going out of her eyes. "My mother was always proud of me but I could never please my father."

"That doesn't mean you weren't worthy," Isaac told her. "It just means that he wasn't a normal dad. You can't blame yourself for his shortcomings."

"I don't, but..."

"No *buts* about it. I've only known you for a little while and I can see you're an extraordinary person. You've overcome adversity to finish college and go on to a rewarding career. You're well liked at work and best of all, Abby thinks you're wonderful. I saw her licking your hands back at your place."

"She's a sweetheart. I was trying to pet her and she seemed to take to me right away."

That makes two of us, Isaac thought. There was something about Daniella that had spoken to his heart the moment he'd met her.

Whether or not that was for the best remained to be seen.

The old farmhouse was far more charming than Daniella had expected. Basically a simplified Victorian, it sported a fresh coat of white paint with red shutters and trim, plus window boxes of early flowers like tulips and pansies.

She grinned. "It's lovely. No wonder you all decided to stay here."

"Believe me, it didn't look half this good when we inherited it," Isaac replied. "Jake has done wonders with the place."

"He must be very talented."

Isaac laughed. "So he claims."

"Sibling rivalry? I have no experience with brothers or sisters. I'd think you'd be proud of him, though."

"I am. We just like to needle each other. You'll see." He gave a soft chuckle. "Our sister, Becky, is the worst."

"You're sure they won't mind my stopping here for a few days, at least until I have new instructions from the marshals? I mean, I wouldn't want to make trouble."

"Believe me, there's no way you'll make more trouble than the three of us can stir up. We love to tease each other and pull practical jokes."

A tall, stalwart man in a T-shirt and jeans appeared at the side of the house, waved and started their way. Daniella could see the family resemblance even though the second man needed a shave. In spite of this one's rugged image, she judged Isaac to be slightly better-looking.

Jake trotted out to the SUV with a hammer in his hand, peered in at Isaac's passenger and broke into a face-splitting grin. "Whoa! Good one, bro. You head for the office to work even though you're stove-in and bring home a pretty lady. That's what I call a good job."

Stove-in was right. Moving stiff-legged on his injured side, Isaac climbed from behind the wheel. Daniella had opened her own door at the same time so he introduced her to his brother with a wave. "This is Jake, as you've probably guessed. Jake, Daniella Dunne. Becky's a lot prettier than he is. And more polite."

Jake wiped his hand on his jeans before shaking hands with her, then looked over at his brother. "Girlfriend or damsel in distress?"

"Damsel, definitely," Daniella answered for him. "The distress part is true, too."

"Sorry to hear that." Jake's grin faded. "How can we help you?"

"I'll take care of Ms. Dunne," Isaac interjected. "I'm going to put her things in Becky's room for now. Later, the women can work out whatever arrangements suit them."

"Ooooh-kay. You play cop while I finish nailing up the new cabinets in the washroom." Jake started away, then stopped and turned. "Don't run off and forget Abby. I'd hate to see you get so involved with a pretty face that your dog suffers."

"I'd never do that," Isaac insisted. Clenching his jaw, he let the little beagle out of the traveling crate he sometimes used and removed her working harness before releasing her and picking up his houseguest's tote.

Abby's sharp yaps brought larger dogs running. Daniella ducked behind Isaac, her hands resting lightly on his shoulders.

"Don't let the dogs scare you," he told her. "They're as gentle as Abs. They just look ferocious."

When she said, "They sound like it, too," her host laughed.

"Stand still and let them sniff you. After that you'll be considered one of the family."

A wiggling brown nose the size of the diaphragm on the business end of a stethoscope touched the knee of her jeans. "I think he smells Puddy."

"That's no problem. We have plenty of cats in the barn and the dogs treat them all with respect, even the kittens."

"You're sure? This one has teeth as big as a wolf."

"The better to protect you with, my dear, to paraphrase the old fairy tale. Make friends with these dogs and any one of them will defend you to the death."

"Interesting choice of words." She rolled her eyes. "What breeds are they?"

"Those two brown-and-black ones are large mutt crossed with very large mutt," Isaac said with a smile. "The third is probably shepherd and yellow Lab. We stick to purebreds for K-9 work because their talents are more predictable, but in private life I like to rescue needy animals."

"Well, I feel like a juicy bone about to be served for supper," she joked, beginning to relax as her furry new acquaintances lost interest in her and dashed off in pursuit of Abby.

Glancing at the open yard, Daniella wished there were more trees and bushes to hide behind. Then again, the lack of a lot of vegetation near the house also meant no one could jump out to pounce on her. On them.

She eyed the long driveway. "You're sure nobody followed us?"

"I'm sure. When I called in to tell my boss what I was doing, I asked for a few of my buddies to run interference, just in case. None of them spotted trouble or they'd have radioed me."

"That's a relief," she said. And it was. Except it was also temporary. Everything in her life was. She was out of a job due to having been identified, she had no home because the apartment was known to her worst enemy, and all her efforts at staying in the shadows had been for nothing. She didn't even have Puddy anymore, and he was the closest thing she had to a real, true friend. One thing was certain. She could not just abandon the cat any more than this K-9 officer would ever give up Abby.

Following Isaac up the wooden front steps to the covered porch, Daniella stopped him with a touch. "Tomorrow, I'm going back to rescue my cat," she said flatly.

"You couldn't find him today. What makes you think you'll succeed tomorrow?"

"Because I'll be going into my apartment alone."

"Over my dead body," Isaac countered.

"Hopefully, it won't come to that," she shot back cynically, calmer now that she'd made a decision to act. Anything was better than feeling helpless and vulnerable.

"Not funny."

"It wasn't meant to be. The more I think about it, the more I realize Puddy was scared of you as well as the dog. If you stay outside and I go in by myself, he should come out of hiding."

"That's assuming he's still in the apartment."

"Yes. It is. I don't buy your idea that somebody let him out. He's always been an indoor kitty. Chances are he wouldn't have run out even if the door was left open."

"Do you have a death wish?" Isaac asked, frowning.

Daniella shook her head. "Tell me. What would you do if Abby was lost in your house and you were about to move away? Would you leave her with food and water and turn your back on her?"

"That's different."

"No, it isn't." She blinked to clear her vision and try to regain more control of her turbulent emotions. "That cat has been my sole companion for over five years. I am not abandoning him. Period. Understand?"

When she saw that she had convinced Isaac, she brushed past him and entered the house. If she failed to honor her commitment to a helpless animal, how could she ever hope to be trusted with the kind of love and acceptance for which she yearned? It was the little things in life that formed a person's character. Sure, traumatic events played a role, but it was small kindnesses and daily thanksgiving that truly shaped people's lives.

And evil acts that tore them apart, she thought sadly. There was nothing she could do to erase the damage her father had done, nor could she forget his wickedness.

But that didn't mean she was going to surrender—to him or to her fear. She wasn't in this alone anymore. Whether he knew it yet or not, Isaac Black was clearly on her side.

Picturing him boldly stepping between her and the news people, despite his injured leg, she let her imagination equip him with armor and weapons and a trusty steed—tricolored, with floppy ears and a wagging tail!

A combination of nerves and a sense of the absurd brought giggles, then snickers and finally tears that rolled down Daniella's cheeks as she doubled up laughing.

"Would you mind telling me why you find my house so funny?" Isaac asked, sounding a tad miffed.

She could not, would not, tell him, of course. What she did manage to say was, "It's not you or your house. It's me. I think I may be wound a little tight."

He nodded. "Come on. I'll show you to your room and you can rest. I may not be technically at work but I have plenty to do on my laptop." He pointed as they passed a ground-floor room. "If you need me, I'll probably be in there."

"If you give me your cell number I can just phone you," she said, feeling quite clever for having thought of it.

He dropped her tote at the foot of the stairs. "You brought your cell phone?"

"Of course."

"Give it to me."

"No. I may need it."

"So your father can call you again or so he can trace your whereabouts through it?"

"What? That's just TV nonsense, isn't it?" Nevertheless, she placed her phone in his outstretched hand and watched as he removed the battery and the tiny information-processing card.

"I'll turn this over to my people and see if they can trace your last incoming call. That would be your father, right?"

Mute and subdued, she nodded. In the space of a few moments she had gone from strong and resolute to scared witless again. Her emotions weren't merely on a roller coaster, they were taking a ride on a spaceship that had run out of rocket fuel halfway to the moon and was now plummeting to earth, where it would smash to smithereens.

Daniella gritted her teeth. The imaginary rocket hadn't crashed yet. The ending wasn't written in stone because she wasn't done fighting. Not by a long shot.

Straightening and thrusting back her shoulders, she stood firm and faced Isaac. "I'm sorry. I didn't know."

Surprisingly, his stern features softened as he admitted, "No, but I did. The error is mine. I should have confiscated your phone back at the apartment and turned it over to the authorities."

"Why didn't you?"

"I'd like to blame my injury or the meds I'd been on for the pain but that won't fly—with my boss or with me." He made a face. "As much as I hate to even think it, I suspect I was concentrating too much on you."

"Me?"

She noted the rosy color infusing his cheeks and guessed what he might mean before he said, "Yes, Daniella. You. Only not as a victim or a suspect, as an appealing young woman who interested me. That was my mistake. I promise it won't happen again."

All she could think to say was *too bad*.

Thankfully, good sense kept her from voicing it.

As far as Isaac was concerned, he was still on the job even if his dog wasn't. He offered his guest a quick tour of the ground floor of the old farmhouse, then suggested she get some sleep upstairs in his sister's room while she had the chance.

What he didn't say was that Daniella might need all her strength and wits in the coming hours and days and should take advantage of any opportunity to recover from the long, trying night before.

Limping to the small room he used as a home office, Isaac was more than ready to get off his feet. He propped his sore leg on a half-open drawer, leaned back in the swivel chair and powered up the laptop he normally carried in his work vehicle. A simple password and he was in.

Most of his emails were inconsequential compared with the files McCord had sent about Daniella. A quick scan told him that the captain hadn't left out anything. The gaps were evident, and now that he knew she'd been relocated by witness protection he wasn't surprised.

Getting the old records of her journey from past to present might be hard to do but learning about her father's crimes and punishment was not going to be tough. Fagan's arrest and conviction were matters of public record. He'd start there, then see how much more help he needed to complete his own file on Daniella.

He'd hardly begun when Captain McCord telephoned. "Black. How are you feeling?"

"Sore. And halfway mad at myself. But the nurse is safe now. She's with me."

"Yeah, so I understand. I thought I warned you to not get personally involved."

"She's not staying here long. I just needed someplace to put her while we get in touch with witness protection and they make new plans for her."

"And when will that be?"

"Very soon. The poor woman's at the end of her rope and there's nothing wrong with letting her unwind here. Once she calls the Feds we'll lose jurisdiction."

"You mean you'll lose touch with her, don't you?"

Isaac took a deep breath before he answered, "That has crossed my mind, yes."

"Well, I'll cut you some slack because of your leg. But while you're home playing babysitter you also need to keep on top of our other cases. General Meyer says the White House wants results on the Michael Jeffries murder, for one. With the congressman back in the news because of the bombing at his press conference, reporters have started asking questions about his late son again."

Despite working diligently on the murder case—and the attempted murder of the congressman himself—the Capitol K-9 Unit was no closer to solving it. "I copy. Has there been any more news about the child who may have witnessed the attack at the Jeffries estate?"

Isaac thought about the child's glove that had been found near the crime scene and the subsequent attacks on All Our Kids foster home, which had resulted in the home being moved to a secret location. The Capitol K-9 Unit surmised that the killer had seen a child watching from the tree line of the woods between the congressman's property and the former foster home, but that the killer didn't know *which* child—hence the attacks on the foster home.

"Some. Tommy Benson admitted he snuck out that night and his caretakers report he's been having nightmares."

"Are the children safe at the new location?"

"Yes. Nicholas interviewed Tommy after the boy got spooked by something and ran away from the home. We're positive he's the kid who witnessed Michael Jeffries's murder and dropped the blue glove in the woods. He did say he's afraid of some guy with white hair. That's about all we've managed to get out of him."

Isaac mentally shook his head at the thought of anyone harming the innocent children at the foster home. He pictured little Juan Gomez, the two-year-old son of Congressman Jeffries's former housekeeper, who'd been found dead at the bottom of a cliff the night before Michael Jeffries's murder. Juan had been staying at All Our Kids until a couple of months ago, when his aunt, Lana Gomez, took him in. "What's going on with Juan Gomez? Is he happy living with his aunt Lana?"

"All reports are very positive," the captain said.

"Good. Send me updates and I'll reread the files to refresh my memory, then get back to you if I see anything that gives me new ideas. I still think there may be a connection between Rosa's death and that of the congressman's son."

"Michael Jeffries was an attorney," McCord said flatly. "They make enemies."

"Yeah, but they don't all end up shot and killed."

McCord was adamant. "There's no way the Jeffries family is guilty of anything except being involved in Washington politics. I've known Harland since I was a kid. If I thought for a minute that they'd actually broken the law, I'd be the first to act."

Which is probably a big part of the reason this case is stalled, Isaac thought. He decided it would be best to change the subject. "Okay. I'll call in as soon as we know where Daniella Dunne is going and when."

"Fair enough. Talk to you later."

The conversation over, Isaac sat and pondered the facts he already knew, sharing them with Abby, who never offered unasked-for opinions.

He smiled down at her. "One, Harland Jeffries is as crooked as a dog's hind leg no matter what Gavin thinks. My apologies, girl." The little beagle wagged her tail and made herself comfortable sprawled on the hardwood floor beside him. Research into the congressman's activities hinted at corruption, the taking of bribes, but nothing that could be proven—yet.

"Two," Isaac went on, "Jeffries's longtime housekeeper took a swan dive off a cliff but left no suicide note."

"Three, whoever shot the son evidently also tried to kill the father. Jeffries could have bled out before help arrived."

As he mused, Isaac was absently tickling Abby's soft, floppy ears with the fingers of one hand.

"Four, Erin Eagleton, another daughter of Senator Eagleton, is believed to have been on the scene during the lethal assault because her jewelry was found there." He took a deep breath and released it as a sigh. "And five, there's a scared kid named Tommy who just may have the answers to everything."

Isaac felt as if someone had put his thoughts in a blender and flipped the switch. Even if they did not yet have all the facts concerning these complicated cases, there was a good chance they had enough clues to at least make some headway.

"Somehow, it all has to hinge on Jeffries. He's the only common denominator."

When a feminine voice behind him asked, "What makes you say that?" Isaac jumped and almost fell off his chair.

SIX

Daniella covered a giggle with her hand. "Oops. Sorry. I didn't mean to startle you."

"I thought you were taking a nap."

She shrugged. "That's hard to do when all I can think about is being blown to bits."

Isaac frowned. "You don't feel safe here?"

"Here? Of course," she answered. "But I can't stay forever. I need to call the US marshals and tell them what's happened so they can relocate me."

"I know. Want to borrow my phone?"

"That won't help much. All the specific info I need to identify myself is either on the phone card you got rid of or in my apartment. They don't just arbitrarily believe anybody who calls and claims to be one of their protected witnesses."

"That makes sense. So, what you're saying is that you need to go back there soon." He began to smile wryly, making her feel as if he believed she'd tried to trick him and failed.

"It's *true*."

"I don't doubt it. I'm also sure you've been racking

your brain to come up with a plausible reason to go looking for your cat." The smile grew. "Am I right?"

"You've never heard of killing two birds with one stone?"

"Sure. I've also heard of pet owners who consider their animals to be family."

"Ha! You should talk." She made sure he saw her staring at Abby. The beagle had rolled onto her back and was lying with all four legs in the air, begging for a tummy rub.

"I told you before. This dog and I are working partners."

"Well, Puddy's my only true friend so he counts, too." She could tell by the way the officer sobered and straightened in his chair that she'd revealed too much.

"I know you have more good friends than one cat."

Daniella shook her head slowly, deliberately. "No. I don't. I didn't dare let myself get too close to anybody in case this very thing happened. My father is too vindictive. If he thought anyone was important to me, the way Mom was, it would be just like him to eliminate that person out of sheer meanness."

She heard Isaac give a sigh as he turned back to his computer and said, "All right. Let's see what else we can find in your father's background that might help us anticipate his next move. How about known associates? Can you think of people he might contact in civilian life? What about the men he worked with before he was sent to prison?"

"Most of them either died or landed in jail, too. Besides, I told all that to the police and the prosecutor before his trial."

"I don't necessarily mean the criminal element. I mean

regular folks. You know, his garage mechanic or the pool boy or yard man. People like that."

She raked her fingers through her hair. "I can't remember. It was ten years ago and I was a self-centered teenager. I hardly noticed those kinds of employees."

"You mean you didn't have a crush on the pool boy?"

Her cheeks warmed. "All I can recall is his dark, wavy hair and nice muscles. Not nearly as nice as yours, though." The warmth of her face increased until she had no doubt she was visibly blushing.

The computer made a chirping noise and drew their attention. Isaac clicked on his email icon and opened the attachment. It contained autopsy photos along with a series of recent reports. "Sorry," Isaac said.

"Hey, I'm a nurse, remember?" She leaned over his shoulder to peer at the screen. "Who is that?"

"Michael Jeffries, Harland's son. Mind if I look at the rest of the file?"

"Not at all. If I hadn't chosen nursing I might have gone into the study of forensics."

As the shots flashed by, she suddenly squeezed Isaac's shoulder. "Stop. Go back. I want to look at that one."

"Looks like Michael hurt his shoulder when he fell."

Daniella pointed. "No, no. That's not an injury. It's a birthmark. I saw one almost identical to it on Harland Jeffries's shoulder just the other night."

"Interesting. Is that kind of thing rare?"

"Not really. Unlike some other types of marks, ones like that can be inherited. It's called a café au lait mark, coffee with cream," Daniella explained. "If I had a picture of Harland's back I could prove it."

"You don't have to prove anything to me. I believe you."

She smiled and gave Abby's stomach a rub.

"About everything," he added. "And I'm going to do my best to see that no harm comes to you."

"Thanks." She didn't pull away when Isaac laid his warm hand over hers and held very still.

He didn't speak again. Neither did she.

There was no need.

Isaac figured he could stall his houseguest and keep her from returning to her apartment for one more day, maybe two. The cat had plenty of food and water so it wouldn't suffer. He simply preferred to keep Daniella away long enough for whoever was after her to determine she was no longer living there.

He sent her out to talk to his brother so he could telephone his sister, Becky, in private. The real estate office answering machine picked up his call.

Instead of listening to the message, he hung up and dialed her cell. "Becky, pick up," he was saying as her "Hello" cut in.

Isaac huffed. "Where are you?"

"On my way to show a house in Arlington. Why?"

"I hope you don't mind having a surprise houseguest."

"Mind? Of course not. Who is it?"

"Daniella Dunne. She's an innocent victim of a crime. She won't be with us long."

"She can stay as long as she needs to. Give her my room if you want. Is there anything else I can do to help her?"

"Come home ASAP," Isaac said. "Daniella acts fine most of the time but I'm getting the idea she's a lot more fragile than she lets on. I don't want her to fall apart with only me and Jake here to comfort her."

Listening to his sister chuckle upset Isaac. "Look, Becky, this is not funny."

"Hey, I was laughing at you, not her."

"Well, fine. Daniella's scared, as she should be, and until the cops can find the person who set explosives under her car, she'll continue to be in danger."

"How can you be sure of that?"

"Because there's more to the story. The bomb construction was familiar, for one. Crude but effective."

"What about the one that went off last night by the monument? Which reminds me, how's your leg?"

"It hurts. Thanks for asking," Isaac said, tongue in cheek. This was not the first time it had occurred to him to wonder why the two recently set bombs were so similar, both in size and destructive efficiency—or in this case, inefficiency.

"We sent the fragments of the first one to the lab at Quantico," Isaac continued. "I don't know what the bomb squad did with the unexploded one under Daniella's car but I'm sure somebody thought to compare the test results. If not, I'll see it gets done."

"Hmm. This is the second or third time you've called her by her first name. Just how close a friend is she?"

"I met her last night," he said flatly.

"And? That doesn't mean a thing if you've fallen for her already."

"Don't be ridiculous. Nobody can get seriously involved that fast. Not even me."

"Okay, okay. I just thought I heard something different in your voice when you talked about her, that's all."

"No way. You're imagining things." But was she? Isaac wondered. There had been something odd, some unexplainable connection, that he'd sensed the moment

Daniella's frightened gaze had locked with his in the ER. They did have an emotional bond of sorts, the kind that appeared once in a lifetime, if ever. He knew it and he suspected that Daniella knew it, too.

Beginning to mutter the moment the call ended, Isaac pushed himself to his feet and made sure he was steady on his sore leg, then limped toward the area of the house where Jacob was currently at work.

As he approached, he overheard his brother's robust laugh, then the higher, lovelier pitch of a woman enjoying the same uplifting emotion. It had to be Daniella, yet the change in her mood seemed so unlikely, he paused to listen.

"So, grab a hammer and give me a hand," Jake said. "I dare you."

Isaac couldn't make out her answer but he didn't care. There was no way he was going to permit her to hang out with his brother when she should be with him and Abby, where she'd be safest.

Careful to smile as he rounded the corner into the laundry room, Isaac stopped. "There you are. I was getting worried."

Her head slanted in a quizzical pose. "Why? You're the one who sent me to Jake," Daniella countered.

"I know. I just needed privacy. You can come back to the den now."

It floored him when she shook her head and said, "I'd rather stay here and help your brother if it's all the same to you. He needs me to hold the level while he nails things in place."

The urge to make a fuss and insist she rejoin him was so strong Isaac almost expressed his disappointment. He saw Daniella look from him to his brother, then back again, as if she were a child trying to decide which flavor of cookie to choose.

He wanted her to come with him voluntarily rather than because he'd ordered it. What little he already knew about her was contradictory, yet instinct told him she could be stronger than she appeared sometimes. She'd have had to be to survive and thrive after her turbulent teen years. Any weakness he was sensing now had to be mostly due to the reappearance of her lethal father.

Having enjoyed a home with stable, loving parents and a peaceful childhood, Isaac couldn't imagine the pain she must have suffered. Must still be suffering.

Perhaps it was his empathy, perhaps his deep desire to look after her, that made the difference. He didn't care how it was defined. All he knew was that Daniella abruptly turned to Jacob to apologize for leaving, then joined him.

He smiled. She took his arm. The warmth of her touch through the fabric of his shirtsleeve was unbelievable. For a few moments he actually forgot the pain in his leg, overlooking everything but her.

When she said, "You know, it's high time I contacted the marshal's office and set up an appointment," Isaac's heart lodged in his throat.

Of course she was leaving DC. He'd known that from the beginning. So why were his emotions taking him for such an impossible ride?

It must be the pain meds that were befuddling his brain, he concluded. No way was he going to actually fall for a woman whose primary goal was to disappear for good. He was smarter than that.

At least he hoped he was.

* * *

Parts of the day sped by for Daniella while other parts seemed interminable. Her biggest concern was for her poor, abandoned kitty.

"I've decided what to do," she began at the dinner table. Becky had arrived bearing several pizzas and the rest of them had set the table. "Do?" Isaac raised a brow.

"About Puddy. You can drop me at my apartment in the morning and I'll go in alone so he won't be so scared."

She saw his gaze rake over his brother and sister before returning to her. "See? What did I tell you? The woman is self-destructive."

"I'm nothing of the kind. I'm logical. Puddy's afraid of dogs. That's why he hid. All I have to do is go in by myself and he'll come right to me. Then I can dig out my private contact numbers for witness protection and I'll be all set."

"Not happening," Isaac muttered.

"Why not?" If she'd been standing she'd have planted her fists on her hips. As it was she almost pounded the dining room table. "You told me there was a watch on my apartment in case my— In case the bad guys showed up again, so unless your cop buddies are slacking off, the place should be secure."

Jake chuckled. "She's got you there, bro."

Agreeing, Becky reached over and patted Daniella's hand. "When you're right, you're right. Would you like me, or all of us, to go with you?"

"Not necessary. But thanks for the offer. Like I said, the cat is kind of shy. Being black, it's easy for him to hide in dark spaces and I'm afraid if I don't coax him out soon he may get depressed and make himself sick."

Laughing softly, Becky winked at her brothers. "Well, guys, I tried to get us invited. Guess you're on your own."

As far as Isaac was concerned this was no laughing matter. He scowled at his siblings. "Coercion isn't necessary. Ms. Dunne wants to survive long enough for the authorities to arrange a new life for her. I'm sure she knows I'm right about not going off on her own." He smiled as if positive she was about to agree. When she did not, he was happy to see the subject dropped, at least temporarily.

He just wished he couldn't see the wheels grinding in her fertile imagination. One look in her eyes told him she was far from convinced.

"Suppose we play it by ear and see what the circumstances are once we get to my apartment," Daniella suggested, eyeing his injured leg after breakfast the following morning. "After all, I know better than to bandage a cut without cleaning it and assessing the damage first. The same should go for your job. It's silly to borrow trouble and react defensively to a threat that may never come about."

Isaac's palms were pressed to the table as if he intended to leap to his feet. Instead, he stood slowly, deliberately. His shoulders were square, his spine stiff and his jaw set, presenting an image of an immovable granite boulder rising from bedrock.

"Ms. Dunne," he began, "I have never lost a person I was assigned to protect and I don't intend to start now. Either you agree to do things my way or we won't do them at all. Am I making myself clear?"

"Perfectly."

Daniella knew she shouldn't fight his good intentions, yet a perverse side of her personality kept insisting she didn't need looking after. Logically, she did, of course. Anyone in his or her right mind could see that. It was just that when Isaac issued orders he got under her skin. Perhaps it was his tone, although it could also be the way he delivered his demands. His body language brooked no argument, actually spurring her to disagree just on principle.

Which is totally unfair, she chided herself, realizing she was being unreasonable—and not liking the picture of herself as a petulant, spoiled child.

Finally she said, "All right, Officer Black. You win. We'll do it your way. Just take me back to find my cat. Please?"

"Of course. As long as you promise to behave reasonably from now on."

Daniella raised her right hand as if taking a solemn oath. "I hereby promise to be reasonable about the rescue of my pet, Puddy." She grinned slyly with a telltale twitch of mirth at the corners of her mouth.

Any vow she took was meant to be kept and there was no way she'd ever agree to promise to do things the officer's way forever. Just getting through the following few days was going to be hard enough without placing further restrictions on her thoughts and actions.

She was her own woman. She'd already given up just about everything that mattered to her. She was *not* going to walk away from her dearest furry friend. Not if she could help it.

SEVEN

Isaac kept waiting for the other shoe to drop. Daniella was behaving so well during their outing back into DC she worried him. Knowing her the way he thought he did, he kept wondering what kind of stunt she was planning to pull before she eventually escaped from Virginia. And from his protective custody.

He wasn't kidding himself. The pretty nurse was not foolish, nor was she fearless. Somewhere between those two extremes was the real Daniella Dunne.

"I've contacted the patrol that was watching your building," Isaac told her. "They haven't seen any suspicious activity."

"Watching it how?"

"Drive-bys and a few closer inspections. They couldn't afford to put men on it 24/7 since no one was actually hurt there."

"I could have been!"

"Yes, but you weren't. Now, settle down. There's no use getting mad at me. I'm not in charge."

"If I'd been a congressman like Jeffries they'd have guarded my apartment."

"That bomb at his press conference was detonated,"

Isaac reminded her. One glance told him she was beginning to adjust to hearing discussions of explosives and
such. When he'd first met her she'd blanched and looked
unsteady every time the subject had come up. Now she
was actually chatting about the subject. Sort of.

"True. I don't suppose there's a snowball's chance in
July of the two bombs being made by the same person."

His head snapped around. "Why do you ask? Do you
think they were?"

"How should I know?" She was studying him intently.
"Wait a minute. *You* think they were, don't you? You've
suspected him ever since you found out he wasn't in
prison anymore."

"I never said that."

"You didn't have to." Daniella's voice rose. "I can see
it in your face. What did the lab reports say?"

"I couldn't tell you if I knew."

She slumped back on the passenger seat of the SUV
and folded her arms across her chest. "Fine. Don't admit
anything. I'll make educated guesses."

"Okay. And while you're at it, maybe you can figure
out why your father might have anything to do with wanting to harm a congressman."

Isaac saw her begin to frown before she said, "He
wouldn't. Our family came from Florida, as you probably already learned when you checked out my father's
arrest record. The only politicians I heard anything about
when I was a kid were local, and those changed regularly
because they were voted in and out of office."

"I suppose it's possible he taught others how to as-
semble the devices while he was in prison."

Daniella huffed. "Or they learned from the internet.

There's nothing that can't be found on there if you search long enough."

"Unfortunately, you're right." He slowed as they approached her apartment and inclined his head toward it. "Looks peaceful."

"Looks can be deceiving."

"You an expert?"

"Yes. I've learned the hard way that it's best to trust no one."

"You're exaggerating."

Her eyebrows arched. "Am I?"

Pulling parallel with the curb, Isaac stopped the SUV. "Here's what we'll do. You wait while I check the hallway and parking areas with Abby. Then we'll go inside together and let her get a whiff of your place from the doorway."

"And then what?"

Isaac could tell his companion was getting testy but it couldn't be helped. He was there to keep her safe and that's precisely what he intended to do.

"Then we talk it over and decide what our next step will be."

"Meaning, you intend to go first and scare my poor cat again. I can't say I'm thrilled about that."

He'd opened the driver's door and placed one foot on the ground when he heard Abby whine and looked around to see why.

His jaw dropped. "Hey! Where do you think you're going?"

Daniella waved to him over her shoulder. She paused on the sparse lawn. "Hurry up and maybe I won't go in without you."

If he hadn't been hurt he could have easily overtaken

her, even if she'd tried to get away. As things stood, however, he figured he'd better comply.

What he wanted was to shout at her for taking even one little step ahead, which, of course, was the direct opposite of the smart thing to do. The more he railed at her, the more likely she was to rebel.

Muttering to himself, Isaac grabbed the end of Abby's leash and joined Daniella, letting the dog lead them both down the hallway.

Abby began to bark before they'd gone all the way. Little wonder. The entrance to the apartment had been smashed in! The wooden jamb was splintered and the door hung half off its hinges.

Someone, somehow, had broken in despite the patrols. And they hadn't been particularly subtle about it.

Daniella gasped. "What? How?"

"Doesn't matter. Just stay back."

She progressed from fear to righteous anger in mere moments. "How *dare* he!"

When she tried to push Isaac aside, she found him immovable. "Get out of my way! I have to go find my cat. He must be terrified."

"That's not our biggest problem." Isaac held on to her forearm and used a tilt of his chin to point to his dog before easing the broken door farther open.

Abby had not only stopped barking, she now sat very still with only her nose twitching, staring directly at the partially obstructed entrance.

"She—she thinks there's a bomb in there?" Daniella knew better than to question the well-trained canine's instincts, yet was having trouble wrapping her mind around reality.

"That would be my conclusion," Isaac said. "I'm not happy she alerted, but I sure am happy you didn't go charging into the place ahead of us and blow yourself up. That would leave a terrible black mark on Abby's spotless record."

Daniella rolled her eyes. "Sarcasm? Now?"

"May as well make fun of a narrow escape instead of letting it paralyze you. You're familiar with that kind of gallows humor in our professions. We've discussed it before."

"Yeah. It's all that keeps us sane sometimes." She gestured at the damaged door. "Well, go get it over with. I want my cat and I'm not leaving here this time until I find him."

Daniella realized that Puddy could have escaped at any time after the break-in but chose to believe that the loud noise, plus whoever may have entered the apartment, would have sent him scampering for cover.

And now? Now it was possible that Isaac and Abby might be seriously hurt—or worse—merely doing their jobs. That thought spurred her to call after them, "Be careful. Both of you."

It was bad enough to believe she'd inadvertently caused her mother's death. She didn't want the responsibility for others on her conscience, too.

She liked Isaac Black. Really liked him. Not only was he amusing and attractive, he loved animals, had a nice family and got along with just about everybody.

Picturing his life brought envy and she immediately quashed it. The man chased down bombs for a living. No matter how much he seemed to have going for him at present, his life was always on the line. Each new day would bring more dangers, more threats, more opportunities for one tiny error to steal all his blessings.

A world without him in it was unthinkable, yet there she stood, imagining that very thing and feeling… Feeling what? Loss? Loneliness? Hopelessness? All those and more. An overwhelming sense of bereavement cloaked her, heart and soul, making her shiver and causing actual physical pain.

Hugging herself, she began rocking and moaning inside, a silent warning trapped behind her closed lips.

It wasn't until Isaac was again standing beside her that she was able to marshal more self-control.

He holstered his weapon and gently touched her arm while the friendly beagle nudged her knees and begged to be petted.

"Are you all right?" he asked, leaning close to speak softly.

"I am if you are."

Intent on hiding her worry and undue personal concern, Daniella figured she'd succeeded. However, the moment she let her gaze meet his and saw the same tender emotional connection reflected there, her confidence began to collapse like a lobbyist's backroom deal.

The final step in the destruction of her will was Isaac's sweet smile. There was something so special, so wonderful about it she could no longer keep her distance.

Without further thought she slid her arms around his neck and stepped into his embrace.

He steadied them both. "Whoa. What's all this?"

"You risked your life for me."

As she felt his arms encircling her and pulling her closer, she heard him say, "In that case, lady, you're way behind. This is the second or third time I've rescued you. You owe me at least one more hug."

That glib comment helped snap her out of her disconcerting tailspin. Leaning away, she gave him a playful smack on the shoulder and grinned. "Oh yeah? Does everybody you protect reward you like this?"

Isaac's broad grin matched hers when he replied, "Nope. Only the damsels in distress."

"Believe it or not, there was no real bomb. All Abby found was a crumpled paper bag that must have contained explosives at one time. It's empty now."

"You're crazy! Why didn't you call the bomb squad?"

"Because a cat was batting the bag around your bedroom like it was a toy and chewing on it while he shredded it with his back feet. I figured, since it hadn't blown up the kitty, it was not dangerous."

"Puddy? You saw him?"

Chuckling, he released her and followed with Abby, thoroughly enjoying the afternoon now that there was no impending danger. "Fine thing. You cancel my reward hug to go looking for a mangy old cat."

"He's not mangy and he's only middle-aged in cat years."

"Look in the bedroom," Isaac said. "And try to get the bag away from him without touching it too much. I don't expect there to be many clues left but you never know. The lab techs might be able to get traces of something besides cat spit from it."

Daniella dropped to her knees by the bed and lifted the side of the bedspread to peer beneath the box spring. Although she didn't indicate she'd even heard his instructions, she straightened with a big, furry, green-eyed black cat tucked under one arm and the remnants of the crumpled paper bag in the other.

"Is this what you wanted?" She held a ragged edge of the soggy paper between thumb and forefinger.

"That's it. Do you have a new plastic bag I can put it in? Otherwise we'll have to wait for our CSIs—crime scene investigators."

"I know what CSI means. I watch TV."

Isaac had to laugh. Daniella looked as proud as a cat presenting a dead mouse, and the real cat looked and sounded ready to pounce on poor Abby and tear her to shreds at the first opportunity.

"In the kitchen," she said. "The cabinet to the right of the fridge."

"Gotcha. Be right back." He hesitated and eyed the hissing, growling animal in her arms. "Are you sure you can handle that monster?"

"We'll be fine. Just take the dog with you."

"Gladly."

In less than a minute he had located the correct cupboard and returned to hold out a large storage bag. "Drop it in here and it won't get damaged any more than it already is."

"Sorry about what Puddy did. Are you positive there's nothing else in here that might be dangerous? I mean, suppose they brought a bomb in that bag? It could be anywhere."

"We checked the entire apartment," Isaac assured her, shaking his head for emphasis. "There is no danger, at least not in here. It would probably be a good idea to let Abs go over your car again if you intend to pick it up from the police impound yard."

"Should I? Could I? I hadn't even considered it."

"If that's what you want. However, I think you'll stay safer if you let me continue to chauffeur you for the present. We can't be sure nobody is watching for your car or maybe planted a bug on it, intending to track you down that way. Then again, I had it towed to the storage yard to convince them you'd moved away."

"Good idea. Didn't you say I should stay at your house for the same reason?"

"Maybe. I don't recall."

"You don't recall? Give me a break. You know exactly what you're doing every second of every day. If you didn't you'd have been killed long ago."

"I think you're giving me too much credit."

"And you're giving me too little! Aargh!"

Her guttural groan of anger and frustration made Isaac jump and startled the anxious cat enough that it wiggled out of her arms. To his surprise, Daniella allowed it to wander off, though she did keep an eye on it.

Giving voice to her emotions must have felt good because she continued making unintelligible grumbling sounds before she finally said, "That's it. I've had it. I'm done."

"Done with what?"

"Being a victim," she said flatly, blowing a noisy sigh. "It's over. I was a scared kid when all this started but I'm not a child anymore. I've built a career and made a comfortable place for myself. No despicable man, father or not, is going to drive me away from the roots I've put down. If Terence Fagan thinks he can scare me off, he has another think coming."

"Whoa. Hold on," Isaac interjected. "It's all well and good to stand up to evil, but you have to be sensible about it. Until we can put him back behind bars, you still need to be careful."

"Fine. I'll report to the marshals and let them help me, but I'm going to make it clear that any relocation they arrange will only be temporary. I love my job here and, believe it or not, I love this city, even if it is full of politicians."

Isaac arched his eyebrows and smiled at her. "Wow. I've never seen this side of you. You really are determined, aren't you?"

When she faced him, hands fisted on her hips, chin jutting stubbornly and said, "Mister, you have no idea," Isaac realized she had made a major turnaround.

He also knew that irrational bravado could prove fatal unless she tempered it with good sense. In his experience, more than one victim had tried to turn the tables on a stalker and had paid for such foolishness with his or her life. That was not going to happen to Daniella. Not on his watch.

The opportunity to hide her and to give her subtle direction was invaluable. He would not waste his chance to influence her choices, even if he had to enlist the help of his siblings. Both of them had military training and were more than capable of defending themselves, as well as the stubborn nurse. She wouldn't have to be made aware of all their steps to safeguard her. As a matter of fact, the less Daniella knew about the defenses arrayed around her, the better she'd probably behave.

Nodding, Isaac made sure she was looking at him, then inclined his head to direct her attention to the closet. "Okay. Pack the last of the things you can't live without and figure out how we're going to transport your wild cat while I call this in, tell them what you want to do and get my orders."

"Be sure you make it perfectly clear that I am not running away this time. All I'm doing is stepping aside so you and your fellow cops can nab my dad. Understand?"

"Completely."

Leaving Abby with her would have made him happier, but in view of prior experience with the unfriendly cat he decided to keep the beagle at his side, where she'd be safe from feline tooth and claw.

A quick call to his office gave him the private contact number for the witness protection program in that area. The rest would be up to Daniella later.

Setting up an appointment for her to be interviewed at his home was easy. Now his only remaining problem was making sure she listened to the advice of the inspectors. Not all the victims in witness protection did. He knew it took an enormous amount of discipline to blindly follow someone else's plans for your daily existence. He also knew that failing to do so was often treacherous. Even deadly.

Daniella had no idea what Puddy would do riding in the same vehicle as Abby, but she hadn't expected what actually happened.

Their crates were side by side. The cat's was made of plastic with a metal door, meaning Puddy's view of Abby was limited. It didn't seem to matter. Daniella heard a low rumble of displeasure that quickly became a roar rising and falling in a discordant wave of sound.

Isaac chuckled. "Is that your cat? He sounds like he's trying to imitate a lion."

She had to smile back. "I suspect he is. I've heard him growl a little before but nothing like this."

Instead of expressing himself and then quieting, Puddy continued. "Oh, dear," Daniella remarked. "I'm sorry."

"Not as sorry as we're both going to be," Isaac managed to say just as Abby joined in the chorus with a "Yip, yip, yip, owoooo…" that rattled the windows of the air-conditioned SUV.

Clapping her hands over her ears, Daniella glanced at Isaac and grinned. "That's *terrible* harmony. They'll never make it in the music business."

"I knew it was coming," he shouted over the clamor rising from the cargo area. "Abs is a beagle. Howling is one of her favorite pastimes."

"Sounds like it," Daniella yelled back. She let go of her ears long enough to reach for the radio, intending to see if recorded music would distract the antagonists.

Isaac's yelp stopped her before she was able to do much. He quickly flicked switches, laughing raucously.

To her embarrassment, the car's communication system crackled and someone said, "Unit Five, dispatch. Are you all right out there?"

"Affirmative," Isaac said. "Abby is singing."

"Sounds more like you're both being overrun by a gang of crazed monkeys," the voice countered. "You sure you're okay?"

By this time Daniella's prior nervousness had contributed to her emotional unsteadiness and she was laughing so hard she was weeping and gasping for breath.

"Hush," Isaac warned, chuckling along with her. "They already think I'm in trouble."

"Mister," she managed between giggles and sniffles, "you have no idea."

He smiled back at her, arched his eyebrows and rolled his eyes. "Maybe I didn't before but I'm starting to get the picture—loud and clear."

EIGHT

Time flew by for Daniella. Puddy had finally settled down about being shut in her bedroom and had quit sticking his paw out under the door, where Abby could try to lick it. Once Daniella had realized the little dog meant no harm, she'd opted to let the animals work out their differences with the partition of solid wood between them.

She'd also done all she could to take over some daily chores and hoped her efforts were appreciated. Something in her nature insisted she must earn her way, participate fully, in order to deserve a place in the small family. There were a lot of things she didn't know how to do, such as wield hammer and nails, but she was a wiz with a duster and vacuum, and could even cook, much to Becky's delight.

Intending to wash a few windows to kill time until her afternoon appointment with witness protection, she had located a bucket, sponge and paper towels, and was searching for a stepladder when she heard a car approaching. More than a little anxious, she looked around and saw a dark sedan kicking up dust on the long driveway.

"Oh, dear. Is it that time already?"

She laid aside her cleaning supplies and headed for the

den to find Isaac, wanting him present when she spoke with the marshal.

"Isaac?" she called down the hallway, one hand cupped at the side of her mouth. "Isaac! Where are you?"

No answer came. Frustrated, she turned toward the front door, brushed her hands on her jeans, smoothed her hair, checked her image in the hallway mirror, then peeked through the narrow windows flanking the main entrance.

As the dark, unmarked car came to a smooth stop in front of the house, she saw only the driver. He paused for a few seconds, apparently speaking on his radio, then opened his car door and stepped out, squaring a broad-brimmed hat on his head and donning aviator glasses as he did so.

"Isaac!" Daniella's shout echoed in the foyer. "The marshal's here."

Still no answer. She gathered her courage and stood tall. If she was going to be master of her own fate the way she'd vowed, it was time to behave that way. Never mind that she was quaking inside. What mattered was how she presented herself and how well she was able to mask her latent fear. The way she figured it, the more she acted poised and calm and in control, the easier it would be to actually begin to feel that way.

Her hand closed on the brass knob and twisted. The door swung open easily. Daniella took a deep breath and forced a smile for the marshal's benefit.

She stepped outside.

Pulled the heavy wooden door closed.

Turned.

Looked up—and saw the leering grin of her father!

* * *

Jake tapped his brother on the shoulder. "Did you hear something?"

"Like what? I can hardly hear myself think when you're running that saw."

"Sorry." Jake flipped the off switch and the table saw blade began a high-pitched whine, its tone dropping as it slowed.

Isaac strained to hear beyond the barn where he'd been holding up the free ends of two-by-fours so Jake could trim them accurately. He glanced at his watch. "I'd better go check on Daniella. Her appointment with somebody from the marshal's office is in a half hour and I don't want her to be startled if she's lost track of time."

"What, exactly, is going on with you two?"

"Nothing. Why?"

The older brother arched his brows and rolled his eyes. "Yeah, right. Tell me another fairy tale. I've seen the way you treat her."

"I'm just doing my job, that's all."

"Uh-huh. So what's her excuse?"

Frowning, Isaac shook his head. "I don't know what you're talking about."

"Okay. Have it your way." Jake shrugged. "But don't waste your breath denying you've seen her making eyes at you. If the attraction were any plainer she'd be throwing herself at your feet."

"That's ridiculous."

"Ask Becky. She agrees with me. And we're both worried about what you may be getting yourself into. I don't care what you say, it isn't only innocent people who end up in witness protection, you know."

"Look. Daniella saw her mother murdered. All she's guilty of is testifying to the truth."

"So who's after her? You gave us a description of the guy we're supposed to look out for, so you may as well tell us the rest. Becky figures to pry the whole story out of her sooner or later, anyway."

Taking a deep breath and releasing it as a sigh, Isaac conceded. "Her own father. That's why Daniella didn't want to talk about it. She's embarrassed to admit that Terence Fagan is her dad, let alone that he swore to kill her because her testimony put him in prison."

Jacob was nodding. "Wow. Okay. I'll buy that. So what's plan B?"

Walking with his brother toward the rear of the house while still favoring his sore leg, Isaac slowly shook his head. "I have no idea. Once we've conferred with the marshal today and discussed the ramifications of Fagan's early release, we should have some kind of a plan. Daniella says she wants to stop running, but taking a stand right now may not be her smartest move."

He felt his cheeks warm as he thought about a future that included the pretty nurse. Such fantasies were likely to be futile, yet he didn't seem able to stop entertaining them. Whatever happened, however their blossoming relationship ended, he would always remember her fondly and pray that she was happy and well.

In his heart of hearts, he wished there were some way for them to remain in contact, but the moment she was forced back into protective custody the invisible chain that connected them would be broken—unless she chose to return, as she'd claimed she would. He wasn't holding his breath. A lot of things could change in the length of time she might have to be away.

The warm spring air was stirring, the sunlight soothing in spite of the sheen of perspiration on Isaac's brow. He halted and raised his arm to shade his eyes. "What's that?"

"Where?" Jacob was beside him, peering into the distance as his brother pointed.

"There. It looks like a dust cloud."

"I don't see anything."

"Maybe I was imagining it. Or maybe it dissipated. It was really faint to start with." Nevertheless, he picked up the pace.

"What's the rush?"

"I don't know," Isaac admitted. "I just have a funny feeling."

"Funny ha-ha or funny peculiar?"

"Funny risky and dangerous."

"I'll come with you."

"No." The seriousness of the order was unmistakable. "It's probably the marshal. You stay outside. Shut the dogs in the barn so they don't get in the way, then keep watch, just in case. I'm going to pick up my duty weapon and find Daniella."

Isaac climbed the wooden porch steps and slowly eased open the back door. In several more limping strides he was standing in the enormous farm kitchen.

By looking down the main-floor hallway he could see through a multipaned window in the room that had been a parlor when the house was new.

Daniella stood just outside. She was fine. His breath whooshed out with relief and he smiled, nevertheless making a quick detour to the den to pick up his firearm, as planned.

In less than a minute he was in the parlor/living room.

It was plain Daniella was upset, but she seemed in control of her basic emotions. He focused past her to the typical dark, unmarked car parked in the driveway. Although he couldn't see him, he figured the marshal had arrived early and caught her by surprise. That would explain her anxiety.

Since the urgency of his earlier worries had abated, Isaac slowed his pace and favored his injury as he crossed the room. It seemed the most natural thing in the world to keep watching Daniella as he walked.

Her back was partially to him so he wasn't able to see her face. Her shoulders were back, her spine straight and she was gesturing with her hands as if expressing herself forcefully.

Isaac froze midstride, put too much weight on his sore leg and faltered. Something had just changed. Something was wrong. Very wrong. Daniella had raised both hands as if surrendering and she were backing away from whoever she'd been talking to.

A man's hand shot out. Grabbed one of her wrists. Yanked her out of Isaac's view.

He threw open the front door and stepped through, his gun at the ready, in time to see her being forced down the stairs toward the black car.

Senses reeling, he realized he was looking at a marshal's car, uniform shirt and standard-issue hat—over faded jeans and dirty running shoes. This man was an imposter!

"Stop or I'll shoot!" Isaac yelled, taking a marksman's stance.

Daniella's captor laughed rawly. "No, you won't. You might hit the girl." He pressed the barrel of a revolver to her temple. "Or this gun might accidentally go off."

"What do you want?"

The fake lawman's grin radiated evil. "Her. But not for long," he said. "I just need to teach her a lesson."

It had occurred to Isaac the moment he'd seen the attacker that he might be Terence Fagan, although it was hard to tell for sure with the hat brim shading most of his face and silvered sunglasses masking his eyes.

"You're Fagan."

"Give the man a medal. He wins the prize."

"Listen, this is crazy," Isaac told him. "You got out of jail legally. Don't put yourself back in just to get revenge."

While the captor continued edging closer to the car, Isaac kept pace, narrowing the distance slightly with each step. The way he figured, Fagan would have to open the door to shove Daniella in before he could get behind the wheel. That should be enough time to launch a counterattack and free her.

And if it wasn't?

Isaac refused to even consider failure as an option.

He just hoped he could survive whatever personal sacrifice he'd have to make in order to bring her through unscathed.

Daniella wanted to do serious damage to the despicable man who was trying to kidnap her. Thrashing, she kicked behind, stomped on the tops of his feet, threw her weight from side to side. Nothing loosened his grip.

"Let me go!" she screeched at the top of her lungs. "Let me go, you dirty..."

Fagan did let her arm go in order to backhand her across the face before she could finish. The blow sent her flying. The instant her hands and knees hit the dirt, she began to scramble away.

Terence Fagan cursed.

Isaac leaped at him as best he could, not even feeling the stitches in his calf. They slammed into the side of the car and went down together.

Isaac's free hand grasped the wrist of his adversary to divert the lethal weapon.

Fagan did the same to him and also began to kick, landing a solid blow to Isaac's leg and causing him to shout in anguish.

Instead of running for her life, Daniella circled the car and leaped onto her father's back, wrapping both arms around his neck and trying to choke him to get him to release Isaac.

In a flurry of arms and legs, screeching and groaning, the three rolled over and over on the ground.

In the background, Isaac heard his brother's shout and a cacophony of barking.

Jacob ran around the corner of the house on the heels of Abby and the enormous mixed-breed farm dogs. He was swinging a shovel like a baseball bat.

Fagan took one look at the slavering, growling canines and screamed, then let go of his gun and everything else, jumped to his feet and dived in the driver's door, scraping Daniella off in the process.

The engine roared. Spinning tires threw a rooster tail of dust and gravel. The big car fishtailed, then straightened and sped away.

"Abby, come. Heel!" Isaac shouted, afraid for the K-9's safety.

The little beagle slid to a halt and the larger dogs did the same, following her back to the yard at a brisk trot, tails waving and looking terribly pleased with themselves.

The sight of Daniella, sitting there in the dirt with her cheeks tearstained and her breathing ragged, tore at Isaac's heart. He reached for her.

She mirrored his actions. In seconds she was in his arms, cradled against his chest, trembling.

He pulled her tighter. Soothed her with murmurs. Wished he'd been there for her when she'd been attacked.

"I'm so sorry," he said softly.

She drew a stuttering breath. "I'm the one who's sorry. I should have recognized my father, even in disguise. Are you hurt? I saw him kicking you."

"It's nothing." He was loath to release her long enough to get to his feet, assuming he could.

When Jacob offered a hand, Isaac took it, pulling Daniella up beside him.

That didn't break them apart. If anything, it strengthened their embrace.

"Is he gone?" Isaac asked his brother.

Jake nodded. "Yeah. Last I saw of him he was turning onto the road and flooring it."

"Terrific."

Keeping one arm firmly around Daniella's waist, Isaac fisted his cell phone and reported the foiled attack, starting with the general direction the fleeing fugitive was headed.

"It was an official car so it shouldn't be hard to locate now that we know Fagan stole it. The uniform, too."

"He—he bragged about killing the real marshal," Daniella added softly, as if loath to say it.

Isaac relayed her information. "Yeah, it's possible. We didn't see any sign of him. His handlers can probably track his movements before he was due here and locate him, hopefully still alive. Tell them I'm sorry I didn't get a chance to examine the car's trunk." He paused to listen. "Okay. Keep us informed."

"What are they going to do?" Daniella asked as soon as the call ended.

"Coordinate a search for the marshal and his car. That has to come first. Then somebody will probably come by here to take our statements. What I can't understand is how Fagan found out when your appointment with the marshal was and how he managed to outwit a professional lawman."

"He told me he put a bug in my apartment and listened to your call to set things up," Daniella explained.

"I should have anticipated that."

Isaac felt her arms tighten slightly, as if imparting moral support, before she said, "Don't beat yourself up about it. There's no way anybody would have suspected what he was up to this time. He's always used indirect action before."

"True. This face-to-face attack changes everything. You realize that, don't you?"

"I do. But I've decided to tell the marshals I'd prefer to handle my relocation myself. The more people who know where I've gone, the bigger the chances of a leak. I don't want innocent people to die because of me."

Isaac didn't totally agree with her logic but decided to save his arguments for later, after she'd calmed down.

It was beginning to look as if destiny had not brought the perfect woman into his life so he could keep her foreve, after all. She was going to have to leave DC ASAP, and it would be more than selfish of him to try to hang on to her.

It might even be lethal.

NINE

To Daniella's relief, Isaac got a call that the injured marshal had been located, hospitalized and was expected to recover.

On the negative side, there had been no sightings of Terence Fagan or the stolen car. She and the Black brothers had given official statements about the attack, but in spite of extensive roadblocks and all-points bulletins, Fagan was still on the run.

She had redressed Isaac's injury after the altercation and had found herself actually feeling his pain. As an ER nurse, she had often done the exact same task, yet this had been the first time she'd winced while tending to a patient. Not only had that reaction been a surprise, it had been unnerving to share such strong empathy with the K-9 officer.

Dinner conversation that evening and the next was subdued, for which she was doubly thankful since she felt so guilty about bringing trouble to such a nice family.

It was Becky who broke the charged silence around the table by asking, "So, Daniella...or should we call you something else?"

Eyes lowered while she pushed peas around her plate

with a fork, she shrugged. "I suppose you could call me Ella if you wanted to, but I really prefer Daniella." Unshed tears filled her eyes and she hoped she could hold them back long enough to politely excuse herself and leave the room.

"Daniella it is, then. Why didn't you fill us in about your past when you first arrived? It would have made a lot more sense if we'd known the circumstances."

"It's not your problem. It's mine. Nobody was supposed to know I was here and I didn't want any of you to be involved if I could help it." She glanced up at Isaac. "Didn't you tell them anything?"

"Enough to keep them from getting hurt and help them look out for you if need be," he replied. "I thought the background-story details were yours to provide if you chose. They knew he was middle-aged and I showed them booking photos."

"He looks much older now, doesn't he?" Daniella asked. "Being in prison really aged him."

"It tends to do that." Isaac looked to his sister. "I should have asked earlier. Did you renew your concealed-carry permit?"

"Yes," Becky answered. "I don't use it inside the beltway but since the trouble started I've decided it would be prudent to be armed when I'm at work, particularly if I'm out showing homes to prospective buyers." She looked to their elder brother. "How about you, Jake?"

He grinned. "Hey, I got enough of that when I was deployed overseas. As long as I have my trusty shovel and these two hands, I'll be fine."

Becky rolled her eyes. "You'd better convince him otherwise, Isaac. You're the one with the badge."

"Ha! Since when does he listen to my advice?"

Daniella reached out, laid a hand lightly on Jacob's forearm and said, "Please? I don't want anybody else to get hurt because of me. There's no telling what my father will try before the marshals either give me the okay to leave or insist on putting me somewhere else themselves."

His grin widened and he winked at his siblings. "Well, since you put it that way, I guess I could load the shotgun."

What a relief. "Thank you."

As soon as she looked away from Jacob and made eye contact with Isaac, she noticed that he seemed out of sorts. Given his concern for his family's safety, she found that off-putting attitude a bit puzzling, particularly since his brother had just agreed to take his good advice, thanks to her.

Becky began to giggle, further confusing matters. When Isaac rose from the table without excusing himself first and stalked from the room, both the remaining siblings laughed.

Counting to ten to make sure she wasn't overreacting, Daniella asked, "What's so funny?"

Becky was wiping away happy tears. "It's a private joke."

"Are you sure? It felt a lot like you were laughing at me and my story. Believe me, nothing about it is the least bit amusing." She shivered. "I still think I see shadows of attackers lurking behind every bush and tree."

"We're not laughing at you," Becky said. "Isaac's the one who's funny. He insists he's not interested in you but he's so jealous of poor Jake it's comical."

"Jealous? That's terrible."

"I wouldn't go quite that far," her hostess said. "Our brother may be too focused on his job and Abby a lot of the time, but he's really a nice guy once you get to know him."

Sorrowful, Daniella shook her head. "That's the worst part of the problem. I can't think of any job that scares me more than his does. Even if I wasn't about to temporarily relocate I'd never consider dating him, let alone getting serious."

"Really?" Becky leaned forward with her elbows on the table. "I think he's very brave."

"Oh, I don't doubt he is," Daniella replied. "But he goes looking for explosives. On purpose. Every day. The gash in his leg is just one example of an assignment gone wrong. Imagine how badly he'd have been hurt if he'd been closer or leaning over it to get a better look." She shivered. "I can still picture every horrible detail of my mother's death. The whole concept of going looking for bombs gives me goose bumps and makes me queasy."

"Then it's probably for the best that you're going to move on," the other woman said. "Tell you what. I'll add you to my prayer list."

"Don't bother. God gave up on me a long time ago."

"You can't really believe that."

Daniella was nodding. "Oh, yes, I do. My mother had strong faith and she still died, even after I prayed and prayed for her."

"That doesn't mean the Lord ignored you. It's possible it was her time to go home to Him. Think about it. You say she was unhappy and stuck in a bad marriage. Her death not only freed her, it gave you a new life, too, and eliminated the cause of her pain."

"But not the cause of mine," Daniella countered. "Terence Fagan is still around, still after me."

"For now," Becky said gently. "Maybe meeting Isaac

and the rest of us is God's way of bringing your father's reign of terror to an end, once and for all."

"Humph. I'll believe that when I see it."

Becky smiled so sweetly it was unnerving when she said, "I pray that we'll all see it before something takes you away from us."

The official K-9 unit vehicles Isaac had been expecting rolled up shortly before the sun set that evening. He had already shut his farm dogs in the barn but Abby was loose because she was familiar with the visitors and highly trained.

He greeted the men, one blond, one darker, with a smile and handshake, then gestured toward the ornate Victorian-style covered front porch, where Daniella waited.

"Adam, Chase, I'd like you to meet Daniella Dunne, aka Ella Fagan. She's the reason I asked you both to stop by with your dogs after work."

Each man nodded politely to Daniella, then they fastened leashes on their canine partners and commanded them to jump down from the areas designed to protect them.

"The Doberman is Ace. His specialty is protection," Isaac said, pointing to Adam and the sleek black-and-brown canine by his side. "The fawn-colored shepherd type with the longer hair and black mask is a Belgian Malinois named Valor. He's trained mostly for search and rescue but both are cross-trained to track suspects and protect their handlers if necessary."

One hand resting on the wooden railing, Daniella descended partway to the yard. "They're beautiful animals." She looked to Isaac. "But why are they here tonight?"

"For added insurance," he replied. "I want them to do another sweep of the property, just in case." Although he'd been trying to broach the subject with nonchalance, it was immediately clear to him that Daniella was not fooled.

"You sensed something was wrong, too? I wasn't my imagination playing tricks on me?"

Isaac was quick to reassure her. "No. I didn't sense anything and I haven't seen a sign of your father, but I did overhear you telling Becky and Jake you were jumping at shadows."

"I thought you'd left before I said that."

"I try to never get too far from you, especially lately," Isaac admitted. "Think of this search tonight the way you do preventive medicine. It's sensible to head off problems, if you can, before you get sick. Right?"

She nodded and folded her arms across her chest, hugging herself as if the spring breeze suddenly carried a chill.

Watching her gaze dart from man to man, ending with him, Isaac smiled slightly and asked, "You can see the logic in that, can't you?"

Her lips pressed together. She squinted. "I can see a lot of things, not the least of which is how worried you are. What are you not telling me?"

"Nothing." He drew an imaginary X over his heart with one finger. "Honest."

"Assuming I buy that," Daniella drawled, "why does this look like an off-duty favor instead of a regular assignment?"

"Because it is." He was unwilling to lie, even if the truth did make her more paranoid. "You met our boss, Captain McCord, at the hospital when I was being treated. His job is a tough one, particularly considering the amount of territory our unit is responsible for, including the White House. He didn't feel that another check on this farm was necessary so he left it up to me to recruit a few volunteers if I wanted it done."

Isaac watched Adam give her a wave and Chase a two-fingered casual salute.

"I want you to split up," he told his comrades, pointing. "Adam and Ace can cover the east side of the house. Chase and Valor can take the west. Abby and I will join you in the backyard and work both sides from the middle. Ready?"

Before giving the signal to begin, he shot a stern look at Daniella. "You wait in the house." He could tell how close she was to arguing and then saw when she made the decision to comply.

"All right. This is your farm, your family and your friends, so I'll do things your way. This time." Her gaze passed over the men and animals. "Please, please be careful. I know Terence Fagan all too well. He's apt to try anything."

"That's why I'm including myself and Abby," Isaac said. "We know what we're doing."

"Remind yourself of that every time the gash in your leg starts to throb," Daniella snapped back. "You may be crazy-brave, but you're not bulletproof."

The blonder of the two other men clapped him on the shoulder and grinned. "No kidding. Some of us have been thinking of taking up a collection to buy you a head-to-toe set of body armor like the guys in the bomb squad wear." He eyed the leg Isaac was favoring. "What do you say, buddy?"

Chuckling, Isaac batted his hand away. "Let's just

concentrate on doing a good sweep, shall we? Becky's out on a date but she left coffee and cake waiting for us in the kitchen."

"Well, why didn't you say so? Let's get at it."

The joking around was a common coping mechanism and usually worked to relieve tension. The moment Isaac looked back, however, his smile disappeared.

Daniella had one arm wrapped around a porch post and was leaning against it as if she needed the added support merely to stay on her feet. Her eyes glistened. Wind ruffled her honey-colored hair that seemed to be getting lighter by the day. The jeans Becky had loaned her had never looked better on anyone, either.

Rays of the setting sun behind Daniella made her fairly glow and seem almost ethereal. For a brief moment he saw her, not as she was, but as he dreamed she could be. Innocent. Unencumbered. Free. Eager to embrace the joys of life, perhaps with him.

Then, his mind cleared and he snapped back to reality.

There was nothing about Daniella that fit his life plan. She was tortured by her past. Threatened by her present. And only half likely to have a future.

It was that future he must defend. With or without a place for himself in it, he had to make sure she had one.

The seconds and minutes dragged by for Daniella. She'd managed to keep one or more of the K-9 cops in sight by moving from window to window inside the old house.

Her final attempt led her to climb to the second floor and peer out her bedroom window so she could see over the barn roof and into the plowed fields beyond. An added comfort was the purring coming from Puddy as she cradled him and gently stroked his long fur.

The dogs and their handlers seemed to be pacing themselves and carefully moving ahead. Abby's nose remained close to the ground while the other two alternated between scents in the air or the soil. It was fascinating to watch, almost soporific, given their methodical back-and-forth movements.

Isaac had had her car checked for bugs, then moved from police impound. He'd stored it under a tarp in his barn rather than disposed of it before they knew what the marshals' plans were.

Not that I care, she mused, slightly disgusted that she hadn't been able to convince herself to simply hop into it and drive away. Part of her wanted to flee while her more sensible side insisted she wait for all the red tape to be finished properly. Logic won. Barely.

A slight movement off to the side in a grove of maples caught her attention. It had been more of a sense than actual sight; a feeling that something had shifted in her usually well-ordered universe. Had it? Or was her fertile imagination merely taking her on another unwanted journey?

Concentrating, she noted that the winged seeds on the tree were shimmering in the evening light. A few were even breaking loose to swirl to the ground like helicopter blades.

Her hand had stilled. The cat nudged her fingers with his head in a plea for more affection.

Although Daniella looked away for only a second, when her focus returned to the base of the trees she realized something had changed. But what?

This scenario reminded her of those puzzles where

minor things are different in similar pictures and the viewer is challenged to figure out what has been altered.

Trees, leaves, seeds, shadows. All seemed identical to her earlier observations.

Then, she saw it. An instant of flash. Sunlight on metal or glass. A gun? Binoculars? Maybe a telescopic sight on a rifle?

It didn't matter. Whoever was down there was now behind the men who were searching the farm fields. When they retraced their steps they'd walk right into an ambush!

The cat wiggled free and scooted under the bed, obviously sensing her tension.

Trembling all over, Daniella let him go his way without a second thought. Part of her brain was screaming *Go! Help them.*

Contradicting orders mingled with her desire for bravery and she pictured herself shinnying under the bed beside her frightened cat.

What should she do? What *could* she do? Becky had gone out for the evening, presumably taking her handgun, and all Jake had to protect himself was that stupid shovel and a shotgun. A lot of good those would do him against a rifle, particularly at a distance.

No. She couldn't enlist aid. She had to handle this situation herself. After all, the prowler was most likely after her. She'd brought the danger here and it was up to her to warn the K-9 officers. *But how?*

Her first thought was to throw open the window and shout at them, until she realized that that would bring them on the run, right into the waiting trap.

"Can I run fast enough to keep from getting shot?" she murmured to herself.

Pressing her lips together, she shook her head. "Not a chance." She'd be doing well to even clear the back porch, let alone make it around the big barn and across the field before being spotted and stopped.

What choices are left?

No easy answers came to her. The sensible thing might be for her to drive Isaac's SUV or maybe Jacob's pickup truck, but first she'd have to lay her hands on the right set of keys. Isaac probably had his with him and if she asked Jake for the truck keys she'd have to tell him why she wanted them, meaning he was bound to interfere, perhaps fatally.

That left only one option. The car in the barn under the tarp. Daniella gritted her teeth and clenched her jaw. That car was where her father had left the bomb for her. Had he been on the premises long enough to have had a chance to repeat his attempt? Isaac had checked, of course, but that didn't mean that someone else couldn't have tampered with her car. She rooted through her purse searching for her spare keys. Where were they? They had to be in there.

Just as she was about to give up, her fingers touched the familiar ring. Fisting it, Daniella ran for the stairs and descended so fast she almost missed a step and fell.

Her pulse sped. Her breathing was shallow. Her knees threatened to fold and drop her to the floor before she accomplished her goal. She would not let that happen. Lives hung in the balance.

Centrifugal force carried her around the newel post at the bottom and headed her in the right direction. There was no time to search for protection or develop a disguise. Besides, the less encumbered she was, the faster she could move.

The element of surprise would be her armor. Dashing through the kitchen, she yanked open the back door and sailed off the end of the porch, not bothering to take the stairs.

Landing was trickier. Momentum pitched her forward. She caught herself on her hands and pushed off like a sprinter, without missing a beat.

The big barn door was closed so she headed for the smaller one at the side farthest from the maple trees that hid her enemy.

In the seconds it took her to work the latch, she kept expecting to hear the crack of a shot and feel its impact.

Instead, she was bowled over by three dogs the size of ponies. Barking and howling, they crowded out the open door and took off around the barn as if their tails were on fire. Would their arrival be enough of a warning? Or would they cause the officers to race back to the house without any thought for themselves? Probably the latter. Unless she acted swiftly.

Daniella paused to take stock. Several cats had made themselves at home atop the tarp covering her car. She shooed them away and whipped it off, then pivoted to free the crude latch holding the larger doors closed.

They swung partially out of the way while Daniella slid behind the wheel, hoping, praying her father had not discovered this vehicle and tampered with it again.

She missed the key slot twice, then grabbed her trembling wrist with her other hand to steady it. The key turned easily. The engine groaned, stuttered, quit! *And the car did not blow up! Praise God!*

Again she hit the ignition. Stomped on the gas pedal. Dropped the transmission into Drive. With a grinding of gears and squealing of tires, the car shot toward the doors.

They hadn't opened fully when she'd released them, but Daniella didn't care. She missed the left one, clipped the edge of the right and spun her car in a half circle, throwing a rooster tail of dust and dirt higher than the top of the car.

Her fingers felt like part of the wheel with her mind directing the engine, her feet urging it on. Nothing could distract her now. Not even being shot at.

The car fishtailed around the corner of the barn and straightened out, heading directly toward the plowed field the K-9 officers were searching.

Shock reflected off Isaac's face, his jaw dropped and he began to wave his arms at her.

Daniella belatedly realized why he had been signaling so frantically. Her hood and front fenders plowed through a barbed-wire fence, snapping the spans and whipping long lengths of spiked, twisted wire behind her.

Her front and rear windows shattered simultaneously, and Daniella let out a piercing scream. Only the windshield stayed together, its surface a tangle of spidery cracks. She hit the brakes, skidded sideways and came to a halt mere feet from the men and all the dogs.

Someone jerked her door open and dragged her from the car. When she landed on the uncomfortable ridges of plowed dirt, she expected to be welcomed.

"You almost killed us!" Isaac roared.

Daniella shook her head and waved away the clouds of dust with both hands, blinking to clear her vision. "I did nothing of the kind. I just saved your lives."

"By whipping us with wire and running us over?"

"No. By keeping you from walking into an ambush when you came back to the house to see why your other dogs were out. I saw somebody hiding under one of the maple trees below my room."

"Did anybody else see this person?"

"No, but… I know there was someone there. I saw a glint of light reflecting off metal or glass. I know I did. I thought it was a gun."

"Right."

She saw one of the other officers tap Isaac on the shoulder and gesture at her car. He stepped closer in spite of the loose fencing wire that was still festooning the hood.

When he turned to look back at her, his anger was gone. So was the color in his face. All he did was point.

Joining him, she understood. It had not been the collision with the fence that had caused her windows to shatter.

A hole as big around as her little finger was punched through the fractured safety glass.

A hole the size of a bullet.

TEN

Isaac kept hold of Abby's leash and slipped an arm around Daniella's shoulders. By unspoken agreement, Adam radioed headquarters, Chase called the local police and Isaac used his cell to notify Jacob.

"Hi, Jake."

"What in the world is going on? I thought I heard a shot."

"You did. Stay inside. Somebody's using us for target practice. Nobody's hurt so far. If you keep your head down, it should stay that way."

"Where are you?"

"Behind the barn. You probably can't see us from the house. Just don't let yourself be silhouetted in the windows, whatever you do."

"Is it Fagan?"

"Can't tell," Isaac said, reluctant to say much in front of the trembling woman in his arms. "Might be."

"Okay. I'll go warn Daniella."

The chuckle Isaac managed sounded more like a cough. "Um, that won't be necessary. She's here with me."

"Outside? Is she *nuts*?"

"Maybe. Probably. The important thing is that you stay out of sight until the cops arrive and you warn Becky to check with one of us before driving home."

"Right. Will do." There was a pause. "You *are* going to tell me exactly what's going on when you come in. I don't care if your girlfriend is embarrassed about her family. I want all the details. Copy?"

"You already know most of them," Isaac argued, "but all right. We'll answer any questions. I promise. Now call Becky for me, will you? My battery's low and I want to save it for emergencies."

Ending the call, he turned his full concentration on the woman at his side and scowled. "Do you have a death wish?"

"Of course not." She leaned away and met his gaze boldly. "I have a life wish, for myself and everybody else I know. If you guys had started back to the house, the sniper would have had clear shots at all of you. I spotted him, but you had no idea of the danger, so I did what I had to do."

"You've never heard of phones?"

He saw her eyebrows draw together in a clear frown. "Yes," she drawled, "but somebody took mine away and never replaced it. I knew if I asked Jake to call you he'd make me stay in the house and put himself in danger. It wasn't his job, it was mine. I brought the problem with me and I intend to face it—as many times as necessary."

"You'd better hope nobody ever gives you a professional psych eval, lady. You sound certifiable."

"Don't raise your voice to me."

"I wasn't, I…" Isaac realized she was right. He had been yelling. Little wonder. Once again Daniella had had a narrow escape and his racing heart hadn't yet recovered. Matter of fact, the more she revealed about her convoluted reasoning, the more concerned he became.

He lightly touched her hand. "Look. I'm sorry. I was reacting to what you'd done and it scared me to death. You may have escaped in the past but that's no guarantee you won't be injured, or worse, if you keep on defying your father."

"I'm as smart as he is."

"Yes, but he's also crafty. You can't expect him to behave rationally. His warped mind won't let him."

"Because he's a sociopath. I know," Daniella admitted. "I spent a lot of time studying about people like him in the hopes I could understand him. He truly believes he's in the right and is allowed to act in any manner that brings him to his goals, no matter who gets hurt in the process."

"Exactly. That was the conclusion of the prison psychiatrist, too. Fagan won't listen to reason because he thinks he's infallible. And he sees you as a roadblock to the perfect life he envisions."

A small smile twitched at the corners of her mouth, taking Isaac by surprise.

"I am a roadblock," Daniella said, speaking softly. "If I'm the only one who can get that awful man off the streets and back into jail, then I'll do whatever I have to do to make it happen."

Left unsaid was the part of her vow that knifed into his gut, his heart, and left him feeling real pain. She meant, if she had to die as her mother had in order to see justice done, she'd willingly make that sacrifice.

Yes, it was brave. It was also foolhardy. There was a big difference between the work he did for law enforcement and her idea that only she could stop Fagan.

If he didn't accomplish anything else while they were together, Isaac vowed he was going to teach her that. Or die trying.

They remained crouched behind Daniella's car, just in case, until they heard sirens and saw flashing red-and-blue lights approaching the house. The officers in the patrol cars slid to stops in the front and rear of the old Victorian, panned the scene with spotlights, then cautiously disembarked, guns drawn.

Isaac stood, causing Daniella to do the same. Or try to. His hand on her shoulder shoved her back down, and she didn't like that treatment one bit. "Hey. Let go."

"Keep your head down until I say you can stand."

"Why? Is your head bulletproof?"

The look he shot her was so disparaging—and so silly looking—she almost laughed. Tension often did that to her. Truth be told, she'd lots rather get the giggles than burst into tears every time she was challenged or felt in jeopardy. That particular thought did make her smile. "I'll take sniper avoidance for a thousand, Alex," she murmured, earning another scathing look from Isaac.

She busied herself petting Abby until Isaac finally gave her permission to rise.

Dusting off her hands and her jeans, she fell into step behind the men and their working dogs while the farm dogs ran circles around the group and barked excitedly. At a whistle from Jake, they headed for the yard and disappeared, presumably confined in the barn again.

Although she continued to stand back a little ways, Daniella made sure to stay close to a refuge such as the barn or the house or a police car so she'd be ready to duck if anybody located the shooter. Instinct told her the man was long gone, but since she didn't want any more safety-protocol lectures from her host, she figured it would be best to voluntarily keep a low profile.

Listening to the K-9 officers reporting the details of the attack reminded her of the Spartan way doctors and nurses kept patient records. Impressions and feelings were unimportant in that context but facts were crucial. The trouble was, they had few to go on in this case.

In retrospect she kind of wished she'd waited a little longer to make a break for it in the hopes she'd have gotten more information about the menace waiting in the trees.

Then again, once Isaac and his friends had started back to the house, she'd have lost sight of them until they'd rounded the barn and by that time they'd have been in the shooter's sights.

Daniella shivered and looked toward Isaac. How special he was. How kind. How attractive. How…perfect.

"Yeah," she muttered, huffing derisively at her own idiocy. "Perfect for somebody else maybe."

He glanced over his shoulder. "Did you want to add something? You spotted the perp first."

"No need." She shrugged and slipped her hands into her jeans pockets so he wouldn't see her fingers trembling. "You guys have covered it. I thought the farm dogs might chase him off when they got out past me but apparently not, since there's a hole in my car."

"If you thought that, why did you risk driving out back?"

"Because I couldn't be sure. I figured you'd take one look at them and come looking to see if I was in trouble. If you had, he'd have been able to pick you off like fish in a barrel."

There was no need for her to wonder if her statement had been nonchalant enough because Isaac's scowl deepened noticeably. *Good.* That meant he would be less likely to realize how scared she really was and coddle her.

How she had managed to do what she'd done without being wounded was beyond comprehension. Isaac had been totally right to yell at her for taking such risks. Given a second chance, she strongly doubted she'd be able to convince herself to repeat the same act, let alone do anything when she knew for sure that the prowler was so well armed.

Basically, she was scared witless. "With *witless* being the operative word," she told herself, remembering how sensible her plan had seemed until now, when she could look back on it.

Edging closer to the others, she admitted needing their support, the comfort of their strength, particularly Isaac's. If he decided to put his arm around her shoulders again she was definitely going to leave it there—for as long as possible.

Adrenaline kept Daniella awake and alert for the next hour or so, then dropped her like a deflating helium balloon. The harder she tried to think up excuses for charging out to the barn and driving her car through a fence, the less she agreed that those actions were wise or necessary.

Back in the kitchen with the K-9 officers and the Blacks, she wrapped her hands around a mug of steaming coffee and faced them. Adam and Chase seemed to have accepted her excuses because their postures were relaxed. Conversely, it was clear that Isaac and his brother had not. They were both edgy and staring at her as if she had committed an unpardonable sin.

"Look," she said, trying again. "I wasn't being careless. I simply didn't see another option that would keep everybody safe."

"What about *you*?" Isaac demanded, his words clipped, his expression accusing her of not thinking at all, let alone making a sensible decision.

Daniella leaned back in her chair and yawned, covering her mouth with one hand. "I started this. I'll finish it."

"You did not!" Isaac started to jump to his feet but Jacob and Adam, one seated on either side, stopped him.

"I think what my brother is trying to say," Jake offered, "is that whatever your relatives did or didn't do, you can't be held responsible."

"Terence Fagan is my father. I testified against him. Of course I'm responsible."

"Who says?"

Her attention swung back to Isaac to answer, "I do."

"You're wrong," he told her, sounding less angry and far more downhearted than before. "That man may have destroyed your mother with a bomb, but she wasn't the only one harmed. You were scarred, too. Deeply. And the only way I know of to help you is to remind you that we're all children of God. All of us are guilty to some extent and all are promised forgiveness. We just have to genuinely ask for it and have faith."

She clenched her jaw muscles and sat up straighter in her chair as if prepping to do battle. "Mom took me to church and Sunday school. I know the rules. I also know I will never be able to forgive that man. Never. He took everything from me. My mother. My sense of family. My home and friends. All of it's gone."

"Then maybe the secret is forgiving yourself first," Isaac proposed.

Speechless to learn that he was so close to understanding her internal struggles, Daniella pushed back from the table and rose.

"Leave your plates and cups in the sink, gentlemen," she said. "I'm too tired to wash up now so I'll do the cleanup tomorrow. Good night."

She made it to the sink without rattling her dishes, then walked stiffly out of the room and began to climb the stairs. Memories of all her earthly father's sins swirled through her mind. It didn't matter what anyone else did or didn't do. She knew whose daughter she was—would always be. Some things were set in stone, like the Ten Commandments, and not subject to change no matter how much she wished they were.

So what about God? she asked herself. There had been a time when she had truly believed she was His child, too. Could Isaac be right? Did she really need to forgive herself the way he'd said?

She clenched her jaw so tightly her cheeks ached. It would take an extraordinary amount of faith to accomplish that, let alone to stop hating the man who had murdered her mother. She not only knew she didn't have the strength for that, but she also wondered if, given the means and opportunity, she would actually consider carrying out the fantasy of retribution by ending his life.

The shock of realizing that doing so would make her just as evil as her father shook her to the core. She paused at the top of the stairs, her hand on the banister, her feet rooted to the floor, and closed her eyes.

Tears slid down her cheeks unheeded. "Please, God," she whispered, "help me. I don't want to be like him."

It was a simple prayer. A child's prayer. And so heart-felt that no other words seemed necessary.

Standing there in the dimly lit hallway, Daniella was astounded to sense divine peace flowing over and around her as if wrapping her in a warm blanket of love.

As she proceeded slowly to her room, she murmured the only thing that felt appropriate. She said, "Thank You, Lord."

It had taken Isaac and the others another hour of spec-ulative conversation before they were satisfied they had done all they could for the present. He had bid his co-workers good-night and was watching them drive away when Becky got home.

She parked in front so the porch light would illumi-nate her way and rolled down her window. "Is it safe to leave my car?"

Isaac nodded. "Yes. Police canvassed the place and so did tracking dogs, until that trail went cold. Whoever was causing trouble before is long gone, at least for the present, but we'll keep an eye out."

"Jake phoned and told me to make myself scarce. I would have come home to help you defend the fort if I'd thought it would help."

"You did the right thing by staying away," Isaac told her as he opened and held the car door for her. "Having Daniella playing cavalry was bad enough. The prowler put a bullet through her car—while she was in it."

"You didn't catch him?"

"No. I doubt we were even close by the time we got organized. My team's dogs tracked him as far as Judson Mill Road but lost the trail there. We assume he had a car waiting."

Becky was through the front door and shedding her light jacket by the time he finished explaining. "One shooter or more?" she asked.

"Can't tell. I'm guessing one, judging by the boot prints under the trees where Daniella first spotted him. It happened at dusk and was really too dark to tell a whole lot without setting up crime scene lighting."

"Why didn't you?"

"Because I didn't want to call more attention to the incident. The last thing we need is a bunch of reporters nosing around out here."

"What harm will it do?" his sister asked, arching her eyebrows at him. "If the assailant was Fagan, like we all think, he already knows where his daughter is."

"True. But there's an outside chance it wasn't him."

"Do you really believe that?"

Chagrined, Isaac shook his head and pressed his lips into a thin line. "No." He looked around to make sure they were alone before he added, "I think it was him and he fully intended to kill her."

ELEVEN

One thing was clear in Daniella's mind in the early-morning hours of the following day. She had to leave the farm, one way or another. If the marshals wouldn't give her an official release in a timely fashion, she'd have to take matters into her own hands. The biggest question was, where would she go? And what would she use to support herself until she got another job?

In the past, government agents had taken care of everything, from selling her meager possessions to giving her a small stipend and helping her finish school.

There had been a lump-sum insurance settlement from her mother's estate, too, but she hadn't been able to convince herself to touch it because of what it represented. Perhaps now was the time. All she had to do was figure out how to ditch Isaac long enough to go to the bank and get the money so he wouldn't try to stop her or talk her out of preparing to leave DC.

There was only one person in the house whom she felt might be willing to help her. Becky. It was worth a try.

Dressing and tiptoeing to the kitchen, Daniella started a pot of coffee and waited. Jake came through, filled a mug and went outside to do chores. Isaac did the same, only he headed for the stand of maples, ostensibly to get a better look at the ground in the daylight.

Becky was already dressed for the office and had her darker hair pulled into a tight chignon when she appeared. "Morning. Sorry I don't have time for breakfast," she said, filling a travel mug and adding cream.

"No problem." Daniella cleared her throat. "Um, would you be planning to go anywhere near Arlington this morning?"

"Yes." The other woman's eyebrows arched and she cocked her head. "Why do you ask?"

"Well, I was just thinking…"

"Bad idea," Becky quipped, smiling and picking up her briefcase. "I heard what happened last night while I was gone."

Reaching out to stop her from leaving, Daniella willed her to understand without a great deal of explanation. "That's why I need a ride to Arlington," she said. "You know it's too dangerous for your family if I hang around here."

"Okay. So?"

"So, I'd like you to help me get away."

She raised her hands, palms out. "Whoa. Why ask me? Why don't you appeal to Isaac? He's the one with the law enforcement connections."

"Because I'm afraid he's part of the reason I'm stuck here. I think he told the marshals to take their time because he wants me to stay."

"He'd never do anything to endanger anyone. He's too conscientious for that."

"I know. But he hasn't pushed it, either, has he? After what happened last night, you and I both know the best choice for everybody is my hitting the road ASAP."

"Can't argue with you there." Becky placed her purse and briefcase on the table and took a sip from her travel mug. "What do you propose we tell the guys? My brothers are smart enough to see right through a ruse."

"We leave a note and don't specify much. I'll just tell them I went to town with you on business. That will be true. I need to visit a safe-deposit box."

"Isaac will blow his stack!"

"Yes, but he won't have much recourse unless he guesses where I'm headed, and there's no clue to that. My father doesn't know about the bank, either. We should be perfectly safe." She began to smile as she realized Becky was no longer coming up with arguments.

"Well, don't just stand there. Go grab your purse, write the note and let's get out of here."

Starting away, Daniella skidded to a stop. "There's one more thing. Will you take good care of Puddy? He loves women. It's men and dogs he's not crazy about."

"Oh, now, wait a minute. You didn't say anything about keeping your cat."

"Please? Just for a little while? As soon as I'm settled I'll send for him."

"You can't do that unless your father's been arrested."

"We can hope that happens soon," she said with a broadening grin and a soaring spirit. "I prayed about it a lot last night."

The incredulous look on Becky's face was laughable. Daniella understood how the other woman felt. She could hardly believe the change in her own attitude, either. She was about to go against the advice of the K-9 officer and probably the marshals' office, too, yet there was an indescribable joy and lightness in her heart that defied description.

As she reached for her shoulder bag and slung the strap over her head to cross her torso, she realized that for the first time in longer than she could recall, she was truly happy.

How the idea of disregarding authority had brought that about was baffling, yet true. She felt free. Unburdened. As if she could accomplish anything if she merely put her mind to it.

Becky already had the car running when Daniella dashed out the front door and down the porch steps and slid into the passenger seat.

"Go, go, go. I think I heard Isaac coming in."

"Did you leave the note?"

"Yes." Daniella nodded rapidly.

Her heart was racing. She refused to dwell on what he might feel when he read her brief sentences. She wasn't doing this just for herself. She was doing it for him, too. And for his family. In the short time she'd known them, they had become very dear to her. Especially Isaac, she admitted silently. He was one of a kind. Someday he'd make a wonderful husband.

That conclusion was both correct and depressing. Her most ardent prayer for the brave man who had come to her rescue was that he find the happiness he deserved—with a woman worthy of his love. Someone with no heavy baggage. Someone who could accept his dangerous job without making herself sick imagining the worst every time he stepped out the door.

Someone…someone…other than her.

The stillness of the house instantly put Isaac on edge. The coffeepot was nearly empty. "Daniella?"

He paced through the kitchen and into the central hallway. "Daniella? Becky?"

No one answered except his brother. Jake came up behind him. "What's the matter. Did you lose the women?"

"Apparently." Isaac was frowning. "Is Becky's car gone already?"

"Uh-huh." Jacob was fidgeting.

"Okay. Spill it. What do you know that I don't?"

"This." Jake produced a scrap of paper and handed it over. "It was on the kitchen table."

Isaac quickly scanned it once, then slowed his mind to read it more carefully. One thing was clear. Daniella was gone. "This is a goodbye note. Do you think she really left here with Becky?"

"Probably. She couldn't see through the broken glass to drive her own car."

"Becky wouldn't help her voluntarily, would she?"

Shrugging, Jacob shoved his hands into the pockets of his well-worn jeans. "Who knows what women will do? They might have decided to band together, you know, like a sisterhood."

"I thought Becky had more sense."

"And I thought Daniella would be too scared to leave after last night. I guess we were both wrong."

Isaac's eyes widened as the full portent of the situation occurred to him. "Do you suppose they were kidnapped?"

"Naw. Becky's armed and dangerous, remember? And I've heard the lungs on your nurse friend. She can howl so loud they'd hear her in downtown DC."

Isaac fisted his phone. "All right. I'm going to call it in as a BOLO—be on the lookout. If they're just acting foolish, no harm will be done."

"And if they didn't leave of their own free will?"

Once again Isaac scanned the note in his hand. "This looks legit to me. I'll run it by the guys in the lab and see if they can tell what kind of mood she was in when she wrote it. That will tell us something."

"Not much," Jake countered.

Isaac glared at him. "You got a better idea?"

"Yeah. I say we head for the city. You deliver the note, then we keep in touch by phone and cruise DC."

"In all that traffic? What makes you think we'll be able to spot Becky's car in a mess like that?"

"Would you rather sit here and stew or be out trying to find them?"

His brother's suggestion made sense. Good thing, too, Isaac mused, since losing Daniella had already turned his thoughts into a maelstrom of confusion.

Abby was circling his feet as if she knew something was about to happen.

"All right," Isaac said. "Let's go. I'll make my call to headquarters from the car, then we'll link up by cell and keep in touch while we drive. They can't be too far ahead of us."

Checking his watch, Jacob agreed. "Want me to start with the real estate office and see if Becky showed up for work?"

"Fine. I'll check in with McCord and brief him in person, then hit the streets if they haven't been located by then. If I were a betting man, I wouldn't give our chances very good odds."

"You were the one telling her that God loved her," Jake reminded him. "Maybe it's time you told yourself the same thing."

Isaac knew his brother was right but spouting platitudes was far easier than actually living as if he had total trust in the Lord. Like all men, he was fallible.

And, like all men, his faith could falter. That didn't mean it wasn't valid. It simply pointed out that he was human. That he could care so much that his heart's desires overwhelmed common sense. He knew the chances of Daniella and Becky getting into trouble in the city were slim, yet he couldn't help worrying.

Ordering Abby into the safety compartment of the SUV instead of her crate, he ruffled her droopy ears before closing the door. Too bad he didn't have the dog's attitude about life. Every day was an adventure to her as long as her partner was along for the ride.

It occurred to Isaac that that was his biggest problem. He wanted his human partner with him, too.

Whether it was sensible or not, he wanted Daniella. It was as simple as that. And as complicated.

Becky chuckled at her companion. "Will you stop fidgeting? We're not being followed."

"How can you be sure in all this traffic?"

"Because I've been watching my mirrors ever since we left home. And, in case you haven't noticed, I've been getting on and off the beltway just for kicks."

Daniella settled back in her seat and folded her arms across her chest. "I noticed. I haven't seen anybody following us, either, but you can never be too careful."

"Is your father really that spiteful?"

"Humph. How would you feel if you'd watched your mother die the way I did?"

"Oh, I get it," Becky said. "It's just that you're his flesh-and-blood daughter. I can't imagine anybody being so callous."

"He probably wouldn't be after me if I had kept my mouth shut about Mom, but I couldn't bear the thought of him getting away with murder." She pulled a sour face. "Too bad my testimony was for nothing. He got out of prison, anyway."

"True. And unfair. What I don't understand is why you have to do this yourself. What did the witness protection people say when you told them you wanted to leave the program?"

"They advised me to wait until they were ready to officially release me." She swiveled to watch her new friend's face. "I really do believe your brother convinced them I was safer staying with him at the farm."

"I can't imagine he'd do that, although not being a guy I'm not positive. Some of them do seem to think they can handle anything and anybody." She smiled. "It's a knight-in-shining-armor complex."

Daniella's head plopped back against the raised seatback and she closed her eyes. "I can see that in Isaac. He really is a great guy."

"But?" Becky's smile grew. "I hear unspoken reservations."

Daniella nodded. "Yeah. He's not my type."

That made her companion laugh. "Sure seems like he is. The way you two look at each other tells a very different story."

"I told you. It's his job," Daniella replied. "There's nothing I hate more than explosives, and he makes a living looking for them."

"And saving lives. You admitted he's brave."

"I know I did. It's not his successes that bother me. It's the times when he makes a mistake. That could get him killed someday. I don't want to have to go through what I felt when I lost my mother."

"You had a double whammy, then," Becky said. "It was much worse because you knew your own father was responsible. Besides, Isaac and the K-9 unit are well trained. They know what they're doing."

Daniella wasn't convinced. "I don't know. I can have two similar patients in ER, give both of them the best care possible and still see one die while the other lives. Sometimes training isn't enough."

"That's because you're not God," Becky said tenderly. "It's up to you to do your job to the best of your ability, then leave the results up to Him. That's the mistake a lot of folks make. They think that they can make a difference when it's beyond human skills."

"Then why even try?" Daniella didn't necessarily disagree, to a point, but wasn't ready to relinquish a sense of control, either.

"Have you ever watched a patient recover after they were told their life was over?"

"Once in a while. Why?"

"Because I happen to believe our days are numbered, as the Bible says. I still think we can choose to squander them or cause an early demise by taking foolish chances, but something in my faith, in my heart, tells me that God has a master plan for me."

She paused, briefly glancing at her companion while she drove. "Think back. Suppose your mother had lived, you had been abused more by your father and maybe never had the courage to become a nurse or moved to DC. You wouldn't have met my family, especially Isaac, and we wouldn't be having this conversation."

"That might have been for the best," Daniella murmured.

Becky wasn't deterred. She chuckled and shook her head. "You might be able to lie to yourself enough to believe that, but you'll never convince me. We're here together, right now, because we're supposed to be."

"If that's true, are you saying that my father didn't really murder my mother?"

"Not at all. I'm saying that your mom was God's child. He knew what was going to happen and what she and her daughter needed. He released her from a life of suffering and gave you a whole new start. It was a gift, not a punishment."

"I still don't get it."

"Neither do I, most of the time," Becky admitted. "The difference is I've placed my life and my trust in God and Jesus Christ. I know He expects me to think sensibly and behave myself, but I also know He's ready for whatever happens and will always be with me."

"Does that help keep away the loneliness?"

When Becky said yes, it was so clear, so firm, Daniella had to accept it.

She retreated into her private thoughts and wondered if she'd been suffering for nothing. Had God been with her all along? Had she simply shut her eyes and her heart and mind to His presence?

There had been a time, years ago, when she'd talked to Jesus in prayer and thought she'd had enough faith to believe. What had happened to that childhood faith? Was it possible she'd been the one to distance herself because of bitterness instead of God withdrawing from her?

If that was true, what about her prayer at the top of

the stairs the night before when she had simply prayed to not end up being like her father? Had she imagined the sense of calm and peace that had followed?

No. Although the feeling had been fleeting, it was as real as the car she was riding in. God *had* heard her prayer and the answer had been palpable. All she needed to do from now on was to remember that even the things she couldn't see or touch could be very real.

Without being careless, she added, leaning to peer into the outside mirror and check the traffic behind them. It was all well and good to put her trust in the wisdom of God. What she must avoid was unburdening herself too much and forgetting that she was also expected to take reasonable precautions.

If Becky was right and God had brought her to DC, that did not mean He had thrown her to the lions. Nor did it mean she couldn't leave, especially for the sake of people she cared about.

Isaac was one of those special people, she admitted, in spite of herself. In that respect she wished she'd never met him because she knew she would worry about him for the rest of her life.

And pray for his continuing safety, she added, realizing she truly believed her prayers would help. That was a breakthrough she had not seen coming and made her wonder what other surprises were lurking in the dusty corners of her heart and mind.

One thing was certain. Like it or not, Isaac Black had started to monopolize her thoughts. She could recall every moment they'd spent together as if watching the same movie, over and over.

The scariest part was that she never got to see the

film all the way to the last reel and be sure everything ended well.

Unfortunately, real life was not like a romantic movie. Sometimes even the good guys didn't make it.

TWELVE

Leaving the SUV running, Isaac dashed into the lab to deliver Daniella's note to forensics, checked his own office, then trotted back out and climbed behind the wheel before he touched base with Jake. "Where are you?"

"Arlington. I swung by Becky's real estate office like I said I would. Nobody's heard from her this morning."

It took monumental effort for Isaac to control his temper. What had his sister been thinking? She knew better than to become involved with his work. Of course, this was the first time he'd taken his job home with him, so part of the blame had to be his.

"Okay," Isaac said. "If they don't know where she is, you may as well head back my way."

"Where shall we rendezvous and when?"

"How about at the Washington Monument at noon? I'd like to have another look at that site, anyway."

"Did the video copied from the TV news cameras show anything interesting?"

"No. A bunch of suits walked by me after Abby finished her sweep but we couldn't get a good look at anybody who was carrying a briefcase."

"You're sure that's what blew up?"

"Oh yeah. I saw it with my own eyes just seconds before the blast knocked me down."

"Good thing you turned away, huh?"

Isaac nodded despite the fact he was alone in the car with his dog. "Yeah." He changed the subject. "While you're at it, keep your eyes peeled for Fagan, too. He probably isn't involved this time but you might spot him."

"Not likely, bro."

"No, but our chances of being the ones who locate Becky and Daniella aren't good, either."

"It still beats pacing the floor at the house."

Isaac had to agree. The only drawback so far had been finding a direct order on his desk giving him an additional assignment.

"Listen, Jake, my captain was called away and left me instructions to go interview Congressman Jeffries ASAP. I'm going to run by the Capitol and see if I can catch Jeffries in his office before you and I link up again. It shouldn't take long. I'll leave my phone on vibrate in case you need to reach me. The local police are covering the city, so why don't you go back by Becky's office and keep an eye out there for a while?"

"That probably makes more sense than driving all over town for nothing, especially since she's not answering her cell. I just hate to feel so useless."

"I know what you mean," Isaac told him. "But now that I'm past the initial shock of the note, I think it's the smartest thing we can do."

Jake huffed cynically. "Having Becky wandering around out here is bad enough. Daniella with her makes it a hundred times worse."

"No argument there. If—when—we locate them I'll let you scold our sister while I read Daniella the riot act."

"Sometimes you sound just like Grandpa Black."

"I know." He chuckled. "From what I can remember about him, I'll take that as a compliment. He was quite a character."

"Stubborn as a mule, as Grandma used to say. Listen, baby brother, be careful out there."

"I will. Bye."

Isaac meant it. He was always careful, always on guard, unless he was relaxing at home. And now even the farm wasn't safe.

"Whose fault was that?" he muttered to himself.

His, of course. He had been the one to insist Daniella stay with him and had also contacted the marshals' office. How was he to know Fagan had hidden a bug in her apartment and listened to the whole conversation? The only good thing about that man's confession was learning that he hadn't been savvy enough to capture their cell signals as first assumed.

That gave Isaac a small measure of peace. A detailed knowledge of electronics would make Fagan's already dangerous bag of tricks far, far deadlier.

Until she actually saw the banded stacks of bills in the safe-deposit box, Daniella wasn't sure they'd still be there. Her hands were shaking as she shoved them into the canvas tote she'd borrowed from Becky and zipped the top closed.

The door to that section of the vault stood open. "I'm finished," she said as she passed the young bank employee who had assisted her.

"Was everything all right?" the woman asked pleasantly.

"Just fine." Daniella knew better than to give any indication of unrest. Considering the acting she'd had to do these past few days, not to mention during the preceding ten years, she figured she should be nominated for a professional performance award, red carpet and all.

The bank seemed unduly crowded as she emerged from the quietude of the vault area. It was hard to keep from scanning the bank's customers so rapidly that she gave the impression of nervousness. In truth, she was growing frantic now that she had her nest egg in hand. It wasn't the money itself that gave her qualms, it was what it could bring to her life, her future. If she left DC on her own, even if she later returned as she hoped to, she'd need cash to set herself up the way the witness protection program had before.

Although she saw no evident threat, her skin tingled and her heart raced. Instinct told her to get out of there as soon as she could, rejoin Becky and hit the road.

Weaving between bank customers and employees, she hugged the tote and her purse close and headed for the heavy glass doors. An elderly security guard near the front exit smiled at her and touched the brim of his cap.

Daniella hardly noticed. By this time the sense of impending doom had burgeoned into a full-blown panic attack. She assumed she'd feel better once she was back outside on the street, but that didn't happen.

On the contrary, emerging into the sunlight and seeing all the foot and vehicle traffic made her feel as if she were being suffocated.

There had been no available parking spots when they'd arrived, so Becky had let her out at the curb and promised to keep circling the block. Where was she?

Scanning passing cars, she forced herself to stand still when what she yearned to do was run. Fast and far. Away from the familiar city and into the oblivion of some place where she wasn't known.

The hair on the back of her neck prickled. She started to turn to go back into the bank to wait for Becky.

No. Don't do that, she countered, not comprehending why she was so sure, yet willing to follow the strongest impulse of the many pulling her right and left like a rag doll about to be ripped apart by warring children.

She hesitated. Almost stumbled. Swiveled back to scan the street once more.

A familiar compact car double-parked right in front of her. "Come on!"

Daniella was off the curb and jumping into Becky's passenger seat in mere seconds. She dropped the tote on the floor beneath her feet.

Whipping back into traffic, Becky dodged the slower-moving cars and made an illegal left turn at the next corner.

Daniella was struggling to fasten her seat belt. "I can't buckle up if you don't stop throwing me around." As she finished speaking, she glanced at her friend. "What's the matter?"

"I don't know. Maybe it was the look on your face when I picked you up or maybe it was something I saw in the background, but all I could think about was getting away."

"Me, too!" Wide-eyed, Daniella looked back over her shoulder. The impression that one of the men in the crowd might be Terence Fagan was intense.

Realizing that her mind could be playing tricks on her, she straightened and forced a smile. "Sorry my jumpiness has rubbed off on you. There's no way my father could have known about my safe-deposit box ahead of time."

"You're probably right," Becky said, "but it's possible that he either had us followed or did it himself, even with all my evasive tactics."

"I'm sure he was the prowler who shot out the window in my car, too." She noted her friend's arching eyebrows.

"After he showed up in the marshal's car and tried to drag you off, do you have any *doubt*?"

"I suppose not." Daniella blew a noisy sigh, then leaned down, pulled one bundle out of the tote and separated the bills. Some she stuffed into her purse, the rest she tried to hand to Becky.

"What's that for?"

"Damages and whatever else you need to stay safe after I'm gone."

"I've been giving that some thought," Becky said. "I wonder if hitting the road on your own is the smartest move."

"Of course it is. It's the only way to be sure my father doesn't continue to harass you."

"What if he doesn't know you've left?"

Growing pensive, Daniella pressed her lips into a thin line. "I'll drive my car. That will tell him."

"Not until we get the windshield replaced," Becky countered. "You have to be able to see where you're going."

"Very funny." Now that they were blocks from the bank and beginning to move faster, Daniella was able to manage a real smile. "I could always hang out the side window or look around those big, radiating cracks."

"Right."

"Or buy a new car. I have enough money to pay cash. Want to take me to a dealership?"

"That won't solve the problem. If you buy a car off a

lot there will still be a paper trail. I think your best option is getting something else from an individual and holding off on the transfer of title."

"Okay. I've never had a car window repaired. How is it done?"

"On scene mostly," Becky said. "I'll stop by my office and place the order."

"Not if it's going to take long," Daniella warned. "I plan to be out of here before tonight."

"I think the glass guy will squeeze you in if I tell him it's an emergency."

"Offer to double his fee," Daniella told her. "Whatever it takes to get it done right away."

"You mean before Isaac figures out you're back at the house, don't you?"

Nodding forcefully, Daniella said, "Oh yeah. Way before that."

The trip to visit Congressman Jeffries's Capitol Hill office building was easy. Isaac parked the SUV in a shady spot reserved for law enforcement, reported his location to headquarters and left the windows rolled partway down to keep Abby cool.

His badge got him past the guards at the entrance without delay. Knowing where Jeffries's private office was saved time, too. Isaac turned right at the second hallway and followed it to nicer quarters than many congressmen managed to get. Space was worth more than gold in DC, and having enough room to turn around, let alone comfortably employ a small staff, was a real boon.

Rather than phone ahead, Isaac had taken the chance he'd catch Jeffries there. Judging by the startled expression on his secretary's face as she took in his full image—uniform, badge, K-9 patches and cap with an identical logo—he had made the right decision.

She blushed, then smiled tentatively. "I'm sorry, officer, the congressman is in conference."

"I can wait." He removed his cap, folded it and looped it through his belt.

"I don't advise waiting. Congressman Jeffries has appointments all day and a state dinner to attend this evening."

"Who is he meeting with right now?"

She hesitated, so instead of giving her time to warn her boss, Isaac strode across the carpeted floor to the heavy mahogany door, knocked once and tried the knob. It turned freely.

The loyal secretary attempted to block his way and failed. "I'm sorry, sir. I told him you were busy."

Two men in luxuriously tailored suits stood with iced amber-colored drinks in hand. The taller, gray-haired one was Harland Jeffries. Isaac recognized the other as Leon Ridge, one of the congressman's longtime aides. Neither appeared overjoyed to see him.

Professional politician to the nth degree, Jeffries left his aide and approached Isaac, offering a hand of welcome. "Good to see you. Leon and I were just finishing up. I can give you a couple of minutes, if that will suffice."

"That should be fine. Captain McCord would have come himself but he was called out of town unexpectedly, so he asked me to fill in for him."

"Fine, fine. Gavin's a good man. Very loyal. We go way back, you know."

"Yes, I know." Isaac stared pointedly at Leon Ridge. "Do you mind?"

Jeffries answered for him. "No problem. Leon was just leaving." He used a glance to direct the younger man to the rear door. "You know what I need done. We're finished for now."

There was something about Ridge that made Isaac's skin crawl. Always had, although he had no concrete reason to feel that way other than the fact that Abby and the other Capitol K-9 Unit dogs wouldn't allow the man to get near them. That judgment was good enough for Isaac.

"Just a few simple questions if you don't mind, sir," Isaac said to Harland Jeffries.

He took the chair Jeffries indicated and watched him settle in on the opposite side of the ornate desk, straighten a few file folders, then lean back and lace his fingers behind his head. The studied pose would have looked more casual if he had bothered to remove his jacket or loosen his tie.

"So, what can I do for you? I hope you've come to tell me that the woman who killed my poor Michael is finally in custody."

"What woman?" Isaac asked, purposely toying with him.

"Erin Eagleton. The one who must have shot him and me. Don't you people talk to each other?"

There was no proof that Erin Eagleton, who'd been Michael Jeffries's girlfriend, shot anyone. Though a charm from her necklace had been found at the murder scene, Jeffries had said several times that he didn't know who had murdered his son and then had turned the gun on him, leaving him for dead. "She's still missing as far as I know. But that's not why I'm here."

Jeffries lowered his arms, rested his elbows on the desk and steepled his fingers. "Oh?"

"You see, sir, it's like this. We're not getting very far in our investigation into the attack during your press conference and we were wondering if you'd had any more thoughts about who may have placed the explosive device."

"Since you haven't found Erin Eagleton yet, what about her?"

"Why would she want to harm you?" Isaac took note of a slight tic at the corner of the congressman's eye, indicating nervousness he wasn't managing to mask completely.

"Maybe she thinks I can identify her. I don't know. It's your responsibility to find out these things, not mine. Do your job." Jeffries got to his feet. "This interview is over."

Isaac nodded and offered his hand, satisfied that he'd made a little progress.

Leaving the building, Isaac was more than happy to get back to looking for Daniella and Becky. Because of Daniella's cryptic farewell note, he wasn't too worried about foul play, but that didn't mean the women hadn't accidentally gotten themselves into trouble. Daniella seemed to have a talent for it, and his sister wasn't much better. Anybody who enjoyed landing jets on a pitching carrier deck in the middle of the ocean the way Becky used to had to be too brave for her own good.

As soon as he was outside on the walkway, he pulled out his cell and speed-dialed Jacob.

"Any sign of them?"

"Yeah. I just missed catching them at Becky's office. One of the brokers said she and another woman stopped by for info on a repairman, then split."

"Did they say where they were going?"

"No," Jake told him, "but I have a good idea I know, anyway."

"Well, spit it out before I go crazy. Where?"

"They called a glass man to have a car windshield and side windows replaced. Where do you think they're headed?"

Isaac let out a whoop. "The farm!"

"That's kinda what I figured. You want me to go see?"

"I'll meet you there. When you pull in, try to block her car with yours in case she decides to make a run for it. I'll do the same."

"You really mean you're not going to let her go if that's what she wants?"

Isaac heard sadness in his voice when he said, "Oh, I'll let her go. I just want to be sure we don't read about her murder in the newspaper. I'll do whatever I have to in order to keep her safe and sound."

"She is going to be madder than a wet hen."

Isaac was so relieved to have learned where to look for the women, it was easy to laugh at his brother's comment. "Now who sounds like Grandpa Black?" he asked with a chuckle. "Just see that you're there, too. I may need backup."

Jake laughed, too. "Bro, if you decide to tangle with those two stubborn women, you're going to need more than me for backup. You're going to need the Virginia National Guard!"

THIRTEEN

Daniella was both elated and depressed, causing untold problems with her psyche. She desperately wanted to run from the danger her father posed, yet the moment she laid eyes on the Blacks' farmhouse she was filled with a sense of home. Friends. Even family.

Wheeling into the familiar driveway, Becky checked her out, frowned and asked, "You okay?"

"Yes. I'm just conflicted. I know it's best that I disappear but I really hate to leave this place."

"Leave Isaac, you mean?"

"Him, too, of course." Knowing that her cheeks had to be aflame, she averted her face and stared out the car windows as if she found the passing fence unduly fascinating.

Becky chuckled softly. "Of course."

"Hey, this is no laughing matter," Daniella insisted, turning back. "I never dreamed I'd someday meet a man who appealed to me the way your brother does, and then when I do, he has the worst job in the world."

"What makes you think you couldn't get used to it if you loved him enough?"

"That's another thing. The more I care about him, the

more scared I get that I'll lose him the same way I lost my mother."

"Like I said, you need to trust God more."

"Why? So I'll have divine comfort when Isaac is blown to bits? No thanks."

"All I can do is tell you what's helped me. The more I tried to figure out my life, the more confused I got. But when I turned it over to the Lord and stopped insisting that everything go the way I'd planned, the results were far better than I'd imagined."

"Let go, you mean?"

"In a manner of speaking. I see it more as rolling with the punches. It's not so much what happens to us as it is how we react to adversity."

Daniella was arguing within, and some of that attitude spilled out into the conversation. "Look. I was only seventeen when I went into witness protection. I've already made up my mind I'm going to run now but eventually return. I have a career that I happen to love and won't abandon. I'm just not going to make the mistake I did the other night in my poor car. I plan to duck, literally and figuratively, then counterattack later, if I have to."

"How do you propose to do that? This is not the Old West and you're no gunfighter."

Agreeing, Daniella nodded slowly, thoughtfully. "I know. I keep thinking there must be some way I can win. I just haven't found it yet."

Becky drove to the rear of the old Victorian and parked, then swiveled to look directly at her passenger. "When I took you to the bank this morning I was positive that helping you hit the road was for the best. Now I'm not so sure."

"Why not?"

"Because it has occurred to me that God may have placed you with us for a reason. Think about it. You're not trained for combat but the three of us are, to varying degrees, and if you stick around it will be like having three bodyguards with at least one of us on duty at all times."

"You're not part of this. You shouldn't have to risk your lives just because my father is out to get me."

"If that's all there was to it you'd be right. But suppose we were put into your life for a purpose? What if we'd be wrong to let you go?"

"Suppose you let me decide about that."

Becky spread her hands, palms up. "Okay. Fair enough. As long as you keep an open mind. I think, while your car is being repaired, you should give the marshals another call. It's quite possible they may be preparing to whisk you away or something."

"I sincerely doubt that. I told them I wanted out of their program. Period."

"You'll never know what's going on if you don't ask. Suppose my brother did pull strings to get them to leave you in limbo?"

Daniella brightened. "Do you really think so?" She stepped out of the car when Becky did, greeted the excited farm dogs with pats on their heads, then led the way toward the back porch.

There was something so special about this farm, this house, she was in awe. There were no adequate words to describe how she felt about the Black family, particularly Isaac, and no amount of internal arguing against those feelings fazed her conclusions.

Sticking close, the largest of the mixed-breed dogs bumped her leg and began to growl. The rumble in his throat was enough to bring Daniella up short. She spread her arms like a human gate. "Becky?"

"What's wrong?"

"This dog is growling."

Becky joined her and bent over the enormous canine to listen. "He *is*. In all the years we've had him, this is the first time I've heard him act mean. Did you do something different?"

"Not me." She eyed the wooden porch. "Shut the dogs in the barn and stay back. I want to take a closer look and I don't want any company."

The notion that a dog that had never been trained for defense was trying to tell her something struck Daniella as improbable. Nevertheless, she had always had an affinity for animals and could read their body language well. This dog was definitely put off by something. It was conceivable that he'd become sensitized to some sights or odors by watching Abby work.

Cautious, purposeful steps brought her around to the open end of the porch. She bent down. Peered into the dimness below the wooden deck.

At first, all she saw were spiderwebs and dust. Then, squinting, she managed to isolate a dark shape that didn't look as if it belonged there.

Daniella gasped, straightened and gaped at Becky. Before she could sound the warning, the rear door opened and Jake stepped out. "About time you decided to show up," he said. "Isaac and I've been all over the city looking for you two."

Becky raised her arms as if sheer willpower could stop her brother's progress.

Beside the porch, Daniella was close enough to grab the hem of his jeans and shout, "Don't move!"

* * *

One thing Isaac had not expected was a call from his sister. The moment he recognized her voice he started to scold. "Do you know what you've done? Jake and I looked everywhere. I can't believe you'd agree to take Daniella into the city, let alone not keep in touch. You…"

Jumbling with the sound of his own voice was the rapid-fire speech of his sister. It was her evident agitation that caused him to hesitate. "What?"

"I said, there's a bomb under the porch and Jake is standing on it. Where are you?"

"Five minutes out. Nobody move. Understand? The slightest jiggle could set it off."

Becky, usually the most levelheaded of all the women Isaac knew, sounded near hysteria. "Didn't you check before you left?" she screeched.

"I was in kind of a hurry, thanks to you. Abby and I went out the back and she didn't alert."

"Well, she would now."

"Somebody must have placed a device when all of us were away. I'm pulling off the highway. Sit tight."

With both hands fisted on the wheel and his siren wailing, Isaac floored the gas pedal. These two-lane country roads weren't designed for high-speed driving, but as long as he stuck to the center line he should be able to negotiate the corners without sliding off into a ditch.

Living in the country rather than the city had made him too complacent. He should have taken more pains to protect his family. It was his fault for bringing trouble home with him, but what else could he have done?

"I could have turned her over to the authorities as soon as Abby detected that first bomb," he murmured. His fist hammered the steering wheel. Why hadn't he? And why, given her father's early release, had he continued to encourage her stay with them? It might not be the dumbest stunt he'd ever pulled, but it was close.

Wheeling into the long drive leading to the farmhouse, Isaac slowed to keep from losing control of the car on the loose dirt and gravel. He parked on the grass before getting too close and jumped out, half running, half limping toward the place Becky had cited.

When he rounded the corner of the house and saw the entire picture, his heart leaped into his throat, pounding wildly.

Jake was just outside the back door all right, and Becky was nearest the barn. It was Daniella's position that tied his gut in knots and floored him. She was standing beside the raised wooden deck with one hand on the closest support and the other clutching Jake's jeans at the ankle.

Even if the bomb detonated and the others were blown clear, there was no chance of Daniella escaping in one piece. None at all.

Thankful that he'd left Abby in the SUV, Isaac boldly approached. Becky spotted him first and screeched his name.

Jake's head swiveled slowly and he quirked a smile.

Daniella was the only one who didn't move, so he called out to her as he drew closer. "If you're not putting any weight on the porch, you can let go of him."

She shook her head, her hair swinging.

Close enough to touch her, he laid a hand lightly on her shoulder and spoke softly so he wouldn't frighten her more. "Let him go, Daniella. Open your hand."

"No. This is all my fault. I'll stay as long as Jake has to."

"I notified my office as soon as I got Becky's call,"

Isaac said, "but they won't send the bomb squad until I report what I've found."

He edged to one side and shined a flashlight into the recesses beneath the porch. "Where did you see it?"

"Under a step. There's a blinking light."

"I don't see what you're describing. Are you sure?"

"Yes. No. I don't know."

Isaac backed out and straightened. "All right. Since you say what you saw was under a step and there's absolutely nothing attached to the porch, Jake can go back inside."

"Really?"

"Yes. Really." He looked to his brother. "Just take it easy and don't slam the door."

Isaac wrapped his arms around Daniella and drew her in the opposite direction, holding his breath until they were in the clear. Then he turned her and pulled her closer, relieved to feel her arms slip around him, as well. Judging by the severity of her trembling, she was good and scared. And foolishly brave.

"Easy. I've got you," he whispered against her silky hair. "What in the world did you think you'd accomplish by getting yourself blown up?"

"I couldn't leave him. I just couldn't." Her arms tightened around Isaac's waist and she laid her cheek on his chest.

The notion that she was ready to sacrifice herself for his brother was both comforting and disturbing. If she cared that much for Jake, perhaps he was the one who was destined to win her heart. Isaac wondered if he would be able to stay close to his family if that did happen. He doubted it. Picturing Daniella as anyone's wife but his was already tearing him apart. To actually see it happen would be sheer agony.

The click of the latch on the front door echoed in the rural stillness. Becky had already joined Isaac and Daniella by the K-9 patrol unit when Jake jogged up and put his strong arms around the group.

Isaac tolerated the closeness for a few long seconds before setting Daniella away and issuing orders. "All of you climb in and wait out here. I'm going to start by working Abby around the house."

Daniella reached out to him, grasped his forearm. "Do you have to go?"

"It's my job. I told you. I need to have the entire area screened and report before they'll start the bomb squad. They may not need to."

Becky had already slid into the second seat. Daniella reluctantly joined her while Jake stood outside. He inclined his head and motioned with his eyes. "Quite a woman."

"Yes." *And I saw her first*, Isaac wanted to add. Instead, he circled the unit. Abby was ready to go, as always. He fitted and fastened her vest, then snapped on a long lead.

One glance back was all he allowed himself before he and his canine partner went to work.

Watching from the car, Daniella was alternately wringing her hands and clamping her fingers together so tightly they whitened.

She squeezed her eyes closed and didn't realize she'd been praying until she heard herself saying, "Please, please keep him safe."

Becky added, "Amen," and joined their folded hands.

"Father, thank You for keeping the rest of us safe today, too, and bless my brother as he does his job."

As soon as Daniella looked up, Becky smiled. "I think it's important to thank Him for the good things, too. Otherwise we sound like spoiled children, always begging for cookies for dessert without being grateful for the whole meal we had before."

"I—I never thought of it that way." She kept hold of her friend's hand. "I guess I should spend more time giving thanks for not being in the car with my mom."

"And for meeting Isaac in the ER," Becky added. "Looking back, I can easily imagine a divine purpose. You needed special friends and allies, and He sent you to us."

"That is a comforting thought," she replied. "I just hope everybody survives our adventure together."

"Even your dad?" Becky asked gently.

Astounded, Daniella didn't know how to answer. What was wrong with her? For years she'd nurtured her abhorrence of that man, so where was the fire in her heart and mind now? Terence Fagan was still causing her trouble and had undoubtedly placed the first bomb under her car, so why couldn't she easily agree that she wished him dead?

Daniella looked over with unshed tears blurring her vision and said, "I don't know anymore."

Becky gave her hands a squeeze. "Good for you."

"But he's just as evil as he always was. What's wrong with me?"

Smiling, Becky too looked misty-eyed. "It's not what's wrong with you, honey. It's more about what's getting right."

"You mean with God?"

"Among other things. Holding on to bitterness can kill a person almost as easily as a bullet. You should know. I'm sure you've had patients who left this earth cursing their fate and the other people they blamed for it."

"A few. It always struck me as a shame that they held on to grudges with their last thoughts. Such a waste."

"Amen, sister," Becky said, dashing away sparse tears and breaking into a smile. "You're really a quick learner."

"Ha! Tell that to your brother. He thinks I'm an idiot."

"No, he doesn't. And I assume you mean Isaac."

Blushing again, Daniella stared at her clasped hands as if they were the most interesting things she'd ever seen. "Yes. Isaac."

"We all have baggage," Becky said.

Daniella met her gaze. "Not everybody's baggage is lethal the way mine is."

FOURTEEN

Isaac was so relieved when Abby didn't alert to whatever was tucked under the back porch he almost laughed out loud. Cursory examination identified the object as an old metal lunch pail that he concluded had probably been left there when the house was far newer. As for the flashing light Daniella had claimed to have seen, he could only imagine sunlight glinting off something nearby.

Following standard procedure, mostly out of habit, he continued the sweep of the yard and shrubbery, so positive that he'd come up empty he smiled at his K-9 partner.

Tail held erect in the position that was called flagging, Abby went gaily about her task, poking her sensitive nose into flower beds and tufts of grass as if playing a fascinating game.

That's what this is to her, Isaac reminded himself. Hers was one of the only jobs he could think of where lack of success was the desired result. He'd much rather reward her for *not* finding a bomb than deal with other possibilities.

Isaac's smile grew. "What's the matter, girl? Do you wish you were out chasing rabbits?"

Snuffling, she kept her nose buried in the grass next

to one of the outdoor entrances that led directly into the basement. That small door closed off a coal chute, a left-over necessity from the days when the old house was heated by a coal-fired furnace.

Isaac frowned. Paused. Gave her more lead and watched closely. He sensed her decision a few seconds before she plopped down into a sitting position and began to quiver all over.

Transfixed, Isaac tapped his ear to activate the radio transmitter in his earpiece. "Capitol K-9 Unit Five," he reported. "Dog has alerted. Send the bomb squad stat." He recited his address, then added, "It's my place. Abby just told me there's a bomb under my house."

Daniella elbowed Becky with a sharp, "Look." Jacob had stopped leaning against the SUV and was clearly on his way to join Isaac. "What do you think?"

"Both of them usually have more casual body language," Becky offered. "If I had to guess, I'd say Abby found something."

"That's what I thought." Daniella hugged herself. "I hope we're both wrong."

"Only one way to find out."

"I thought you'd never get around to saying so. Let's go ask."

They clambered out and joined ranks, shoulder to shoulder, to approach the brothers. Daniella began, "I was right, wasn't I?" It shocked and puzzled her when Isaac shook his head.

"Well, if you didn't find anything, then why do you look as if you're mad at the world?" She made a face. "Or is it me?"

"I'm not mad at you," Isaac assured her. "Not for convincing me to search for explosives, at any rate. I'm still pretty steamed at the goodbye note and disappearing act, though."

"Never mind all that. What did Abby find?"

"I'm not positive. We won't be until the bomb disposal squad arrives. But she did alert. It just didn't happen to be in the place that scared you."

"What?" Daniella's head snapped around and she scowled at each of the others in turn, beginning and ending with Isaac. "There was something under the porch. I saw it myself. It was rectangular and about this long." She held her hands parallel to demonstrate.

"That was nothing but an old rusty lunch box, probably an antique from the looks of it. It was the other side of the house Abby told me was dangerous."

"Oh, my…" She swayed as the truth hit home and felt Becky grab her arm. "I have never been happier to be proved wrong, even if I do feel foolish."

Slowly shaking his head, Isaac told her, "You may want to rethink that. If you hadn't spotted what you thought was a bomb and called me, we might all have lost our lives."

"A blessing in disguise?" his sister asked.

"Yes. And not that well disguised if all the perp did was slide it down the old coal chute into the basement. We're fortunate it didn't accidentally detonate when it hit bottom."

The full significance of his words sank in slowly, making Daniella wish she didn't understand quite so well. Once again she had brought her personal troubles to others and once again they had narrowly escaped.

It took her several minutes to calm herself enough to speak her mind. She reached out to Isaac. Touched his arm for a brief moment. "I was going to just hit the road, for your sake, but since it's gone this far, maybe I should recontact the marshals' office like Becky suggested and see what they say."

"You actually *want* to leave."

"I have to. Don't you get it? As long as I'm here, Fagan will keep trying to hurt me and you'll all be in his crosshairs."

"Okay. Two things," Isaac said, looking deeply into her eyes and making her feel like a butterfly specimen displayed in a collector's box.

"Go ahead. But I'm right and you know it."

He massaged the back of his neck with one hand while continuing to make direct eye contact. "First, there's no way for Fagan to know you've moved away from us unless we post a big sign on the lawn and he believes it. Second, we need to figure out how he knew we were all going to be gone at the same time so he could plant this new bomb."

"He couldn't have known. I only thought of my traveling money and asked Becky for a ride to Arlington this morning." She paused, eyes widening. "Could he have lied about leaving a bug in my apartment just to make us feel complacent about other options?"

"That had occurred to me," Isaac said flatly.

"Uh-oh."

Isaac agreed. "You can say that again. If he has different means of eavesdropping we'll have to be a lot more careful about what we say. I'll put the Capitol K-9 Unit's tech wizard, Fiona, to work on the problem as soon as we're cleared to reenter the house. She can check cell phones and our computers to make sure he hasn't tapped into those systems."

"I could just hit the road and check in once in a while," Daniella offered.

"How? From where? With what, a compromised cell phone?"

"Email, maybe? I could stop at coffee shops or libraries and use their computers."

"Only if you're sure your father didn't learn any new tricks in prison. It was your idea that he might have taught other inmates his skills. Suppose they shared theirs with him? If he's half as smart as you are, I wouldn't put it past him."

"Thanks—I think."

"You're welcome. There's also the possibility he contacted another relocated witness who managed to get him the information he needed."

"Now you're really reaching."

"I know. But we can't overlook any possibilities, no matter how remote."

"Look. It's not that complicated," Daniella insisted. "My father saw me on the TV news."

"And reached your apartment while you were still at work, set a bomb and got away clean? I strongly doubt that was all the time he had."

"You think he was already closing in?"

Isaac soberly agreed. "He had to be. The newscast may have helped with the final details, but it's hard to believe he could have come to DC and accomplished all he did, like planting that bug in your apartment or the bomb on your car, if he hadn't had some prior knowledge."

"I—I don't know what to say." Daniella was speaking softly, hesitantly. How could she argue with a professional? Besides, wasn't one branch of law enforcement supposed to have an in with the others? If that were the case, how could she be certain that somebody in *Washington* hadn't tipped off her father?

So, who else would care about her true identity, let alone suspect she was in hiding? Was she sending signals that told people she was a fugitive from injustice and homicide? Could she possibly be that transparent?

A blurred picture began to emerge. How difficult would it be for a man with underworld connections like Terence Fagan to find the weakest link in a chain and either bribe or threaten enough to coerce someone into giving him access to her personal files?

Considering what she knew about her father and what she'd witnessed growing up, she was surprised he hadn't knocked on her door and exacted his revenge months ago.

Her gaze locked with Isaac's. "Are you positive you want me to stick around? I mean seriously. Think about it. You'll be risking your homestead and folks you care about. That makes no sense to me."

"Maybe that's because you've never belonged to a close family. We stand up for each other and for our special friends. They'd do the same for me."

"Am I a special friend? Is that what you're saying?" Daniella managed to ask the question without showing too much emotion, but by the time he got around to answering she was starting to feel the welling of unshed tears.

Stepping closer, he said, "If I have my way, you'll be an official member of my family someday. In the meantime, consider yourself adopted."

She didn't answer. Couldn't speak, let alone reply with any degree of confidence. Was he intimating that he had serious feelings for her? That was awful. And wonderful. And everything in between.

Isaac closed her gaping mouth with one finger under her chin, then leaned and kissed her gently.

Maybe it was the thought that they had just cheated death that made her so willing to accept his show of affection. At that moment, that precious moment, Daniella didn't know or care. She merely kissed him back and let herself enjoy the closeness, the rare sense of total approval.

He knew her background, her family troubles, and yet he was inviting her into his private circle. That, alone, was such a beautiful gesture she could hardly take it in.

For those brief moments when Isaac's lips caressed hers, she was the person she had always dreamed of being. And she was no longer alone.

Isaac had stayed outside with the others while the bomb squad had entered his cellar, located the device and defused it. To nobody's surprise, it matched the design of the ones Fagan was known to favor. If the fingerprints were his it would be a slam dunk.

He didn't want to break bad news to Daniella but saw no alternative. Unfortunately, their already tenuous relationship had grown even more strained since he'd given in to his heart's desire and kissed her. At the time he'd done it he'd known it was a fool's move, yet the chance she might favor his brother over him had forced him to act or perhaps pay for his inaction for the rest of his life.

Once he'd kissed her, however, he'd realized that his tender feelings were reciprocated, making him glad he'd made the move, yet sorry he'd pushed things ahead so rapidly. Under less stressful conditions, she might not have responded quite so eagerly. Then again, maybe their trying circumstances were meant to help them develop a deeper relationship more quickly than normal.

It was later in the evening, after they'd eaten supper, when Isaac heard from his boss. As he'd expected, his frank report on Jeffries's cynical attitude and nervousness during their interview had not been well accepted.

"What were you trying to do," Gavin McCord demanded, "give the man a heart attack?"

"I just asked him if he knew anything else about the bomb at his press conference. I was under the impression you sent me to question him because I have no personal ties. And speaking of bombs, I should tell you there was another explosive device planted at my farm today. The preliminary details will be coming from the bomb squad after they process the evidence." Isaac heard papers rustling in the background.

"I just got that report. Hold on."

More rustling sounds were followed by an exclamation. "Whoa. That's not what I'd expected."

"What? What did they find?"

"Fingerprints on the inside of the casing. The outside had been wiped clean but there were several good partials on the works, not that the assembly was very sophisticated. Basically just a few wires, a detonator and old-fashioned gunpowder."

"Humph. That sounds like Fagan's work."

"I'd have to agree with you if the prints were his. They're not."

"Were they able to ID the maker?"

"This says so, but there must be a mistake."

"Who was it?" Isaac wished he was face-to-face with his captain so he could judge his facial expressions.

"Not over the phone. I'd rather look into the identity question myself. I'll get back to you."

"Wait!"

McCord had ended the call. Deep in thought, Isaac decided he owed it to Daniella to inform her that her father had apparently not set this particular device. Yes, it was still possible that he'd had someone else do the construction for him and had then wiped the exterior of the box clean, but the chances of that were slim. Fagan would have wanted her to know where the bomb came from in order to increase her angst.

Isaac climbed the stairs and knocked on her closed door. "Daniella? It's me."

When an answer didn't come promptly, he knocked again, warned, "You'd better be decent because I'm coming in," and opened the door, half expecting to find her gone and the room empty.

Instead, he saw Daniella sitting on her bed, legs crossed, amid bundles of cash. Her enormous black cat was curled up atop part of the pile of bills.

Eyes wide and lips parted in surprise, she stared at him.

"What in the…?"

"This is the traveling money I mentioned. Becky took me to get it."

His heart hardened despite his tender feelings for her. "Is *that* what your father is really after?"

"Of course not. He'd have no way of knowing I'd stashed it away instead of spending it"

He saw her face change as he demanded, "Where did it come from?"

"I could tell you but I don't think I will. If you don't trust me, there's no point, is there?"

Their raised voices sent Puddy under the bed seeking sanctuary.

"I never said I didn't trust you," Isaac insisted.

"You didn't have to. I can see it in your eyes. You think I was involved in something criminal like my dad, don't you? Is that why you're spying on me?"

"I'm not spying," he said, trying to salvage the conversation before their friendship was further undermined. "I came up here to bring you good news."

Although she didn't speak, he could tell she was interested enough to let him explain.

"It's about the bomb Abby found in the basement. The prints on it weren't your father's. This time, we can't tie the bomb to him."

She unfolded her legs and slid to the edge of the bed, where she sat very still, apparently absorbing what she'd just learned.

Finally, she met his gaze. "That doesn't make any sense."

"I know." Shoving his hands into the hip pockets of his jeans, he struck a casual pose, hoping to encourage her to do the same by example.

"Whose prints were they?"

"That's another strange thing. My boss got the report of a match but he wouldn't tell me."

"Could he be the one who gave away the time of my first appointment with the marshal?"

Isaac was adamant. "No way. I've never met a more honest man. Gavin's just being cautious, that's all. He acted like he might be acquainted with the suspect and said he wanted to do more investigating before he made the lab's findings public."

Sighing, Daniella nodded. "I suppose he knows thousands of people in DC, including the White House staff."

"We all do. Our Capitol K-9 Unit is under the command of General Margaret Meyer. She has an office there as well as at unit headquarters."

"All right." She eyed the jumble of money. "You don't happen to have a big safe here, do you? I'd hate to lose the only thing my mother left me."

"That's where all that cash came from?"

Her "Yes" was faint as she raised her eyes to search the depths of his.

"I'm so sorry, honey. I assumed you were struggling to make ends meet because of where you lived and the older car you drove, and when I saw all that cash... I shouldn't have jumped to conclusions." He took a step closer, hoping she wouldn't throw him out.

"Another hazard of your job?" Daniella asked.

"Apparently. I meet a lot of criminals when I'm working. I guess it's made me cynical."

Rising, she slowly approached until she was close enough to slip her arms around his waist and step into his waiting embrace.

"Well, get over it, Mister," she said, laying her cheek against his chest. "The bomb-chasing problem is bad enough without adding a distrustful nature on top of all that constant danger."

"It's what I do," he said, kissing the top of her head and inhaling the floral sweetness of her shampoo. "I'm sorry, but it's my calling."

"The same as mine is to do all I can to nurse folks back to health. I know."

As her hug tightened and he felt her begin to tremble, Isaac realized how truly frightened his job made her.

Part of that fear was understandable because of her traumatic past, but that wasn't all there was to it. He knew her well enough now to see that she was also selling herself short. There was a good chance that, even though she was attracted to him, she'd eventually pull away for good, thinking she was doing him a favor.

He knew he couldn't make her fall in love with him. However, he didn't intend to sit back idly while she forced herself to leave for all the wrong reasons. If, in the end, she wanted to disappear again, he'd support that decision. He might not like it, but he would not stand in her way.

As Isaac saw it, his most important task besides protecting her was to convince her that she could trust her own instincts. Rely on herself. Believe she deserved the happiness that had eluded her for the past ten years.

Nothing in Terence Fagan's thick file indicated that he had the slightest affection for his only child, so no one could count on him seeing the light, so to speak. What Isaac did hope was that Daniella would be able to stop identifying so strongly with her father's sins and begin to focus on the love her mother had imparted while she was alive.

Having grown up in a close family with loving parents, Isaac had trouble imagining any father developing lethal enmity for his offspring, not to mention going so far as to actually murder them.

That was one reason why so many in law enforcement doubted that Harland Jeffries could have shot his only son, Michael. That, and the fact that Jeffries had taken a bullet that night, too. Yes, it was troubling that they hadn't been able to find the gun or a second bullet that had passed through the congressman's shoulder to test for matching ballistics, but all that did was open the possibility of an additional shooter. Or more.

What must it feel like to know that your father wanted you dead? Isaac's arms tightened around Daniella and he kissed her again, letting his lips linger before he rested his cheek against her hair.

There had to be a way to help her heart heal enough to fully trust again. And he was going to find it. No matter what he had to do.

FIFTEEN

The open door to Daniella's room kept her from feeling as if she and Isaac being together might cause his siblings to question their innocent motives. That was ridiculous, of course. The man was merely comforting her after apologizing for his gaffe about the money. And she was accepting his demonstration of friendly concern by returning his hug.

Ha-ha, her mind countered. *You may be able to fool everybody else, but don't try to fool yourself.*

She forced herself to loosen her grip and ease away from him in spite of the tender look in his eyes. Nevertheless, he released her without argument.

"Sorry," Isaac said quietly.

"For what? You didn't do anything wrong."

He shrugged. "Okay, whatever you say."

In the background a door slammed. Jacob's voice echoed up the stairwell. "I've closed and locked everything and put all the cars in the barn."

Isaac turned toward the door to answer, "Thanks."

"No problem."

He took another step away from her, leaving Daniella wishing they had remained closer. She was toying with the notion of actually saying so when she heard a familiar yip. Abby was hot on the trail of something, probably her human partner.

A smile lifted the corners of Daniella's mouth while the canine's exuberance lifted her spirits. "I think somebody is looking for you."

"Undoubtedly."

"Well…"

"Yeah, I'd better be going."

Before he had a chance to step into the hallway and shut her door, Abby barreled past in a blur of brown and white, barking all the way.

Daniella moved to try to block the dog. She may as well have tried to halt a flooded river with a teaspoon. Abby weaved past her without slowing a bit and dived under the bed!

The roar Puddy answered with was punctuated by hissing and growling.

Moving nearly as fast as the beagle, Daniella lifted the hem of the spread to peer under.

Isaac did the same.

All she could see was a flurry of tooth and claw. The combatants rolled around and around, popping out the opposite side for a moment, then back under the bed.

"Get him!" Isaac yelled. "Before he kills her."

"He's just defending himself. You grab your dog."

"I'm trying to!"

From behind them came laughter and shouts of encouragement. Jake and Becky were standing back and enjoying the melee.

Isaac didn't take his eyes off the tussle but Daniella did look up. "Help us!"

"No way. You two are doing fine." Jake guffawed.

"I've got her leg," Isaac shouted. "Pull your cat off her."

"How?"

"Grab him like his mama would, by the scruff of the neck."

The solution seemed too simplistic but she was willing to try anything at this point. She closed her fist on the loose skin behind Puddy's head and held tight while he struggled to reach the whining dog that Isaac was sliding in the opposite direction.

The cat's growling continued after the separation. Daniella began to speak soothingly to him, almost in baby talk, and he quieted in her lap, although he kept glaring at the excited beagle.

"Is Abby all right?" she asked, afraid to hear that Puddy might have injured the valuable animal.

"Yes, thankfully." Sitting on the bedroom floor, Isaac was scowling at both her and her pet. "How about your monster. Is he hurt?"

"I don't think so. Puddy was just scared because Abby showed up so unexpectedly."

"She's right," Becky offered from the doorway.

Isaac was scowling. "You would."

"I agree," Jake chimed in. "Abby's fine with the barn cats. There's no reason to believe she'd hurt this one."

Rolling his eyes, Isaac cradled his dog and watched the enormous cat. Its fur was puffed out, making it look as large as its antagonist and twice as formidable.

Abby, on the other hand, had begun to pant and drool and try to wiggle loose.

"See? She wants to be friends," Daniella said. "Put her down and see what happens."

It was evident that Isaac didn't want to follow anyone's orders, particularly hers, yet he did finally lower the dog's paws to the floor. Trembling with excitement, Abby strained against her collar and began acting like a sprinter, eager to break out of the blocks at a track meet before the starting gun fired.

Daniella offered her fingers for the beagle to sniff. "Since I was holding Puddy, this will give her an idea of what he is and calm her down."

"I didn't know you understood dogs so well."

"I get along with most animals," Daniella assured him. "A neighbor's dog was one of my best buddies when I was a kid. I wasn't allowed to have a pet of my own so I'd sneak down the street to play with Buster." Remembering more, she sobered. "I had a kitten once, when I was about seven. My dad told me it ran away and Mom suggested we not replace it. As an adult, I came to the conclusion that Dad was responsible for its disappearance."

"I'm so sorry."

"Yeah. Me, too." She shook off her doldrums and smiled while scratching behind Abby's ears. "I think you can let her loose now."

To her delight, once the dog was free, she merely stood there, sizing up her new enemy. Puddy did the same. His tail was so puffy it resembled a stiff brush.

This was the way animals met in the wild. If one felt cornered, it was natural for that one to fight. Since they were both free to advance or retreat, she believed they'd find neutral ground and call a truce.

Sure enough. Puddy made the first move, practically tiptoeing closer. One step. Two. Abby's tail began to wag and she lowered her chest to the floor, paws spread wide in a play pose, pink tongue lolling.

The cat lifted a paw and touched the dog's muzzle, then danced sideways on the tips of his toes, the end of his bushy tail beginning to twitch the way it did when Daniella dangled a toy on a string.

She held up a hand and smiled at Isaac. "Hang on. It's going to be fine."

Abby yelped.

"I think you're right. That's a play bark."

Puddy leaped, bounced off the middle of the beagle's back as if it was a trampoline, and ended up on the bedspread.

"There. See?" Daniella said. "Now we can quit worrying about them. All is forgiven."

"Apparently." Isaac got to his feet and called his dog to heel. "I think it's time we put an end to these fun and games and all went to bed. It's late and it's been a long day."

Daniella walked him to the door, where they joined Becky and Jacob. "I still need a safe to store my money. Any suggestions?"

"I can drive you back to the bank tomorrow if you like." Becky eyed her youngest brother. "Unless Isaac wants to take you."

"I'd be glad to—right after I go interview the boy from All Our Kids foster home who witnessed the shooting at Jeffries's place."

"I thought that had been done several times," Jake said. "What else can you hope to learn?"

"I'm not sure. I've had a couple of new ideas and I'd like to ask the boy some questions myself. It may not amount to anything." He looked toward Daniella. "How about riding along with me? I'm sure I can get my captain's permission. You'll have to be blindfolded for the final few miles of the approach but it won't last long."

Smiling, she agreed. "I think I can stand doing that.

Could we go to the bank first? I hate to carry all this loose cash around."

"No problem. We'll escort Becky to work in Arlington, visit your bank, then head to the safe house where the children are staying."

"Will that take you too far out of your way?" Daniella asked.

Becky caused subdued laughter when she piped up with, "Honey, I suspect my brother would go to the moon for you if you asked him to. Just take his offer of a ride and say thank you."

The grin splitting her face grew so broad her cheeks ached. Aiming it at Isaac, she repeated, "Thank you."

Isaac had decided it would be best to handle his upcoming visit to the children's home the way he had the recent one to the congressman. He'd drop in the following morning, unannounced, and trust that Cassie Danvers would be able to arrange for him to question Tommy.

He used the time trailing Becky to Arlington to mull over the details of his upcoming mission, not dreaming that his tension showed until Daniella spoke up. "Okay. Your sister is safe at her office and you're still frowning. Are you nervous about carrying all this money? You are armed, you know."

"It's not that. I'm thinking about the little boy I plan to interview."

"I can help if you'd like. I'm pretty good with kids. Most of the ones I treated in ER were either hurt or traumatized or both. They settled down fast if I kept my tone soft. They had to stop fussing in order to hear what I was saying to them."

"I guess it wouldn't hurt to let you go in with me, as

long as you don't interrupt. If I need your help I'll ask for it. Okay?"

"Okay. Now suppose you tell me more about why you're wound so tight this morning."

He didn't nod but he did exhale as if he'd been holding his breath. "It's complicated."

"I'm listening."

"Cassie Danvers, housemother of All Our Kids foster home, is my captain's significant other."

"His girlfriend, you mean?"

"More than that. They're engaged. She's bound to tell him what Tommy and I talk about, especially since I plan to bring up the congressman's name."

"Why would that bother anybody?"

"Because McCord was mentored by Harland Jeffries years ago when he was a resident at the same home—and afterward, too. No matter how I handle the meeting with Tommy, it's liable to ruffle feathers. I'm already in the doghouse for pressing Jeffries about the bomb that went off near the monument."

"Their inconvenient friendship can't be helped, can it?"

Isaac huffed. "No."

"Then you have to proceed."

"Easy for you to say." He thumbed his cell phone until he'd retrieved a file of photos. "These casual pictures are what I plan to show the boy, instead of mug shots, to see if he reacts."

"And if he does?"

"Then I'll report it to my captain and take the flak, even if it costs me my job."

"Aren't you the guy who keeps telling me it's not my fault that my father was a terrible person?" She ignored his deepening scowl and continued. "Well, think about it. If McCord is one of the good guys and his buddy Jeffries is the problem, don't you think the captain will thank you for exposing a crime, no matter who's guilty?"

"It still won't be a picnic."

Daniella chuckled. "Who ever said that doing the right thing was easy? Certainly not me. So, tell me more about this children's home we're going to."

As Isaac began to fill her in on the details surrounding the attack on Cassie and the kids she cared for, he was aware that some of his apprehension was easing. It was as if Daniella's presence and empathy had infused his thoughts and helped bring peace about the difficult task he was about to undertake.

Yes, he sometimes got similar results when his team met to discuss their work, but this was different. Stronger. More defined.

He glanced over at her as he pulled up to the guarded gate that protected the safe house where the children were temporarily located. A conclusion had suddenly formed. Daniella was in the process of not only accepting a part of his job, she was getting enthusiastic about it!

It was a small, first step, Isaac realized, grateful as well as awed. Nevertheless, it was a beginning for her. For them. If she could clearly see how much it meant to him to save lives and clear the streets of criminals, perhaps she'd one day be able to tolerate the dangerous things he was called upon to do for the sake of others.

Like these innocent children, he added silently before turning his thoughts to prayer.

"Help me find the truth," Isaac whispered, circling the SUV to hold the door for his passenger. The moment his gaze lit on her face and she smiled at him, he added, "About everything."

It wasn't God's failure to hear his pleas that concerned him. It was knowing that his idea of the right answer and the Lord's actual reply might not be anywhere near the same.

Trusting Him no matter what was the hardest part.

"Aren't we taking Abby in with us?" Daniella asked, pausing before starting up the walkway to the front door.

"Not this time. There are some strange guard dogs here, helping patrol, and I don't want to risk a dogfight."

"Makes sense." She saw the front door open and two women step out. One was petite, with long reddish hair. The other was not only older, she seemed about to jump out of her skin.

Isaac took Daniella's arm and nodded to the women. "Cassie, this is a friend of mine. Daniella, meet Cassie Danvers, the foster mom I told you about, and Virginia Johnson, her helper and cook."

The redhead offered her hand. "Pleased to meet you."

"Same here." Daniella didn't even try to shake hands with the other woman for fear she'd bolt in fear. "I've worked with children before in my job as a nurse. Isaac let me come with him in case I could be of assistance."

"Nobody here is sick," Cassie insisted. Her brow knit as she focused back on Isaac. "I take it this isn't a social call?"

"I thought maybe I could have another word with Tommy."

"Don't you think he's been through enough?"

"Yes. I also think he knows more than he's told us. Like you, I want to see justice done. You and these kids can't go on living in an armed camp forever, and we don't dare let you go back to your real home until everything is solved."

It was clear to Daniella that Cassie was unsure so she stepped forward, reached for her hand again and clasped it gently. "Why don't we all go inside and discuss this?"

The housemother agreed. "All right." She gestured toward the door, where several small faces with wide eyes peeked out at her before quickly disappearing.

Daniella took special pains to smile without focusing on a particular child as she walked into the comfortable living room. There was a long sofa covered with a wrinkled throw, three small side chairs and one larger scuffed-leather one filled with what looked like hundreds of small stuffed animals.

When Cassie treated her like a valued guest and began introducing the children who were present, Daniella crouched to greet each one personally. A little waif named Rachel was the tiniest and immediately stole her heart.

"And over here is Tommy," Cassie continued, pointing to the chair with the pile of toys. "Trust me. He's bound to be under there somewhere."

A reedy, muffled voice insisted, "Uh-uh."

Smiling broadly and trying not to laugh, Daniella said, "Well, what do you know. Those animals talk!" as she perched on the matching ottoman. "My kitty talks to me sometimes, but I have trouble understanding what he says."

The pile stirred.

Daniella sat very still. "It goes like this, 'Mrrrow' or 'meorrrr,' or sometimes he hisses, but that's only when he's scared."

"I never get scared," came from the pile of animals.

"Good for you, Mr. Monkey." She picked up the closest toy and looked into its shiny black button eyes. "Or was that you, Mr. Bear?"

When the child buried under the pile of animals didn't reply, Cassie offered, "His name is Bearie."

"Good to know. My name is Daniella, Bearie."

A head of tousled, sandy-brown hair appeared amid the toys and one blue eye peeked out.

She made her reaction melodramatic, clutching the bear to her and gasping. "Oh, my." Grinning, she asked, "Are you Tommy?"

She could sense his painful shyness, see it in the way he immediately eased lower in the chair, letting only the top of his head and eyebrows show. No wonder the poor little guy was so reticent, she thought sadly. If he had witnessed the actual shooting at the congressman's estate, as Isaac believed, he'd have trouble trusting any adults. Add to that the family upheaval that had landed him in foster care in the first place, and she could easily see why he'd prefer the company of harmless stuffed toys.

Daniella held up the bear again. "I'd love to meet your friends, Bearie. Will you please introduce me?"

To her delight and surprise, Tommy's faint, childlike voice proceeded to name each stuffed animal while she held it up. She listened intently, hoping he wasn't going to ask her to repeat many of them.

"Wow, you have a really good memory, Bear. Or was that Mr. Monkey? Tell you what. Will one of you ask Tommy if he'd like to play a game with us?"

The boy's head eased out above the pile of fur, felt and stuffing, sending some of the toys sliding.

Daniella caught the closest ones. "Careful. We don't

want anybody to get hurt like that poor man did who got shot. You remember seeing him, don't you, Bearie?"

The boy shook his head and averted his gaze. She'd almost lost him by going too fast. One quick glance at Isaac reassured her, so she proceeded, taking pains to guess incorrectly and thereby build up the child's confidence.

"Let me see how well I can remember something. This is Bearie in this hand, right? And Mr. Monkey over here?"

Tommy gave her a look that indicated she was not only wrong, she wasn't too bright. Again he shook his head.

"Okay. My mistake. Now it's your turn." She took care to present a few animal toys and let the child answer for them before returning to their primary reason for visiting the home.

"Good job. I think this is too easy for all you animals. How about trying something harder?"

The spark of interest in the boy's eyes convinced her she was going to succeed this time.

Daniella lowered her voice and cupped a hand around her mouth so he had to lean closer to hear. "I know how smart you all are. You can tell good guys, like me and Officer Black over there, from bad men, can't you?"

"Uh-huh." Tommy was barely whispering.

"Good for you. How about the man with the white hair you saw that night when David's blue mitten got lost in the woods?"

Tommy retreated and drew some of the toys to his chest, where he hugged them close. "I don't wanna play."

"But how are we going to tell you won if you stop playing? Just once more, okay?" Instead of pausing to give the child time to think over his reply, she plunged ahead, holding out a hand toward Isaac and asking for his smartphone. By concentrating on its screen and hiding it from the boy, she was able to distract him again.

"Uh-uh, no peeking. I haven't found the pictures I want yet."

The first time she held up the phone for him to see, it displayed a picture of Abby.

Tommy pointed at Isaac with one of the tentacles on a green octopus. "His dog. She likes me."

"I'm sure she does." Daniella continued to work the phone, hoping she'd be able to access the file Isaac had shown her on their drive over.

"Here we go." She held up the phone with one of the pictures of a toddler Isaac had told her was named Juan.

"I know him!" In the background, Rachel clapped her hands.

"That's Juan Gomez." Cassie explained. "He used to live here."

"Right." Daniella offered Tommy a high five which he almost accepted.

Carefully paging through the photos, she found one of a smiling younger man standing beside Harland Jeffries. The only other time she'd seen an image of his son, Michael, had been in the postmortem pictures, but she wasn't about to show those to a child. If she showed this one to Tommy, there was a good chance he'd shut down again, but at least they'd know he'd seen Michael, perhaps even on the night he was shot to death.

Before turning the phone toward the boy, she held it up so Isaac could view the photo and got his silent okay.

Tommy was on his knees on the chair seat, eagerly waiting for his next test. Daniella hated to trick him but if his information cleared up the murder and freed the others in the home to return to a normal life, as Isaac hoped, it would be justified. At least she prayed it would.

Slowly pivoting, she prepared for the worst, deciding at the last minute to cover half the photo with her hand, leaving only Michael visible.

Tommy's jaw dropped. His blue eyes widened. Tears began to glisten.

Her heart broke for the frightened child. In order to reach out to him, to comfort him, Daniella had to use the hand that had masked off part of the picture.

When she did, Tommy screamed and pointed. "That's—that's the bad man with the gun!"

He burst from the pile of toys and ran straight to Cassie. She lifted his small, wiry body into her arms in spite of her diminutive size.

Daniella swallowed past the lump in her throat and stood to face Isaac, still displaying the same photo.

"He wasn't pointing to Michael Jeffries," she said with conviction. "The man he saw holding the gun was the congressman!"

Before they left the children's home, Isaac took Cassie aside and begged her to let him be the one to break the news to Gavin.

Cassie shook her head. "It will be easier for him to accept coming from me. Besides, we can't be certain Tommy is right about who was holding a gun."

Isaac gritted his teeth. He didn't want to believe the worst, either, yet couldn't help wondering. If only they could come up with a plausible motive for Michael's murder maybe the clues would start to make more sense.

"Okay, how about agreeing to give me three hours?" Isaac asked Cassie. "I should be able to get my men in place by then and find a judge willing to issue a search warrant for Jeffries's estate and office."

"Harland Jeffries founded All Our Kids foster home. He hired me. He mentored Gavin when he was an angry teenager about to go wrong. He saved him from a life on the streets and led him to the right side of the law." She took a shaky breath. "Michael was his only son. How can you even suggest he did such a horrible thing?"

Isaac was trying to come up with a valid rebuttal when Daniella stepped forward and grasped Cassie's hand. Both women were trembling so badly he couldn't tell which was worse.

"My own father killed my mother right in front of my eyes," Daniella told Cassie, obviously speaking softly to keep from further upsetting the children. "The reason I'm with Isaac now is because my dad got out of prison and came after me. It's not unthinkable that some men might kill if they thought it was necessary for self-preservation. Maybe Harland fired by accident. Maybe he did it on purpose. Only God knows for sure."

By this time Cassie was weeping. So was Daniella. Isaac yearned to go to her and enfold her in a comforting embrace. Instead, he waited for the drama to play out.

"I'll give you two hours," Cassie finally said. "After that, I'm calling Gavin and telling him everything that happened here today."

"Fair enough." Isaac was satisfied that that was the best he could expect.

A small hand tugged at the leg of Daniella's jeans. She swiped at her cheeks and sniffled, then smiled down, surprised to see who wanted her attention. "What is it, Tommy?"

"A picture. We were swimmin'."

"I can see that. There's you, and Rachel and…" Her gasp caught Isaac's immediate notice. She was pointing at the framed photo of a group of small children in a wading pool. "Who's this?"

Tommy grew solemn. "That's Juan. I wish he'd come back. He likes my animals."

Straightening, Daniella showed the picture to Cassie, then to Isaac. "Do you see a faint birthmark on this boy's shoulder or am I imagining things?"

"He had a good-size mark on his back, near the shoulder," Cassie said. "It was kind of hard to see against his darker skin but it was there, all right."

"Café au lait," Daniella murmured. She stared at the other woman. "Was Michael Jeffries his father?"

Cassie shook her head emphatically.

"How can you be so sure?"

"Because, Michael wrote an article for the Washington Post promoting adoption, and confessed he couldn't have kids of his own."

Isaac cupped Daniella's elbow to turn and guide her toward the exit. He didn't want to waste one second of his two-hour window, so he exerted gentle pressure. "We really do have to go. I'll bring you back later if you want and you ladies can have a good cry together."

They were seated in the SUV before Daniella responded with words. She blotted her damp cheeks first, then said, "We don't choose to cry, Isaac. Our female brains make more of the natural chemicals that cause us to weep than men's brains do."

"I've seen guys lose it," he countered.

"Yes, but it usually takes a lot more to bring a man to tears than it does to affect a woman the same way. It's not a weakness, it's the way God made us."

"And He never makes mistakes, right?"

"Right. Seeing a woman's tears has a tendency to also alter a normal male's brain chemistry and make him more sympathetic."

"Humph."

What he wanted to do was counter her claim with a macho comment that would disprove that hypothesis. He could not. Truth to tell, his own emotions had been affected by seeing the women so upset, particularly Daniella. He had brought her to the foster home and allowed her to become involved in his work again. He should have known better.

There was no question that he could control his emotions. After all, he'd already seen plenty of suffering and there was undoubtedly more waiting in his future. What he could not deny, however, was the tugging at his heart and the boulder that sat in the pit of his stomach every time he saw joy leave Daniella's face.

She might never know the entire truth, but he did. There was not a shadow of a doubt.

Her pain was his. It always would be.

Instead of relying on the earwig, Isaac picked up the mic, identified his unit and told the dispatcher to switch to another channel while Daniella sat in the passenger seat and listened.

"I have a credible witness to the shooting at the Jeffries estate and a probable motive for Rosa Gomez's murder, too, when we get time to look into it," he reported. "I'll need a search warrant for Harland Jeffries's property and a task force assembled ASAP." He paused. "One more thing. This is vital. Do your notifications by cell or in person. Do not let Captain McCord find out what we're doing if you can possibly help it."

The voice on the radio said, "That's against protocol."

"I know. I left an urgent message for General Meyer, and I'll brief her as soon as she calls me back. If anybody gives you trouble, tell them to check with her and mention my name."

Daniella could tell he was really torn by having to act behind McCord's back. "Maybe it would be best to tell the captain before Cassie's two hours are up," she suggested when he was finished on the radio. "He has a right to know everything, even if the suspect is an old friend of his, and that way you can express your conclusions so he'll be more likely to understand."

"No. I don't want to take a chance on being stopped until we've searched the congressman's house and grounds."

"What are you hoping to find? Surely he wouldn't have kept clues around if he did shoot his son."

"Probably not. I suppose the shooter could just as easily have been Erin Eagleton, like most people thought. Tommy didn't say he saw Harland actually pull the trigger."

"The trick is going to be convincing him to speak up and comment more on that night without putting any notions into his head. Kids can be very impressionable."

"That's what I figured. By the way, thanks for your help. I never thought of making my interrogation into a game the way you did."

"You're welcome." The compliment warmed her to the core and brought a slight smile. "I don't want the poor kid to be scarred for life because of seeing something awful, but I do wish he hadn't run away before the actual shooting."

"Yeah, if that's what he really did."

Driving back to DC, they approached the hospital where Daniella had worked and she felt a pang of nostalgia. No matter how trying her job had been at times, she'd enjoyed doing it. She was about to comment along those lines when Isaac's cell phone sounded.

"Maybe that's your big boss returning your call."

"I hope so."

She saw his face change when he looked at the ID on the small screen. "Becky? What's wrong?"

Daniella didn't have to hear the answer to know it was something dire. Isaac clenched his jaw muscle. His eyes narrowed. He pulled to the shoulder of the road just before they reached the beltway and handed his phone to her.

"Becky?" she said, wishing they were together so she could read her friend's face as well as she was reading Isaac's. When the connection stayed quiet, she pleaded, "Talk to me. Please?"

The sound of shuffling in the background was all that was coming through. Then she heard what had to be a slap, a gasp and a thud, followed by a shaky "Daniella?"

Clearly there was something terribly wrong. Cradling the small cell phone, she motioned to Isaac to shut off the SUV's engine so she could hear every nuance.

When Becky did start to speak, it was rapid-fire and barely understandable. "Kidnapped. Don't come after me. I'm…"

Again there was the smacking sound of flesh against flesh and then a scream. "No!"

The evil-sounding cackle that followed made Daniella physically ill. She held out the phone and stared at it rather than keeping it pressed to her ear. One look at Isaac told her he already knew who had taken his sister.

Becky was with someone even worse than Harland Jeffries was suspected of being.

She'd been abducted by Terence Fagan!

Isaac reclaimed his phone. "Where's my sister, you useless…?"

"Now, now, is that any way to talk in front of a lady?"

"What do you want?"

"A simple trade," Fagan said. "My woman for yours."

"No trade. We don't negotiate with kidnappers."

"In that case, say goodbye to your sister."

"Wait." He eyed Daniella, looking for a sign of approval as he said, "How about a ransom? Your daughter has a lot of money stashed away."

She was nodding rapidly, clearly in agreement, and leaned closer to Isaac to put her ear next to his and eavesdrop on the conversation.

Fagan chuckled. "It's a tad too late for that. I'm afraid this conversation is over. If you won't trade my daughter for your sister, she's of no use to me anymore."

Shouting "Wait" into the phone, Daniella tried to wrest it from Isaac. He held fast so she resorted to yelling. "I'll come. I'll take her place. I promise I will. Just don't hurt her."

"No, she won't," Isaac insisted, pulling away and stepping out of the car to distance himself from her interference. Pacing, he continued to argue with Fagan, hoping the man would listen to reason or at least be tempted by the big payday Daniella could provide.

"I figure it must be close to half a million," Isaac told

him. "I can get it and deliver it to you. Just tell me where and when."

"I thought you didn't negotiate."

"Officially, we don't."

"But my having your sister makes a difference?"

"Yes." It galled him to admit weakness, yet he had no choice. The only way to rescue Becky was to stall her kidnapper until he could set a trap for him, probably at the site of the exchange. As long as Fagan kept him busy on the phone he couldn't arrange a thing. Not a thing.

Isaac motioned for Daniella to join him and once again shared the phone with her.

She clapped a hand over her opposite ear. "What? I can't hear you."

"Where's the cop?"

"He's right here. We both are."

Isaac affirmed her claim, making a rolling motion with one hand to indicate she should keep talking and stall. Then he slipped back into the SUV to radio headquarters and inform them of the kidnapping. He was taking a chance by trying to trick a wily criminal like Fagan. Daniella's wits were going to have to keep them both out of hot water.

He laid down the mic when he saw her motioning wildly for him to return to her.

"Noise is bad here. Say again?" Isaac asked. His heart fell when he heard Fagan's demand.

"Look, I can't get home that fast. We were headed back to DC. We're clear on the opposite side of the beltway right now and traffic is almost at a standstill."

"Excuses? You don't want your sister back, do you?"

"Of course I do." The phone cackled as if it had a

mind of its own, and the hair on the back of Isaac's neck prickled.

"I'll give you one hour to get back to your farm," Fagan told Isaac. "Any longer than that and your sister dies." Another laugh grated. "And when you call your brother to tip him off, make sure he understands that I'll be ready to put a bullet in her the second I think something's wrong, so he'd better behave himself."

"Why rendezvous at the farm?" Isaac asked. "Why didn't you just blow up the house with the last bomb and get it over with?" Dead silence on the other end of the line was confusing.

Finally, Fagan spoke. "I don't know what you're trying to pull, but I didn't have time to place explosives at your house when I was there. I was too busy shooting at my ungrateful kid. Almost got her, too. And you and your buddies and those ugly mutts."

Before Isaac could question him further, Fagan added, "Look at your watch and get moving. The hour starts now."

Grabbing Daniella's arm and half dragging her with him, he raced for the car. "Hurry. We only have an hour to get home and I have a lot of preparations to make in the meantime."

"Do you want me to drive?"

"Only if you've had a defensive driving course."

She climbed in the passenger side and slammed her door, then reached for the buckle ends of the seat belt. "Can we make it?"

He flicked on the lights and siren and eased away from the curb. Most of the passing cars gave him the right-of-way as soon as they could find a place to pull over—which wasn't easy.

In the clear, Isaac floored the accelerator. They'd get home in under an hour. They had to.

The only thing he didn't like was keeping Daniella with him. If he could think of any safe place to drop her, or imagined for one second that she'd stay out of trouble on her own, he'd gladly leave her standing at the curb and speed off.

One glance at her determined expression and the way she was clenching her fists told him they must stay together. Leaving her to her own devices, the way she had been when she'd driven her car into the path of rifle bullets, was out of the question. He didn't know how he was going to control her once she saw her father and Becky. He simply knew he had to try.

And keep trying.

Until there were no more chances left.

SIXTEEN

Daniella didn't think this was a good time to mention that Isaac's erratic driving was making her carsick, so she bit her lip and endured.

Radio traffic had come at them so fast she was pretty confused. Not that it mattered. She'd do whatever Isaac told her to do. She clenched her jaw and amended that promise. Common sense had to take precedence over orders if there was no doubt he needed her help.

She was about to ask him what her role was to be when he turned to her and explained. "Jake is going to be upstairs, out of sight, when we arrive. He'll be armed with the .12 gauge shotgun. That will mean he can't make distance shots but it'll be fine for defense if it comes to that. Unless he calls to tell us Fagan beat us to the farm, I want you to make a run for the house as soon as we get there and head straight for Jake. He'll protect you. Got that?"

"Yes." Daniella's mouth was so dry she could hardly swallow. Her immediate goal had to be a facade of calm, for Isaac's sake if not for her own.

"Culpeper police are already on scene. They know about Jake and to watch for this vehicle."

"So they don't shoot us?"

"Ideally, yes," Isaac said, grimacing. "I'd prefer to have men I've worked with backing me up but they're still fifteen minutes out. If we wait for them…"

"We may be too late to save Becky."

"Exactly."

Daniella could tell how concerned Isaac was, and the guilt piled on top of her like tons of sand being unloaded from a dump truck. No matter how hard she tried to rationalize, this kidnapping and whatever followed was her fault. When she'd had a chance to hit the road again and hadn't followed through, she'd made things worse.

In view of how hard her companion was concentrating and the speed of his driving, she decided to keep any negative thoughts to herself. Isaac needed to focus on freeing his sister. Period.

Yes, she would run upstairs and join Jake. And, yes, she would stay out of the way while the police surrounded her father and made him surrender. But if things started to look bad for Isaac, Becky and Jacob, she was *not* going to stand idly by and observe.

As far as Daniella was concerned, the plan of trading her for Becky was viable. Terence Fagan was not going to win. Not if she had anything to say about it.

"I don't see the cops," Isaac muttered, wheeling into the driveway and barely slowing until he reached the sheltered area next to the barn.

"They're supposed to be hiding," Daniella reminded him.

"There should be an officer I can talk to, somebody who can brief me on their plans."

"Shall I wait?" she asked.

Isaac's "No!" was gruff and loud. He tempered his

anxiety as best he could and pointed at the back door. "Sorry. Just go."

If this had been a regular assignment, not involving his loved ones, he'd have carried out his orders with calm assurance and technical expertise. For the first time since the academy, he could understand why agents who were personally involved with a situation were pulled off that case. Knowing the victims too well did change a person's reactions and hamper judgment.

With no sign of Fagan or Becky and the knowledge that the other man may have been within viewing range of them in the city, Isaac assumed he'd arrived first. Therefore, it made sense to use Abby one more time, just in case. Fagan's choice of the farm as a meeting place seemed odd. In case he'd already been there and planted explosives again, hoping to get rid of all of them at once, this was the ideal time to conduct a quick sweep.

He released his dog, then started to work his way around the house. Jake would take care of Daniella, he would face Fagan and get Becky back, and the police, wherever they were, would take the convicted felon into custody.

That was how it all worked in textbooks. Right now, Isaac would have agreed to any scenario that would bring his loved ones out alive.

He pictured Daniella and took a deep breath, releasing it with a whoosh. Yes. His loved ones. *All* of them.

"How long have you been up here?" Daniella asked Jacob.

"Since Isaac called."

"You've been able to watch the road that whole time?"

Jake nodded. "Yeah."

"Have you seen any local cops?"

"A patrol car cruised through the yard, then left. Either they didn't understand what was going down or they decided it wasn't important. I ran downstairs to talk to them but they were already gone."

"Didn't you report it?"

"Oh, sure. And whoever took my call acted as if I was overreacting." He snorted derisively. "Apparently they were expecting to drive up and see a gunfight. When the place was quiet, they thought the threat was over."

"Are they coming back?"

He shrugged. "They said they were but I sure haven't seen any sign of them."

"What are we going to do?" She grabbed his forearm. "We can't leave Isaac down there all alone to face my dad. What about Becky?"

He laid a warm, strong hand over hers. "Look. I know you want to help, but we won't do Isaac any favors if we get in his way and mess up his plans."

"Ha! I listened to him making plans on the drive home. It sounded more like the script for a sitcom. He won't know what to do until he sees Becky and that awful man."

"At least, thanks to Abby, we'll be sure there's no bomb this time."

"Big whoop. Where there are bullets, who needs a stupid bomb?"

Knowing Jake didn't deserve her sarcasm, she reined it in. "Sorry. I'm getting to the end of my rope. I didn't mean to take it out on you."

"Holler all you want," he told her with a slight smile. "Believe me, I've felt like it today."

"I'm going down the hall to use the restroom," Daniella said. "Be right back."

The fact that Jake let her leave his side without complaint proved that he believed her. And she hadn't lied, exactly. She was going to splash cold water on her face from the bathroom sink. Her only secret was she didn't intend to go back to him before checking on a couple of other things.

She glanced at her watch. Less than ten minutes until the meeting. Everything would soon be over.

And, God willing, the good guys would win.

A nagging voice in the recesses of her brain kept asking, *What if they don't?*

That premise was unacceptable. She didn't have a gun as Becky did and wouldn't have known how to use it if she had. Knives were also out. After helping care for victims of knife fights, she knew she'd never be able to hurt anyone that way. Besides, she'd have to get too close, and anybody with a gun could cut her down before she had a chance.

So what was left? Visions of armored knights on horseback wielding lances led her toward the familiar kitchen. In medieval days, castle defenders had dropped burning logs or poured pots of boiling oil down on their enemies. That would work only if her foes happened to stand below one of the upstairs windows, but she figured it was better to prepare *something* than to stand there like a lamb waiting for slaughter.

Isaac was no longer visible in the yard. There was no sign of her father and Becky yet, either. Live coals were out because they might ignite the whole house. Would she have time to get a pot of cooking oil hot enough to burn someone?

There was only one way to find out. She turned on a burner, grabbed a pan and started to fill it with corn oil.

Watching it heat, she berated herself for trying such a silly idea. She would gladly have done something else, something far more clever, if anything had come to mind.

Most of all, she yearned to know the unknowable, that they were all going to survive. Closing her eyes, Daniella turned to the only source of comfort available. She took her heartfelt appeal to the One who was always there, always faithful, her heavenly Father.

This time there was no sense of peace, no unusual result, no amazing realization. This time, she saw that part of the answer was up to her. First, she must trust the Lord of the universe. Then, she must employ the wits He had given her and be ready to act in whatever manner He presented. Bravely. Quickly. Without thought for self-preservation.

Was she afraid to risk her life? Of course she was. But she needed to take part in the rescue in order to redeem herself. How that might happen was yet to be determined.

Peering out the window over the kitchen sink, her breath caught. Isaac had returned and was standing firm, feet apart, one hand hovering over his holstered gun like a sheriff in an old Western.

A green van fishtailed around the corner, heading straight for him.

He never flinched.

Clamping her hands over her mouth, Daniella stifled a scream. She could not move, could not force herself to look away. Not even if…

The tires of the green vehicle threw up clouds of dust as it slid to a halt mere inches from the K-9 cop.

Round one to Isaac, she thought with heart-stopping relief. Should she stay where she was and continue watching, praying, or should she grab the hot pan of oil and take it upstairs?

That question was answered when she saw her estranged father climb from the van. He hauled a bruised, disheveled Becky out after him, wrenching her past the steering wheel as if she were of no consequence, and pointing toward the house.

Daniella realized she'd run out of time. If she'd gone back to Jake sooner she'd already be in place with the oil, ready to pour it on Fagan.

Instead, she turned and raced up the stairs, calling herself all sorts of names for not acting promptly enough. What good was a weapon if she wasn't in the right position to use it?

On the second floor again, she tiptoed to the rear bedroom, where she'd last seen Jacob, and soundlessly pushed open the door.

She froze. Her feet felt glued to the floor.

Jacob—and his shotgun—were gone!

The kitchen door slammed.

Becky gave a muffled cry of pain as she was shoved into a chair.

Isaac spun around, reaching for his sister, and felt a sharp pain slice through his temple.

He dropped to his knees, dazed.

If it hadn't been for Fagan's pistol and his sister's vulnerability, he would have jumped the older man outside. "Where's my rich little girl?" Fagan drawled.

Still kneeling, Isaac raised up, supported by one arm while the other probed his scalp wound. "I told you the money was in Arlington. If you wanted it, you should have met us there."

"Naw. My Ella and I can pick it up later. Or I can go by myself after she tells me which bank it's in."

"She put it in a safe-deposit box," Isaac informed him, hoping that news would help keep the hostages alive a little longer, himself included.

"Think you're smart, don't ya?" Fagan wielded the pistol like a club, barely missing Isaac's forehead when he swung this time.

That error left him a fraction off balance. His arms cartwheeled.

Isaac rocketed up off the floor and hit him squarely in the midsection. They both staggered backward.

Becky was too battered to do more than raise one foot and trip her captor as he passed.

That, coupled with Isaac's weight, was enough to down him and send the gun sliding away across the smooth vinyl.

Fagan writhed, twisted, stretched toward his pistol.

A shrill "No!" echoed through the house and into the kitchen. If Fagan recognized the woman's voice, he gave no indication of it. Isaac, however, knew exactly who was shouting.

"Get out of here," he yelled, breathless from grappling with her nefarious father and angry that she would so blatantly disobey a sensible order.

"Becky, grab the gun!" Daniella screeched from the foot of the stairs.

Fagan's straining fingers brushed the pistol grip too hard and pushed the gun farther away instead of capturing it.

Isaac saw a flash of movement as someone dashed past and for a moment thought the stubborn nurse was going to follow his instructions to flee.

That instant of inattention was nearly fatal. The man he'd had pinned to the kitchen floor threw himself sideways and flipped Isaac onto his back, grabbing his wrists and holding them immobile, keeping either of them from getting to the loose pistol.

Isaac had a holdout gun in an ankle holster he couldn't reach. His quarry, being heavier and having a clear head, had gained the advantage. His sister was groggier than he was, and to make terrible matters worse, Daniella was somewhere nearby.

Didn't she know how dangerous it was for her? Hadn't she seen enough of her father's deeds to guess what he'd do to her the first chance he got?

Struggling mightily, Isaac raised his shoulders off the floor, preparing to head-butt Fagan, even if it knocked them both out.

A primal roar from above and slightly behind made him freeze. There was a flash of metal. A swish of air. Followed by a hollow-sounding *bonk* that reminded him of the time Jake had dropped a ripe watermelon on their mother's living room carpet.

Fagan slumped forward, unconscious.

Pushing the man's limp body off his chest, Isaac struggled to his feet, expecting to see that his brother had come to his rescue.

Instead, Daniella stood off to one side, armed with a cast-iron skillet that was older than their combined ages. Her muscles were quivering and her eyes enormous. Nevertheless, she had taken the stance needed to repeat the blow and was clearly ready to do so.

"I'll take that," Isaac told her, stopping to scoop up Fagan's gun.

His other fist closed around the handle of the skillet.

Daniella released it so easily he almost fumbled. "What did you think you were doing?"

"Saving your life." She leaned past Isaac to look at her father. "Did I kill him?"

"No, honey. I imagine you gave him a corker of a headache, though." He guided her to a chair and urged her to sit so he could turn his attention to his sister.

Becky looked black-and-blue but she was also grinning at Daniella. "Good one. If I wasn't so whipped right now I'd borrow your pan and give him a whack myself."

Isaac glanced at the prone figure. Fagan hadn't moved a muscle but was breathing regularly. "Looks like he'll be out for a while. I'll cuff him, anyway." He reached for his duty belt before recalling that he'd been forced to drop it outside after he'd been relieved of his weapon, as well.

The sound of distant sirens was rapidly growing louder so Isaac opted to tend to his injured sister for a few more moments. Rinsing a dishcloth in cold water, he folded it and laid it on her forehead. "Better?"

"Mmm, thanks. That feels good." She closed her eyes and sighed.

Daniella was also concerned with Becky's condition. "We need antiseptic and gauze squares to clean her cuts and scrapes. She should see a doctor, too, as soon as possible."

"We'll let the EMTs handle those details." He straightened, glancing toward the unconscious man and expecting to see the same scene as before.

Instead, he watched as Terence Fagan stood. He was brandishing a different weapon—the gun he'd taken from Isaac when he'd first arrived at the farm.

Isaac shouted, "Look out!"

Becky screamed.

Daniella ricocheted off the edge of the kitchen counter, unsuccessfully trying to thwart her father's attempt to grab her.

Isaac had pulled his reliable holdout gun, but Daniella was in the way of a clean shot.

All he could do was stand there and watch as Fagan dragged her, kicking and screaming, across the kitchen toward the back door.

SEVENTEEN

In Daniella's mind she'd been captured by the most evil person in the entire world. Every fiber of her being raged against his touch. Her wrist ached and her skin burned where his fingers were clamped. Screams filled her throat, erupting in a cacophony of earsplitting wailing accompanied by a degree of physical resistance far beyond her normal strength.

Bracing herself, she labored to gain traction. Her gaze raked the room, searching for any weapon or means of escape, while her soles skidded on the vinyl.

The stove! Could she reach it? Every second took her a little farther away. She lunged, jerking until her captive arm gave with a pop and she suspected she'd dislocated her shoulder.

No amount of pain was enough to stop her. Not when she was so close. Panic muted the worst of the pulsing agony, allowing her to continue to strain. So close. So very close. Her extended fingers trembled with the effort. Another inch. That's all she needed. Just one more try. She could last that long. She had to.

A groan started low in her throat, emerging with an

urgency that fit her fight for life better and better as the pitch and volume rose, surprising even her.

Fagan's grip relaxed very slightly. That was enough. Daniella twisted. *Free!*

Her fist closed on the handle of the pan of oil. She didn't stop to wonder if the contents were hot enough to do damage. She just swung.

Centrifugal force carried the pan in an arc toward Fagan and left a trail of spilled oil in its wake.

Daniella continued to attack. The pan failed to make contact with the man's head, as she'd hoped, but the hot oil splashed across his face and chest.

Both arms flew up to shield his eyes, temporarily destroying any opportunity for an accurate shot.

Seeing her chance, Daniella prepared for another swing. Off to her left, she saw Isaac taking aim. She thought she heard him bark an order to her, but Fagan's screeching and cursing made it too hard to hear.

He had pivoted away and was scrambling for the door, slipping on the oily floor. Common sense pulled her the opposite way in spite of a burning desire to keep after him, to make sure he was captured and put back in prison where he belonged.

"Stop or I'll shoot," Isaac roared.

Terence Fagan ignored the warning. He jerked open the door and stumbled out, raising his firearm in front of him as he did so.

A loud bang shook the windows. Fagan's body was driven backward off the porch as if he'd been lassoed around the waist by a giant and given a mighty yank.

Frozen in place, Daniella saw plenty through the doorway. She didn't know what kind of weapon had made the booming sound, but she could guess. Jake must have left the house and sneaked around to find a better vantage point. When her father had aimed the pistol at him, he'd shot first.

Shouts outside mingled with those of the uniformed officers who burst into the kitchen. Some were local cops but the majority wore the patches and gear of Isaac's K-9 unit. Most had their dog partners by their sides.

At this point, Daniella wanted nothing more than to be in Isaac's arms regardless of who might see them together and question his motives. He welcomed her with open arms.

"Is—is he dead?" Daniella asked.

"Medics are checking him," Isaac told her. "He probably is."

She clung to him, listening to the rapid pounding of his heart and wondering why she felt so odd.

He gently stroked her back and murmured his support. "Are you okay?"

Raising her face to look directly into his eyes and draw more comfort, she nodded. "It's very confusing."

"What is?"

"My feelings. My reactions. I thought I'd be overjoyed when that man died, but I'm almost sad. That makes absolutely no sense. He tried to kill me. I should be happier now. What's wrong with me?"

"Not a thing." Isaac bent to kiss her lightly on the forehead. "I wondered if you'd stay bitter after all the horrible things he did to you and your mother. I'm glad to see you were able to forgive him enough to go on with your life. Hate can cripple a person as badly as a broken bone."

"Hmm." He was right, of course. And nobody was more surprised by her tempered attitude than she was. The emotional roller coaster might not be over yet, but

Isaac was right. She could see an end to the grudge she'd been holding and the undeserved guilt that had accompanied it.

Settling against him with her arms wrapped around his waist, she wished they could stay that way indefinitely. It was the aching, prickling soreness of her shoulder that snapped her out of that lovely daydream.

"When the paramedics are done with Becky, I'd like one of them to take a look at my arm and shoulder. I may have dislocated something in the struggle."

"Why didn't you say so?"

Daniella looked up at him, touched by his evident concern. "Because you were hugging me and I didn't want that to end," she whispered for his ears only. "I really like it."

Isaac arched a brow, his dark eyes glistening. "Me, too. Do you think that might be another good sign?"

Because they were surrounded by officers and dogs, she cupped a hand around her mouth to speak aside. "I think it's definitely worth discussing, preferably in private."

"*After* we get your injuries looked at," Isaac said firmly.

"You are one bossy cop, you know that?"

"I think you're up to the challenge, don't you?"

If the atmosphere in the room had not been so somber she would have smiled, although it seemed wrong to even consider doing so. Not only were her thoughts scrambled, her emotions were, too. What she needed to do—what they all needed to do—was calm down and process everything slowly and sensibly.

Daniella was already positive she loved Isaac in spite

of his job. The notion that he might love her in return made her giddy.

So which was it to be? she asked herself. *Do I let myself admit how much I care and face the threat of losing him every time he goes to work, or do I listen to my cowardly side and push him away?*

There had been a time, not many days before, when she would have let her fears govern her choices. Today, having repeatedly cheated death and survived, she was far less certain.

"What do you mean you found another bomb?" Isaac could hardly believe his ears.

The rookie officer looked very pleased with himself. "No lie. We nabbed the perp red-handed. Might have missed him if a cute little dog hadn't flushed him out of the bushes."

"A beagle? With a playful attitude?"

"Sounds about right, except she wasn't acting playful when she latched on to the guy's ankle."

Isaac smiled. "Abby's actually a police dog but she's trained to use her nose, not her teeth. She must have been watching the attack dogs being worked."

"Well, wherever she learned the trick, it worked."

Hesitant to leave the scene, even for a few minutes, Isaac glanced over at the blue plastic sheet covering Fagan's body, then at the nearby ambulance where Daniella and Becky were being treated. Fagan had seemed genuinely surprised when he'd insisted he hadn't placed the previous device in the farmhouse basement. Was it possible he'd had an accomplice? If that man had decided to take matters into his own hands, it was a good thing he'd been captured or they'd still be in jeopardy.

"Take me to your suspect," Isaac ordered.

When he rounded the house with the other officer, his jaw dropped. Captain McCord was standing next to a patrol car, holding Abby in his arms. The handcuffed prisoner beside him was dressed like any other rural worker, but that was where the similarity ended. Isaac recognized him instantly. It was Leon Ridge, one of Congressman Jeffries's aides!

Struggling to make sense of what he was seeing, Isaac frowned at his captain. "What's Leon doing here?"

"That's a good question," McCord replied, passing Abby to her partner. "He's not talking."

"I was told there was a bomber in custody."

Nodding, McCord pointed to a shoe box that was currently being examined by a team of experts wearing heavy protective suits. "According to your dog, there is. Leon was caught trying to slip that into your basement through the coal chute. Since that's how the last bomb was delivered, we assume that's what's in this box, too."

As Isaac puzzled over the proof, he saw a member of the bomb disposal unit wave.

Leon Ridge spoke up. "Hey, I'm just an innocent bystander. A guy named Fagan left that. I happened to see him do it and just wanted to take a look."

Turning to his captain, Isaac shook his head emphatically. "Impossible. Fagan took my sister from work in Arlington, then hung around DC to make contact with me because he was after Daniella. There's no way he had time or opportunity to place another bomb."

Ridge shouted, "I saw him, I tell you," while one of the local officers secured him in the rear of the closest patrol car.

"If I hadn't been so worried about Becky I'd already

have a report on your desk," Isaac told McCord. "Daniella and I talked with Tommy Benson this morning." He hesitated, wishing he didn't have to be the one to tell his boss about Tommy's identification of the congressman.

"And?"

"I'd rather think it through and type it up for you."

The captain huffed. "Yeah. I have an idea I'd rather not hear it, either, but lay it on me. We may as well bring everything out in the open, starting with the lab finding Leon's prints on the first bomb we took out of your basement."

"Jeffries!" Isaac was astounded.

"I've had my suspicions about Harland for some time. Finding Leon here confirms them, although I can't understand why he'd send an aide to frame Fagan and do away with you."

"Yeah, there is that." Isaac was shaking his head as some of the pieces of the puzzle fell into place. "Jeffries must have gone over the edge. No totally sane person would think that eliminating me would stop any of his secrets from getting out." He paused before saying, "Tommy said he saw Harland pointing a handgun at Michael the night of the murder."

"That still doesn't explain who shot Harland."

"Doesn't it?" Isaac nodded at the prisoner waiting in the patrol car. "Leon is his fixer. I think, once we get through interrogating him, we'll know if Harland's crazy enough to tell somebody to put a bullet in him just to keep from looking guilty."

To Isaac's surprise, the captain said, "Now that I'm beginning to see the whole picture, I think he just might be. He's definitely in over his head."

"Don't forget Rosa Gomez. Leon or another of the

congressman's aides may have done away with her, too."
Isaac paused. "I think it's highly possible Harland ordered her killed, especially if we're right about Juan's birthmark being inherited from Harland instead of Michael."

"I suppose that's part of another unwritten report?"

"Yes." Isaac filled in his captain about Juan Gomez having the same birthmark as Michael and Harland Jeffries, that Michael was reportedly unable to have children and that Harland Jeffries was very likely Juan Gomez's father. Isaac could see his captain's mind working—that Harland may have had Juan's mother killed to keep her quiet since an "illegitimate" child from an affair with his housekeeper would have hurt his chances for reelection.

What was less clear was why Harland would kill his own son. What was the motive there?

Since little Tommy didn't see Harland Jeffries pull the trigger, and since Harland had been shot, too, the Capitol K-9 Unit still had more questions than answers. What they did know for sure was that Harland Jeffries wasn't the man everyone thought he was.

Isaac laid a hand of comfort and support on Gavin McCord's shoulder. "I'm sorry."

"Yeah," the captain replied, "me, too."

"Please, let me go with you?"

"Don't you want to hang around here and nurse Becky?"

"She's sleeping and Jake is watching over her. There's no reason for me to stay here when I can go with you."

"You could mop the kitchen floor."

"I've done that twice and we're out of grease-cutting detergent. Try again."

"You'd be bored silly. Trust me, it's not the way you see it on TV. There's very little excitement at police stations." Isaac smiled at Daniella and slipped an arm around her shoulders, using a light touch where a sling supported her left arm. "How are you feeling?"

"Frustrated and tense," she answered.

"Why? The danger's over."

"For me, maybe. You're still in somebody's sights. If I stay behind while you go into the city, I'll worry myself sick."

"So, what else is new?"

She took a playful swing at him. "That's not what I mean. We both know my father couldn't have been responsible for everything. With the congressman's aide in custody, you may find out enough to tell who's behind the rest of the terrible things that have been happening."

"And we may not. Leon's a pro at lying. After all, politics is a good teacher."

Daniella quieted and made a decision that would probably affect her whole future. At least she hoped it would. She looked up at Isaac, reveling in the way he gazed back at her and astounded by how rapidly her heart had opened to him.

"Okay. Let me put it this way. I thought I was going to die when my father tried to drag me away from you. Then I thought we might *all* be out of time, which was even worse."

When Isaac opened his mouth to speak, she stilled him by placing her fingertips on his lips.

"Let me finish. Please?"

He assented.

"I used to think I'd never consider falling for anybody like you, no matter how attracted I was."

"Are you saying…?"

"Hush!" Daniella's growing smile mirrored the joy she was seeing on his face. "What I'm saying right now is that I do not want to be away from you for even a second. It may not make much sense, but that's the way I feel."

"You just lost a parent. Naturally you'd look for an anchor."

"Ha! The only anchor my father would have considered providing is one he could tie around my ankle right before throwing me overboard. It's not that, Isaac. It's you. And me. And if you won't let me ride along with you this time, I'll throw a hissy fit that will curl your hair."

"Is that so?"

"Try me."

Instead of being angry at the threat, he started to laugh and pulled her into his embrace. "I'd love to see you revert to acting like the younger kids at the foster home, but your tantrum will have to wait."

"We're going?" If her shoulder hadn't been throbbing, she'd have jumped up and down.

"We're going. Together. Grab your purse and meet me at the SUV. I'll go tell Jake I'm taking you with me and pick up Abby."

Daniella assured herself she couldn't have been happier if he'd dropped to one knee and proposed. That thought stopped her in midstride. Her decision to admit feelings of affection hadn't gone quite that far.

She knew she wanted desperately to be near Isaac. Being away from him caused true pangs of longing and made him seem so appealing, so amazingly right for her, that it took her breath away. Was that love? Was it enough?

More important, would it be enough for the rest of

their lives? She didn't want to commit to anything until she was sure. So, how long would that take—and would she recognize it if and when it occurred?

Daniella grabbed her purse, gathering the strap in her hand rather than chance bumping her sore shoulder, and proceeded to the K-9 unit vehicle.

The yard was empty, as if the earlier mayhem had never occurred. Her glance kept returning to focus on the door. Watching. Waiting.

It swung open. Abby nosed out ahead of Isaac. A grin split Daniella's face and her heart leaped the moment she laid eyes on him. Yearning built within her until she could hardly contain her exuberance.

His eyes met hers. He smiled that amazing smile she so adored, and it was meant for only her.

No more questions remained. She loved Isaac Black. That was all there was to it.

Instead of climbing into the passenger seat on her own, Daniella paused until he'd secured Abby in the rear compartment and looked for her.

"Need some help?"

"Yes, please. My arm hurts," she said, which was the truth as far as it went.

Isaac approached. Opened and held the door.

Daniella tossed her purse in first, then slipped her uninjured arm around her hero's neck and stood on tiptoe to kiss him gently.

His lips softened. He slid an arm around her waist, lifted and steadied her, as he deepened the kiss.

That ideal response was all the proof she needed. Isaac loved her. Now all she had to do was convince herself to accept that unexpected gift and adjust her plans accordingly, which might be tough to do after spending the past ten years insisting she was perfectly content to spend the rest of her life alone.

To Daniella's astonishment and dismay, she discovered it was far easier to fall in love in the first place than it was to deal with the changes that that love might be bringing.

Isaac seemed to tremble slightly as he set her away and guided her into the SUV.

When she tried to fasten her seat belt one-handed and failed, she realized that most of the unsteadiness was coming from her.

And when he reached across the seat to secure her belt for her and their fingers brushed, she wondered if it was possible her anatomy instructors had been wrong when they'd taught that bones were so strong.

She was positive hers were about to melt.

EIGHTEEN

It didn't surprise Isaac that the interrogation of Leon Ridge was lengthy. It took hours of constant questioning before Ridge caved and implicated the congressman at all. When he did, questions about corruption and taking bribes were answered and some suspicions confirmed, but law enforcement was far from done grilling Leon.

Although they now had a plausible motive for Rosa's murder, namely Juan and his birthmark, they were still working on the details of Michael's shooting death. All Leon Ridge would admit was his part in the wounding of Harland Jeffries and he claimed that had happened after Michael was already dead. The fact that Erin Eagleton's name was also mentioned bothered Isaac, yes, but nowhere near as much as it bothered Chase Zachary, another member of the K-9 team, who was better acquainted with her.

After Daniella's first trip to headquarters, she had quit asking to go along again, much to Isaac's relief. The hardest part for him was seeing her at home with his siblings and not picturing her as part of the family. He'd hinted about it over and over, trying to judge her level of commitment and ending up more confused instead.

She was an enigma; one day kissing him as if she were head over heels in love and the next treating him with no more casual affection than she displayed toward his brother and sister.

Becky counseled patience while Jake urged him to make his feelings clearer. Stuck somewhere between the two extremes, Isaac tried to find balance.

It seemed only fair to share some details of his work with Daniella, particularly since she'd been directly involved in the past and he wanted her to understand how vital his job was.

They were sitting together on the porch swing, slowly rocking, when he decided to bring up Leon Ridge. "Looks like we were right about Harland Jeffries being dirty." Isaac was leaning forward, elbows resting on his knees, fingers clasped between them. "Leon's started talking."

"Was he an eyewitness to the shootings at the estate?"

"Not exactly. He claims the congressman called him in a panic, though," Isaac told her.

"That's something. Maybe we won't have to bother poor, scared little Tommy again."

"Probably not. Apparently, the boy didn't see much more than what he's already told us. Nobody did. Two men were yelling at each other and the white-haired one had a gun. That's about it."

Isaac straightened and slipped an arm over the back of the swing, ready to lay it across her shoulders if she seemed agreeable, particularly since she wasn't wearing the sling.

"So, what did happen?" Daniella asked.

"If you can believe Leon, Jeffries insisted he hadn't meant to hurt Michael. They'd been arguing about taking proper care of Juan, the little boy with the birthmark in the photo we saw at the foster care safe house. Michael was supposedly threatening to go public about his father's affair with Rosa Gomez and Juan's birth, for the sake of the child's future. They struggled. The gun went off and Michael was wounded."

"Why didn't anybody call for help?"

Isaac shrugged. "Good question. Maybe Michael died too quickly. We can't be sure. Anyway, Harland phoned Leon and together they figured out an alibi. Leon swears he was only supposed to lightly wound the congressman so Harland could claim the same assailant was responsible for killing Michael. He almost overdid it, though. Harland passed out before he could call 911 and could have died before he regained consciousness."

"But—" Daniella was frowning and slowly shaking her head "—where does my father fit in all of this? He wasn't working for Jeffries, was he?"

"No, not according to Leon, and everything we've been able to substantiate so far has proved true. It looks as if Harland was so mentally unbalanced after shooting Michael he wasn't thinking straight. When I recently interviewed him about the bomb that went off during his press conference, he figured I knew he was responsible, which was correct. Unfortunately, to his twisted mind, my visit to his office also meant I knew more about his other crimes than I actually did, including the death of his son. Leon says the guy was convinced that getting rid of me and blaming it on Fagan was the answer to all his problems."

"That's crazy."

"Uh-huh. Very. I had already reported most of what I knew. Besides, you and Cassie both heard Tommy ID the congressman as the armed man, so logically, you two should have been on his hit list, too." He paused, thinking about all that had taken place and how blessed they were to still have each other.

"So, what now?"

"Captain McCord has requested a search warrant for the Jeffries estate and the congressman's office. We're planning to raid both at the same time."

"When?"

Isaac checked his watch, then replaced his arm behind her shoulders and pulled her closer. He sighed deeply when she snuggled against him. "In a few hours. We'll wait until dark to minimize the danger to bystanders."

"Surely Harland won't be in his office then."

"We hope not. We'd like to confine the risk to his estate."

"And to yourselves," Daniella added as she laid her palm on his chest. "I wish you didn't have to be involved."

"You mean you wish I had a different job?"

Leaning away slightly, she studied his face for a few moments before starting to smile. "No. I can see you're doing exactly what you were meant to do. It's Jeffries who worries me. If he's as mentally unbalanced as you say he is, how can you be sure you won't be greeted by a hail of bullets?"

"Like I've said before, Gavin—my captain—has been close to Harland ever since he was a teenage resident of the foster home on the Jeffries estate. He'll go in first and make sure the congressman is unarmed, if he's home."

"This must be really hard on your captain."

"It is." Isaac clenched his jaw as he considered that truth.

"Um, speaking of hard jobs, I want you to hurry home. There's something I'd like to talk about."

"So, talk." He glanced at his watch again. "I've got a few minutes to spare."

"Oh, no, you don't." She shook her head so hard her silky hair swung back and forth over her shoulders. "I've seen you use your job as an excuse to run off in the middle of an important conversation, and I'm not taking any chances."

"You're serious?"

"Totally."

Isaac leaned closer and used one finger to tilt up her chin before giving her a tender kiss. "In that case, here's a little something for you to think about while I'm gone."

Abby was part of the assault team that entered the Jeffries mansion on McCord's signal. Other officers raided the congressman's DC office at the same time.

Gavin McCord was standing in the center of the ornately furnished living room and holding a small black book when Isaac and Abby approached him.

"I want you to check the whole house for any trace of explosives," McCord ordered. "I don't think you'll turn up anything like that, but it never hurts to play it safe."

"What about Harland? Did you find him?"

"No. The few servants he has left swear they haven't seen him since breakfast."

"Do you believe them?"

McCord nodded, disgust and disappointment evident. "I suppose the political grapevine warned him somehow. I should have anticipated that."

"Well, at least his focus is off Washington. He has to know his political career is finished. Where do you think he went?"

"Probably overseas, wherever he's stashed a getaway

fund." The captain waved the notebook. "It looks like it's all in here, the bribes, the deals under the table, the coconspirators. He even orchestrated the plot to steal George Washington's golden arrow from the American Museum a few months back. I've already ordered the arrest of his other aides."

"All of them were crooks?"

"No. He apparently kept a few on payroll who were squeaky-clean, probably in case he needed an alibi or a handy scapegoat. We'll sort them out."

"Where did you find a book like that? I can't believe he'd be careless enough to leave it lying around."

"He didn't. It was hidden in his safe room, the last place I checked when nobody could locate him." McCord started off and motioned Isaac to follow with Abby. "You can start in there, then work the rest of the house with the team while I coordinate with Fiona and our other techs to search his personal online records."

"What about Erin Eagleton? Did Ridge exonerate her?"

"No." McCord stared at Isaac before pulling out a cell phone and punching a number, then holding up a hand to signal Isaac to wait.

"Fiona," he barked, "get me everything Jeffries had in his records that has anything to do with Senator Eagleton or his daughter, Erin, I don't care how obscure."

Isaac could hear her forceful, enthusiastic "Yes, sir" and that made him smile. If anybody could dig out the truth, it was Fiona. For all her quirks, she was the best computer tech in the business, although she'd had more than a few moments of inattentiveness since she'd fallen for one of their secondary K-9 officers, Chris Torrance.

Remembering how clues had pointed to Erin being on

the scene when Michael was shot and how the congressman had implied that she must have pulled the trigger, Isaac was worried. Judging by the expression on the captain's face, he was, too. Without the murder gun to check for a ballistic match or fingerprints, placing blame was anybody's guess.

Was Jeffries thinking of his own escape at this time or had he disappeared because was he bent on finding and harming Erin so she couldn't refute his claims?

Only time would tell. Isaac just hoped nobody else had to pay for the crooked congressman's sins.

The body count was already far too high.

Daniella was sitting on the front porch, wearing a quilt like a shawl and waiting for Isaac, when he finally got home.

Parking, he let Abby loose and plodded wearily up the steps. "Do you know what time it is?" he asked.

"Yes. It's after two a.m. If you'd let me come with you we could have had our little talk on the drive home."

"Can't it wait until morning? I'm beat."

She laughed lightly. "It is morning."

"So it is. Okay. Got room for me on that swing?"

"I'll make room." She patted the slatted bench next to her. "This shouldn't take long, unless you make the mistake of arguing with me."

"You know I'd never do that." He was sending a look at her that was half scowl, half smile. "You're not getting up the courage to tell me you've changed your mind *again* and are leaving, are you?"

"Don't bother putting on that hurt expression. You won't need it. I'm not going anywhere. I'm just nervous."

"Why should you be afraid? Your sworn enemy is

dead, Leon Ridge is in jail, there's a warrant out for Jeffries and the case against him is coming together. We'll have him in no time."

"I'm not concerned about criminals. Your unit and the other cops can worry about them. From now on I'm staying out of it."

"So…?"

She laid her fingertips over his lips, ostensibly to silence him, and he kissed them instead.

"Stop distracting me."

"Why? You keep distracting me."

Daniella blew a noisy sigh. "I want to talk about the future—our future."

"Ours?"

She laughed again, her cheeks blooming in the dimness of the single porch light. "You shouldn't be surprised. I've done everything I can think of except come right out and ask you if you love me."

"Of course I love you!" Watching tears glimmering in her emerald eyes, Isaac couldn't decide whether to kiss her into silence or let her keep talking.

He was about to choose the kiss when Daniella began to whisk away sparse tears.

"Okay," she said, sniffling and smiling. "So when are you going to tell me what you plan to do about it?"

"What do *you* want to do?"

"Uh-uh. No fair. If I have to tell you that I want you to sweep me off my feet and ask me to marry you, it won't be as romantic."

Stunned by both her boldness and the way her ideas had meshed so perfectly with his, Isaac laughed. "Suppose I surprise you one day soon with a ring? Will that do?"

"It might, if you don't wait too long."

"I'll do my best," he said, sobering. "I'll always do my best for you, honey. You know that, don't you?"

She reached up and cupped his cheek.

Isaac placed his hand over hers, then drew it down to kiss her palm. There would never be a dull day married to this extraordinary woman, he realized, counting his blessings again and again. And he would guard his life for her sake as well as his own.

"I think your sister was right when she said the Lord brought us together," Daniella whispered. "So it's a good thing we fell in love. I sure wouldn't want to disappoint God after He went to all that trouble."

Isaac gave her a heartfelt kiss. "I agree. Prepare to say yes when I pop the question."

He saw her lips tremble, her eyes glisten, as she smiled and said, "I can hardly wait."

* * * * *

With over seventy books published and millions in print, **Lenora Worth** writes award-winning romance and romantic suspense. Three of her books finaled in the ACFW Carol Awards, and her Love Inspired Suspense novel *Body of Evidence* became a *New York Times* bestseller. Her novella in *Mistletoe Kisses* made her a *USA TODAY* bestselling author. Lenora goes on adventures with her retired husband, Don, and enjoys reading, baking and shopping…especially shoe shopping.

PROOF OF INNOCENCE

Lenora Worth

Before destruction the heart of man is haughty,
and before honour is humility.
—*Proverbs* 18:12

To my fellow authors in this series: Shirlee McCoy, Terri Reed, Lynette Eason, Margaret Daley and Valerie Hansen. I love and appreciate all of you!

ONE

An urgent heartbeat pounded through Erin Eagleton's temples each time her sneakered feet hit the dry, packed earth. She stumbled, grabbed at a leafy sapling and checked behind her again. The tree's slender limbs hit at her face and neck when she let go, leaving welts across her cheekbones, but she kept running. The sun slid in a shimmering-gold descent beyond the trees to the west as dusk settled like a vivid red orange blanket over the sticky, hot Virginia hillside. Soon it would be full dark and she would have to find a safe place to hide.

Winded and damp with a cold sweat that made her shiver as it snaked down her backbone, Erin tried to catch her breath. Did she dare stop and try to find another path?

The sound of approaching footsteps behind her caused Erin to stare through her nonprescription black-framed glasses into the growing darkness. Making a split-second decision, she took off to the right and headed deeper into the woods. She had to keep running until she came to a highway or a hideaway. But she was so tired. Would she ever be free?

Dear Lord, I'm so lost. I don't know where to turn.

Memories of Chase Zachary moved through her head,

causing tears to prick at her eyes. Her first love. Her high school sweetheart who now worked as a K-9 officer with an elite Washington, DC, team. A team that was investigating her.

From what she'd read on the internet and in the local papers, Chase had been one of the first officers on the scene that horrible night.

She'd thought about calling him a hundred times over these past few months, but Erin wasn't sure she could trust even Chase. The last time they'd seen each other, on the very evening this nightmare had taken place, he hadn't been very friendly. And why should he be kind toward her? He probably hated her for breaking his heart when they were so young.

But then just about everybody else along the Beltway and possibly even in the entire metro area surrounding DC hated her right now. Erin had been on the run for months. She knew running made her look guilty, but she'd had no other choice since she'd witnessed the murder of Michael Jeffries, and she'd almost been killed herself. The authorities thought she was the killer and until she could prove otherwise, Erin had to stay hidden.

The media had already condemned her with a relentless assault that had her face plastered all over television news reports and newspaper headlines. Whole hours of cable news had been dedicated to dissecting her life. How could anyone stand up to such scrutiny?

The reports had at first painted her as an allegedly scorned ex-girlfriend who'd possibly murdered prominent Washington lawyer Michael Jeffries because he'd broken up with her. None of which was true. Michael had been too caught up in his crusade against corruption to even have time to break up with her, and besides, their relationship was mostly for "show," to please their political families. Tired of the ruse, *she'd* actually gone to dinner with Michael on that cold night to break things off with *him*. But Michael had been too upset about another situation in his life for her to tell him it was over between them, publicly and privately. He'd found out he might have a young relative living in a foster home and he'd insisted he had to get home and do some more digging for the truth.

Erin still remembered Michael's frantic attempts to explain the situation. "I can't tell you everything, Erin. I don't want to accuse anyone of wrongdoing, but I *will* find out the truth. I think I can prove I'm right. I need more time. And I'm going to talk to my father and make him tell me the truth."

They'd parted ways, and Erin had decided to go for a walk.

Later, concerned about his state of mind, she'd searched for Michael and found him at his father's estate outside the city.

At least the news reports had one thing right about that night. Michael had been murdered.

And she knew who'd killed him because she'd witnessed the whole horrible scene. But no one would believe her if she told the truth—that Congressman Harland Jeffries had killed his own son, had worked to pin the murder on Erin and had tried to have her killed, too.

Now Erin Eagleton was a wanted woman.

And if she couldn't get away from the man chasing her so she could prove her innocence, she'd soon be going to jail.

Or—she'd soon be dead.

* * *

Chase Zachary held the delicate cashmere scarf to his nose, the lingering scent of the expensive floral perfume making him remember the touch of her lips on his. Chase remembered way too many things about the girl he'd loved and lost years ago in high school. But right now he'd give anything to find Erin once again.

Help me, Lord. Help me to find her before it's too late.

She was out here in these woods, lost and afraid. Chase had been searching for her for close to five months, while on duty and often on his own time, too. He'd never believed Erin capable of murdering Congressman Jeffries's son Michael and shooting the congressman, so he'd been trying to find enough evidence to disprove the original theory that had her as the scorned girlfriend who'd been at the scene of the crime. So many things about this case didn't add up, but at least now they had a witness who said the congressman *had* shot his son.

That witness, an aide named Leon Ridge, was now in custody. After being caught a few days ago after planting a bomb, he'd finally caved and explained that the congressman had accidentally shot Michael and then, in an effort to cover it up, he'd had Leon shoot him so he could insist that some unseen assailant had attacked both of them. And the congressman had hinted that Erin might be involved. Crazy, but Leon had done a good job following orders. The congressman's injuries had been severe enough to make it look real, but Leon Ridge swore his version was the truth.

"And what about Erin Eagleton?" Chase had asked the bouncer of an aide. Rumor around the city was that Leon's only qualification involved handling delicate matters for the congressman.

"I don't know anything about her," Leon had retorted. Then he'd started fidgeting.

"You mean you haven't heard all the news reports alleging she was the shooter? She's missing, in case you didn't know."

"I don't watch the news."

"Right. But you probably know that Congressman Jeffries is wanted on corruption charges. He's missing. Could have left the country."

Shock had turned Leon's skin a sickly pale.

The captain had stood up. "Let us know when you're ready to tell us what really happened that night, Ridge. Think about it long and hard because until we find Erin Eagleton and the congressman, you're our main suspect."

"Hey, I told you the truth. The congressman accidentally shot his son."

"And you were forced to shoot him at his request to make it look like an unknown assailant did it," Chase had reminded him. "That's a tall tale, for sure." Then he'd asked Leon Ridge the one question burning through him. "Was Erin at the congressman's estate that night?"

"Like I said," Ridge had insisted in a quick rush of breath, "I don't know anything about Erin Eagleton."

Ridge still maintained he was telling the truth, but Chase didn't believe him. More like, he was covering his own hide until Erin turned up. Ridge had clammed up even more when two fancy lawyers had visited him.

Now Erin was still out there on the run, afraid for her life. Chase needed to find her to tell her that they had new information that might clear her name.

And he wanted to tell her that it had all started with a two-year-old boy.

A maid named Rosa Gomez who worked for the congressman had been found dead the day before Michael Jeffries was shot. The congressman was wounded the night Michael died and at first claimed he hadn't seen the shooter. Erin's starfish necklace was found at the scene of the shooting—Chase had verified that since he'd seen her earlier on the night of the shooting. After that, everything pointed to Erin as a witness or person of interest, but no one had been able to find her.

Then a kid named Tommy Benson from the All Our Kids foster home not far from the congressman's estate confessed that he'd sneaked out that night and witnessed the congressman holding a gun. But the kid also said Michael was still alive when he was there. Tommy hadn't seen Erin there. He didn't even recognize her in a picture. Chase couldn't imagine Erin arriving after that and committing such a cold-blooded crime. No way.

But things were unraveling for the pompous congressman. The dead maid had left behind a little boy who carried the same scallop-shaped light brown birthmark as the congressman and his son Michael. Strong evidence that the rumors about the boy being Harland Jeffries's son could be true. And maybe…it was one of the reasons Michael had been murdered. Congressman Jeffries stood to lose everything if he'd been having an affair with his maid and had a secret child whom he'd let languish in foster care.

But would that alone force him to kill his adult son?

The team had finally found evidence of corruption by the congressman…in his own meticulous records. They'd also had a break when they'd arrested several of his top aides, but no one wanted to talk. They'd planned to bring in Congressman Harland Jeffries on corruption charges and to question him about the murdered maid since the evidence was mounting on that one, too. But the congressman had fled. No one could locate him and Leon Ridge talked only about his version of what had happened the night Michael had died.

But Ridge had admitted to planting a bomb to kill K-9 team member Isaac Black and DC General Hospital nurse Daniella Dunne, trying to make it look as if Daniella's mobster father, Terence Fagan, had done the job. Congressman Jeffries knew the nurse had seen his birthmark, the same birthmark that Michael and little Juan Gomez had on their shoulder. More evidence that Juan was a Jeffries.

That admission at least showed Leon Ridge as a henchman for the congressman and proved that the congressman wanted the Capitol K-9 team to stop this investigation.

Ridge was a witness to whatever really happened the night Michael was murdered, but he refused to even discuss Erin's involvement.

Someone had put a muzzle on Ridge. Why?

Was the congressman trying to get to Erin before she could finally tell the truth about what happened at his estate that night?

"I know you didn't do this," Chase said, his gaze scanning the countryside. Fiona Fargo, who worked as a technician for the team, had been helping to track any chatter regarding Congressman Jeffries or Erin Eagleton, and had seen some interesting search efforts in the internet cafés in and around this area. When she'd found a Wi-Fi hot spot at a local hotel, she'd let the team know some of the searches might be coming from Erin. And she'd found evidence that Erin was picking up work there as a waitress. That explained how she had cash to carry her through.

Chase hoped he could find Erin soon, and he wished he could have helped her the night of the murder, or at least stopped her from going to the Jeffries estate. But they'd bumped into each other near the Washington Monument and the tension between them had somehow overshadowed any clear thinking.

She hadn't even realized Chase was jogging along the path until he stopped and called her name. "Erin?"

Erin had whirled, her honey-blond curls collapsing in a silky waterfall around her face and shoulders. She wore a patterned scarf bundled loosely around her shoulders and a short wool jacket over jeans and high-heeled boots. A gold necklace sparkled against her skin and the blue pattern in the cream-colored scarf matched her deep blue eyes.

"Hey, Chase." Her gaze moved over his fleece hoodie and back to his face, surprise masking her obvious discomfort. "Still staying in shape, huh?"

He jogged in place, and then relaxed. "Yep. Part of the job."

She walked closer, her arms wrapped against her midsection to ward off the winter chill. He could see she'd been crying.

"Are you okay?"

Lowering her head, she looked down at her boots. "I'm fine. Just working through some things." She stared off into the lights twinkling all around the city. "I wonder if it'll snow tonight."

Her tone suggested she didn't want to talk about anything but the weather.

Chase had never known when to give up, however.

"Erin, are you sure you're all right? You shouldn't be out here alone."

"I told you, I'm fine."

He tried one more time. Seeing her made his life hard, but he cherished their brief encounters all the same. "Anything I can do?"

She shook her head and wiped at her eyes. "No, nothing. I have to go." She pivoted, her eyes holding his. "It was…good to see you again, Chase."

Chase reached out to her, his fingers brushing against her scarf. "Erin, you know I'd do anything for you, no matter what."

"I don't need your help," she replied, ripping away from his touch. "Not anymore."

That comment brought out a pent-up bitterness in Chase. "You mean, because you don't need me in your life now, right? I saw you with Michael Jeffries at that recent White House dinner. I guess your father is still calling the shots."

"I have my own life now, Chase. No one tells me what to do."

"Okay," he said, hating himself for caring. "Or maybe you still don't have the courage to stand up to your daddy."

The hurt in her eyes as she turned away made Chase want to take back that accusation. But it was too late for that. Too late for a lot of things.

"Erin?"

"I have to go," she'd said, her expression as chilly as the night wind blustering through the bare branches of the nearby cherry trees.

She'd taken off so fast her scarf fell away from her

jacket. The soft material fluttered toward the ground like a dying butterfly, but Chase caught it up in his hands.

Chase had held it and called out to her. "Erin?"

But she'd already slipped out of sight.

Chase had been one of the last people to see her the day of the murder, and he'd beaten himself up over that tense conversation. What had she been crying about that night? Why hadn't she let him help her?

A few hours later, he'd seen her broken starfish necklace in an evidence bag and Chase had become obsessed with finding Erin. It might be too late for them, but he wouldn't let time run out on saving her.

This latest lead from Fiona and the research team had brought him to a rural area of Virginia about forty miles southwest of DC. Months ago, someone matching Erin's description had been seen by a couple, Edward and Mavis Appleton. The elderly Virginia husband and wife had helped Erin in the days after the murder, but they'd been attacked by some thugs also looking for Erin. Since then, no one had come forward with any concrete sightings, but the team had proof that she'd been using internet cafés and remote libraries to do some online research, all of it pointing toward a strong corruption case against the supposedly upstanding Congressman Jeffries. Smart. She'd tried to bring down Jeffries on her own.

Since the man was now wanted on said corruption charges, Erin had obviously been onto the truth. Because the congressman had fled and was now missing, Chase wanted to find Erin before one of the congressman's henchmen did.

The big dog at his feet whimpered and danced around, dark eyes staring up at Chase with anxious clarity. Valor was ready to get on with things, too.

"Yeah, boy, I know," Chase said to his K-9 partner. Trained in search and rescue, Valor knew only that he was needed to find someone. But how could Chase explain to his faithful companion that they'd gone off the grid—way off the grid?

Leaning down, Chase allowed the fawn-colored Belgian Malinois to sniff the now-familiar cream-and-blue patterned cashmere scarf.

"We need to find her, Valor," he said, praying that after so many months of uncertainty regarding Erin Eagleton's whereabouts, one of his leads would finally pay off.

Valor sniffed the delicate material, then started trembling. The big dog was ready to go. Chase held tight to the leash and made sure Valor's protective vest was secure. Then he gave the command to "Find."

Valor took off into the Virginia woods located along a jogging trail near a narrow stream. Chase held tight and ran along with the animal. Had they hit on something so soon?

Was Erin somewhere nearby?

TWO

She was running in circles. Every tree hulked like a giant monster waiting to grab her. Every snap of a branch caused her to whirl in a dizzy spin of fear and slap at some unseen assailant. Earlier, unable to sleep, she'd heard someone outside her room—and she'd seen a man dressed in dark clothing and carrying a gun. Erin hadn't stayed around to see if he'd come to call on her. She was used to mysterious assailants trying to kill her. Going out the back and over the balcony, she'd taken the first path into the dense woods, thinking she could circle back and hide somewhere in the small town and then board a bus out. Somehow.

Now it was dark and she was soaked with sweat and the bugs were trying to finish her off. The short dark auburn wig she wore seemed to be shrinking on her head. It pressed into her skull like a wet mesh helmet and had her whole head itching with a fire that burned all the way down her backbone. The few possessions she managed to carry around bounced together in the deep pocket of the old jeans she'd been wearing for days now. She had a little cash left and she had her research notebook. She sure didn't want to lose that since it had all her memories and all of her questions and, maybe, a few answers. Erin had to get somewhere safe before morning. Another hotel with a front and back entry, so she wouldn't be cornered, more attempts to search online for information and clues, news articles and tips.

This was her life now, a never-ending nightmare of always looking over her shoulder with an ingrained fear that might not ever leave her. She was pretty sure she'd finally outrun her pursuer, so she planned to hike out of the woods.

Searching for any sign of the lights toward the town, she shifted in the gray moonlight and slid behind a big tree. What was that sound? Was someone running toward her again?

Footsteps echoed out over the woods and the swish of bushes being shoved aside followed. Someone was still after her.

Holding her breath, Erin closed her eyes and prayed for guidance. She would survive this. She'd heard the news reports regarding the vast array of corruption charges being brought up against Congressman Jeffries. Now he'd been indicted for some of his crimes. But surprise—he'd fled like the coward he was. At least she wouldn't have to be the one to prove he was corrupt. But she still had to prove she hadn't killed Michael. She knew the truth and she intended to tell that truth once she…once she what?

Turned herself in and tried to reason with the police?

Or maybe gave a long statement over the airwaves and screamed to the world that she was on the right side of the law?

Or maybe she could call her powerful father and hope that the scandal of having a fugitive daughter hadn't ruined his position in the Senate or severed his strong ties with the Washington elite. But she'd been careful about not having contact with her father so she couldn't start now. He'd have to report hearing from her. Knowing that being involved in such a scandal could indeed ruin her father's career right along with any thoughts she had of her life going back to normal, Erin didn't know where to turn next.

She dropped her head and stood there, defeated and exhausted. When she heard pounding footsteps coming toward her, she knew she had no choice. She had to run as fast as she could.

But a thought occurred to her. In the cover of darkness, she could at least try to stop the gunman in his tracks before she took off. She'd trip him up and try to hit him over the head, maybe use some of the self-defense maneuvers her father had his security team teach her. That had worked when the congressman's aide Leon Ridge had tried to kill her the night of the murder. Maybe she could find the strength to fight off this latest assailant.

Erin crouched behind a huge live oak's aged trunk, a broken limb her only means of protection. She waited, holding her breath, her mind whirling with the vision of her hitting her stalker over the head, tripping him with one foot while she hit at him with all her might. Then she'd run. As fast as she could.

But when she turned to put her foot out, a dog's woof caused her to stumble. Right into two waiting hands.

Erin started fighting, kicking and screaming as she tried to gain a foothold.

The dog started barking but stood back in a frenzied dance.

And the man holding her did something that surprised her and caused her whole world to tilt.

He shouted "Heel" at the big dog, and then he called her by her name. "Erin? Erin? It's me. It's Chase."

Erin stopped fighting, her fists relaxing against his solid chest, her gaze halting on the face she remembered so well. Her voice cracked and she blinked to clear her head. "Chase?"

"It's okay," he said on a whisper. "You're safe now, understand? You're with me now and I won't let anything happen to you."

"Chase." She said his name on the wings of a prayer and thanked God for sending her a hero. *Chase Zachary.* A hero who had once been the love of her life, her high school sweetheart.

A man who'd also been after her for over five months.

Should she try to run from him, too?

She hadn't asked for this and she wasn't prepared for what seeing Chase now could mean, but for a few brief seconds, she was so very glad to see him again. "Chase? Is it really you?"

"Yes." His fingers gentled on her skin. "Relax, okay?"

Then he pulled her into his arms and held her close while she cried. Somewhere in the back of her frayed mind, she heard the big dog woof again. But this time the sound only reinforced how relieved she felt. Relieved and safe—unless he planned to take her into custody.

"Where are you taking me?"

Erin couldn't quite wrap her brain around Chase finding her in these lonely, isolated woods. But when she glanced ahead at the dog leading them through the overgrown bramble and tangled vines, she understood. He'd had a little help from a friend. She could try to run again, but the dog would track her down. A weight of fatigue pulled at her like a heavy, stifling blanket. The enormity of Chase finding her caught up with her until panic set in. She had to run. These people would kill her and Chase, too.

Did she really want to go back out there alone? No. So she asked again, "Chase, where are we going?"

"Away from this place," he said, his words just above a growl.

Earlier when she'd explained someone had been after her, Chase had quickly checked the woods before moving on, and then he'd made sure he and the dog guarded her at all times. They'd zigzagged back and forth, the dog stopping here and there to sniff the wind and the ground, but never alerting. Chase hadn't made any small talk. He was intent on doing his job—which she figured now meant keeping her alive until he could get her under lock and key. Maybe the gunman who'd stalked her was gone. But she knew others would keep coming.

She thanked God the dog had led Chase to her at a time when she'd been out of options. But that joy was short-lived. "You tracked me."

He nodded, his hand still on her arm. But then he stopped and tugged something out from under his shirt and shoved it at her. "I believe this belongs to you."

Erin took the soft white-tinged bundle, but it was hard to see what it was in the dark. The material glistened in the moonlight and she let out a gasp. "My elephant scarf. How did you—"

"You dropped it the last time we talked."

Erin swallowed back the emotional agony that scraped across her frazzled nerve endings. Their chance meeting so many months ago had stayed with her all this time. They'd had a brief argument that night just hours before Michael had died. Chase had made a sarcastic remark about seeing her at a White House dinner with Michael. He'd accused her of never being able to stand up to her formidable daddy. And he had been right. She was such a coward, she'd been afraid to tell anyone what had happened later that same night—the night she'd watched the congressman shoot Michael.

She'd been afraid to contact her father, afraid the congressman would make good on his threats to kill her father or ruin his career. And she'd been afraid to reach out to the one man who could have possibly helped her. The man now guiding her out of the dark woods.

And yet Chase had kept her scarf. "You've had this all this time?"

"Yep. I asked your father if I could hold on to it—to help track you."

Chase had gone to her father? Of course they'd have to cooperate with each other regarding her whereabouts. She wondered how many times the authorities had questioned the senator. She could never be sure of her father's true motives, but she loved him dearly and since her mother had died, Erin had tried to be the good daughter everyone expected her to be. She wanted to believe the senator would tell the truth no matter what. He'd taught her that much at least. Erin had managed to stay away from her father while on the run, so he wouldn't be forced to lie on her behalf. But she missed him so much.

"Is he okay?" she asked, tears hot in her eyes. She'd heard her father had been injured in an attack a few weeks ago, and she'd managed to sneak into a DC hospital to check on him but only long enough to make sure he wasn't seriously hurt. He never knew she was there. But she wasn't ready to admit that to Chase.

"Your father is fine," he answered. "He's concerned about you, of course."

Chase obviously didn't want to discuss the man who'd come between them when they were so young and full of idealistic love. But then, Chase wasn't one to discuss his feelings with anybody.

"I'm sure he's concerned," she replied, wishing she could explain everything to Chase right now. "And the Eagleton Foundation? Any word on that?"

"Kind of in a holding pattern from what we've heard. We questioned everyone who works for the foundation. No one knew anything about your whereabouts." He gave her a quick glance. "They're all concerned about you."

She'd probably be voted out as CEO of the Eagleton Foundation. If that hadn't already happened.

"I couldn't contact anyone. It would have put them in danger, too."

He didn't respond to that, but he shot her a cautious glance and guided her over a tree root.

Holding on to the scarf like a lifeline, Erin loved the softness it brought back into her life. Knowing Chase had carried her scarf all these months gave her renewed hope. But the memories the exquisite piece of her past life brought out made her want to weep. She was no longer that girl and she was no longer a part of Washington's elite society either. The nation's capital was a very unforgiving place.

But she had her memories, good and bad. "My dad gave me this scarf for my birthday a few years ago. You know how I love animals."

Chase glanced over at her. "Yep. I remember you going on a safari…one summer."

The summer after they'd broken up.

Erin wrapped the delicate cream material stamped with blue elephants around her neck. "Chase, are you taking me back to DC?"

"No."

Thinking he'd never been a man of words, she tried again. "Where are we going?"

"Where were you before?"

And so like him to answer a question with a question.

"In a hotel up on the highway." They wound around a curve in the path. "I've tried to stay in cheap hotels to save cash. I've worked odd jobs to keep me going."

Which he had to have known. He'd found her, hadn't he? Was he testing her for the truth?

If so, he didn't let on. "Then we won't be going back to any of those places. They'll be looking for you at every cheap motel in the area."

They finally emerged from the woods and she saw a white SUV with official trim work and the words *Capitol K-9 Unit* stamped in dark letters on its sides. In bright red underneath, it stated *Caution. Police Dog.* Chase and the dog he'd called Valor stopped, both of them shielding her while the man did a visual of the area and the dog lifted his nose for any air scents.

"He's beautiful," she said after Chase used his key fob to open the high-tech vehicle. He helped her into the passenger's seat, where what looked like an assault rifle was mounted inside the console between the seats. Valor jumped into a clean metal compartment right behind the two front seats, his doleful dark eyes washing over Erin with a certain curiosity that belied his training.

She automatically held her knuckles to his brown nose and allowed him to get to know her. "Hey there, Valor. Thank you so much for finding me."

Valor whimpered a reply and did a little dance to show he understood. Chase patted the dog's head and made sure he had some water. Then he closed the side door and got into the SUV.

"He's a hard worker," he said while he buckled up and checked the area again. Once he appeared satisfied that no one was lurking in the woods, he let out a sigh. "Erin, are you okay? Really?"

Did he actually care how she felt? "I am now."

He nodded and she could almost feel his gaze hot on her skin. She'd thought about his green eyes a lot when she'd been trudging through lush hills full of birch and hickory trees and old mushrooming oaks. Her heart lifted, but a solid dread brought it back down to earth. Would Chase understand her predicament?

He watched the shadows around the vehicle and then glanced over at her. "Then tell me what's going on."

She was so glad to be able to talk to someone she needed to trust that she pulled off the offending wig and tugged at the fake eyeglasses. Her now chin-length hair tumbled out in damp dark tufts of mixed brown and blond highlights. "Someone was chasing me. Again."

"We've established that," he said, his gaze moving over her hair. "I need to know the whole story, starting with the night you went missing."

Erin tried to detangle her curls. "You might not believe the whole story."

"Try me."

She wanted to tell him everything so he could help her piece it all together. "Can we find someplace else to discuss this? I've been hiding out so long and I hate these woods." She glanced out the window. "I have a mortal fear that someone is always watching me."

He cranked the big SUV. "Okay, but... I'm about to make a call to Captain McCord and... I need to know one thing first and what I tell him will depend entirely on your answer to my question."

"What do you need to know, Chase?" she asked, already understanding. Already seeing reluctance in his doubtful, hopeful gaze.

He held on to the steering wheel with both hands, but his gaze held hers. "Did you murder Michael Jeffries?"

Erin understood he had to ask, but her heart hurt at hearing that question coming from his lips. "No," she said. "No, Chase. I didn't murder Michael. But I know who did."

Then she went on before he could say anything. "And before you make that call, I need to know if I can trust *you*." She slanted her head and stared him down. "Do you believe me?"

"Yes," he said without hesitation. "I told you—you're safe now."

"Okay," she said, her shoulders feeling as if a great weight had been shoved off them. "Make the call."

He heaved a breath then took out his cell and asked to speak to Captain Gavin McCord. Erin listened and held her breath while Chase gave the captain his location.

His next words startled her. "I have Erin Eagleton with me and I hope to be able to...bring her in soon." Chase listened and then replied, "Yes, sir. I understand. It's late and she's exhausted. I plan on stopping for the night to throw anyone off our trail."

Erin lifted her chin and pivoted on the seat. Had he tricked her? Would he turn her over to the DC authorities and just walk away?

She'd get out of this car and take off again if he planned to do that.

But when Chase ended the call, he turned to her. "Okay, I bought us some time, but Captain McCord is probably calling General Margaret Meyer right now to read her in on this. Meantime, I'm going to find us a safe place to stay tonight so we can talk. Just you and me."

Just you and me.

His stoic, matter-of-fact words held a hint of intimacy that only reminded her of their time together.

As if to cover that, he said, "I need to hear the whole story from you before things get chaotic."

Erin put a hand on his arm. "Thank you."

He didn't say anything, but she saw the way he glanced down at her finger curled against his arm. The heat between them radiated like a warm wind that rivaled the humid summer night. She moved her hand away and he put the vehicle in Reverse and took the bumpy dirt path to the main road. Soon they were speeding away into the night.

Since she didn't have to watch over her shoulder at every turn, Erin relaxed for the first time in a long while. Chase was here. But so many questions remained between them. Maybe Chase would help her sort out all of this before Congressman Jeffries found her and silenced her forever.

"Rest," he said. "We'll figure this out, I promise."

Erin leaned her head against the car door, his words echoing in her head as she drifted into the first peaceful sleep she'd had in months.

THREE

Chase put his hand on Erin's shoulder. She'd fallen asleep almost immediately after they'd left the deserted park about twenty miles back. He'd driven in circles for at least an hour and he'd watched the road for anyone who might be following them. Now he was on a remote back road where a sign boasted a bed-and-breakfast that promised privacy.

He'd have to do a quick sweep with Valor after they checked in, but maybe this place would be safe for the night at least.

"Erin?"

She jumped and grabbed at his hand then started hitting and slapping him, a scream tearing through her throat.

"Erin, it's me. Chase!"

She gulped in deep breaths, her eyes wide with fear and then awareness. Her whole body relaxing, she asked, "Where...where are we?"

"An old inn. Way off the beaten path." He had to take her inside and find her some food and a good soft bed so she could get some sleep. Handing her a generic navy-colored ball cap he kept in the SUV, he said, "Put your hair up underneath this and put those glasses back on."

"I have the wig," she said on a groggy note.

Chase did a visual and saw nothing but dark woods and the winding road up to the inn. "But someone's seen you in that wig," he retorted. "Put on the cap until I can get you in a room."

"Okay."

Her meek tone tore through Chase. Erin wasn't one to be meek or subdued. She was honest and frank and smart. Never afraid and never this quiet. She'd gone on the run for a reason and Chase believed that reason consisted of staying alive so she could prove her innocence. But it also showed him that right now, she didn't trust anyone. Especially not him.

Trying to ignore the disturbing feelings being near her seemed to be unleashing, he helped her with her now-mismatched hair. She'd obviously dyed it a couple of times. And she'd cut it. Still shorter than he remembered, it hit in soft waves against her chin. He remembered the softness of her hair, remembered pulling the light caramel-colored strands through his fingers so he could tug her close. Now he had to keep a safe distance. And keep her safe.

He had to stop reliving the past and start focusing on keeping her alive. That was his duty.

Your duty was to find her and bring her in for questioning.

He planned to question Erin. A lot. He'd report in again after he'd heard her side of things.

But he wasn't letting her out of his sight until he knew the truth. He figured there was much more to this story and he didn't know whom he could trust right now.

So Chase did what he'd always done when he had doubts.

He went with his instincts. And his instincts told him that this woman would never hurt another human being. Much less kill one. Now he just had to match her story with what Leon Ridge had told them. Maybe soon, they'd all know the truth.

The Moonlight Inn lived up to its name. The big Victorian house glistened with an eerie grayish-white wash from the light of a crescent moon. Surrounded by towering old live oaks, it looked at once both welcoming and sinister.

Erin loved the quaint old white clapboard exterior with the wraparound porch, but she wasn't so sure about the isolation of the place. Still, being away from the main road allowed Chase and her some time to get all the facts straight. If she could keep her eyes open long enough to talk to him. It took all she had to put one foot in front of the other.

"You look plum wore out," the cheerful lady behind the front desk said, her concerned brown eyes washing over Erin's soiled T-shirt and jeans with a keen interest. "Did you two go on a long hike today?"

"Yes," Chase answered with a smile. He glanced down at Valor. "And we chased this fellow around a lot. We're ready to settle in for the night."

The woman's gaze moved from Erin to the dog at their feet. "What a beautiful animal."

"Thank you," Chase said. He'd already removed Valor's working vest so no one would ask too many questions. "He's tired, too. He loves to…search the countryside."

"Chasing squirrels, huh, boy?" The lady chuckled, her white hair as stiff as the fake pink flowers clustered in a pretty red vase next to the antique cash register.

The woman glanced at Erin, causing Erin to realize that she hadn't spoken.

"Yes, always chasing something," she said, her tone forced. Chase hadn't clarified anything with the desk clerk. Erin wondered how he'd handle the room situation.

"If it's available, we'd like the deluxe suite with the sitting room," he said, pointing to some pictures underneath the glass on the counter.

The old lady nodded. "Our best suite. Roomy and private."

Chase didn't respond. He simply paid the bill and kept smiling. Erin took in her surroundings, a habit she'd developed after being forced to watch her back. The inn was clean and uncluttered with the front entrance and lobby here and a long hallway to the back of the house. If she had to run…

"All set," the woman said, handing Chase a receipt. "I hope you have a good stay."

Chase glanced toward Erin, his green eyes going soft. "Thanks. I hope so, too."

Erin managed a smile to hide the way her throat tightened and went dry at that glance. Now that they were inside, the glow from the lamplight clearly showed her all the features of his face for the first time.

He'd aged into someone she recognized and yet didn't really know. His dark blond hair was cut in a crisp military style that stood in curling spikes across his forehead, and he had a few laugh lines, or maybe worry lines, around his eyes. He was buff and tan and healthy. Her heart, which had shriveled up in a corner to die when she'd lost all hope, seemed to unfold like a blossoming rose. She didn't want to depend on this man. She could turn and bolt out the door, but she was so weary. She felt safe just being near him.

Chase looked as good as she remembered and then some.

While she was dirty and tired and mousy. And then some. A far cry from her sorority days and the whirlwind social life of the nation's capital.

But she was relieved. She couldn't help the relief that pushed through her numb system like a cooling wind to prove she was still alive. This kind of comfort could come only from knowing someone she'd once loved had found her when she thought she'd be lost forever. Erin glanced at a still life on the wall of a stream flowing down a mountainside. This was how she felt each time she sat in the dark and prayed, the image of Christ front and center in her frazzled mind. Lately, she'd almost given up on that image. But Chase stood here, an answer to a prayer she hadn't even known she'd prayed.

"There you go," the woman with the name tag that said *Janey* told them. "You're all set. Breakfast is from six until nine each day and if you'd like, I can send up a midnight snack to tide you over. Since you're arriving so late and all." She glanced at the go bag Chase had grabbed from the SUV and then she let her gaze sweep over Erin's torn, dirt-stained jeans, old hoodie and ratty T-shirt. "There's a washer/dryer combination in the hallway to my left if you need to wash some clothes."

Chase didn't take her up on that offer. "We'll take the snack. With hot tea and coffee."

"And I'd like some water," Erin added, touched that he remembered her preference for hot tea. "With lots of ice."

"Okay. I'll get right on that." The woman smiled at Erin. "And you can enjoy a good, long bath, honey."

"That sounds perfect," Erin replied, true joy racing through her heart. It had been a long time since she'd had a bubble bath.

But when they got upstairs, she watched Chase checking all the windows and doors and decided that in spite of the wonderful, old-fashioned claw-footed tub in the adjoining bathroom, she might not get that bath. A quick shower would have to suffice.

Because they didn't have time for the luxuries. Chase was here on a mission to either bring her in as a wanted murder suspect, or to help her prove her innocence.

And tonight was all about her convincing him on which option he should choose.

Chase took Valor for a quick walk, telling the way-too-interested Janey that the big dog needed to have a bathroom break. She nodded and explained where the dog walk was located. That was fine by Chase since it allowed him a chance to patrol the perimeters of the property and check around bushes and shrubs. Satisfied that the place was secure for now, he glanced up at the window where the deluxe suite was located. The room where Erin sat right now, jotting down notes she wanted to present to him when he got back. A small balcony was centered near two French doors, but it should be safe since it would be difficult for anyone to climb up the side of the house to get in. Difficult, but with a big oak tree nearby, it could be done if a person was determined. He and Valor would keep watch all night.

When they turned back toward the front door, Chase heard a twig snap down past the slope in the yard. Valor's ears went up while Chase's system buzzed with a new awareness.

He could release Valor to search, but this could be a trap, a means of distraction to draw them away from the house.

Not wanting to take any chances, he kept an eye on the front entrance and hurried Valor along so they could get back. He'd already had a quick shower, but a new sheen of perspiration worked its way down his spine, and not from the snap of a twig. Erin Eagleton had always made him sweat.

It had been obvious from their first glance several years ago that Erin was way out of his league. She'd been the popular socialite cheerleader at the small, private high school they'd both attended. And Chase had been the poor kid who'd been given a football scholarship to the school where all the politicians' children had first dibs on everything. She'd lived in one of the gated estates that dotted the countryside surrounding Washington and he'd lived in a standard farmhouse that his hardworking family had hung on to for nearly a century.

First class meets middle class and love at first sight for him. Maybe even for her. They'd both fallen hard, and then they'd been torn apart way too soon.

But that was all over now. Erin had been dating Michael Jeffries for years. No way she could have killed him.

It had been common knowledge that Erin and Michael were considered a power couple along the Beltway. She was the beautiful daughter of a popular senator and Michael was the son of Congressman Harland Jeffries. She and Michael were often seen together all over Washington, attending high-level parties and dinners. The kind of parties that a rookie K-9 officer who was former Secret Service usually patrolled rather than attended.

Reminding himself that he was part of an elite unit of officers, soldiers and special agents who had been hand-picked by the president's special in-house security chief, Margaret Meyer, Chase hoped he could earn his merit by bringing Erin back alive so they could get to the truth.

She was here and safe for the time being. He hurried back upstairs, remembering how she'd looked in a huge white terry cloth robe she'd found in the closet, thrown over a pair of black running shorts and a T-shirt he'd dug from his go-bag. At least the extra clothes had been clean. Baggy and cute on her, but clean.

And she looked…beautiful.

Tired, worried, fragile and beautiful.

It had taken a lot of willpower for him not to rush across the room and hold on to her forever. They might not have forever if he couldn't clear her name. They might not have a forever even after he cleared her name. Erin would want to go back to her posh life and leave him to get on with his simple life.

Which now only reminded Chase that he didn't have time to go down memory lane and he sure didn't have time for daydreams of how Erin looked all fresh faced and blushing.

Waving good-night to Janey—did the woman ever go to sleep?—he took the stairs two at a time and rapped on the locked door twice. "It's Chase."

Erin opened the door with a cup of tea in her hand. Someone from the staff had brought up food earlier. He'd checked the waiter and the food and waited for her to come out of the bathroom so they could eat. But his appetite had disappeared at the sight of her. Using the excuse of walking the dog, he'd bolted out of the suite with a terse order for her to lock all the doors and stay put.

Now he was hungry. For food. For her story. For just being with her again. "Mind if I eat while we talk?"

"No," she said, motioning to the pushcart full of tiny crustless sandwiches along with fruit and cheese and two giant chocolate chip cookies. "Your coffee is in that little pot." She pointed to a silver carafe.

Chase settled Valor with a treat and then came to sit on a cushiony blue love seat across from her cream-colored leather chair. After downing two of the ham-and-cheese sandwiches, he poured some coffee and rubbed a hand over his hair. "Everything looked okay outside. We should be safe for the night."

She nodded. "I can't seem to stay awake."

"That's the letdown," he explained. "You've been living on adrenaline for months now."

"Oh, and here I thought I was just tired." She bit into a slice of rich cheddar cheese and grabbed a couple of plump grapes.

"You *are* tired, but… Erin, before things get crazy tomorrow, I need to hear the whole story and then I'll tell you what I know."

He didn't want to give her any details that might color her own perception or blur her story. They could compare notes after he got her statement down.

She put down her tea and pushed away the plate of food. "Okay." Then she took a deep breath and tugged the big robe around her. After picking up her crumbled notebook, she opened it as if she were about to read a book. Then she slapped it shut and lifted her gaze to meet his.

"I had planned to break things off with Michael," she began. "Our fathers pushed us together in our last year of college, but honestly, we never got past being friends. We had fun together and I guess you could say we looked good together, according to the tabloids anyway, but it was mostly for show."

Chase took that in as he remembered Erin in flowing formal gowns and on the arm of the man known as "The Capitol Crusader." Michael Jeffries had been a bit cocky and smug, but the man at least had a good heart since he fought for less fortunate people. He sure didn't deserve to be shot even if he had made Chase jealous at times. Chase always told himself Erin was better off with someone who had as much money and clout as her father. That's the way the senator saw things anyway.

"So you did see Michael on the night that he died?"

Erin took a sip of tea and then continued. "Yes, I did. That morning he called me and asked if we could go to dinner and…well, he was so upset when he picked me up I didn't have the heart to break up with him."

Chase jotted notes since this was a new development. "Why was he upset?"

She pushed at her still-damp hair. "He said he'd found out a young relative of his was stuck in foster care and possibly living at the All Our Kids home—you know the one that his father started years ago. Michael was determined to get the child out, but he wouldn't tell me who the kid was or why doing this was so important to him." She shrugged and looked down at her hands. "We parted at around nine or so, but later—not long after I saw you— he didn't answer my calls and I got worried about him."

Chase checked his notes. "You and I spoke around ten that night," he reminded her. "I remember glancing at my watch and wondering why you were out walking so late."

"I needed to think about things," she replied. "I was

worried about Michael's frame of mind and I was upset that… I couldn't make it work with him. I went to his condo to check on him and he wasn't there. I figured he'd driven out to his father's estate to possibly discuss getting the congressman's help with this child he was so worried about. He told me he needed to talk to his father, so I headed out there."

Chase held up a hand and decided he could tell her what he knew for a fact. "Let's stop for a minute. We've confirmed that Michael was talking about a two-year-old boy who belonged to his father's housekeeper, Rosa Gomez—"

She shook her head and held her hand toward him. "But then the child couldn't be related to him."

Chase hated to spill things to her in this way, but he had to get all the facts straight and he had to feed them to her one by one. "Erin, the little boy—Juan Gomez—is the son of the congressman. We've pretty much established that he's Michael's half brother."

FOUR

Erin went still, her eyes widening. "I can't believe this. Do you think… Michael went to his father's house to confront him or to at least ask him to take Juan out of foster care?" Then she gasped. "They were in a heated argument when I came around the corner to the patio. What if that's why the congressman shot Michael?"

It was Chase's turn to be shocked. Leon Ridge had told them it was an accident. "Are you saying that's what happened that night?"

She nodded, tears forming in her eyes. "Yes, Chase. I went there to find Michael and… I walked up on them arguing. The congressman said something about Michael ruining everything. He reached for a gun and then they were struggling, pushing and shoving, and the next thing I knew the gun went off and… Michael fell to the ground." She put a hand to her heart. "Then blood went everywhere and… I screamed and ran toward Michael."

Chase saw the terror in her eyes. "And then what happened?"

"I took off my jacket and tried to stop the bleeding. Congressman Jeffries stood there in shock, or so I thought. He tried to explain that it was an accident, but

I saw him hold that gun to Michael's stomach and pull the trigger.

"After that, I didn't know what to say, but I kept begging him to call for help. He didn't move and then he turned nasty and pointed the gun at me, telling me if I told anyone what I'd witnessed he'd swear that I shot Michael. When I took out my phone, he grabbed it from me and even threatened to kill my father."

She gulped in a breath. "When I begged him to call 911, he said he'd ruin my father, that he'd frame him and destroy his career. He asked me if I wanted that on my conscience." She put a hand to her mouth and shook her head. "I didn't know what to do."

Chase got up and came to kneel in front of her. "Hey, it's okay. If you're telling the truth and Michael did know about Juan Gomez, we have more than enough information to prove his father had a strong motive for shooting him."

"I am telling the truth," she said, pushing him away. "Why would I lie?"

Chase didn't think she was lying, but he had to keep questioning her. "Why didn't you call your dad or even me? Why did you run, Erin?"

She lifted her head and stared at Chase, her dark blue eyes still moist. "One of the congressman's goons showed up when I was trying to help Michael. Leon Ridge—that creepy aide who was always hanging around. I asked him to help me and that's when the congressman told his aide to rip off the starfish necklace Michael had given me for my birthday and to drop it near Michael's body—and then he demanded that Leon shoot *him* in the shoulder so it would look like I'd done it. But before he let that stupid man shoot him, he told Leon to *take care of me*.

He never wanted anyone to hear what I had to say about that night. He made it look as if I'd shot Michael and I'd run off. Only, he never figured I'd live to tell the truth."

Chase could understand the fear in her eyes. Leon Ridge had pretty much told them a similar story. Funny that Ridge hadn't mentioned that he'd taken Erin out to be shot. Ridge refused to even talk about Erin or her whereabouts. He said he had no idea where Erin was and he didn't care.

When Chase thought about how close she'd come to dying, he asked the obvious. "But you got away?"

"Yes, but only after Leon Ridge put me in a car and took me out to the woods. The minute he dragged me out of the car, I kicked him and used one of my boot heels to dig into his foot. He shot at me and missed. Then I ran and ran and… I've been running since then, hiding out all around Maryland and Virginia." She grabbed at Chase's shirt. "Now do you believe me?"

Chase lifted her up and tugged her into his arms. "Yes, Erin. I believe you. And now that I've heard your side of the story, we'll compare notes and I promise I'm going to do everything I can to clear your name."

Erin nodded. "I've blocked out a lot of that night. Michael wanted to tell me something." She closed her eyes. "He said something. He kept looking over my shoulder and he whispered a word." She gasped and grabbed at Chase's sleeve. "I thought he was trying to say *gone*. That he was telling me I needed to leave. But Chase, what if he was saying a name?"

"Juan," Chase said, the horror in her words chilling him in spite of the hot summer night.

She bobbed her head again, tears falling down her face. "Juan."

Chase drew back, deciding he needed to be honest. "We have Leon Ridge in custody and he told us Jeffries shot Michael, but we found that hard to accept. He claims the shooting was an accident, and that the congressman and he came up with an alibi. He said he shot the congressman to make it look as if an unknown assailant had done it, but he never mentioned that he saw you that night. And he refused to discuss Juan Gomez and the boy's connection to the congressman."

"What? Why didn't you tell me that before now?" Her expression changed, an angry frown clouding her face. "Let me guess. You were waiting to see what I'd tell you, right?"

Chase tried to calm her down. "I had to be careful, Erin. I didn't want to confuse you or upset you."

"You don't believe me after all." She pushed him away. "You probably think I'm lying about him taking me out to kill me."

Chase tugged her back around. "I told you, I believe you. Ridge never told us he'd even seen you. He clams up when we ask about you being there that night."

"That's because Jeffries will have him killed if he says anything else. I'm surprised he said that much, He was there when the congressman decided to pin the whole thing on me, but I got away from Leon. The congressman can't be too happy about that."

"Ridge is obviously the fall guy," Chase explained. "We interviewed the congressman about Juan and the murder, but he denied any involvement. He tried to convince us that Juan was Michael's child."

"That's not possible," Erin exclaimed. "Michael couldn't have children. It was…always a sore subject between us."

"We know the child isn't Michael's for that very reason. Leon tried to convince us of that, too. We reminded Leon of the opinion piece Michael wrote for one of the local papers, promoting foster care and adoption. The congressman got tripped up in his own lies on that one. He's wanted on corruption charges, but…now we're talking murder, too."

"I asked you to trust me," she reminded him. "You have to trust that I'm telling you the truth. The congressman shot Michael and Michael was trying to tell me why. It's all about that little boy. That makes sense now that I know he's the congressman's son. Leon Ridge planned to kill me, but he won't admit that. And since he failed, Congressman Jeffries will keep sending people to do the job."

"You don't need to convince me anymore," Chase said. "We've all been concerned about your safety. That's why I asked my captain to let me get you somewhere safe for the night."

"Are you sure? Or is that a ploy to take me into custody?"

"Listen, Erin. If we do take you into custody, it will be for your protection. You won't be safe out there on your own. You have to see that."

"I do," she said on a weary voice. "I… I don't know who I can trust, who I can turn to. The congressman obviously always finds me. Jeffries's reach is far and wide."

"So is General Meyer's power," he reminded her. "Let me do my job. Let me help you."

"Thank you," she said on a soft sigh. "I don't have any choice. If I can't trust you then I'm doomed already."

Chase held his hand to her chin. "I'm here and I'm doing everything I can for you."

She wrapped her arms around his neck and held tight.

Chase guided her toward the love seat and pulled her down and back into his arms. He believed Erin's story completely, but…he wasn't sure how to go about proving her innocence to the world. They were fighting a very powerful enemy. He couldn't let his emotions and his involvement with Erin get in the way of his job.

So he held her tight and prayed to God to give him the strength to keep the promise he'd made. And he remembered that with God on his side, he could fight all enemies.

Much later, after he'd sent Erin to bed in the adjoining room, Chase lay awake on the sofa, Valor by his feet, and went back over this case and tried to make a plan of action. First, he needed to let the team know that he'd heard her statement. They'd want to question her, too. Then he needed to go back to Leon Ridge and interrogate him about what had really happened that night and he also wanted to once again interview some of Michael's friends and coworkers. They'd have to go from there, but Chase wasn't sure what might happen.

He was a rookie, only a year into being on the elite handpicked K-9 team. What if they took him off the case? How could he protect her then? Chase was former Secret Service, so he knew how things worked. But he also knew he had a duty to protect Erin, no matter what.

He said a little prayer for guidance and hoped General Meyer would allow him to continue protecting Erin. She would be in a lot of danger once word got out that she'd been located.

Chase finally gave in to his fatigue and dozed on the uncomfortable little couch for a while. Around 2:00 a.m. Valor alerted with a low growl and Chase was up and holding a weapon toward the French doors out to the upstairs porch. The doors he'd believed no one would breach.

A few minutes later, the intruder broke into the room and found them waiting for him. Chase gave Valor the "Attack" command and Valor leaped into the air and went for the man's throat while Chase circled the culprit.

The man screamed and covered his face, causing Valor to go for his arm. Chase let Valor hold the culprit until he could move in. The man squirmed and writhed in pain, which only made Valor's teeth sink deeper into his bleeding wounds.

"Drop the weapon," Chase said, motioning to the gun the man held in his right hand. Valor backed him up with a low growl and another show of his teeth sinking into the man's left arm. But the man wasn't ready to give in. He pulled the trigger and a shot hit the ceiling with a loud ping. Chase fired back and the man crumbled onto the floor, Valor still holding his arm.

"Release," Chase said. "It's too late for this one, Valor."

When he turned around, Erin was standing in the open door to the other room, her gaze falling across the dead man at Chase's feet.

"You okay?" he asked over his shoulder while he checked the man's pulse and found none.

"Yes," she said behind him, the one word breathless. "That's the man who was chasing me in the woods."

Chase looked back to make sure Erin really was all right. She stood inside the door, wearing the oversize robe, her arms held tightly against her waist.

Chase commanded Valor, "Stay."

Erin advanced a step into the room, her gaze still on the dead assailant. "He was wearing a hat, but I saw his face when I was running away from the hotel. I don't recognize him."

A knock shook the door. "Hey, what's going on in there?"

Janey. Chase gave Erin a warning glance. "Let me handle this."

He opened the door and showed the wide-eyed Janey his badge. After explaining things, he told Janey he was about to make some calls. "I'd appreciate it if you inform the other guests about what's happening and keep them out of the way," he told the frightened woman.

"This won't be good for business," Janey whined. "A dead intruder in the best suite we have. That's a first."

Chase turned to Erin after Janey left and tugged her across the room away from the body. "I need to call this in."

Her eyes narrowed, a flicker of fear deepening them to midnight blue. "You can't take me back. I'll go to jail for something I didn't do."

Chase leaned close, his hand on her elbow. "I don't believe that's gonna happen now. Think about it, Erin. The congressman fled because of the corruption charges and…we now know that Juan Gomez is his son. That's enough to bring him in on murder charges, too, since we have witnesses who say Rosa Gomez was shaking him down for more money right before she died." He also reminded her about Leon Ridge. "We have him in custody and when he hears you're alive and well even though they sent someone to kill you yet again, he's gonna panic."

"But…none of that can help me, Chase. Leon will

accuse me since the congressman is pulling his strings. He's too scared to tell the truth and we both know it."

"I'm going to make him tell the truth," Chase said. "Now we have one of Jeffries's thugs breaking in on your room—a room only you and I should have known about. Why would he go to all of this trouble if he isn't trying to kill you?"

"He could convince everyone that he wanted to bring me in to prove I did this."

"But the congressman hasn't told any of us that he was conducting his own investigation and he never fully admitted to seeing you at the scene. We'll question Ridge until he gives us what we need."

"And in the meantime, what happens to me?" she asked.

Chase glanced back toward the dead guy and then turned to her again. "In the meantime, I'm going to make sure you stay safe."

Erin sat on the sofa and watched as law-enforcement people tramped back and forth in what had started out as a beautiful suite in a quiet country bed-and-breakfast. She'd been questioned and prodded and interrogated and analyzed to the point that she was no longer coherent. All she wanted right now was a soft bed and sleep. Lots of sleep without nightmares or visions of people chasing her through the woods.

"How you holding up?" Chase asked, sitting down beside her for a brief moment. Valor had stayed by her side while his human partner did his job and filed his own report.

"I'm okay," she said. Then she shook her head. "No, that's not true. I'm tired, scared and worried that I'll be hauled away the minute they're done here. Poor Janey is probably afraid they'll take her in, too. I think every branch of law enforcement sent several representatives to gawk at me and get me to confess to anything and everything. I'll probably be blamed for Leon Ridge's confession, too." She lifted her hand toward the window. "Not to mention the reporters already gathering out there. I'm the topic of the day."

"Janey can use all of this as PR," Chase said, obviously trying to make her smile. "She's handling the reporters with cookies and coffee. I don't even want to think about what she's telling them. She'll have gawkers driving by for weeks."

"At least someone will profit from my notoriety," Erin replied with a frown.

Chase touched his hand to hers in a quick gesture. "It's going to be all right. Oh, by the way, your father's on his way, too."

Erin moaned and held a hand in her hair. "I was hoping I'd see him back at his town house in DC. He shouldn't drive all the way out here. We're at least two hours away from the city."

"He's bringing lawyers," Chase said, his eyes full of understanding and sympathy. "I tried—"

"—to talk him out of it," she finished. "I know how that goes." Then she turned serious. "Will I have to be arraigned or post bail or whatever comes next?"

Chase's smile was soft and swift. "Hold on, Sherlock. You aren't going to be charged with anything right now. But you will be questioned."

She pushed at her hair. "Again?"

"And again," he said, his eyes holding hers. "You are

innocent until proven guilty, remember? Leon Ridge did tell us that the congressman *accidentally* shot his son."

"I am innocent," she said, hoping he really did believe her. "But Chase…if it's all over the news that… I've been brought in, what do you think Congressman Jeffries will do?"

Chase glanced around to where Captain Gavin Mc-Cord stood talking to two FBI agents. They'd already taken the dead man away, but Erin wondered what they would do with her. Did Chase really think he could stop this steamroller?

"Chase?"

He turned back to her. "The congressman will come after you."

Erin tried to ignore the shudder creeping down her spine. "He'll be in a panic knowing Leon's been arrested and that another of his minions is now dead. He still wants *me* dead. I can't see that changing. I think it'll only get worse."

"He's running out of options so he's getting desperate," Chase said. "Look, let's get done here and…if you don't want to go back to your place or to your father's house, you can come home with me."

"That won't be necessary, Officer Zachary."

Erin cringed and turned, recognizing her father's stern voice. She shot Chase a glance and saw the dare in his green eyes. Getting up, she hurried to her father before Chase said anything. "Dad."

"Baby." Her father pulled her close and for a moment, Erin felt like a little girl again. Tall with hair that had once been dark brown but was now mostly a silvery white, Senator Preston Eagleton had always been a handsome man. And right now, with the scent of expensive cigars and spicy aftershave engulfing her, Erin felt safe again. It was good to be back in her father's strong arms. Her dad drew back to look at her. "Are you all right?"

"I am now," she said, tears pricking at her eyes. "I'm sorry I worried you all these months."

Her father looked her over. "My doctor will meet us and give you a thorough checkup after we move you out to our house. I thought you'd have more privacy out from the city."

"That's not necessary," she said, shaking her head at the thought of heading to her father's vast country estate. "I'm tired and I have a few bug bites, but—"

"My daughter, hiding out in the woods." Her father gave her a harsh glance. "Why didn't you call me, Erin?"

"I had my reasons," she said, "and I don't want to talk about all of that right now."

FIVE

Seeing the formidable Washington attorney her father kept on retainer, Erin's pulse escalated. "Do you think I killed Congressman Jeffries, Daddy?"

"Or course not," her father retorted. "I only brought my lawyer with me as a precaution." He glanced at Chase. "I've had my own team working on finding you since General Meyer didn't want to divulge her K-9 team's investigation with me."

"For your own safety and protection, sir," Chase said, stepping forward.

He held out a hand and her father shook it, but Erin saw the gesture was out of politeness and nothing more. "I know how to take care of myself and…my daughter," her father said to Chase. "Now, if you're done with her…"

"Erin, what do you want to do?" Chase asked, his tone firm and sure. "We can take you to a safe house right now."

Torn between staying secure near Chase and wanting to visit with her father, she glanced between the both of them. "I'll be okay, Chase," she finally said. "That is, if I'm free to go."

Her father's lawyer stepped forward. "Erin, I'm so

glad you're all right. Let me go and talk to Captain Mc-Cord and the other officers and we'll have you out of here in a few minutes."

Chase gave her a reassuring look. "I'll speak to Gavin, too." He leaned close. "I'll explain things to him. We need to know you'll be safe."

Her father frowned after Chase hurried away. "What was that all about?"

Erin didn't want to argue with her father so soon after seeing him again, but she had to be honest. "I'm still in danger, Daddy."

Her father glanced around as if someone in the room might be after her. "Oh, and how's that?"

"I didn't kill Michael, but... I know who did."

Shocked, her father pulled her close. "What are you saying, Erin?"

"I'm not sure, but I think Congressman Jeffries will keep sending people after me."

"Are you suggesting that Harland Jeffries is trying to kill you?"

"I *know* he's trying to kill me," she retorted, wondering if her own father doubted her. "That's why I had to go into hiding. I saw him murder Michael."

Her father's features were schooled in a calm facade, but she'd seen the disbelief in his eyes. "All the more reason to get you away from the city and home where we can talk in private."

Erin glanced over at Chase. "I'll go with you if they let me leave, but I might have to go to Capitol K-9 headquarters for more questioning."

"Not tonight," her father replied. "You need to be checked over and you need to rest." He shot a condemning glance toward Chase. "After all, he didn't do a very good job of protecting you."

Erin had learned a thing or two out there on her own. One being that if she didn't stand up to people, she'd never learn how to survive anything. "Dad, Chase did more than protect me tonight. He's been searching for me since the night Michael died. He found me and he saved my life. You might consider that before you dismiss him completely."

Her father looked suitably chastised, his gaze moving from her to behind her. When Erin looked around, Chase was standing close enough to have heard what she'd said.

He gave her a look of appreciation then turned to her father. "You're free to go, Erin," he said, his eyes on Senator Eagleton. "Sir, we're depending on you to keep her close to home for now since we'll need to interrogate Erin again. Captain McCord will send some officers to help patrol your estate." Then he glanced back at Erin. "I'll come by first thing in the morning to check on you."

"That won't be—" the senator began, then he changed his tune. "Don't be too early, son. She needs a good night's sleep." He reached out his hand to Chase. "And… thank you for finding my daughter."

Back at headquarters early the next morning, Chase was questioned by everyone from the president's special in-house security chief, General Meyer, to Metro Police Detective David Delvecchio and Secret Service Agent Dan Calvert. All of the interagency big guns wanted in on this one. And his boss, Captain Gavin McCord, wanted a play-by-play of everything leading up to Chase finding Erin and what happened afterward.

"Someone was chasing her when I found her so I had

to make the choice of protecting Erin instead of going after the perpetrator. After that, it was late and she was tired, but I called you right away to report I had her," he repeated for about the tenth time. "I was pretty sure we were being tailed so I took her to the inn until morning. But the tail obviously followed us since the assailant showed up where we were staying."

"She could have easily escaped again," Captain McCord pointed out with an intimidating frown. "I should have ordered you to bring her in right away."

That same frown shadowed just about every face on the entire Capitol K-9 team. Metro Police Detective Delvecchio cleared his throat in what could have been a skeptical snort. The cynical detective had cooperated, but he hadn't been happy with having to share information with the K-9 team. Captain McCord had managed to get past that, at least.

"She didn't run," Chase retorted. "Valor was on alert and besides, she was so exhausted she fell asleep as soon as she went to bed. I took her statement and I caught yet another man trying to kill her."

"Or at least breaking into her room," General Meyer said, her vivid blue eyes nailing Chase to his chair. But he'd also seen a hint of compassion in those all-knowing eyes. The general was a smart cookie and this team had her heart. Maybe she'd cut Chase some slack since he'd been working this case since the night they'd found Michael Jeffries dead and the congressman wounded.

"Yes, you did bring in our key witness," Captain McCord said. "Good work." He scrolled through his phone. "I'm waiting to hear if we have an identity on your intruder."

Chase hoped that identity would give them another piece to the puzzle.

"I have reason to believe Erin is still in danger," he said. "I'd like permission to be put on her protection team."

"You'll continue this investigation," McCord said in a tone would brook no argument. "I know you were once close to Erin, but Chase, you're *too* close now and besides, Erin will be safe with her father out at his estate. He understands she's a person of interest and possible witness in this case so his lawyers are advising him to keep her close. We'll send some of our people to patrol the perimeters, too."

"Agreed," Chase said, figuring now was not the time to argue. "Where do you want me?"

"I want you to try to get in touch with some of Michael Jeffries's friends. Ask them again if he seemed upset about the Gomez boy, find out if they talked to him that day. We've questioned a lot of people already, but now that we have Erin Eagleton's statement, we start back at square one. If you hear anything about Erin and Michael having words or acting in any unusual way, you'd better report it immediately." His gaze moved around the room. "Leon Ridge left out everything Miss Eagleton has told us. I'll be questioning him on that, too."

Chase wondered if the captain was even now still willing to vouch for Congressman Jeffries. Maybe he was also too close to this case to see what was obvious. The do-good congressman had fooled a lot of people, including Captain McCord. The captain's former mentor needed to come forward and face the music so they could all get on with things. So Erin could get her life back, at least.

General Meyer continued the conversation. "And talk

to Cassie Danvers again." She glanced at Gavin as if daring him to disapprove since Cassie and the captain had become a couple after the foster home had been vandalized and almost burned down. They were now engaged to be married. "You can find her at the temporary safe house where Gavin placed the All Our Kids foster children and house mother Cassie when they were in danger. She might remember something about Michael coming by to see the little boy that week."

"Captain?" Chase waited to verify the approval since the captain seemed unsure about Chase's motives right now.

"She's at the safe house," Captain McCord said. "She's been through a lot, but Cassie's strong. If anyone can help us, she will."

Chase itched to call Erin, but he had his orders, and at least this footwork would keep him busy. Besides, maybe he did need to distance himself from her so he could stick to the facts. Hadn't he been trained to study the evidence and keep his personal judgments to himself? But when he thought about what Erin had told him, Chase went with his instincts and remembered the captain had commended him several times on doing just that. Chase had always believed in Erin's innocence and now the facts were beginning to back him up.

Capitol K-9 Unit member Adam Donovan stood in a corner of the briefing room with his partner, Ace. The big Doberman's head moved from side to side while Adam, a former FBI agent, didn't seem to move at all.

Chase gave Valor a silent command and walked over to greet Adam. Valor needed a good rest and so did Chase. He hadn't slept very well last night and this would be another long day of work.

Adam nodded as he approached. "Tough morning, Rookie?"

"You got it," Chase replied. "I'm being given grunt work to keep me away from Erin."

Adam gave him an understanding smile since he'd fallen in love with Lana Gomez, the sister of the late Rosa Gomez, who'd been Congressman Jeffries's housekeeper and the mother of his toddler son. "Well, you did tell us right up front that you and Erin had a past. Captain doesn't forget things like that, you know."

"Yep. Full disclosure—that's my game," Chase replied. "I'm worried about her, though. I think Jeffries will try to come after her again."

"So you believe her story?" Adam asked on a low tone.

Chase had racked his brain over this and his gut kept coming back to the same conclusion. "I do, yes. Erin has always been honest and I can't see why that would change. Her story supports what Ridge told us. He just left out the part about her being there, of course. She's been through the worst, Adam."

Adam lifted off the wall. "Then, man, you gotta follow your gut like the captain always says. We train our animals to do just that, right?"

"Good point," Chase replied. "Meantime, I'm going to pound the pavement to get to the truth."

Erin woke with a start. For a minute, she thought she was still out there in the dark, running for her life, and a sick panic set in. But when she blinked and sat up, she realized she was back in the room she remembered so well, her room in her father's Maryland house miles away from Washington, DC. Her father had been shot right here in the backyard, near the gazebo. One of his favorite spots since her parents used to dine out there during good weather.

Thank goodness he'd survived. He surprised Erin when he told her that her cousin Selena had come to eat lunch with him the day an attempt had been made on his life. Erin was happy that her father had reached out to Selena, since he and Selena's late mother had a rocky past. But Selena had been in danger, too.

Was someone determined to kill everyone in her family?

Would they go after Chase, too?

In her mind, she was now about a thousand memories away from Chase.

Did you expect him to follow you out here?

Chase had done his job and brought her back to face her accusers. Was he one of them?

No. Chase believed in her. She'd seen it in his eyes and in the way he'd protected her and trusted her last night. But what about now? They had a confession from Leon, true. But Jeffries wouldn't like being betrayed and that was probably why Leon refused to confirm that Erin had been at the murder scene. Jeffries thought he could pin Michael's death on her, but now she had become a credible witness instead.

Because of Gavin McCord's original devotion to Congressman Jeffries, the Capitol K-9 team would pursue this case until the bitter end. She prayed they'd find Jeffries before he made another move toward her.

Michael deserved justice.

Tears pricked at her eyes as she remembered Michael lying there, so still, his life blood running out of his body while his own father did nothing to save him.

The house phone rang, causing her to jump. When her

father's secretary told Erin that her cousin Selena Barrow was on the private line, Erin took the phone receiver and got out of bed to go over to the mint-green chaise longue by the big window overlooking the backyard.

"I've tried all morning to get through," Selena said when she heard Erin's voice. "I'm so glad you're all right, Erin. Nicholas and I have been so worried."

"Who's Nicholas?" Erin asked after thanking Selena.

Selena's light laughter surprised Erin. "It's a long story, but…he's Nicholas Cole—a member of the Capitol K-9 team who's on White House detail along with his partner, Max. We…uh…met when someone broke into General Meyer's office—"

Erin had briefly talked to General Meyer late last night or maybe it had been early this morning. They'd met at several Washington functions and she liked the stoic older woman. "Wait, she's the head of the K-9 team, right? She's the boss."

"Yes, and she has a long title, but she's also a retired four-star general so everyone calls her General," Selena went on. "Anyway, someone also ransacked my office at the White House that same day."

"I am behind," Erin replied, remembering how she'd tried to draw her less fortunate cousin into her circle of friends, but her father had frowned on that. He'd never forgiven Selena's alcoholic mother—his deceased sister—for always calling him for help through the years. She'd embarrassed him one time too many in public, so he'd distanced himself from his only sister and his niece. But Erin liked Selena and wanted to rekindle their relationship. "Why did someone break into your office?"

"They took my electronic notebook," Selena replied. "The one I've kept for months…on you."

Erin's heart clanked against her ribs. "Why me, Selena?"

"I believe you're innocent," Selena said with such conviction it brought fresh tears to Erin's eyes. "I tried to do whatever I could to help prove that, but I finally had to back off and let the authorities do their thing, including the entire Capitol K-9 team. Nicholas can't tell me much, but he says things are looking up for you." Selena's soft sigh lifted across the silence. "I know you didn't kill Michael, Erin. And if I have my way, I'll make sure the whole Capitol K-9 team and everyone up to the president himself feels the same way. This team is amazing. They'll keep hammering that shady Leon Ridge until he tells them the whole story. The human team members are about as tenacious as their canine counterparts. Like a dog with a bone."

Erin didn't know what to say. Over the years, she and Selena had lost touch and had seen each other again three years ago at Selena's mom's funeral. After that, they'd tried to have lunch here and there, but they'd truly reconnected late last year when Erin had spotted Selena at the White House during a charity event. But it hadn't been easy trying to get together, mainly because Erin had gotten caught up in the whirlwind world of Washington, keeping up with the Eagleton Foundation and also maintaining a good facade so her father would never have to be involved in any scandals. The irony of that was not lost on her. They were both up to their eyeballs in this particular scandal.

And yet even after the way Erin's father had treated Selena, her cousin had believed in her. "I'm sorry my dad and I haven't stayed in touch with you," she said.

"Oh, but your dad and I have grown close," Selena

replied. "I was out at the house when he got shot and I saw him in the hospital later and he asked me to forgive him. Then I sat with him at the town house once he came home. Everything is forgiven, Erin." At Erin's silence, she added, "Everything, okay?"

"Thank you," Erin said again, her voice husky with emotion. "I'm so glad to hear that and I hope we can see each other soon. I'm kind of under house arrest right now. Hard to get away."

"Don't try," Selena retorted. "The press has even begun calling me for sound bites. But… I'm *not* biting. You're in the safest place you can be right now. Your dad hired some serious security after our scare in the garden."

Erin reluctantly agreed then asked, "So…you and Officer Cole are…close?"

Selena let out a sigh that sounded contented. "Yes. Very close. As in—engaged. We hope to get married soon."

"That's wonderful news," Erin replied, thoughts of Chase circling through her tattered brain. "I wish you the best."

"You'll be at the wedding," Selena said on a sure note. "I hope you'll agree to be one of my bridesmaids."

Erin wasn't so confident. "I'd be honored. I hope I can do that."

Selena said, "You will. We have to have faith." Before Erin could respond, she added, "And by the way, the news reports are saying you were brought in by Chase Zachary. Is this the same Chase Zachary you dated in high school?"

"Yes, it's him," Erin replied, wondering if she'd ever hear from Chase again. And wondering why she'd confided in Selena about that. Not that she minded Selena knowing. It was just hard to accept that Chase was back in her life in such a strange way—bringing her in under a cloud of suspicion. "He found me, somehow, and he saved my life the other night."

Selena gasped. "We need to talk more, but I have to go. And I know you're exhausted. I just wanted you to know—if you need me for anything, and I mean anything, call me at this number."

Erin grabbed a pen and notepad and took down Selena's cell number. "Thank you again, Selena. I can't tell you how much this means to me."

"Hey, we're family," Selena replied. "Remember that."

SIX

Erin hung up and stared out the window, but she didn't notice the manicured yard or the perfectly trimmed trees and shrubs or even the lush woods beyond the grounds. She couldn't believe she was back here after all these years. Or that her cousin had tried to come to her defense.

Dressing quickly, she decided she wouldn't hide in her room all day. Too many memories were crashing down around her, many of them involving Chase. They had been teenagers then, and now they'd been thrust back together as adults. She should have run away from him last night, too. But…when he'd tugged her close and told her everything would be okay, she'd believed him.

He'd told her that once before, too, and that hadn't turned out so well. He hadn't trusted her enough to believe she'd come back to him after her trip to Africa the summer of their high school graduation. Erin had had every intention of coming home to Chase so they could plan their college agendas and later…their wedding. But he'd been so angry at her for going in the first place, he'd broken things off.

"This will save you having to do it," he'd said. "We

both know we'll never make it. We're too different, from two different worlds."

She'd left, heartbroken but determined to win him back come fall. But Chase had refused to even talk to her.

Their high school sweetheart love affair had ended all too soon. And she still regretted letting that happen.

Would a murder case that had the whole nation talking bring them back together, or just tear them apart again?

Erin didn't know what to think about that. She prayed that soon all of the facts could be made public and that she could go back to her life and the responsibility of running the Eagleton Foundation. And maybe if nothing else…she and Chase could be friends.

"He's sure lawyered up."

Chase stood outside the interrogation room where they were holding Leon Ridge, thinking the same thing his friend and fellow officer Nicholas Cole had just stated. "Yeah, but he's lying and we all know it."

Captain McCord came out of the room, looking grim. "He claims he doesn't know what happened to the murder weapon," McCord said, a hand slicing through his dark brown hair. "A small-caliber handgun was used to kill Michael Jeffries. But he won't budge much on anything else, especially regarding Erin Eagleton and her missing car. Says he didn't move Erin's car, but he's suddenly insisting the congressman told him *later* that the shooter was Erin Eagleton and that's why he went after her. But the congressman told us he didn't see the shooter." The captain put his hands on his hips, his expression full of fatigue. "Leon claims he only confessed to help out the congressman, who's like a father to him. He must think

Jeffries will help him out of this jam, but I don't see that happening. We seem to have conflicting reports here."

"It makes sense that Ridge shot both of them and is now trying to finger Erin as the shooter," Chase said. "But she says she walked up on the congressman and Michael arguing, and that the congressman held the gun to Michael's stomach. She thinks it was an accident, but the congressman wouldn't help save his own son."

McCord rubbed a hand down his five o'clock shadow. "So Ridge might be willing to take the rap for the congressman or he's just buying time, maybe giving the congressman more time to get wherever he thinks he's going."

"Ridge won't talk anymore now that the fancy lawyer is back," Chase said, disgusted. "And can I just guess who managed to send that lawyer?"

McCord glared at him. "Congressman Jeffries?"

"You got it. Probably to intimidate Ridge, if nothing else."

"I agree with you, Zachary," McCord said with a grudging admiration and a solid acceptance. "But we need more evidence. So I suggest you get back out there."

"Yes, sir." Chase sent Nicholas a raised-eyebrow glance then silently commanded Valor to "Come."

The next few hours were spent calling Michael Jeffries's friends and coworkers and, sometimes, finding them in person. Chase had left his contact cards with half a dozen people. He got a call from McCord that the man he'd shot at the country inn was a low-level hit man who had a long criminal history. But he'd never talk now and they didn't have any leads on who had sent him.

At around sundown, his cell phone rang again. Chase had just stopped to grab a bite and he was still parked, with Valor in the back eating his own dinner. When he answered, he was surprised to hear Cassie Danvers's voice. He'd left her a message earlier since she still ran the All Our Kids group foster home that for now was being housed in a safe location out of the city.

"You wanted to speak to me?" Cassie asked. She sounded breathless and he could hear voices in the background. He had to admire the woman. She had a tough job trying to keep several children of all ages contained and safe.

"Yes. Thanks for returning my call." Chase crushed his cell phone between his shoulder and ear, and scrolled through his paper notebook. "I wanted to ask you a few questions regarding Michael Jeffries. Specifically, if you or anyone on your staff talked with him the week or so before he died."

"I already told the DC police and the FBI that I didn't talk with Michael during that time and as far as I know, no one on my staff did either. But you have to realize, Michael and the congressman both stopped by the foster home a lot."

"Could you check again?" Chase said. "It's really important. Several of his friends say he was upset right before his death, allegedly that he'd found out Juan Gomez might be related to him."

"And we've established that," Cassie said, her tone kind if not weary. "I don't recall talking to him, but my assistant, Virginia Johnson, might have. She sometimes filters visitors while I'm dealing with one of the kids."

"Could I possibly speak to her?" Chase asked. "I need any information that can help establish that Michael was extremely upset and that he went to his father's house to possibly confront him about Juan Gomez."

"I'll tell Virginia you'd like to question her—maybe tomorrow morning." When he heard a crash, she said, "Look, I can't talk right now, but I'll call you soon, okay?"

Chase ended the call with about as much information as he'd started with this morning. How could he prove Erin was telling the truth if he couldn't find one person to corroborate her story? Deciding to call it a day and take himself off duty for a while, he headed out toward Senator Eagleton's house to check on things and hopefully visit with Erin for a couple of minutes. He exited the interstate and cruised along the scenic country road dotted with huge homes. He'd never fit in with Erin's world, and that was one reason he'd let her go.

He'd never been good enough for her.

But he had to be good at his job in order to save her.

Erin glanced up to see Chase and Valor walking toward where she sat with a guard nearby on the back veranda, watching storm clouds gather over the horizon. She knew this was serious by the way the other three guards her father had hired accompanied him. The stoic guards were always dressed in black, complete with bulletproof Kevlar vests, and they carried radios and semi-automatic rifles. Similar to Chase, but not nearly as comforting.

"Hi," she said when he approached. Valor was with him, so she waved the overbearing guards away. "What are you doing here?"

She hadn't seen him since two nights ago when he'd turned and walked away after her father had come to the inn to insist she come home with him.

"Hi." He motioned to two wrought iron chairs. "Mind if we sit and talk?"

"Have a seat." She couldn't ignore the relief washing through her after seeing him again, but from the brooding expression on his face, she dreaded what he'd come here to say to her. He waited for her to sit and then ordered Valor to do the same. The furry dog curled up between them, his dark eyes following Erin.

She held her hands fisted at her side. "You must have a really good reason for coming all the way out here to see me."

He glanced around the yard, his gaze landing on the shimmering pool. "I'm not here in an official capacity. Just wanted to make sure you're okay."

Erin started to protest until she noticed the dark circles of fatigue hovering around his eyes. His green gaze danced over her with concern, but the dark clouds hid his face in silent shadows. Chase had to be every bit as tired as she was.

"I tried to argue with myself to stay away," he said. "But I think being here with you might be good for both of us. I needed a break."

The edge in his voice caught at her. "Do you still have doubts about me?"

The split second of hesitation before he answered told Erin the truth, but she let him speak.

"I have never doubted you." He slanted his head. "Can't we just…talk? I needed to see you, Erin. And it has nothing to do with this investigation."

"Or maybe it has everything to do with this investigation."

Chase stood and came to kneel in front of her. "Listen. I have to go on facts. I don't mean to doubt you, but this is a big case and we need to have everything in order. Even your testimony. Because if we capture Jeffries, you will be a key witness in what happened the night of the murder at his house."

Seeing the sincerity and concern in his eyes, Erin tried to relax. "I understand. You have a job to do. I want this to be done right, too. It just seems as if I keep coming up against a wall with every attempt to make things right."

"It's more than just doing my job," he said, his hands over hers. "I want to protect you and stand by you, too."

And he'd been trying to do that at every turn. When she'd been the one doubting him and everyone else at every turn.

"I'm sorry." Erin's gaze met his. "And I'm being rude, trying to pick a fight with you. You're right. I need a break, too. Since I've been back, it's been crazy. Reporters, officers, lawyers, you name it. I've had calls from all of them. Thank you for coming."

Chase did a neck roll and Valor half rose in high hopes they were going into action. "It's nice to just sit in the shade and enjoy the day. I'm tired."

"I get that," she said, the warmth of his hands bringing her comfort. "I can make us a grilled cheese sandwich."

"Mmm. Sounds good."

She moved an inch closer. Pushing at her short ponytail, she said, "Since doing things on my own hasn't helped me all that much, I think I have to trust in the people who've tried to protect me, no matter what. That's you and your team, Chase. And I have to trust in God and pray that with His grace, my innocence will be clear once and for all."

"We can all agree on that."

When Chase signaled Valor, the canine got up and

came to sit by Erin. She reached down and petted the big dog and gave Chase a thankful smile. "At least Valor seems to like me."

"He's one smart animal," Chase said, grinning.

There was so much between them. She wanted him to know that she now understood God's love in her life. They could both apply that to their life together and, maybe, at least be friends again. But she worried that she'd never have any friends at all.

Chase got up and pulled her to her feet. "Hey, don't go down any gloomy roads, okay?"

She smiled up at him. "In spite of those summer storms brewing in the sky?"

He glanced behind them. "A good night to stay in and pop popcorn and watch one of those sappy movies women like, right?"

"Right." She reached for his hand. "My dad's working late, so other than the four horsemen over there, we're alone."

Chase tugged her close. "Well, we can sit here and watch the storm roll in. Together. Okay?"

Erin nodded but resisted touching a hand to his cheek. "I'd love that."

Meantime, she would pray that it wasn't too late for them to have a second chance.

The next evening, Chase drove through the country-side, remembering how much they'd reconnected last night. A couple of hours of catching up and talking had helped him to relax and refocus on this investigation. Erin was still the sweet, smart girl he remembered. Only now she was a grown woman, a strong woman who wanted justice for Michael Jeffries.

So he'd been going back over any contacts who might help him figure out something to connect the dots on this case.

When his phone rang again, he hoped Cassie Danvers had thought of something along those lines. He still hadn't heard back from her.

But it wasn't Cassie on the line.

"Chase, it's Erin."

"Erin? What is it?"

"I...someone's in our house. I mean, I saw someone in the garden, down by the pool. A prowler."

Chase gunned the truck and headed out into traffic. "Where are your father and the guards?"

"My father had a commitment in the city and I don't know where the guards are. They're not responding to my calls. The whole house is quiet."

"I'll be there in a few minutes. Meantime, take your phone and hide. Do you hear me, Erin? Hide."

"Okay. Can I stay on the phone with you?"

He warred with how to answer that, his heart slipping and sliding in the same way his truck was skidding through traffic. "Call 911. Stay on the line with them, okay?"

"Someone's coming," she said. "Chase?"

"Stay with me, then," he shouted, the burger he'd eaten too fast congealing in his stomach. "I'm on the way. Just hang on. I'll put you on hold while I call this in."

"No. Don't...just hurry. I hear footsteps."

Chase didn't dare hang up now. "Erin? Erin, are you there?"

No answer. The connection was abruptly cut off.

Erin listened, her breath coming in quick gasps, as someone moved through the rooms downstairs. Where were the armed guards her father had hired to patrol the yard and house? Where were the officers Captain Mc-Cord had sent out to the estate?

Since she'd tossed her cell phone long ago, she'd been carrying the cordless phone around her room all day. Now it had gone dead. The backup battery must have run down.

But when she hurried to the cradle to check, fear coursed through her veins. It didn't matter if she put the phone back to the cradle since someone had cut the phone lines right along with the electricity and, apparently, the state-of-the-art alarm system that her father had promised would keep her safe.

Chase is on the way, she kept telling herself while she locked her bedroom door and then searched for a viable weapon. He'd alert some of the team members patrolling the grounds, too.

Weary that she was once again in danger, Erin refused to give in or give up. She was home now and… after months of being isolated and surviving with her wits only, she wasn't about to go down without a fight when she was so close to finding hope again. So when she heard the footsteps moving up the spiral staircase toward the second floor, she found her way by moonlight and hurried to the big closet that still held a lot of her old clothes and shoes, and groped in the dark for anything she could use as a means of protection.

When her hand hit on an old tennis racket, Erin's heart stalled and restarted in a sputtering gulp of air. It wasn't much, but it could hurt if she remembered to swing it as if she were serving a ball to an opponent. Then she pushed boxes and storage bins up against the closet door as a barrier between her and whoever came after her. If she could hit the attacker over the head or trip him at least, she'd be able to run.

Crouching in a corner behind some boxes and old boots, she prayed that no spidery creatures were living inside her closet, and that whoever was coming up those stairs wouldn't find her before Chase and the police did.

He'd call for backup. That much she knew. He'd have Valor with him, too. And that smart and capable animal would rush to save her. All she had to do was protect herself before the intruder found her. But she could hear each creak of the house, and she knew every board on those old stairs. The intruder would be here before she could find a way to escape.

Erin took deep, calming breaths and willed herself to become small and invisible. She'd played hide-and-seek as a child, but she'd never imagined she'd have to hide from a real culprit who might do her harm or finish her off for good.

But she'd learned something since she'd left life as she'd known it and become a hermit. She'd found a strength she never knew existed and…she'd found her faith again.

How much longer can I live like this, dear Lord? Please help me to find a way out of this. You know my heart. You know I didn't kill Michael and You know who's behind all of this. Help me, Lord.

Her silent prayer looped through her head in a hundred different ways while the seconds ticked off like a time bomb about to explode. With her sweaty hands gripping the aged handle of the once-expensive tennis racket, she envisioned what she would do when that door opened.

And then she heard the crash of her bedroom door as it burst back against the wall. Someone was now inside her bedroom. Thinking she should have tried to make it out of the house, Erin centered her thoughts so she could use every self-defense tactic she'd ever learned. She'd been able to save herself several times because she refused to be a victim.

That was one thing her mother, Gayle, had taught her. *"You are strong and capable, Erin. Never play the victim. Never blame your troubles on someone else. God will see you through. He will give you strength, but in this world, you have to learn to stand up for yourself and your beliefs."*

Her mother's words, spoken in such a cultured, sure way, made Erin sit up and prepare herself for the worst. She'd lost her mother years ago when she was in middle school. Thinking of her now gave Erin the strength she needed.

Holding her breath, she slid up against the hanging clothes, the scents of a thousand old perfumes surrounding her in a cloying grip. The door handle shook and rattled, causing Erin to lift the racket up to shield her face.

And then she heard sirens off in the distance, heard the squeal of tires in the driveway below. Gasping in a long breath of air, she moved forward, the tennis racket her weapon.

The doorknob jiggled again. Was he going to try to kill her before someone found him?

Erin stepped behind some old coats, sweat pouring down her back, her T-shirt clinging to her rib cage. When the door was shoved open, she heard a man cursing and heaving a groan.

And then, all of her barriers were pushed aside and he was inside the closet. Erin almost screamed, but she waited…one, two, three heartbeats.

A dog's angry bark stopped the invader, who was now only a foot away from her. She could smell the foulness of his sweat, could hear his low curses and his hurried breathing.

Then the man turned and ran out of the closet, out of the room and down the stairs.

Erin clung to the tennis racket and hurried out from under the weight of her old clothes. Valor barked and snarled as the front door of the house was shoved open. The big animal's growls and barks continued while Erin ran to the door of her bedroom. She heard another door slamming somewhere deep inside the house and guessed the intruder had gone out the kitchen or garage door.

"Erin?"

Chase!

"In here," she called, her whole body beginning to shake. "I'm in here, Chase. He…he got away."

SEVEN

More police officers nosing around, more K-9 officers searching the woods behind her father's estate, more questions coming at her from all directions. More tense glances from Chase as he updated her father, the DC police and the ever-present FBI and Secret Service. Maybe now at least, they'd all believe someone wanted her dead.

Erin sat on a couch in the formal living room, shock and exhaustion trying to take her under, trying to drown her. Valor was stationed at her feet. They'd brought the dog in a few minutes ago. But the others were still out there looking. Out there searching in this never-ending nightmare.

They'd never catch these people. She might not ever be completely free. Not until they found Congressman Jeffries at least. But he'd put his politician's spin on this. She could rest only when they had his full confession.

Chase's clear emerald-green eyes held her, lifted her back up. He came and sat down beside her, his expression pinched with fatigue. "Just got word. We lost him in the woods near a creek."

Erin nodded, unable to speak until she took a drink of water. Holding the glass with both hands so she wouldn't shake, she said, "I… I didn't get a good look at his face, but he was tall and dressed in black. Oh, wait, I've already told you that."

Chase gave her a patient smile. "It's okay if you repeat things. It only means you saw what you saw, but you might add details as you remember."

"I'm glad my father wasn't here," she said. Casting a glance toward where her dad stood with two officers, she let out a held breath. "The guards my father hired—"

"One was knocked out and one stabbed," Chase replied on a grim note. "They've both been taken to the hospital and we hear they'll be okay. We questioned one of the other two. He got blindsided, too."

"Didn't we all?"

"Yes. Whoever did this knew his way around this place. He waited until our two officers made the rounds and when they walked down to the gate to do a sweep, he came in the back way and cut the electricity, phone lines and security. Then he attacked the first guards to come up on him and got away from the one guard who came up on him late." He leaned close. "I want to make sure this doesn't happen again. We need to take you to an undisclosed location."

"Selena," she said, her heart sputtering. "She said to call her if I need help."

Chase drew back, concern flashing across his face. "Your cousin? I don't think that's a good idea since she had some trouble at her place a couple of months ago." He remembered all of the details since he'd been following anything that might involve Erin. "She actually got close to your father after we questioned him about another case that Michael had been working on. After he was shot, she stayed in his town house and helped him plan a gala."

Erin felt a rush of surprise mixed with a heavy guilt when she remembered Selena telling her the same thing. "I've caused both of them so much trouble. I'm glad Selena was there when Dad needed her, and I don't want to put her in danger. She's been through a lot on my behalf and she is planning her wedding. Maybe involving her is a bad idea."

He sat there doing the Chase thing in his head, calculating, analyzing, deciphering. He lowered his head, scratched Valor behind his ear. "Yep, a lot of engagements happening these days." Then he gave Erin a direct green-eyed stare that spoke of things neither of them was ready to say.

"I think we'd better just take you to a safe house."

"Yes. I don't need to bother Selena."

He nodded. "Maybe you and Selena can have a long phone visit. The entire team will help protect you." He touched her hand for the briefest of seconds. "And I'll be around."

"Will your captain agree to that?"

"I'll convince him."

She had no doubt he'd do just that. Chase had always been stubborn and sure, but she sensed a need in him—a need to prove himself, to help a friend, to do this job.

"Should I call Selena?" she offered.

"Let me…clear this with the higher-ups. Even phone calls can be monitored for your location."

Erin gazed around the crowded room. "Might want to clear it with my father, too."

He didn't look worried about that. "I'll make him understand that the estate is no longer safe for you."

Their eyes held, memories pulling her to the surface, holding her tight. "Thank you."

Then her father came over, his expression full of rage. "I can't believe this happened. What good is security if it doesn't work?" Giving Erin an apologetic glance, he said, "I'm so sorry, honey. I thought any attacks against me were long over…after Carly Jones was arrested."

Erin shook her head. Her father had explained how his chief of staff had been taking bribes from lobbyists for years. When someone tried to blackmail her, she tried to frame Selena for her crimes. "I'm so sorry I wasn't here with you, Daddy."

Her father held her close. "Well, you're here now, darlin'."

"Chase is moving me to a new location. Undisclosed," she replied, hoping her father wouldn't fight this. "I won't put you in danger anymore."

The senator's expression changed from sympathetic to furious again. "I don't think—"

"It's my decision, Daddy."

Chase stood, his fists tight. He looked as if he were in fight mode. Valor's ears went up.

Her father's gaze moved between them in a silent power struggle. "What's the plan?" he finally asked Chase.

Chase seemed to relax and Valor went back down on his belly, but kept his head up. "I've got to clear a few things with my captain and General Meyer, but… I think it best if we hide Erin until we can locate Congressman Jeffries."

"Where?" the senator asked.

"I'd rather not let anyone outside of the team know," Erin said before Chase could speak. She stood, straightened. "The fewer who know, the better," she added. "But I'll keep in touch, Daddy. I promise."

"I don't like not knowing," her father said on a low growl. "I need to know you'll be safe."

"Daddy, from what I've heard you've been through a lot, too. Your chief of staff, Carly Jones, was a murderer who let a man go to prison for her crimes…and for a while it seemed that scandal was all tied up with this one. She tried to kill Selena—because Selena was getting too close trying to prove my innocence when no one else cared—just to hide what she'd done. You can't risk much more, and I won't let you. Just tell the press I'm resting in an undisclosed location until the real killer can be brought to justice. I won't skip out anymore, no matter what."

Her father looked nonplussed. "I can handle scandal, Erin."

"She's right, sir," Chase said. "We don't need a trial by media and we don't need any vigilantes. Word will get out that someone broke in to your house, and we might get even more press out here, not to mention curious bystanders who'd love nothing more than to be heroic on their own. We need to keep Erin safe and out of sight until we have a solid case against Jeffries."

Her father stood silent for a moment and finally nodded and glanced around. "Honey, you witnessed a murder. I just worry—"

"I've survived this long, Daddy. Let Chase do his job. I'll be okay, I promise."

"You can't promise that," her father retorted, pain moving through his eyes.

Erin hugged him, knowing he was remembering her mother. "I'll do my best and…so will Chase."

"I'm counting on that," her father said. Then he shot Chase an unrelenting stare. "You hear me, son?"

"Yes, sir." Chase turned as Captain McCord entered the front door. "I'm going to clear the way right now." He glanced back to Erin and her father. "And Senator, I could use your backup on this decision."

Her father nodded, a grudging admiration flickering through his concern. "I'll make sure of it."

"Don't make me regret this, Zachary."

Chase took in Captain McCord's scowl and the gruff command. The Eagleton estate had settled down now that most of the law-enforcement officers who'd arrived on the scene had gone back to their offices in town.

"I don't plan on it, sir." He took off his black cap and slapped it against his leg. "Look, I had a relationship with Erin in high school, but we're both adults now and…that's over. I can do my job and I'd like to stay on her protection detail."

He wanted to add that he'd done his job both by bringing in Erin Eagleton and by alerting the proper authorities tonight. He'd just have to prove he could handle guarding Erin while he guarded his heart.

"Right." The captain didn't look so sure. "General Meyer believes you *will* do your job, and I'm counting on you. If you need backup or you get in too deep, you'd better come to me, understood?"

"Understood."

Chase turned to check for Erin. She was upstairs with Brooke Clark, a member of the K-9 team, and her golden retriever, Mercy, packing a few clothes for the trip across the countryside to another location. Brooke would drive ahead of them to the safe house. They'd have to get past the press crowding around the gate, but the local police and some DC police officers would handle that. Erin would be in disguise to protect her identity and to keep anyone from following them.

Chase and Officer Nicholas Cole had a plan to get Erin out and then switch cars midtrip to throw the press, or anyone else watching, off their trail. Nicholas was a former navy SEAL, so he could do this in his sleep. Chase was glad he had Nicholas on his side since Nicholas was engaged to Erin's cousin, Selena. Since Nicholas and Selena had fallen for each other, they'd continued to find proof of Erin's innocence.

Chase planned to turn that up a notch. Nothing had panned out with any of Michael's friends. None of them had known about Michael's discovery of a young relative living in the All Our Kids foster home. Either Michael hadn't confided in anyone but Erin, or the rest of his friends just didn't want to talk about it with a law officer for fear of being in danger. Sometimes the Washington elite made things hard for mere commoners.

He needed to ditch the attitude and concentrate on this case. His wariness toward Erin and her father had become tempered now that he was back near her again. And so should his memories of loving Erin for so long. He had to put the way she looked, the way she smiled, how she seemed so broken and alone, out of his mind. For now. Maybe forever.

He headed to the foot of the stairs to wait for Erin, but he stopped in the big foyer to check his phone messages. A few from work, one from his mom checking on him and...one from Cassie Danvers.

Chase listened to Cassie's message as he watched Erin and Brooke coming down the curving staircase, Mercy leading the way. "Hi, Chase. It's Cassie Danvers. One of my workers remembered something about seeing Michael the day before he died. You might want to hear this."

Chase glanced at his recent calls. The call had come in around 9:00 p.m. He'd call Cassie first thing in the morning.

And he prayed she had information that could help prove Erin's side of the story.

Erin didn't know what to expect when they arrived at the safe house. But the small out-of-the-way town house looked like just about every other house in the neighborhood. Two-story and brick, with a small front yard.

"We're here," Chase said over his shoulder. He'd placed her in the backseat to avoid anyone seeing her.

Erin glanced up at the modest house. From what she could see from the porch light shining through the trees, it was trimmed in white with dark shutters around the windows. The small yard looked neat and manicured and the raised porch held hanging baskets and ferns in pretty stands. A facade.

Seeing this quiet, unassuming home caused something to tug at Erin's heart. She'd lived in a high-rise postage stamp–size apartment near the Potomac River. What would it be like to have a nice house on a quiet street, a house with a pretty backyard and flowers growing in big pots? Flowers she could plant herself, a house she could love and decorate and raise a family in? A house with a husband and a dog to keep her company at night?

Chase opened the door and their eyes met. Erin wondered if he could see the longing in her gaze, but she managed to pull a blank face before he reacted. No need to go there. Her future was shaky at best. Chase couldn't be a part of it, no matter the outcome of this mess. He'd told her once long ago that he didn't think they could make it, that he couldn't live in her world and he didn't expect her to live in his. End of story.

"Ready?" he asked, his gaze sweeping over her like a beam of light.

Unable to speak at first, she nodded. "I hope I'm doing the right thing coming here."

"You should be safe here for a while," he said. "We have several places all over the area and we move people from place to place as needed."

"But you think this will last longer than a while, right?"

"I can't say."

No one could say, so Erin left it at that. Chase helped her out, then went around and let out Valor. A second later, another vehicle showed up and Nicholas Cole and his Rottweiler, Max, came around to join them.

"All clear?" Chase asked, his hand guiding Erin toward the house.

"Clear," Nicholas retorted. "No one followed us."

Erin had learned enough in the past few days to understand members of the K-9 team had their own stoic language. When they didn't want to talk, they didn't. They communicated only the necessary details with no fanfare.

A sharp contrast to the always-talking heads along the Beltway, but this team sure gave her a sense of security. Chase gave her a sense of security just by looking at her. But those intense glances also gave her a shivering sense of need.

She needed him to understand so many things.

She needed him to forgive her.

She needed him, period.

They hurried her onto the porch and Nicholas used his phone to alert Brooke Clark that they had arrived. The spunky K-9 officer was good at calming scared witnesses and good at protecting them, too. Then Nicholas backed away and stood guard with Max while Chase ushered Erin through the door.

Brooke greeted her with a curt nod. "Hello, Erin. How're ya holding up?"

Erin held her own in spite of rocking on her feet. "I'm fine. Just…tired."

Brooke went into action. "Well, I'm here for as long as you need me. I'll make you a sandwich or get you something to drink."

"That's not necessary," Erin said, worried that she'd already become a problem. "I'm sure you have more important things to do than wait on me."

"I'm planning my wedding," Brooke replied. "While we're here confined together, maybe you can help me with that. You seem to have a great sense of style."

Again that sharp pang of regret mixed with envy, but Erin pushed it away. Chase was right. A lot of wedding plans going on around here, in spite of the gravity of their work.

"I think I can help with that," she said as she mustered up an encouraging smile.

Brooke gave Chase and Nicholas her own encouraging smile. "Good, but first let's get you settled in. There are two bedrooms and a bath upstairs. I'm putting you in the bedroom on the right, close to the guest bathroom. And…we have a security light that shines on that corner of the house. A motion-detection light." To assure Erin, she added, "We also have a good security system."

The unspoken threat of danger hung in the air, but Erin

ignored it. She was so tired she could hardly blink, let alone think about someone coming for her again.

"That sounds perfect," she said on a weak croak.

Chase went ahead of her up the stairs. "I'll show you the way."

Erin knew what he was doing. He was allowing Valor to sniff things out. Because no matter where they hid her and no matter how many people they put on her protection detail, Congressman Jeffries wouldn't stop until he found her. The man truly thought he could still wiggle his way out of murdering the mother of his little boy and his son Michael.

For a moment, she considered leaving again. She needed to run so no one else would get hurt or possibly die because of her. But common sense stopped her. If she ran, all of these people would have worked in vain. She had to stay and somehow find proof of her innocence.

EIGHT

Brooke showed Erin the bathroom. "It's stocked with fresh towels and toiletries. Sleep as late as you'd like. No pressure here."

"Thank you," Erin said when they'd reached the bedroom. A lamp on a bedside table brightened the room.

Erin glanced up at Chase, but he only gave her a grim nod and said, "Looks good. I need to talk to Nicholas and then I'll come back and check on you."

"No need," she told him, wondering why he seemed so tense. But then, why wouldn't he seem that way? He'd gone out on a limb for her since she'd returned, so he might regret that already. Probably regretted ever getting involved with her again.

But he searched for you...for five months. He found you in spite of the odds and he's been fighting for you. Chase was putting his life on the line for her. He'd always fought for what was right. Maybe that's why he'd walked away from her.

He'd believed he was doing what was right for her.

Erin wanted to tell him how much she appreciated him, but Chase didn't give her a chance. "Okay, then. See you in the morning."

He whirled, ordered Valor out, and they stomped down the stairs.

After Chase left, Brooke's eyebrows shot up. "He sure is focused on protecting you."

"He's focused on getting to the bottom of things," Erin corrected. "I'm not sure he fully trusts that I'm telling the truth."

Brooke turned at the door. "Oh, and I think you're wrong about Chase. From what I can tell, he's very concerned about keeping you safe. Which is probably why he and Nicholas will be patrolling the front yard for the rest of the night."

Erin woke to the smells of coffee and bacon, and the light of a bright sunbeam slicing through the closed wooden blinds. Glancing at the ornate little clock on the bedside table, she saw that it was past nine. Somehow, she'd managed to fall into a deep sleep.

Voices downstairs brought her up out of the bed. Grabbing some of the clothes she'd packed last night, she hurried to the bathroom and freshened up. Wearing a button-up cotton shirt and jeans with sandals, she shook out her hair and opened the bedroom door.

Valor lay in front of the door. The dog glanced up at her and woofed a greeting. She heard a "Come" command from downstairs, and Valor stood and hurried ahead of her.

Surprised, Erin had to smile. Valor was her protector, too. But like Chase, the faithful dog was trained to protect her. She couldn't get attached to either of them.

She moved down the stairs and steeled herself for seeing Chase again in the light of day. He and Nicholas sat at the kitchen table, nursing big mugs of steaming coffee. Brooke moved between the stove and the table with a plate of toast and a bowl of scrambled eggs. A plate of bacon was already on the table.

Chase stood and gave Erin an appreciative appraisal, but his expression stayed close to stern, the half smile tight with unspoken tension.

"Good morning," Brooke said. She went about her business as if it were a perfectly natural thing to be here with two other K-9 officers and their furry partners, along with a "person of interest" in a scandalous murder case.

"Hi." Erin felt as if she'd walked in on something. "You didn't have to cook for me, Brooke."

"I didn't," Brooke said. "They cooked. I'm just serving it up."

Nicholas sat up and then politely stood at the sight of her. Chase shot her a probing glance then sent what looked like a warning to Nicholas. Had something else happened last night?

"What's wrong?" she asked. Brooke handed her a cup of coffee and Erin gladly took it.

"Nothing," Chase said, moving to help her with a chair. "How'd you sleep?"

"Fine." She sank down, her gaze moving from him to Nicholas. The tall blond with the golden-brown eyes nodded curtly but didn't give anything away.

"Chase, is something going on, something I need to know about?" she asked, her hand curling around the warmth of the coffee mug.

"Nothing for you to be concerned about," he said. "We had a quiet night." He leaned up and grabbed a piece of toast. "I need to…visit some people…regarding the case."

"Who?"

"I can't tell you who," he said. "Just wanted you to be aware that I won't be able to hang around much today."

Well, he did have a good excuse to give her the brush-off. "I don't expect you to hang around."

"She'll be fine with us," Brooke interrupted. "Right, Nicholas?"

"I'll be here," he said, his tone as calm as the blue sky outside, his demeanor steady and secure. Did Nicholas resent her because Selena had been put in danger a couple of months ago, too?

"Why can't you tell me anything?" Erin asked Chase, needing to know if he trusted her yet. "Since I'm at the center of this investigation, I think I have a right to know."

Chase put down his half-eaten toast. "Look, Erin, we've got a lot of angles to cover on this case and I'm not at liberty to keep you posted on what I'm doing. I have my orders and—"

"And babysitting me isn't a high priority. I get that and I understand why you brought in Nicholas for backup. And maybe even that's why you brought in Brooke, so I wouldn't feel so isolated. But if this involves me, I'd like to hear it."

"It doesn't," Chase replied. "Just routine questioning. I'm trying to establish a few things—timelines, people who talked to Michael—"

"You mean, people who talked to him besides me? Are you trying to prove I'm right or show that I'm wrong?"

"He believes you're right," Brooke said. "We all do." She took a sip of her coffee. "But he has to do his job, Erin."

Erin realized she'd raised her voice, and she immediately regretted her tone, given how they'd all helped her. "Okay. Sorry."

She didn't press Chase anymore. But she didn't have an appetite either. So she grabbed a piece of dry toast and mumbled "Excuse me," then took her coffee to the front of the house.

Standing at the window, she stared out at the deserted street and tried to center herself in prayers. Until a hand on her arm pulled her around.

"Don't stand by the window," Chase said, taking her coffee out of her hand and carefully placing it on a nearby table. "Erin, I'm sorry. I have to follow a few leads I've been working on and I didn't want to worry you with details that might not pan out."

"Okay." She wanted to believe he was doing this for her, but she still worried that history would repeat itself. Would he walk away because he still didn't believe *in* her?

"Erin, I need you to understand—"

"That you're just doing your job. Got it." She shut her eyes for a moment. "I wish this could be over."

"It will be. We're all working toward finding the truth." He touched her, lifting her chin with the pad of his thumb. The tenderness in that act made her want to crumble against him and absorb some of that quiet strength. "Hey, we all believe you and we're getting closer to the real story every day. Your life has been threatened several times over."

"It's hard to let go of…running," she admitted. "I let everyone down. My father. Michael. You."

"You don't owe me anything," he replied, his tone quiet, his eyes full of regret. "I mean, who knew we'd wind up together again, like this?"

Erin regretted acting like a spoiled brat. "I'm sorry. I'm still reeling from everything that's happened over the last few months." Tears she'd tried to hold back spilled down her face. "I haven't even had time to grieve Michael's death. I feel horrible that I wanted to end things with him, that I couldn't…love him enough. But I never dreamed that the last time I saw him would turn out to be our last time together. That he'd be dead before that day ended."

Chase gave her an understanding stare and dropped his hand away. "It must have been hard, watching him die that way."

"Yes. Awful. I begged the congressman to help him, to call 911, to do something." She stopped, grasping at a memory. "He called Leon Ridge instead of 911."

Chase's expression darkened. "So Ridge wasn't already on the estate?"

"No. I was holding Michael's head on my lap and… I placed my jacket over him, trying to stop the bleeding." She pushed at her hair, memories hitting her full force. "I remember glancing up at the congressman and when I saw him on the phone, I thought he was getting help. But… I think he pretended to be doing that because instead of giving our location, he barked an order. 'Do it now,' he said. Then he hung up and that's when he pulled the gun on me."

Chase jotted notes in his pocket notebook. "We're searching his phone records to check on who he called. We checked Michael's records, but we didn't check the congressman's records since he insisted Michael was the target, or so we thought. A 911 call came in later, so what you say makes sense. If he called Leon Ridge that means Ridge not only helped the congressman try to hide what he'd done, but your testimony with a phone record to back it up can help prove Ridge was there at the same time you were."

"He showed up right after that call so he had to have been nearby," Erin said. "Michael...wasn't responding. I couldn't get him to wake up."

"I'm sorry you had to go through that."

They stood there, inches apart. Chase reached out his hand toward her again and then dropped it. "I'd better get going. McCord needs to hear this, and I'll get the crime-scene techs' help with going back over the timeline and the evidence we have so far."

"Of course. You need to do whatever it takes to prove that Congressman Jeffries isn't the man everyone thinks he is."

"I'm working on it," he said. Then he did reach over to touch her face one more time, his fingers brushing at her tears. "I failed you once, Erin. I won't do that again, I promise." With a muffled sigh, he tugged her close, his fingers tangling in her hair. "I just need you to keep the faith, okay?"

She nodded and pulled away, too shocked and emotional to be coherent. She couldn't depend on anyone right now, not even Chase. But she wanted to trust him, so she agreed with him. "Okay." Then she crossed her arms against her stomach to keep from rushing into his arms. "Chase, be careful."

He winked at her. "Always."

She watched as he loaded up Valor and headed out for the day. When she turned around, Brooke was perched against the wall across from the kitchen.

"You and Chase...sure have a history."

Erin let out a gulp of a chuckle. "Yeah, you could say that." Embarrassed, she brushed at her tears.

Brooke lifted off the doorjamb and came to stand in front of Erin. "I think you two definitely have some unfinished business."

"I hope you don't mind interviewing Virginia here in the kitchen," Cassie Danvers said to Chase later that afternoon. She slapped peanut butter and jelly onto thick slices of bread and then threw them together before she moved on and stirred some sort of fruity drink into a giant pitcher, all without batting an eye at the constant interruptions from several kids of various ages. "It's almost lunchtime so we have to stay on top of things."

"I don't mind at all," Chase said, glancing at his watch. He'd stationed Valor out on the porch with a command to stay. Had over three hours passed since he'd left Erin back at the safe house?

"In a hurry, Officer Zachary?" Cassie asked, giving him a firm smile.

"No, no. Just wondering where my morning went," he admitted. "I've been filing reports and fielding questions all morning. Not to mention, trying to track down people who might be able to shed some light on this case."

"You don't look too pleased."

"I haven't found anything substantial," he replied, fatigue tugging at him like a wet fog. He was waiting to hear back about Congressman Jeffries's phone records, too. Everyone had been focusing on Erin's missing phone and Michael's records up until now.

Cassie dried her hands on a dish towel and came over to him with a fresh cup of coffee. "On the house," she said on a droll note. Then she got herself a cup. "Sorry you have to wait a few more minutes for Virginia. It's been a busy morning around here."

Chase could see why Captain McCord had fallen hard for Cassie. The two had met when an intruder had tried to set the foster home on fire, and McCord and his K-9 partner, Glory, had tracked a kid's blue glove back to the house. One of the kids, whom they had now identified as Tommy Benson, had sneaked out that night and he'd seen the congressman holding a gun. Apparently, someone had spotted the kid there and decided to torch the foster home to make sure none of the kids talked. Which was why they were all still here in a safe house until this case was wrapped up.

Chase got sick to his stomach, thinking how any man would deliberately set fire to a foster home to hide his crimes. Especially if that man had actually started the home and had remained its champion throughout the years.

At least something good had come out of that horror.

After the captain and Cassie had been around each other through attacks and near-death experiences, they had bonded and fallen in love. Cassie was down-to-earth and smart, not to mention kind of pretty with all that red hair and those flashing green eyes. She'd been a rock throughout the past few months. Chase figured it'd take a certain kind of woman to measure up to his formidable captain. This one obviously did.

"You've had to deal with a lot lately," he said, taking the coffee with gratitude. "I guess you'll be glad to get back to normal one day."

"I gave up on normal a long time ago," she replied. A ball rolled by and she stuck out her foot to stop it. "Hey, not in the kitchen, remember?"

A young boy gave her a sheepish grin then grabbed the ball and darted to the other room.

"Summertime," she said to Chase. "I will be so glad when we're back at a place we can call our own, hopefully before school starts up." Her smile radiated strength. "If Gavin has his way, that could happen sooner than later." Then she put a finger to her lips. "But I can't talk about that right now."

Chase lifted one eyebrow. "Oh, okay." Then he held up his hands, palms out. "Captain doesn't talk about anything much anyway."

"He is the strong, silent type," she quipped, clearly in love.

"I hear that." Chase wanted to find some peace with this case, too. And he kind of wished he could find someone to share his life with. Erin came to mind, but his feelings for her were as scattered as the old oaks sprinkled across the countryside.

He blinked and refocused. "Now…what do you think Virginia needs to tell me?"

Cassie glanced around to make sure they were alone. "Virginia will be in soon. She's on the phone talking to Lana Gomez, checking up on little Juan."

Juan Gomez. The little boy at the center of this mystery and the young son of Congressman Jeffries. His mother had been tossed away like a bag of garbage, killed for having an affair with the wrong man.

"How's he doing?"

"He's great. Lana loves him and well…she and Adam are engaged and talking marriage. That kind of thing seems to be in the air these days."

Chase grinned at her smile. "So I hear." He grinned, then thought about how he'd touched Erin's face this morning and remembered how much he'd wanted to kiss her. But all of those feelings he'd tried so hard to bury would have to wait.

He wouldn't make a move toward getting Erin back until he had Harland Jeffries behind bars.

NINE

A slender woman with brown hair and matching eyes hurried into the kitchen and let out a breathless sigh. "I'm so sorry. Got carried away talking about Juan. I miss that little boy so much."

Chase stood and shook her hand. "Thanks for agreeing to meet with me, Ms. Johnson. I won't keep you long."

Virginia sank down with a look of fear mixed with duty, kind of as if she might be facing a firing squad. "I wish I'd remembered this earlier, but it's been completely crazy these last few months."

"It's okay," Chase said, hoping to reassure her. "You've all been under a lot of pressure. I'm glad you remembered it now. So…what *do* you remember? Did Michael Jeffries come by here at any time during the week he died?"

Virginia bobbed her head, her eyes widening. "Yes, he sure did. It was earlier on that day—the day he died."

She averted her eyes, but Cassie gave her what looked like an encouraging glance. "Virginia, just tell the truth."

"I was trying to calm Juan. He had just come to us that day and we were all concerned since he was so young and alone. I was nervous and I guess Juan was sensing that. Mr. Jeffries stormed in the door and stood there, staring at Juan and me." She glanced over at Cassie. "Cassie had taken one of the kids for a checkup so I was there alone with some of the younger kids."

"Did he say anything about why he was at the foster home?" Chase asked.

"No. It was the strangest thing. He made small talk and said he was just stopping by to check on us and see if we needed anything and then he asked me about Juan. Where did he come from? Did I know his parents? I told him Juan's mother had died in a terrible accident." She shrugged. "We had just heard about his mother's death and we didn't know at the time that she'd been...murdered. I was still sad about that so I didn't say much more."

"What happened next?"

"He came toward Juan and asked if he could hold him."

"Did you let him take the boy?"

"No. I'd changed Juan and he only had on a diaper. I wanted to get him into some clean clothes first." She shook her head, her hair flying out around her face in brown ribbons. "Two of the kids started fighting so I took Juan with me into the kitchen. When I came back to the living room, Mr. Jeffries was gone."

Cassie leaned forward. "She got on with her day and then later everything changed. We got attacked and... we had to move."

"I know I should have remembered earlier but... I was so scared when all of this happened I never connected on that moment until Cassie asked if I remembered Michael ever coming by here right before he died." She shrugged. "He and the congressman both came by a lot anyway since we were so close to Congressman Jeffries's estate. They were around so much, I never thought about that day."

"Understandable under the circumstances," Chase replied, thinking Virginia could be attractive if she wasn't so uptight. But she seemed like a nice lady and nothing about her indicated that she was lying. Virginia Johnson probably didn't know how to lie anyway. She definitely cared about these kids.

Chase thanked the two women and headed back toward DC, his thoughts swirling. It wasn't much, but it did prove that Michael had been upset about something and that he'd come to verify Juan's being at the foster home. Had he seen the birthmark on little Juan that matched his own and his father's? If he had gone to confront his father about this the night he died, Erin had to be telling the truth about walking up on their altercation.

But what if Michael had confided in her at dinner? She and Michael could have argued. They'd been seen leaving the restaurant around nine, and the stamp on the restaurant receipt verified that. Chase had seen Erin at the National Monument around 10:00 p.m. The call to report the murder had come in around 11:30 p.m.

Had Erin gone to see Michael again that night after she'd stopped to talk to Chase? She'd told them over and over that she'd arrived at the estate a little before eleven and witnessed the congressman and Michael struggling. Then the gun went off and Michael fell to the ground. After she and the congressman had argued, he'd threatened her, held the gun on her. He'd called for help and Leon Ridge had shown up, and after shooting the congressman, he'd put her in his car around eleven twenty. She remembered that from the clock on the car's dash.

The congressman had waited for them to leave, but

according to his own statement he'd passed out briefly before he'd called for help. He could have died and everyone would have assumed Erin had killed both of them.

But they still needed to find her car and they needed to find the murder weapon. Some of the team members were on that right now, along with the FBI and the Metro Police. Leon Ridge could make things a whole lot easier if he'd just give them the rest of the story. Fat chance on that one, especially if he was being coerced to take the rap.

Deciding to check in with the forensic team, Chase dialed up Fiona Fargo, the technician dynamo who helped the whole team. She'd know if the techs who'd been going back over Ridge's car had found anything. And she'd tell Chase what she knew since Fiona was a romantic at heart. Fiona had her own thing going with fellow officer Chris Torrence. She wanted Erin to be exonerated and she wanted Erin and Chase to find each other again.

Fat chance on that one, too.

"Hey, I was just about to call you," Fiona said without preamble.

Chase held his breath. "Tell me something good, please."

"Good and better," Fiona replied in what sounded like a happy tone. "They found strands of honey-blond hair in Leon Ridge's car. In the front passenger seat."

"And?"

"They're a positive match for Erin's DNA."

"Okay, but that doesn't show she was forced into the car."

"Does blood on the door handle count then?"

"Yes, yes, it does, but whose blood?"

"They found two different types of blood," Fiona said. "One is a match for Erin—just a smidgen on a door handle. But we also found a print on the door handle, kind of out of sight. The fingerprint belongs to Erin. But the rest of the blood belongs to Michael Jeffries."

Chase let out a whoop. "That matches what Erin told me this morning. She said she tried to stop Michael's bleeding with her jacket. She must have had his blood all over her clothes and hands." But he wondered about finding *her* blood. "Maybe she injured herself since she was forced inside the car."

"Makes sense to me," Fiona replied.

Chase asked her about the congressman making a call to Leon. "Find out who he called for me, okay?"

"We're on it," Fiona replied. "We're gonna get this thing figured out, Chase."

Chase hoped she was right. "Great. Anything else to make me smile?"

"Nope. But as soon as we search those particular phone records, I might have more. We've already pulled his records regarding the corruption charges, of course. We might find something there to link to the night of the murder, too."

"Keep me posted," Chase replied. "I'm heading back to check Erin and to relieve Brooke and Nicholas."

"I have one more thing," Fiona said.

"I'm listening."

"The techs did a really thorough search of the car and they found an old photo pushed up underneath one of the floor mats."

"A photo of what?"

"Not what, but who," Fiona replied. "The image looks a lot like Rosa Gomez."

"Really?" Chase's pulse jumped. "Maybe we need to ask Leon why that photo was in his car."

"Yeah, I think that's a good idea," Fiona replied.

"Okay. Thanks, Fiona."

Chase ended the call and let out a sigh of relief. Now they were getting down to the details. Important details.

He needed more than his gut instincts and a sketchy account from a paid henchman to prove that Erin didn't have anything to do with Michael's death. Captain McCord and General Meyer could allow for only so much before they started buckling down on him to end this thing.

Chase wanted nothing more. But he wanted to end it with the truth and he wanted to prove Erin's innocence and catch Congressman Jeffries and get his confession, too. If they could get the truth out of Leon Ridge, they'd be halfway there.

But he needed to find Congressman Jeffries, and soon. A man like him would become desperate when his carefully controlled house of cards came tumbling down. And that scared Chase.

By the time he arrived back at the safe house, Chase was tired but hopeful. Valor looked bored. He liked doing his job, not traipsing around with his partner. Chase had taken a few minutes at the foster home to show the kids some of Valor's best moves. A good workout, but no real action. A good night's sleep would be nice for both of them, however. Chase knew a lot of action could be around the corner.

Three days later, Erin had read two books, flipped through several bride magazines and made notes to help Brooke and Selena and whatever other bride might come along. And she'd cooked twice, a Mexican casserole for dinner last night and a chocolate cake for the guards who'd been watching over her day and night.

So far, the days had become almost mundane and ordinary, except for officers and K-9 partners moving around the perimeters of the house and yard. For the hundredth time, she checked the clock and wondered where Chase was. This had become her routine.

Brooke and her partner, Mercy, kept Erin company during the day. Or rather, stood watch over her, to protect her and to keep her contained, Erin had decided. But she didn't mind having Brooke and the lovable Mercy with her. They talked about weddings and marriage, and then compared other girlie things. Brooke was dedicated to her job and now, to a veterinarian named Jonas Parker and his son, Felix. Another happy ending that only left Erin sad and confused.

"I don't think I'll ever get married," she'd said this afternoon after they watched a romantic comedy. "Men are too hard to figure out."

Brooke laughed at that comment. "I so agree. But you know they can be worth the trouble. And besides, figuring them out is part of the fun."

"Hmm. I suppose you're right."

"Chase has done some fancy footwork on your behalf," Brooke reminded her. "We're slowly gathering evidence to prove you did witness the death of Michael Jeffries— not commit it."

Erin was thankful for that, at least. "He told me about the hair follicles inside Leon Ridge's car. My hair." She told Brooke how the hit man had grabbed her by the hair and shoved her onto the front seat. "I really thought he'd shoot me and toss me out the door."

"And they found traces of your blood," Brooke said, shaking her head.

"I skinned my knuckles," Erin replied, remembering how excited Chase had been on Monday when he'd asked her about that. Chase had been careful in what he could say, so she suspected he knew much more than he'd told her. But Leon Ridge refused to confess to anything other than what he kept repeating—that the congressman had accidentally shot his son and then he'd panicked and called Leon for help. True enough, if you didn't consider that Erin had witnessed the whole thing and that she wasn't supposed to be alive to tell the truth.

"He's running scared," Chase had explained about Leon. "He knows he'll be next if he squeals the rest. You're a solid eyewitness, so Leon would rather take the fall than admit that."

"Good thing you did skin your hand," Brooke said over lunch. "It supports your statement. Ridge forced you into that car and sooner or later, he'll have to tell us why he did that."

Slowly, one by one, the Capitol K-9 team members were beginning to see that Erin had been telling the truth from the beginning.

She had to wonder still if Chase truly believed her. He'd been in and out, taking turns with Nicholas and Brooke, and several other team members to make sure she stayed alive.

Was he avoiding her now that he had her safely tucked away?

When she heard his truck pull up, she let out the breath she'd been holding. He was safe for now. Chase was working day and night to help her, so he couldn't doubt her. She sent up a prayer of thanks for everything he'd done for her, but Erin was beginning to depend on him way too much.

What would happen once this case was solved, once they caught the people responsible? Would Chase walk away again? Would he forget all about her? He loved his job and he had built a good life without her. Why should that change once this was over?

She wouldn't think about that right now. Knowing she couldn't hide out here forever, she asked God to protect those who worked to protect her. What else could she do right now?

Trust in God, she reminded herself again.

For a few hours, she'd have Chase mostly to herself. For now at least, he was home. Home, where they could be together for what was becoming very precious time.

TEN

Home. In spite of the constant watchfulness of several interagency law-enforcement teams guarding her around the clock, Chase figured Erin was probably ready to go home. But when he walked in and saw her each day, she did look healthier and happier than when he'd found her in those dark woods. Having this quiet reprieve had helped her a lot, but with Captain McCord and General Meyer demanding daily reports and reminding him that she was technically still under suspicion, Chase had tried to stay on the job so he could prove them wrong. Which meant he hadn't been able to spend as much time with Erin as he would have liked.

"I think Selena wants Erin to be in our wedding," Nicholas had told him earlier. "So we need to keep at it and get this case over with and done. She won't plan our wedding if Erin can't be her bridesmaid."

Chase agreed with that notion. But with Leon Ridge refusing to talk in spite of the evidence mounting against him, Chase was beginning to feel hopeless again. No one had seen hide nor hair of Congressman Jeffries either.

"He's out there," Captain McCord said at an early morning briefing. They'd watched his estate and his apartment near the Capitol building, but both remained closed up and vacant. "We've had leads that place him in New York, Costa Rica and even Europe, but none of them have panned out. I want him brought in as much as the rest of you do."

Chase wanted that, too. The congressman probably *was* down in the Caymans or somewhere in Europe by now. But Chase also wanted to spend time with Erin, time that didn't require a constant watch and the tension of knowing someone wanted her dead. He valued the precious moments they'd spent together over the past few days, but he could tell she wanted to go back to her apartment in the city, back to her life before...

Before Michael's death?

Or way back to the day she'd told Chase she was going on that summer safari with several of her rich friends? A trip her father had given her for graduation and had insisted she needed to take...to expand her horizons. The final straw for Chase since she'd been willing to go and leave him behind.

They'd broken up that day, but Erin had tried to reach out to him, hoping Chase would forgive her, when she returned a few weeks later. But...he'd left early for college and...he refused to return her calls after that. Didn't see the point. They weren't meant to be together anyway.

Who was the stupid one now?

Who would have believed all these years later they'd be tossed back together in such a strange way? Or that his feelings for her would come back so sure and strong?

Trying to see this time of forced confinement as a blessing, Chase wondered how Erin felt about him. Did she still care? They talked late into the night, sitting together on the couch until she got sleepy. Then she'd go upstairs and he'd stay there with Valor, guarding the house and getting very little sleep since his mind was all wrapped up in this investigation. He didn't care about sleep right now. He cared only about Erin. He cared only about keeping her alive.

Maybe…after this was over, they could have a second chance with each other. He'd changed and so had she. Surely with prayer and hope and a new maturity, they could start fresh.

She only wanted a do-over, a second chance with Chase.

In spite of the circumstances, Erin loved waiting for him to come here each night. It almost felt like normal life. Almost.

When he came in the door today, Valor on his heels, Erin glanced up from her perch at the kitchen table, her gaze meeting his. "Hi," she said, relief sweeping over her. She worried about him when he was out there working.

Chase nodded, a half smile playing across his lips while he assessed the room and her. Valor gave Chase an expectant glance.

"Go on. Tell Erin hello," Chase said. She loved how this had become an endearing part of their routine.

Valor trotted over to Erin and she went down on her knees to give the big dog a pat and a hug. Even though Valor still had on his protective Kevlar vest, Erin managed to snuggle against him. "Hello, my sweet boy. How you doing?"

Valor's dog smile widened. The big dog glanced back at Chase as if to show his partner he was Erin's favorite.

Chase cleared his throat. "We're both fine, thank you."

Erin lifted her eyes to stare at him and saw the need

in his eyes, the same need that caught hold of her each time she was around him. "How…how was your day?"

It *was* a normal question, asked on a normal summer day with the sun shining outside and the smell of dinner wafting from the stove. But the hope tearing at her heart was anything but normal. Her longing had changed from wishing she could prove her innocence to wishing she could make Chase love her again.

That was a wish that might not come true, a future that couldn't be seen, but a longing that couldn't be denied.

Trust in the Lord. Have faith. Do not despair.

The words from Psalms came to her in a rush of awareness.

Chase must have seen the calamity forming in her eyes. He reached down and pulled her up, his gaze holding hers, his silence speaking more than words ever could.

"Erin—"

"I'm back," Brooke called as she opened the laundry room door and came into the kitchen. "Bath towels are all folded." Taking one look at them, she stopped, her mouth falling open in surprise, and then turned and headed the other way. "And now I'm going to check on the cleaning supplies."

Erin smiled at Chase and then started giggling. "I've never seen her so embarrassed before."

He chuckled back, looking relaxed for the first time in days. "Her timing stinks, but dinner does smell good."

Enjoying the moment, Erin said, "And what would have happened if Brooke hadn't interrupted us?"

"This," he said, lowering his head to hers.

Erin waited for his kiss, waited for his touch, waited

for what seemed like a lifetime to see forgiveness in his eyes.

And then the air was pierced with a boom and she heard barking outside and boots hitting the hardwood floors.

In the next moment, she found herself down on the floor with Chase covering her and Valor dancing in an angry circle, his barks matching the woofs coming from another officer's dog.

Brooke came charging in from the laundry room, Mercy on her heels. "Someone's shooting at us."

Chase went into action, leaving Valor with Erin. He radioed Dylan Ralsey, the team member who'd relieved Nicholas today. Dylan and his partner, Tico, were out front.

"I'm on it," Dylan replied. "Not sure where that shot came from."

"I'll check the back," Chase reported in response. He motioned to where Brooke crouched by the back door of the kitchen. "Keep her here, okay?"

She bobbed her head and crawled toward Erin and Chase. Chase turned and checked on Erin. "You okay?"

"I think so. I'm sorry they keep coming after me."

"We'll talk about sorry later," he said. "Right now, I need to get out there."

"Be careful."

Chase rushed to the back door, gun lifted, and opened it before he crouched low and sent Valor out.

Brooke slid to the door and locked it. Then she rushed back to the safety of the cabinets across from the other counter. She held her revolver in the air.

Erin glanced at the weapon and then back at Brooke. "What do you want me to do?"

"Don't get shot," Brooke said on a reasonable note.

Erin let out a breath. "Agreed. I need something—" She spotted a rolling pin and reached up onto the counter and grabbed it. Not exactly a gun, but a weapon she could hurl at someone or use to trip them up.

Another shot pierced the dusk and shattered a nearby window, the echo reverberating out over the neighborhood. Then every dog along the street joined in the barking.

Erin lifted herself up to sit against the kitchen cabinets. "Are you all right?" she asked Brooke.

"Fine," Brooke said on a winded breath, her gun held with both hands now. "I'm kind of used to this." She checked her weapon. "Someone wants to shut you up permanently."

"It's him," Erin said on a hiss. "Congressman Jeffries won't stop until I'm dead. I'm the only witness to what really happened that night, and if he can't frame me for Michael's murder, he'll make sure I never talk to anyone again."

"We lost the scent," Chase said thirty minutes later to Dylan. Same song, second verse. Or maybe the third or fourth verse. Someone had managed to trace them again, but how? "I'm thinking they've planted a GPS or bug on one of our vehicles or maybe somewhere on Erin's clothes." She always wore a dark hoodie, but he couldn't figure how anyone could have planted a tracer on that old thing.

"We need to read in McCord and the general," Dylan

said, his weapon lowered while he scanned the street behind the house.

Patrol cars roamed the streets while officers went around the neighborhood on foot to question potential witnesses, but the yards here were wide and spread apart. So far, no one had seen the shooter.

"That'll go over real well," Chase retorted, his cell already out. Then he noticed a car parked haphazardly in a driveway down the street. "Hey, I don't remember seeing that car before."

"Those big hedges blocked our line of sight," Dylan replied, already heading that way. "But you're right. The patrol cars had to have come by here. No reports, so I think this is a new development."

The navy blue sports car looked familiar, but it also looked dirty. Too dirty.

Dylan turned to scan the street. "Maybe a neighbor heard the shots and got out of the vehicle and ran in the house."

"Maybe," Chase said, alerting Valor. "Let's check it out."

Valor started his ground-to-air sniffing again and immediately alerted when they reached the car. The big dog trotted to the open driver's door and stopped to stare. But when he whimpered, Chase got a tingling sensation alone his neck.

"Interesting," Dylan said, his weapon at the ready.

"Yep." Chase held his service revolver out in front of him, but he had a sick feeling that Valor had alerted on this car for a reason. If Chase took a guess, he'd say Valor knew the owner of this car.

He came around the sleek, mud-encased hood, thinking he'd probably find something inside this car to make his day go from bad to worse. "I know this vehicle," he said on a low whisper.

"Oh, yeah?" Dylan walked so silently, Chase turned to find him looking over his shoulder. "*Oh*, yeah," he said again as they both stared into the front passenger's seat.

"This is Erin's car," Chase said, his heart doing a fast drop to his feet. "Valor must have picked up on her scent or maybe the scent of whoever left it here."

"Sure is a mess," Dylan retorted on a dry note. "Almost like it's been hidden in the woods for…say…months."

"Yeah." Chase did a quick scan of the houses lining the street. "I think someone is sending us a message."

"The shooter?"

"Or the congressman who sent the shooter." Chase figured someone had deliberately left the car here. "Maybe the congressman did this." He nudged closer. "Or maybe someone else."

"And the bloody jacket inside?"

"That's Erin's, too," Chase said. "She was wearing that the night I saw her. The night Michael Jeffries died." He did a sweep of the area and then stared back into the car. "Only, Erin left this covering Michael at the scene. Ridge grabbed her and put her in his car, but our techs found Michael's blood in the car. That matches what Erin told me about the jacket."

"Hmm," Dylan said. "Then how did the jacket get in her car?"

"Good question. I'd guess Leon put it there, but… he's in jail."

Quiet. And then Dylan stated the obvious. "So that's not her blood but Michael Jeffries's."

"I think so," Chase replied as he carefully checked the cramped backseat then headed around to the trunk.

"Which proves she was definitely there when he got shot. We need to look inside this trunk, too."

Dylan radioed their location then turned back to Chase. "Right, but…let's go back to all the blood on that jacket. What do you think?"

Chase lowered his weapon and turned to face his friend. "I think, just like Erin told me, that that's Michael's blood." Then he pulled out his phone again. "And I think we need to get this vehicle processed as soon as possible. I don't like this." He started back toward the house.

"Hey?"

"Stay here," he said to Dylan. "I have to check on Erin."

"Got it. Make sure she's okay."

"On my way," Chase called, running now with Valor by his side.

He had to get back to Erin, and he prayed he wouldn't be too late.

Mercy growled low.

Erin's cell buzzed, but it was high up on the kitchen counter. Too dangerous to reach right now.

Brooke glanced at Erin and pointed to the front door of the house. Erin held on to the rolling pin then mouthed, "If anyone comes up this hall, I'm going to throw this and then you can—"

"Shoot them," Brooke replied, her calm as clear as the two words she'd just spoken.

Erin felt that same calm. They had Mercy with them and she was so ready to pounce. That lock wouldn't hold if someone wanted in here and…with even the alarm sounding, someone could easily shoot at them and run.

Too late to worry about that now. A *pop, pop* hissed over the house.

Someone had just shot open the front door lock.

ELEVEN

Chase could hear Mercy's frenzied barks now mixing with Valor's. Radioing for backup, he hurried through the backyard and tried the kitchen door. Locked. Because he'd told them to lock it. He headed toward the basement door. It stood open.

When he heard a crashing sound, he moved around to the front of the house only to find the front door wide open.

"Erin?" he called out. "It's me. It's Chase."

Valor's snarls and barks settled to a low growl. "Search." Chase carefully went through the door after the eager dog, noting the lock had been shot off.

"Brooke?"

"We're in here," she called, her voice firm.

Chase hurried to the kitchen and found Erin and Brooke crouched near a counter with Valor now standing guard.

Valor whimpered a greeting and both women jumped up and started talking.

"All right, one at a time," Chase said, lowering his gun. He reached out and grabbed at Erin. "Are you both okay?"

Brooke stood and did a neck roll. "Affirmative. A man dressed in dark clothing with a mask over his face. Mercy scared him off."

"And Brooke shot at him," Erin replied, terror still in her eyes.

"Erin pinged him with a rolling pin. He should have a really big knock on his head."

Amazed, Chase radioed Nicholas that everything was okay, then explained to Brooke that they had a situation.

"What kind of situation?" Erin asked, worry edging her eyes as the whole house became flooded with law-enforcement personnel.

He'd have to tell her sooner or later. Might as well be now. "We found your car."

She let out a gasp. "What? Where?"

"Someone left it down the street," he said. "It had your jacket in it. And Erin, there was blood all over the jacket."

Erin leaned back against a cabinet. "I... I used it to try to stop the bleeding. That's Michael's blood, Chase. Remember I told you?" She put a hand to her mouth, tears misting at her eyes. "Who would leave it here knowing someone would find it?"

"Someone who *wanted* us to find it," he said, pulling her close. "Someone who's running scared."

"And determined to make me look like a murderer," she retorted, turning away to stare out into the growing darkness. "But...this could also prove I'm telling the truth, right?"

"Whoever planted that jacket in your car probably thinks you're either dead right about now since they sent a hit man to kill you or...that you haven't told us everything."

She glanced beyond him. "You mean, they sent the

shooter and then they left my car here, thinking I'd be dead, but the evidence would be here for all to see."

Chase's radio buzzed. "We'll talk more later. I have to help process the scene at the car," he said. "And... don't clean up anything. We need to check for prints at the front door, in here and in the basement. Brooke, do a search for any bullet fragments or slugs. You'll both have to give your statements, too."

Brooke started moving around the room, already doing her job.

He motioned to a nearby patrol officer. "Don't leave this room."

The officer nodded, his expression somber.

"I'm taking Valor with me," he said, giving Erin one last glance. "Stay safe."

Erin lifted a hand. "I left that bloody jacket lying by Michael. Leon dragged me away. I didn't take the jacket with me."

Chase came back over to Erin. "We'll get this figured out." Then he gave Erin what he hoped was a reassuring glance. "We're going to stop this, I promise."

She only nodded and then turned away again. When Chase glanced back, he could see the dejection in her body language. She'd folded over into herself as she tried to shut out yet another horrible reminder of that night.

"We need to bring her in," Captain McCord repeated later that night after they'd finished up with the crime scene. "The only place she's going to be safe is in protective custody."

Metro Police detective David Delvecchio grunted and looked bored. "The man's got a point, Zachary. This woman has been hiding out all over the countryside and up until you brought her in, she's been pretty resourceful out there. Now whoever's behind this has upped the ante."

"Erin *is* the ante," Chase said, glancing around the briefing room to see who else wanted to argue with him. "But you're right. She has a better chance of surviving if we move her to a place he can't figure out. I want to take her out away from the city. He somehow finds out where we're keeping her. He knows she's in our custody, but… we're running out of options."

"Then let us protect her," Secret Service agent Dan Calvert said. He'd been involved in this investigation since General Meyer's office and the White House had been breached. "Don't be so stubborn about this. You've tried and…they keep coming."

"And they will find her again," Chase said, afraid to let Erin out of his sight. "Or do you still want her under wraps because she's still high on the list of suspects?"

"That's one way to look at it," Captain McCord said. "Blood on her jacket and left in her car, hidden for months. Something doesn't add up."

"It does add up, sir. She left that jacket at the scene. We found Michael's blood in Leon's car, along with her blood. She fought against being taken and got a slight injury. Plus, she said she had Michael's blood all over her hands." He slapped his right palm on the table. "Whoever moved her car took the jacket, too. Which means that on the night of the murder, the wounded congressman was able to call someone else after Leon left with Erin."

Nicholas spoke up. "And tonight he called someone to kill her and to make sure we found that car."

"But still no sign of the murder weapon," McCord replied. "Maybe they'll gift us with that next time."

"I don't want there to be a next time," Chase replied.

McCord's grudging nod confirmed the obvious. "Okay, I can see that scenario about someone placing the jacket in the car. Fits right in with her being set up." He shook his head. "But we have to look at the facts and follow the evidence. So far, we know Erin Eagleton was at the murder scene and inside Leon Ridge's car, and now we have her car and a blood-caked jacket that matches the one she described to you."

Chase wanted to tell them about the things that didn't add up. "And someone brought that car to the safe house because they sent killers in first. They figured Erin and possibly Brooke would both be dead before we found the car."

"And that would have been that." McCord grunted and rubbed his face before he lifted off the corner of the table. "We need to beef up the search for the congressman. He can't get away with murder and attempted murder no matter where he hides. I hate to admit it, but he looks guilty of more than just corruption."

"He needs to step forward like a man," Chase retorted.

McCord's stare pinned Chase to the floor. "You've done a good job, but…you're too involved. Should have known it might come to this."

Chase couldn't argue with that. He was involved. He wouldn't let Erin become a scapegoat for a man who'd fooled a lot of people in the past. "Look, Captain, the evidence is mounting against Leon Ridge as possibly being an accessory to murder. We need to get him to talk again. I believe he's still hiding a lot, especially the part where he took Erin against her will."

The captain studied Chase for a moment. "Let me go back in and tell him we've found the car and the jacket. That's all he needs to know right now. Once the techs get back to us after examining the jacket, we might find something more to push at him."

Chase had to follow orders. "What can I do in the meantime?"

"Go home and rest," McCord suggested. "We'll make sure Miss Eagleton is placed in a new safe house."

Chase dug in his heels. "With all due respect, sir, I can't go home and rest."

McCord didn't bulge. "Zachary, you're running on fumes. That means you go home and rest up."

Chase nodded and left the room. But no way was he going to get any rest.

Erin didn't know where they were taking her. She'd been at K-9 headquarters all night and now she only knew she had to leave quickly and in the dead of night. Without Chase or Valor with her.

"Don't worry," Chase had whispered in a quick, cryptic tone. "I'll be watching out for you."

"But—"

"Just do as they say, Erin. We have to move you and… they think I'm going home to twiddle my thumbs."

But he wasn't. That's what he was trying to tell her.

"Don't get fired over me, Chase. I'm not worth it."

"Believe," he said. "Remember? We need to believe in each other and in God's grace and goodness. I'll make sure I know where the captain takes you."

She wanted to believe. She did have faith. Her faith had held her together even in her darkest moments. But faith without action was just a facade. Chase had shown her how to believe in another human being, to trust another person to help her. To trust him the way she had when they were so young and in love.

Could she go back out there without Chase and Valor by her side, guiding her and protecting her? Erin hated the shudder of fear curling against her spine.

"I'll be okay," she said, trying to remember the boy she'd loved long ago in the mature, handsome face she saw now.

"Yes, because this team is the best in the world." He winked at her and turned. But she saw something there in his eyes, just a flicker of awareness that seemed to light her from inside. Chase had turned into a good man and he was good at his job.

If he said he'd find her, he would. She had no doubt of that.

"Ready?" Nicholas asked, Max at his feet.

"I think so," she replied. "I travel light these days."

Except for the tremendous burdens she carried on her shoulders. So much baggage, she felt weighted down. Too many *if only*s and *might have been*s. If only she'd stayed that summer and gone off to college with Chase in the fall, things might have been so different now. If only she'd tried harder to get Michael to open up about what had him so upset, she might have been able to save him.

As she was smuggled into a waiting car, she had one more *if only* to add to that list. If only she could be free again.

Completely free and clear to be near Chase again.

TWELVE

Erin didn't like this. While her new guards were nice and well trained, she missed Chase. John Forrester and Dylan Ralsey both seemed as capable as Chase and the others. These two hunks had adorable four-legged partners that were trained to attack and protect. She should feel safe.

She only felt lonely.

The house was plain and three-storied, one of those Georgetown brownstones that blended in with all the others around them. But it was apparently off the beaten path and so nondescript, no one would even notice she was here. The tall narrow house sat apart in what looked like an unoccupied row of four other side-by-side houses, far from the others on the street, probably to avoid any neighbors getting too close. Same as the last place.

Did Chase know where she was?

Would he really come for her or would he realize he was better off being taken off her protection detail? He'd come so close to being killed too many times, she wouldn't blame him for letting the other team members take over for a while. But he'd also saved her life several times.

Would these two officers do the same? Of course they would. They were handpicked by Captain McCord. The man might not believe her, but he sure took his duty to protect Erin seriously. Maybe because her powerful father was breathing down his neck. She'd even heard the president himself wanted this over. No more than she did.

Or maybe because Gavin McCord was every bit as good at his job as the team under him. If her father and their boss didn't give them all commendations after this was over, Erin sure would.

If this ever ended.

"Do you need anything, Miss Eagleton?"

Erin whirled from where she stood in front of an empty fireplace to find Dylan Ralsey and his dog, Tico, both staring at her. The man had straight dark inky hair and dark, almost black eyes to match, while the dog had dark fur around his ears and nose and a silky lighter brown coat that reminded her of Valor.

Erin glanced at the half-eaten piece of toast she'd left on a tray. "No, thank you. I'm fine."

"Did you sleep last night, ma'am?"

"Yes, I did." She hadn't, but that wasn't his problem.

"Would you like more coffee?"

She eyed the coffee carafe sitting by the tray on a nearby table. "I can get it myself. Would you like a cup?"

"No, I'm good. I'll be in the hallway if you need anything. And John and his partner, Guard, are at the back door."

"Got it, thanks," Erin said, not meaning to sound so harsh. Officer John Forrester and his German shepherd, Guard, were both just as serious as this one. And just as attentive.

But how could she explain that she was about to crawl

out of her skin? How could she keep living her life like this, on the run for close to six months and still being stalked and shot at? Pursued? What next?

She'd been back in DC for little more than a couple of weeks and Jeffries was still coming at her. What could he possibly gain if everyone knew he was trying to kill her? Did he think eliminating her would save him, give him redemption, or maybe lessen his guilt?

Erin stood there and prayed for the Capitol K-9 Unit and all the team members who'd dropped everything to solve this case. She prayed for Chase and hoped he'd get the rest and peace he needed. She prayed for her father and Selena and everyone else who believed in her.

And she asked God to help her find the way. How could she end all of this and get on with her life, get on with her grief and, maybe, get to know Chase all over again?

Then she remembered something very clearly.

No one had ever found the murder weapon. She'd heard Chase and the others discussing that particular detail time and again.

It was hard to prove anything without the murder weapon.

"And I think I know where it might be," she whispered into the cold, dark fireplace.

But she wasn't sure how she'd ever get anyone to believe her or take her to that particular place.

Chase had been cleared to help watch the safe house.

Now he was guarding the street behind the house, a plain brick three-story sitting away from the other homes on a quiet cul-de-sac. He knew the place since he'd brought an informant here once to be called as a witness in a drug lord's trial.

It had a front door and a back door with steps down to the small yard and a back-street entrance, and a basement entrance much like the last house. They usually kept the basement locked and off-limits just in case an occupant decided to bail out on them.

Which this particular occupant just might do.

Chase wouldn't blame Erin if she did run. They hadn't done a very good job of hiding her. Chase certainly hadn't done his job to the best of his ability.

But he couldn't shake the feeling that someone, somewhere was always watching and reporting back to Congressman Jeffries. It wouldn't be hard to pay a mole to tell the congressman their every move. Chase didn't have time to pursue that angle, but he had asked Fiona to keep eyes on everyone in and out of headquarters. Deliverymen, carriers, temps, anyone.

Fiona had managed to find the calls the congressman had made before he'd contacted 911. One number was a match to Leon's cell number. The other matched that of the man Chase had shot at the inn. Another tiny break.

Maybe they'd get a break on whom the congressman had watching them, too.

Meantime, he hoped to get Erin out of this city if this place was breached. He'd gone over the plan with the captain. But they all agreed that, sooner or later, this had to stop.

So he watched, knowing a team of the best K-9 officers had been assigned to guard her. During the day, that meant Dylan Ralsey and John Forrester. At night, Deanna White and Tasha Lamant took over. All great at their jobs.

Chase was just glad to be involved. He and Valor

waited in an unmarked car behind the house each day. He was to report anything he thought might be suspicious to those inside the house. Three days in and nothing.

Until today.

When he looked up a half hour before the shift change at dusk, he saw a man dressed in black moving up the stairs to the kitchen entryway. Chase didn't get out of his car, but he kept his eyes trained on the man. Valor's ear pricked up, but he remained as quiet as a church mouse.

He had to alert the officers inside, so he radioed Dylan.

Dylan listened and then replied, "We'll get her out of here."

"Wait." Chase lifted his binoculars and watched the man hovering on the tiny porch stoop, a package of some sort in his hands. What he saw sent a chill down his spine. "All of you need to get out of there. He's wiring the kitchen door with what looks like some sort of explosive."

Erin was learning to listen when the officers compared notes. She'd heard things over the past few days.

"No news on Jeffries, no sightings of him anywhere in the city. We've got eyes on his apartment in town and his estate, but we've heard he's long gone and out of the country. We've had reports from the FBI that they've done another sweep of both places."

"He won't come back to either residence. Too hot. He's probably in Switzerland or the Caymans by now."

"We might not ever find him. And with no murder weapon, we might not ever solve this case."

Where did that leave her? Erin wondered today while she waited for the changing of the guard. No word from Chase either.

If something didn't happen soon, she would have to

find a way to get back out there on her own. It might be the only way she could stay alive to prove Harland Jeffries killed his son.

Then she heard Dylan talking on his phone. "We'll get her out of here."

After that, everything shifted into motion. One of the dogs started growling and both men went into action. Dylan rushed back to the living room with his dog, Tico, while Officer Forrester held his position at the front of the house, his partner's hackles raised. Then he said something into the radio he carried. "Got it. What's your location?"

Whom was he talking to?

"Front door about to be breached. Stay there. We'll get her out the back."

"What's going on?" Erin asked, already dreading the answer.

"Follow me, ma'am," Dylan answered, grabbing her by the arm to guide her toward the back of the house. Another noise and he slipped his weapon out of its holster.

"I think we have visitors at both entryways," he said into his radio. "I'll take care of our guest. Tico will escort us."

"Roger that," Officer Forrester shot back, his voice full of static. "Basement?"

"Sounds like. I'll get her out that way."

"Go. I got this."

Officer Ralsey signaled to Tico. "Go."

The big dog barreled toward the basement door and waited, then went ahead while Dylan got it open and took Erin down the narrow stairs.

"We're gonna get you out of here and when I open this

door up to the street, Tico and I will make sure it's safe and then we need to run to the right. Got that?"

"Yes," Erin said, her heart rate increasing with each step they took. "What are you going to do?"

"I'm going to protect you from whoever is trying to get to you," Dylan answered in a no-nonsense voice. "Don't panic but they've wired this house to explode."

"A bomb?"

Dylan nodded and whispered, "We have to get you to safety. A car will pull up out back and no matter what, you need to get in that vehicle, understand?"

"Yes."

Erin wasn't surprised that she was being attacked again, but she sure wished Chase were here, too. She trusted these two men and she didn't want anything to happen to them, but…she and Chase seemed to have their own unspoken language.

Dylan had her at the basement door to the street now. Unlocking it, he peeped outside. Tico scratched at the door, his nose in the air. The dog went ahead, sniffing and growling.

"Ready?" Dylan asked, guiding Erin toward the door.

"Yes." But she wasn't ready. She wasn't ready at all.

Dylan turned to her. "Listen to me. This is very important. If anything happens to me or Tico, you keep running to the right up the street. You understand?"

"Yes, I mean, no. I won't leave you."

"You have to, Miss Eagleton. Just run to the right."

"Okay."

They crept out the door and up the concrete steps to the street. Erin stayed behind the tall officer, but Tico alerted and headed up the steps toward the back-door stoop, his growls and snarls vicious now.

A man stood on the stoop over them. Tico advanced and growled low. She gasped, causing the intruder to spot them.

"Stop," Dylan shouted to the intruder. "Stop right there or I'll shoot."

The man turned to run down the steps, a gun in his right hand. Halfway down, he stopped again. "This place is about to go up in smoke." And then he held up what looked like a cigarette lighter. Tico jumped forward, still growling. "Tell the dog to halt now or this place will blow. You need to give me the girl."

Dylan whispered to Erin, "On three, you run. Just run."

Then he rounded the wooden steps, his gun raised. "Put down your weapon and take your hand off that switch."

"Can't do that."

The intruder stood with the gun trained on Erin, his other hand holding the denotation device.

"The bomb squad and a SWAT team are headed this way," Dylan said in a calm voice. "And that K-9 officer will eat you alive before you ever activate that device."

"I'll take my chances," the nervous man said, his eyes now on Tico.

Dylan gave Erin a nod. "One, two, three—"

After that, everything happened so fast, Erin couldn't breathe. The intruder fired off a shot. Dylan shot back and she heard another shot. The man hit the button and then fell off the steps and into the street. Erin screamed and turned back, thinking the whole place was about to explode.

Dylan gripped his left shoulder and called to Tico.

Blood was seeping between his fingers. "Run," he said to Erin on a weak breath. "Hurry."

Erin glanced around and saw Tico rushing down the stairs to guard the man who'd been shot. "No, I have to get you away—"

And then, she felt herself being lifted into the air. Another man, dressed in black. Grabbing her, dragging her toward a waiting van.

"Let me go." She kicked and screamed and tried to get out of his grip. More shots, but not from Dylan. Erin wasn't sure where they'd come from. The man holding her collapsed in front of her feet, his eyes open to nothing.

He was dead.

Erin scanned the street then turned back to where Dylan lay, still holding his bleeding shoulder. The basement door swung open and John Forrester and the other K-9 named Guard came running up the steps to the street. She could hear sirens off in the distance.

John glanced at her. "Go. Run!"

What about the bomb? She stared up at the door above them. A hissing sound filled the night and she smelled something acrid and chemical.

Then another hand on her. She swung around and came face-to-face with Chase. "Let's go," he said, dragging her up to the street.

A car sat idling beside the old fence. Chase opened the passenger side door. "Erin, get in. Hurry."

Chase! He'd been in on this.

She looked back at where they'd left Dylan and John and then she got inside the car.

Chase immediately radioed back for an update. "Ralsey, Forrester, report."

Nothing.

Chase stopped the car. "I'm going after them." But before he could get out, John Forrester appeared on the street behind them, holding up his wounded friend. Dylan grimaced but gave Chase a thumbs-up.

"Get her out of here," John called, waving them on.

They were a block away when the house exploded and a huge mushroom of flames and smoke filled the night air.

THIRTEEN

Chase kept checking Erin for signs of shock. "Hey, you still with me?"

"I'm okay," she said, her voice still and flat. "I'm okay."

Chase pulled out his cell. He'd warned Forrester and Ralsey about a possible bomb.

"I have to make sure they're all right." He pulled out his phone and waited for his contact to answer and then said, "Can you give me an update?"

Deanna White sounded winded. "Everyone is safe. Did you get the package out okay?"

Chase looked over at Erin. "Yes."

"Good," she said. "John's ears are ringing and Dylan's gunshot wound will heal. A through-and-through in his left shoulder." Another beat then she added, "And Captain McCord is surveying the scene. You are to proceed as planned."

He ended the call and put away his phone. "The two officers are okay. They know I have you."

Erin lifted up to stare over at him. "That's good, but where are we going now?"

"Out of the city," he said, his hands clutching the steering wheel. He'd picked her up in an unmarked car and now he watched to make sure no one was tailing them. "But first, I want to take you back to headquarters with me. I need to interrogate Leon Ridge again, but I can't do that and worry about you, too."

"So I get to watch you work him over?"

He smiled at her dry humor. "No, you get to stay in the conference room, where we can all watch out for you."

"But won't your captain be mad that you took me away from the safe house?"

Chase shook his head. "He knows I took you. We planned for this. Did you see what happened back there? Erin, they've been coming after you for months. They were after you the night I found you and they found you at your father's heavily gated estate, and then the first safe house and at yet another safe house handpicked by Captain McCord. Enough is enough."

"I agree," she said, her hands together in her lap, her head down. "I agree. Every time I get shuffled to another location, I think about running again. And now I wish I had left. You can't be involved in this anymore."

"I've been involved since the night I found your necklace at the crime scene."

"Do you still think I killed him, even after Leon Ridge admitted Jeffries accidentally shot Michael?"

"I know you didn't kill Michael," he said. "I believe you, but the congressman and Leon don't want anyone else to know the truth. They don't want to admit that you were there that night. You won't be safe until we can force Jeffries's hand." He watched the dark road and then added, "I want to clear your name, Erin. No questions left, no regrets."

"And how do you suggest we do that?"

"I don't know yet, but… I'm starting with pinning Leon Ridge to the wall, and then after I've talked to him I intend to get you out of DC."

"Do you know more than you're saying?"

Fatigue dragged at him like a heavy fog, but he wouldn't give up. "No. I'm still trying to find a way to prove beyond a doubt that you are telling the truth. I believe the congressman accidentally killed his son and then when he realized you'd witnessed it, he panicked and refused to call the authorities. Then he decided to pin Michael's death on you to save his political career and to hide the corruption he's gotten away with for years. That's what I need to prove, Erin. That he's trying to frame you to save himself."

"Yes, he is," she said after a long sigh. "Chase, I appreciate how you're willing to help me, but we can't keep doing this."

"I don't much care about all of that right now," he said. "I'm taking you to what I consider to be a safe, secure place."

"Where?"

"I'd rather not say."

She hushed for a few moments and then asked, "Is this how I'm supposed to spend the rest of my life? I can't go into witness protection because I'm still a suspect of sorts. I've told the truth but with Jeffries in hiding, I might not ever be safe. I don't want to look over my shoulder anymore, Chase."

"You won't have to," Chase told her. "I've beaten a path over and over every lead, Erin. I've talked to anyone who might remember something from this investigation. I'm slowly building a case against Jeffries."

He let out a breath and continued. "We know he is

Juan Gomez's father. We know Michael made inquiries all that week regarding Juan's parentage and his father's possible involvement. We know someone killed Rosa Gomez on Jeffries's orders. And we've established that Tommy Benson snuck out of the foster home that night and saw Congressman Jeffries holding a gun. This whole chain of events—Rosa's murder, Michael's murder, the All Our Kids home being attacked and almost burned down, break-ins at the White House and attacks on Selena, the museum where Rosa's sister, Lana, was attacked, crooked aides being paid off and even using Danielle Dunne's mafia father coming after her as a means for a cover-up, and then Leon Ridge planting bombs to scare off Isaac Black—all of these things lead back to Congressman Jeffries."

Chase glanced at her. "We only need to piece together the part where you come in, and I think Leon Ridge will crack on that one, too. We need a little more time and I'll have it figured out." He shifted in his seat and checked the rearview mirror. "First, I'm going to sit down with Leon again. As soon as possible."

"Well, remember to ask Leon Ridge where he hid the murder weapon," she said, her tone firm and sure. "Better yet, take me with you since I have an idea that it's on the Jeffries estate somewhere. I'd like to watch Leon squirm when he figures out I'm alive."

Chase nodded on that. "Oh, don't worry. You will definitely go with me. I'm not letting you out of my sight. But you will not get to watch us interrogate Leon."

"As long as he confesses everything, I can live with that," she replied.

Chase wanted her to live for a lot more reasons than making Leon Ridge cave.

* * *

An hour later, Chase and Captain McCord sat in the interrogation room at the Capitol K-9 headquarters, both staring across the table at Leon Ridge. Ridge didn't look so hot. He was built like a linebacker, but his pallor spoke of being confined too much. Maybe prison life didn't agree with him.

Chase leaned forward. "I'm not going to waste time, Leon. We have a problem. Erin Eagleton is alive and in our custody. Her story matches yours in spots, but we need to make both versions match up to get the real story. If you have any hope of coming out of this with a lesser sentence, now is the time to spill it because Jeffries is still trying to kill her."

Chase halted and put his hands on the table. "Do you want another woman's death on your conscience?"

Leon looked blasé at first, but he started twitching. "What do you mean?"

Chase hit a palm on the table. "I mean, you're looking good for concocting this whole scenario. You'll be the fall guy for murder if Jeffries isn't located. And if Erin Eagleton is harmed in any way, her father will make sure you're not only in jail. He'll make sure you suffer for possibly aiding and abetting a fugitive. Suffer, Leon. Really suffer. Think about that."

Leon scratched his nose and sweated. "I told you, I don't know anything about Erin Eagleton."

But Chase saw something in his eyes. A sadness that pushed through the disregard that shouted at Chase. Chase decided to start with the one thing that had been bugging him. And this one thing might sway Leon. "Why did you have a picture of Rosa Gomez in your car, Leon?"

Leon's head came up and his face reddened with anger. "I don't know what you're talking about."

Too late to lie. The man had reacted too quickly to that question. McCord's gaze narrowed, but he didn't react. The captain sat as still as a rock.

Chase pulled out the picture from a folder. Covered in clear plastic, the aged photo showed a smiling Rosa standing in what looked like the garden at Jeffries's estate. "We found this underneath the front seat of your car. The same car you used to kidnap Erin Eagleton."

Leon strained at his handcuffs. "Did she tell you that?"

Chase refrained from screaming out his frustrations. He had to focus on this for Erin's sake. She was sitting in a guarded conference room across the hall right now.

"Erin? Yeah, she told us a lot of things. Said you helped the congressman out that night. Shot him with his own gun to make it look as if she'd done it and then you pushed her into your car with orders to kill her."

Chase lifted the picture and waited for a moment. Leon's demeanor had changed. He was jittery and visibly shaken.

Chase kept pushing. "Congressman Jeffries allegedly had an ongoing affair with Rosa and we have evidence that he hired someone to kill her."

Leon's eyes widened. "I don't know nothing about any of that."

Maybe not, but he kept staring at the picture of Rosa. "Did you know Rosa, Leon?"

Leon lowered his head and pushed a chained hand through his thinning hair. "Yeah, of course. I saw her around the estate. Nice lady."

"How nice?"

"What do you mean by that?"

McCord gave Chase the one-eyebrow-up frown. Probably wondering where Chase was going with this.

Chase tried again. "I mean, was Rosa nice to *you*? Did you ever eat in the kitchen, chat with her or discuss the weather or what a wonderful boss you both had?"

Leon's frown made him look as if he'd swallowed nails. "I liked her, yeah. She was good to me."

"Did the congressman know you two were close?"

A light of rage fused through the criminal's eyes. "What? What are you saying? What have you heard?"

McCord grunted. "I'd like to hear that myself."

Chase's stomach burned with the sure knowledge that he was on to something. "Did you have a thing for the congressman's secret lover, Leon?"

Leon went molten, his gaze firing a black hostility across the table. "I don't have to answer that."

Captain McCord stared at the picture and then looked at Leon. "I think maybe you should answer that since it might help your case." He glanced from Leon to Chase. "But you think about it while we step out for a break, okay?"

Chase didn't want a break, but the captain's scowl told him he'd better take one. Once they were out in the hall, he turned to McCord. "Sir, I think Leon had a thing for Rosa. If he did, then he might turn on Jeffries. I mean, what if he really did try to kill the congressman that night?"

McCord stood as silent and still as a statue. "That's a stretch, Chase. But I have to admit, you're making him sit up and take notice."

Chase nodded. "I'm going to check on Erin and then we'll go back in."

McCord looked through the one-way mirror to where

Leon sat staring at the picture Chase had left on the table. "Okay."

Chase hurried to find Erin. She was sitting curled into an office chair, a magazine open in her lap and Valor at her feet. When she saw him, she stood up, a questioning expression lighting up her face. Valor did pretty much the same.

"Hi." She slid her hands inside the pockets of her jeans.

"Hey." He moved toward her, wanting to touch her and hold her tight. Instead, he patted Valor on the nose. "We took a break, but... Leon's beginning to see the error of his ways."

"Has he corroborated what I've told you?"

"We're getting there." Chase moved an inch closer. "How you doing in here?"

She gave him one of her sweet smiles. "Valor and I are sharing a lot of secrets. He's a good therapist."

"Yeah, I tell him all of my troubles," Chase admitted. "And we compare notes on you, of course."

She leaned close. "All good, I hope."

Chase moved way too near, the floral scent enticing him. "We both think you're special. And... I gotta get back in there."

"Okay." She stepped back and pushed at her hair. "Chase, thank you."

Chase nodded and went back to grill Leon Ridge a little more. But he held being near Erin over his heart like a shield.

"Okay, so what's the deal, Leon?" he asked a couple of minutes later. "Tell us about Rosa and we'll get to the rest later."

Leon swallowed and shifted in his seat for a few more

minutes, his expression changing from dark resistance
to clear resolve. "All right, okay, so I cared about Rosa."
He looked down at his big hands. "She was good to me
and…he treated her like dirt."

"*He* being the congressman," Chase said.

"Yeah." Leon turned conversational. "After she had
the baby, I tried to help her out. She didn't have much
money and her only sister wouldn't have anything to do
with her. She cried a lot and she was always tired. Didn't
get much sleep with the boy always crying and needing
attention. I felt sorry for her."

"So you didn't feel this way until after the child was
born?"

Leon shook his head. "I treated her bad, too, at first.
But then, I saw how he treated her, how he wouldn't even
acknowledge the baby. His baby. So I started bringing
her supplies and, sometimes, flowers and candy. I had
to hide it from him, of course. But I got to know her and
I liked her." He sniffed and looked down at the table. "I
loved her."

"How did she feel about you?" Captain McCord asked.

"She cared about me, but she was afraid to…end things
with him. She went to him right before she died, hoping to get some help for the boy. Juan was sick and even
though she had nice presents from Jeffries, she could
barely afford a doctor. I don't think he liked her asking
for more money."

Chase exchanged glances with the captain. "I can see
how being around each other and both of you having to
take orders from a man like Jeffries could bring about
a strong bond." Then he tapped his fingers on the steel
tabletop. "Did you know they were going to kill her?"

"No, I swear I didn't or I would have stopped it. The

man you killed at the inn, he pushed Rosa off that cliff. After that night, I wondered…and then everything happened so fast the night Michael died." Leon's vacant eyes went misty. "They didn't have to kill her, you know. She just needed more money. For the boy."

"You're right on that one," the captain said. "Which is why you shouldn't have to take the fall for a rich and powerful man who's probably sitting somewhere on a beach laughing at us."

McCord kept staring across the table. "And, Leon, if you think those suits who keep visiting you are here to save you, guess again. The DA can twist this to make a strong case against you even for Michael Jeffries's murder. You had motive and you had opportunity. Maybe you went to the estate to confront the congressman about Rosa's death and Michael got in the way. The congressman said he didn't see the shooter, so…he could easily pin it on you. You shot the congressman and you kidnapped Erin Eagleton and planned to kill her on his orders, right?"

"Yeah, right." Leon realized he'd just confessed. "I mean, he made me do all of it. I didn't kill Rosa or Michael, but the congressman had me shoot him and take the girl." He shook his head. "Erin Eagleton saw too much, knew too much."

Chase frowned at the fidgety criminal. Leon had just proved what Erin had known all along. "Leon, he's trying to kill a senator's daughter. A woman who hasn't done anything evil or criminal in her life. You can help us stop this."

Leon's glare had fizzled to a feeble frown. "I told you, I was trying to help the Eagleton woman. But she ran away from me. And I can't stop what's already been set in motion."

Chase started to stand, but the captain's hand held him in check. McCord leaned in toward Leon. "Maybe you can tell us where the murder weapon is. Anything to redeem yourself."

Sweat beaded on Leon's forehead. "I threw it away, after the woman ran." He lifted his head, his anger now directed toward the man who'd brought them all together. "It ain't right, but I'll go down for this, no matter what. I've got a target on my back. I'm already a dead man, so what does it matter what I say or do?"

Captain McCord scrubbed his hand down his chin. "So...what have you got to lose? Do something decent, Ridge. Tell us everything you know. Avenge Rosa's death and help us save Erin Eagleton."

Leon Ridge glared at the captain, but the flare of rage returned to his eyes. "I don't know what to do."

Chase pushed his chair back so hard, it fell to the floor. "He's going to kill her because she was there that night, but if your story matches hers, we can help you. We can go from there."

Leon lowered his head and stared at his handcuffs. "Okay, all right, I'll tell you the rest. So she was there that night. The congressman accidentally shot his son. That's the truth. And the woman did see it happen." He stopped, took a deep breath, his beady eyes going dark. "Jeffries panicked when Erin Eagleton wanted him to call for help and then he kind of went haywire and decided he needed to pin this murder on Miss Eagleton. He ordered me to shoot him to make it look like he was a target, too, and he ordered me to take Miss Eagleton out and kill her after I shot him."

"And where did you take her?" the captain asked, disgust sharpening his question.

"I stopped somewhere way back in the woods up near a hill."

"Did you shoot *at* her?" Chase asked.

Sweat beaded on Leon's upper lip. "Maybe. I mean, man, I had to do my job. It's always about cleaning up messes, you know." He leaned back in a slump. "But she got away, and she kept running." He finally looked up and straight into Chase's eyes. "And I let her run. I let her get away. I didn't want to kill her."

Chase kicked at his chair again. "That's some comfort then, isn't it?"

Leon gulped and glanced around as if someone might be listening. "The thing is—I haven't heard from Jeffries, but I know he's watching me. He must have found someone else to do his dirty work after you killed the man who murdered Rosa. And after you took me into custody." He shrugged. "Being in jail is the only thing keeping me alive right now."

Chase left the room and headed across the hall to Erin. "He told us just about everything."

Her eyes grew wide. "Thank goodness for that. Now what?"

"Now I take you to another safe place."

He hoped.

They were at a small cabin deep in the woods. She hadn't recognized any signs or markers since he'd taken the back roads in the wee hours. The night was black, with dark clouds looming overhead. The sticky air shouted for release. Lightning danced off in the distance, hiding the coming dawn. Chase had picked a perfect spot.

Even if she wanted to leave, Erin would only wind up lost in the woods. A shiver of apprehension climbed up her backbone and caused her neck muscles to tighten. She didn't want to go back into the woods. So she turned and tried to focus on being here with Chase, safe and away from the evil that seemed to follow her.

A muted lamp on a small desk spotlighted the sparse, clean cabin. Paneled walls, a huge fireplace and old but comfy-looking furnishings filled the quaint space, along with an efficiency kitchen that held only the essentials. All flannel and wood without a trace of feminine influence. A hunting cabin. She did detect the slight scent of furniture polish and fabric freshener, however.

"So you get the bedroom down the hall and I'll bunk out here in the den," Chase explained. "Valor will guard you. He'll sleep at the foot of the bed."

"And who will guard you?" she asked, pushing at her always-messy hair.

He stopped and held his hands on his hips. "I'm trained to guard myself."

She wondered about that. Did he have anyone on his side? He never talked about his personal life. She didn't dare ask about his family, but she knew Chase had always been close to his parents. He was prickly tonight, on edge.

"Are you hungry?" he asked now.

"No."

"The kitchen's stocked with crackers, cheese and some fruit, soup, sandwich meat. Sodas and coffee and plenty of water."

"Someone knows we're here?"

"Someone brought supplies."

"Oh, I see. You thought of everything."

Chase roamed around the cabin while Valor lay in

front of the cold fireplace with eyes that followed his partner. "Let's talk about locating the murder weapon, Erin."

Oh, that had to be the reason for the mood. That and another harrowing experience that had almost gotten his team members killed. When she'd talked about searching for the missing gun the congressman had used to shoot Michael, instead of asking questions, he'd gone quiet. But now he knew she'd been telling the truth. Still, he had to keep pushing. He'd kept her at headquarters until it was safe to travel again.

Sitting down because she didn't know what else to do, she said, "I know the murder weapon is still missing."

"That's right," he said, finally taking a stool by the fireplace to sit near the sofa, where she sat with her legs curled up. "Leon said he threw it away somewhere in the woods. Is that what you remember?"

Erin nodded at that analysis. "He's one of the top dogs on the congressman's staff. Always hanging around, slipping in and out of rooms. He knows where all the bodies are buried and he knows that estate inside and out. He could probably take you right to the place where he hid the gun."

"Did you notice anything odd when he forced you into his car?"

Wondering why Chase asked that question, she said, "No. It was dirty. Lots of old food wrappers. I mostly watched for road signs and a way out. I remember the gun, though."

She closed her eyes for a moment. "The congressman had blood all over his hands and I saw blood on the gun, too. Michael's blood." She lowered her head and closed her eyes. "I've tried to block it out of my mind, but…it keeps coming back."

Chase thought back over what he knew. "Michael was shot at close range. We know the congressman had blood on his clothes. His and Michael's. We thought because he'd tried to help Michael."

"He didn't." She pushed at her hair. "Splatters. He had splatters from when the gun went off."

Chase's gaze locked with hers. "Let's go back to Leon's involvement." He came over to sit down beside her. "So where do you think he hid the gun?"

His nearness only reminded Erin of how much she'd missed him. He looked tired and…aged. But his question shouted out the doubt he still had about her involvement in that horrible night.

"I don't know for sure," she admitted. "I'm guessing. But the congressman was a gun advocate and an experienced hunter and marksman. He valued all of his weapons, some of them antique and expensive. He would have realized Leon might still have the gun, and he would have asked Leon about it so they'd have all their bases covered. If Leon hid it in the woods, the congressman wouldn't be happy about that."

Pushing up off the sofa, she pivoted at the fireplace and turned to Chase. "The congressman would want to get that gun back because he's that arrogant and panicky. Leon probably planned to go back and get it when things cooled down."

"Why wouldn't he just throw it in the river or hide it away from the estate?"

"Leon could use the murder weapon to blackmail the congressman." She stared at the cold fireplace. "I think that in all the commotion, Leon injured Congressman

Jeffries worse than either of them had planned. The congressman passed out and he realized later that the gun was gone. Leon had it." She glanced down at the dark socks covering her feet. "He must have gone into a panic, but I'm sure he came up with another lie in case he had to answer questions regarding the gun."

"So maybe you're right on the blackmail thing. Leon says he tossed the gun, but maybe he knows exactly where it is. He has motive. He was in love with Rosa Gomez."

Erin wondered how she hadn't seen this before. "Michael used to complain about him hanging around, always flirting with the women on staff and bragging about his new car, new motorcycle and things such as that. Leon liked to talk up his position on the congressman's staff. He impressed the lesser-paid help."

"We found a photo of her under the seat of Leon's car along with the traces of Michael's blood and your blood."

"And you're just now mentioning this to me?"

He got up and came to stand in front of her. "I haven't had a spare minute over the last few days to discuss anything with you. But Leon told us a lot last night."

Erin accepted that and remembered to be grateful for even the smallest things. "Well, you're here now and I appreciate that and how you're working so hard to help me," she said, her emotions crashing with the same intensity as the growing storm rumbling all around the cabin.

Chase stood a foot or so away, his gaze tugging at her, his eyes searching her face. "Yes, I'm with you now." Then he reached a hand around her waist and tugged her close. "I don't want to be without you ever again."

"I'm here," she said on a whispered plea while she forgot their conversation, forgot everything but Chase.

"Believe in me, trust me. I need to know you can do that, Chase, no matter what."

"Let me show you, then."

Erin welcomed the closeness, accepted his gentle kiss with a sigh. And then, she was in his arms, her hands moving over his jawline and into his soft, clipped hair.

Outside, the rain began to fall. Chase pulled away to stare down at her. "This is dangerous. It's late. Maybe you should try to get some sleep."

"Yes." Forcing herself out of his arms, Erin took a calming breath. "You, too."

His hand on her wrist tugged her back around. "Erin, I promise you I will find Harland Jeffries. And when I do, I'll make him tell the truth."

"I know you will," she said, taking his hand in hers and lacing their fingers together. "I just don't want you to die doing it."

FOURTEEN

A couple of days later, Chase and Erin were back to business and skirting around the pull that kept the air between them charged with lightning bolts of awareness. But after going over the woods behind the estate, the crime-scene techs hadn't found the gun that had killed Michael Jeffries.

Chase broke the news to Erin as yet another rainy day turned into a stormy night. "No news on the gun, but we won't give up. If you think of anything—"

"Leon took me out the back way. That much I remember. Take *me* out there, Chase. Maybe I can find the spot."

Chase listened to Erin's emphatic plea again but disagreed. "That is not going to happen."

"Leon has admitted the congressman told him to kill me." She shrugged and held her hands down.

"Yes, and in a court of law, Jeffries's lawyers could twist that to make it look like you shot Michael and got away with Leon, and they could make it look as if you two are trying to frame the congressman."

"That's ridiculous. I've only been in the same room with Leon Ridge maybe four times in my life and we were with other people. I've never had a decent conversation with the man and I sure don't like him now."

"I understand that, but high-powered lawyers can make things stick even when they're ridiculous."

"What about all the other evidence?"

"It should hold. That and your testimony coupled with Leon's confession should be enough." He shrugged. "But we need all of it. If we can locate Jeffries and get a confession from him, this will all be over. But…that's asking for more than we might ever find."

Erin toyed with the zipper on her hoodie. "I wish I could find something more substantial to add. My memories are fuzzy, but I'm sure there's a missing link I've forgotten."

Chase stood near the window, the habit of checking outside making him antsy. "They know you're alive, Erin. And they're scrambling to cover their tracks because they have to believe you've told us the truth. Even your memories are dangerous."

She got up off the couch and stalked across the cabin like a mad feline. They'd been holed up here for two days and he'd seen every mood of Erin Eagleton.

She paced and sighed, stared into the cold fireplace and sat in an old armchair and read paperback books. Then she fumed and studied the notes in that little notebook she guarded like a hawk. Somehow, she'd managed to keep the mangled, frayed thing with her no matter how fast she had to run or whom she had to hide from. He wanted to take it and read it, but Chase was afraid it might contain more than just the details of her trauma.

His head came up. "Erin, what kind of things do you write in that pocket journal?"

She whirled, her hand checking the old cotton hoodie

she wore. "Dates, events, thoughts. Mrs. Appleton gave it to me along with an ink pen. She saw me scribbling on a napkin. Told me to use the notebook as a journal." She shrugged. "She didn't even know my real name or why I was running, but she knew I needed to remember."

Erin had always loved her journals. And her doodles. He'd figured it was more personal than informative. More about Jeffries's unethical deals than the night of the murder.

"Have you actually gone over it?"

"Not too much until now. I've been busy trying to stay alive." Glancing toward the door, she said, "Every place you've brought me, I've thought of running. Just leaving it all behind. I've certainly written about that in my journal. I'm afraid to remember, Chase. Does that make sense?"

He wondered what she'd recorded about him. Maybe she was afraid to let him see that, too.

"You've been through a lot. Maybe that's why you've been hesitant to read your notes."

They looked at each other for a split second.

"Let *me* see that notebook," Chase said. "Maybe together, we can piece things into place."

Erin reached in her pocket and pulled it out and handed it to him. "I *have* looked over my scribbled notes several times while we've been here, but it's mostly what I could remember that first night at the bed-and-breakfast."

"We need to read it together and compare notes," he said. "With any investigation, you always follow the evidence, Erin. We have evidence. Just not enough."

She gave him a hopeful glance. "Anything to find the last piece. Jeffries's gun. If Leon tossed it, it's in those woods somewhere."

Chase wondered how she could be so certain that the gun was hidden near the Jeffries estate, but his gut was burning, so he went with her theory for now. What did he have to lose?

An hour later, Chase's eyes stung with fatigue and his mind was boiling over with too many details that didn't add up.

"I told you this notebook has everything I could find regarding what I believed to be his hidden corruptions—"

"And those notes back up what we have on him," Chase interjected. "We need more. One tiny gem of evidence. Something that can substantiate your claim that Leon had the gun. He could always change his tune on that."

Erin grabbed the notebook back from Chase and began searching again. She went back to the beginning and studied each page, her eyes flashing with an intensity that had him worried.

"I ran and ran after I got away from Leon Ridge," she said. "It didn't seem as if he took me too far." She studied her scrawled words. "I found the Appletons' house in the middle of the night, and they took me in and gave me food and clothes."

She checked the first few pages. "My notes don't even make any sense to me."

Chase watched her, his heart aching for this incredible, brave woman. A woman he'd tried to put out of his mind for most of his adult life. But here she sat, back in his life and fighting for her innocence and her freedom. He wanted to help her, to prove she was telling the truth. He had a new hope for them, too, after seeing her doodles and notes.

She'd mentioned how he'd found her.

Chase is back in my life. It's amazing and scary, but if anyone can save me from this, Chase will.

He'd seen other notes about him, but she'd glazed over those like a bird fluttering away from danger. She didn't want him to see that part of her scribbling.

"I *was* right," Erin said on a little squeal that brought him out of his daydreams. "Here."

She sank back and pointed to some doodles on the third page of the lined notebook. "See that little box in the corner of this page?"

Chase nodded. "Yes. I didn't notice that much before. I thought maybe it was the Appletons' farmhouse."

"I forgot about even drawing it," she said. "But now I remember why I drew it."

"And?"

"Leon Ridge used the congressman's gun to shoot him in the shoulder," she said. "I saw that up close because Leon held on to me while he shot the congressman."

"Right, but you said Leon still had the gun when he forced you into the car, and he admitted that."

"The old square barn," she said, pointing to the little doodle. "The congressman had most likely been at the back of his property on a shooting range and that's why he had the gun with him that night. He and Michael used to go out there after work a lot. There's an old barn back there."

"Are you sure?"

"I drew that box while I was reliving the horror of that night." She turned to face Chase. "Leon held the gun on me until we got out to the woods, and he would have shot me with it, if I hadn't maimed him enough to get away." She jabbed a finger at the box. "Chase, I ran right past the barn, but I remember him firing at me in the dark. I heard the bullet hitting wood a few feet from my head. This little square is that barn. It has to be."

Chase wanted to celebrate with her, but he had to be sure. "So you're saying we might find a slug embedded somewhere in the wood?"

"Yes. Yes." She got up and moved around, excitement in her eyes. "And possibly the gun around there somewhere."

"We didn't search too far back in the woods that night," Chase said. "We focused on the scent we picked up that took us to the foster home. We didn't even know you were missing until the next day."

He stood to touch a hand to her cheek. "Erin, it's been six months since that night. Leon could have easily gone back to the scene to make sure he covered his tracks. Our techs haven't found anything out there."

She looked dejected and then shot up again. "But we can at least check it out, right? I mean, they might have looked all around the barn but they didn't know about the bullet hitting the wood. Have them look again. Let me go with them."

Chase jotted his own notes. "It's worth a shot, but you're not going."

She didn't look happy about that.

Chase went back over everything to keep from kissing her.

"We had no idea until last month when that boy— Tommy Benson—said he saw the congressman with the gun, that the congressman had used his own weapon, or we would have checked him that night for gunshot residue." He thought back over the evidence. "Michael's sweater and entry wound revealed what we call 'stippling,' which is soot and gunpowder burns that show the victim was shot at close range."

"Yes," she said, moving her head in agreement. "Michael and his father struggled, and his father grabbed the gun and held it to Michael's stomach." She put her hands to her mouth, her eyes going dark with terror. "Then Leon held me with one hand, and he shot the congressman from about fifteen feet away, maybe. They both shot that weapon."

Chase pulled out his phone and called Fiona. "Let's check once more. If we find the gun, we might also find some blood embedded in the barrel and maybe even the inner workings. We'd have to dismantle it, but it might be worth a shot."

"Chase, slow down. I'm working as fast as I can," Fiona said in an instant greeting. Chase pictured her red hair standing up in tufts stiffened by a substance they were all too afraid to ask about. "Got all that. What do you need from me?"

"Erin's jacket. It's too late to prove there was any GSR on it, but it tested positive for her blood and Michael's."

"Yes, we confirmed that—no gunshot residue but her blood and Michael's. Next?"

"The congressman's clothes contained bloodstains, right? But were they tested for GSR?"

It had been chaos that night and it was a long shot, but maybe someone had checked for GSR on his clothes after he was taken to the hospital.

Fiona mumbled to herself and then replied, "Okay, according to the lab report, yes. Traces of GSR on his jacket and shirt, and his blood and Michael's on his clothes. We believed the gun powder residue came from the congressman being shot."

"Thank you, Fiona," Chase said. "How are things?"

"Good for you," Fiona retorted. "General Meyer told everyone to keep working on finding the truth. And she said to leave you and Erin alone for now."

Chase closed his eyes and sent up a silent prayer. The savvy general knew where he was keeping Erin. The whole team did and they were guarding the woods all around this place.

But due to his stint with the Secret Service, General Meyer *knew* Chase. That made his job easier and gave him the confidence to stay the course.

"Thanks for that information," he said. He ended the call and turned to Erin. "They found GSR on the congressman's clothes."

Erin squealed again. "So that proves he used the gun, right?"

"Yes and no. No one tested his hands because at the time we didn't know he'd touched the murder weapon. Now we do, of course."

She pushed at a cushion. "And he didn't volunteer that information."

"If he'd already been shooting the gun earlier that night, he'd have plenty of GSR on his clothes *and his hands*. But now he can deny all of that and keep pinning the murder on you."

"But Leon said he accidentally shot Michael and I saw him shoot Michael. So it's his words against Leon's and mine." Erin got up and ran her hands through her hair. "Tommy Benson also saw him with a gun."

"His lawyers would dispute that twenty ways to tomorrow." Chase followed her and turned her around. Valor watched them and waited for his cue. When none came he settled back to stare at them.

"Hey," Chase said, his hands moving through her hair. "It's not all bad news. If a slug is buried in that old barn wood, we need to find it and match it to the type of small-caliber gun we believe was used. A lot could go wrong, but it would be another piece of the puzzle."

Erin looked up at him with trusting eyes. He'd fought hard to earn that trust. And he'd tried to stay out of any kind of emotional tangle while he searched for answers. But being here with her 24/7 was both a joy and a challenge.

"Hey," she said. "How are *you*? I mean, really?"

He tugged her into his arms. "Right now? I'm good."

He put the investigation away and took another kind of risk. He pulled her into his arms and kissed her, slow and easy and with a deliberate gentleness so she'd feel that he would never leave her again.

Erin sighed against him and returned that same gentleness. He could tell she wanted to be in his arms.

Then she lifted away, her eyes dark with longing. "Chase, I want this to be over so we can…begin again."

"Me, too," he said, bringing her back. "Me, too."

Two nights later, Chase's cell phone buzzed. He got up from his spot on the couch and grabbed it, sleep making him sluggish. Valor sat up, always ready for some action.

"Zachary, we got trouble."

Nicholas Cole. Nicholas and Adam Donovan were helping to guard the perimeters around the cabin.

"Armed men combing the pasture and headed for the woods."

Chase was up and at the window. Valor followed suit. "Who and how many?"

"I can't tell. Looks like some sort of SWAT team but

only a few. Maybe three or four." Nicholas paused and then said, "I don't think they're friendly."

A sinking feeling hit Chase in his solar plexus. "How did they get this far?"

"Waited and watched," Nicholas said. "It's dark and hard to see anything. Max alerted. They could be headed to…the other house on the property, too. But we won't let them get that far."

Chase went cold. With Valor like a shadow on his heels, he hurried to the bedroom and woke Erin. She sat up in a shot, her eyes wide. "Have they found us?"

"Someone's possibly nearby or at my parents' house."

"We're on your parents' land?"

"Yes," he replied, not bothering to explain. "Get dressed."

She stood up and shook her hair out. "I am dressed."

She slept in her clothes out of habit. A good thing she did, too. Even with the warm temperatures outside, Erin clung to her old hoodie and jeans like a shield. He remembered her wearing classic, preppy clothes before, but Chase didn't try to stop her quirky wardrobe habits now. Whoever that was would be here pretty soon. He prayed they didn't hurt his parents.

"Stay here while I check the front yard," he said, hurrying to the window in the other room. "Stay," he said to Valor. The eager dog settled and watched Erin's every move.

Why had he thought this was a good idea?

Too late to worry about that now. He had to get her to safety and go check on his parents. But when his phone buzzed again, Chase stopped and stared.

Captain McCord's number flashed like a laser across his phone screen.

"Sir," Chase said, his tone full of resolve.

"Kid, you need to move her again." A long heave of breath. "I have to admit, you sure picked a good hiding place this time. Took a few days for them to figure it out."

"But they keep coming."

"Yes, and I just found out why. Seems someone on Jeffries's staff—what's left of his staff—hired the same security company as Erin's father did."

Chase rubbed his forehead with two fingers. "A mole? That would explain why we never found the intruder who came into Erin's room. Our dogs would have been familiar with the scents already, too."

He heard a grunt of agreement. "Yeah, well, too late to discuss the variables now. I'm with your parents. They're safe. Just sit tight and we'll take care of your family."

Chase lowered his head, his gaze on the coming storm. "I'll do my best, Captain."

McCord grunted. "We've got your back on this. I should have had your back from the first day."

"It's okay, sir." Chase hung up and turned to get back to Erin. Then he heard Valor's low, aggressive growl, followed by angry barking.

Chase hurried to the back of the cabin.

Erin wasn't in the bedroom. The bathroom door stood open. Empty.

Valor stood on his hind legs, scratching at the heavy curtains over the window.

Chase rushed to the curtains and pulled them back. The window was partially open, the screen gone. Had Erin gone through this window? Had she decided to run again?

He stared out into the rain. Nothing.

He turned to check the room. Erin had left. And she'd taken her hoodie and her notebook.

The shock hit Chase like a battering ram.

Even after everything they'd been through, she still couldn't trust him? She'd walked away from him long ago while he'd been willing to fight, and now they were reliving history but in a much more dangerous way. If she'd run from him now after everything they'd been through together, maybe they weren't meant to be in each other's lives after all. She still couldn't trust him enough to believe in him, and this time her lack of trust could get her killed.

The pain he'd held in his heart for so long came back to Chase with a sharp slap.

She should have waited to see who was out there. Maybe she'd never truly trusted him and she'd only been waiting to escape—from him. Maybe Erin Eagleton just didn't need anyone to protect her and love her. Or she didn't want him in her life again, even if it meant saving her life.

Sick at heart, he radioed back to Nicholas while he worked to open the window wide. "I think Erin's on the run again. She's gone and I can't find any evidence that she was forced to leave."

Nicholas started shouting. Dogs started barking. "Go. We'll catch up."

Chase and Valor were already out the window.

FIFTEEN

Chase stalked through the trees, the dark woods he'd roamed as a child suddenly sinister and dangerous. In spite of his best efforts, Erin had become too afraid to stay with him. He'd tried so hard to protect her, and yet again he'd failed. Would he always be that country boy who'd had a chance at a life with her and missed it?

They were reliving history, but this time neither of them wanted it to end this way. He'd let her get away once and now he regretted that even more. She was in danger but she didn't want to let him help her, maybe because she'd never believed in him. So many times she'd talked about running, but he'd convinced her that he'd take care of her. But he hadn't done that.

Erin was better off without him after all since he hadn't done a good job of protecting her. But he'd keep doing that job tonight, so he put his personal feelings aside and concentrated on protecting the person they'd all worked so hard to shield.

He followed Valor into the thunder and lightning of yet another round of storms. A heavy rain hit at them, but Valor never stopped pushing through the woods. Would they be too late to help her?

His cell buzzed. Chase held it close.

"Location?" Captain McCord shouted over the clash of thunder.

Chase named the area. "The trail behind the cabin. Headed toward the river."

"We're spreading out," McCord replied. "We'll back you up and meet up with you on the dirt lane."

Back him up.

The captain was doing his job. Once this was over, Chase would probably be suspended or fired for messing this up. What then? All of his hopes and dreams had failed, and he'd have to start from scratch.

And the worst of it. He'd lose Erin. Again.

The rain slashed at him like a whip. The sky raged its own pain. Chase ignored the sharp needles of rain and kept trudging behind Valor, his mind churning with another kind of anger.

But somewhere in his tormented mind, his faith caught hold.

Maybe sometimes people had to be apart for a reason. He was stronger now, trained to protect and serve. He was tight with his team members and they'd all rallied around helping Erin, even when they'd doubted her.

Maybe God put you in this exact place at this time to save the woman you love. The woman you were meant to be with.

"Suffering produces perseverance, and perseverance, character, and character, hope."

The verse from Romans shot through Chase's mind like a bolt of lightning. He couldn't give up hope now. Now was the test of truly finding the courage he needed to do what he had to do. He'd save Erin, no matter the outcome, no matter what the future brought. That was his first duty. Save the one in danger.

Determination and a need to succeed caused him to push through the woods. Valor was on the scent, his nose in the air, the hairs on his neck and back bristling.

"Find her, boy."

When he heard other dogs barking, Valor whirled on the trail. Chase gave him full rein. "Where are you taking us?"

And then Chase heard a motor cranking and the roar of a movement through the trees.

Back toward the cabin they hurried, Valor leading the way. When the motor's whine came to a stop, Chase feared the worse. Erin must have taken the four-wheeler his dad kept at the remote hunting cabin. But then he thought he heard another sound. A vehicle cranking? And then, the muffled sound of a gunshot.

He urged Valor on, both of them running now.

He ran right smack up on Captain McCord and his German shepherd, Glory, followed closely by Brooke Clark and Mercy. Chase halted Valor and glanced around. No sign of Erin. When Valor alerted toward the trail, Chase almost let the big dog keep going.

But he held back. "Have you seen her, sir?"

The captain took off his wet cap and scratched his head. "She's gone. They used a four-wheeler to breach the trail by the river. Must have doubled back here while we were back there."

"What do you mean?" Chase asked, adrenaline shooting through him. "From what I could tell, she left on her own."

The captain gave him a surprised glare. "I don't think

so. She didn't run away, Chase. Someone took her. And we're almost certain some of those involved were on the team who pretended to protect her at her father's house."

Chase's whole system changed course. Erin wasn't the one at fault here. He was. She kept reminding him he needed to believe in her. Had he failed at that, too?

"What happened?" he asked while Valor sat waiting. Chase didn't think his heart could pump any faster. "I heard the four-wheeler cranking in the woods."

Isaac Black stalked up, wet and fuming with frustration. His beagle, Abby, lowered her nose, her long ears brushing the mud. "They used the off-road vehicle to get her here and then took her out in a big van, Chase. Happened so fast, threw all of us off guard."

Chase slapped at the raindrops on his face. "I'm going after them." He'd track that van clear across the country if he had to.

"And how do you plan on doing that?" Captain McCord asked, sympathy in the question.

"Did we get a good description, a license plate?" Chase asked, dread weighing him down.

"I got a partial on the plates and the van was black, nondescript and long. No side windows." Isaac pointed toward the muddy road. "Already put out a BOLO. And we took down one of them. He's dead."

"So let's go over the scene," Chase said, walking Valor along the muddy tracks leading from the woods to the road. "They must have parked here behind those trees."

"Tracks lead from that area to the road," Isaac said.

"The rain's gonna wash away any evidence we might find," the captain called. "Do your best to find any trace you can before it's too late. We've got patrols out, watching for the van, and we've got ears to the ground. We've alerted Senator Eagleton about the security company. And we've sent team members and a cruiser to his house."

"Get someone out to the Jeffries estate," Chase said, his gaze sweeping the woods. If Jeffries had Erin, he'd probably try to kill her father and her, too. Unless he planned to take her hostage long enough to get away.

"You think *he* took her there?" Adam Donovan asked.

"Yes, I think he took her and yes, he might have taken her back there," Chase retorted, his impatience etched in a solid fear for Erin's safety. "He's been after her for six months and somehow, he's known our every move. He must have paid a pretty price to lure someone from that security team to his side."

The captain's expression sizzled with rage. "I think he knows too many people who have access to information that should have been kept quiet." He marched up to Chase. "What has she told you, Zachary? Anything that might shed some light on where he'd take her?"

"She wanted to go to Jeffries's estate," Chase said. "She remembered some more details of that night. Leon Ridge might have tossed the gun near an old barn on the back of the property."

"We can interrogate him again," Captain McCord said. "But he's pretty much told us everything. Of course, he could be lying about how he got rid of the weapon."

Chase nodded on that. "I had every intention of talking to Ridge again after she remembered the old barn. He didn't take her far from the crime scene."

"Do you want another go at him?" the captain asked.

Chase stared into the night, torn between going after

Erin and trying to get the truth out of Leon Ridge. "No. I want to find Erin. Just see if he'll come clean on where he might have hidden that gun. If Jeffries knows the gun is still missing, he'll want to clean up that loose end right along with killing Erin."

SIXTEEN

Erin sat in the dark, inside the big cold van, and hoped Chase would find her soon. They'd blindfolded her and tied her hands, but after they'd stopped on a dark road in the middle of nowhere, they'd removed the covering from her eyes. She had a bad feeling her journey through this nightmare was about to be over.

He'd kill her.

The congressman had pursued her since that night, sending assailant after assailant, and now she'd run out of time. Not surprisingly, she'd recognized the voice of one of the men who'd been waiting when she came out of the bathroom. They'd forced her through that window with the threat of killing Chase and his family.

The man who'd whispered those threats while he held a gun to her ribs had been on her father's security team. A mole who'd probably been sent to kill her at her father's estate and at all the other locations where she'd been kept. It all made sense now. They'd been watching her since the night she'd run away.

Chase, I love you.

She wished she'd said those words. Tonight, she'd had

a chance, but they'd circled and backed away, too afraid to take things to the next level.

Now she sat here in the dark, lost and afraid. Chase didn't know they'd forced her. He probably thought she'd just left again.

He found you once. He'll find you again.

Dear Lord, I'm so tired. I've tried to stay strong. I need to let this burden go and let You take over.

Erin squinted into the storm. She could find the strength to run one more time. She had to fight until her last breath. She owed that to Michael and...to Chase.

As the darkness surrounded her and the two men who'd abducted her paced back and forth outside the van, Erin remembered her shock that night. She'd almost blacked out a couple of times, especially when she'd realized the congressman truly had gone mad. Had she heard something somewhere in that fog of horror, something she'd blocked out? Maybe she'd remember some other detail that could help her.

She started crying and hated herself for doing it, but she'd reached the point of no return. "Enough," she whispered. "Enough."

She had to remember Chase and how they'd somehow found each other again. *We tried to stay apart, but God brought us back together.* Surely that had to mean something.

If I ever break free from Harland Jeffries, I will find you and I will never let you go again.

That silent promise to Chase echoed inside her head while she waited for whatever came next. Her pledge to Chase gave her the burst of strength she needed to survive.

But then a long black car pulled up and a man got out.

Erin's pulse slammed against her temple, her heart rate rushing ahead so fast, she felt dizzy. She would run one more time to get away from this man. She had to try.

One of the goons opened the door for the man. He leaned in, a dark smile on his haggard face.

"There you are," he said, concern in his voice, censure in his eyes. "Are you hungry? I suspect you didn't have time for dinner."

"I don't have an appetite." She stared at the dark, wet night.

"Erin, you need to keep up your health," Congressman Jeffries said. "Life is too short to become malnourished."

Erin stared into his gleaming eyes and prayed her life wouldn't be cut short tonight.

Captain McCord stood with most of the team around him. They'd all been brought in with their K-9 partners after McCord had called Chase to tell him they'd located the van that had taken Erin. It was parked on a logging lane behind the Jeffries estate. Small hope, but it was a start.

While Chase and a couple of others searched the Jeffries estate and the woods, the rest were going to guard the one person who might be able to find the missing murder weapon.

Leon Ridge.

He wasn't happy about this field trip. "Y'all are using me as a decoy. He's gonna kill me. He knows I hid the gun because I tried to kill him with it. Now you're protecting the woman and putting me out here with a bull's-eye on my back."

"Shut up," Adam Donovan said. "You made some bad

choices and that's why you're standing here. Help us out and see where it goes from there."

Chase checked his weapons and made sure Valor's protective vest was securely buckled. Valor sat still, his ears up and his eyes watchful.

"Come on, boy," Chase said to the eager canine. "We're going to find our favorite person." Then he took off with Valor along the trail toward the woods. Being with Erin again had brought out something else he'd tried to hide. He loved Erin. He would always love her. But he had to get this case done and out of his system before he could tell her that. He should have told her tonight when they'd been so close. He'd believed she'd left again when she'd been taken. When would he learn that she loved him, too? That she needed him to believe in her, too?

Taken once by social status and prestige. Taken tonight by an evil man who wanted to hang on to both those things. Chase would find her and he'd never let her go again, no matter what.

That's what she'd said to him. *Believe in me, no matter what.* He clung to that now and held tight to the hope of finding her alive.

SEVENTEEN

Erin's pulse quickened as the driver turned the dark vehicle onto the winding paved road up to the Jeffries estate. Thunder boomed over the hillside and gray clouds made the wee hours of the night seem desolate and dismal. Dark memories swirled around her like black lace, tickling at her consciousness with hisses and taunts.

Her words to herself. *You let him die.*

Congressman Jeffries, talking to her in that patronizing, controlled tone the night he'd killed his son. *"I can't let you live, Erin. I'll have to make it look like you did this. It's the only way."*

Her voice screaming into the night. *"Please, please, let me call someone. Let me help him. He's going to die."*

He did die. He died right in your arms.

You could have saved Michael.

You should have run away before it was too late.

The congressman shouting orders to Leon Ridge. *"Shoot me in the arm, so it'll look as if she did it. Then get her out of here. And take care of her. Permanently."*

She'd relived the angry words and her own guilt over and over for the past six months. Michael's dying gaze had stayed with her. And even now as she dreaded being back in this place, she remembered details she'd tried hard to forget.

He'd tried to say something.

Erin could see it clearly now. Michael's bloody hand gripped her jacket. His frantic gaze moved from her to the table.

"Juan."

He'd called out Juan's name. That forgotten memory shouted out at her with each twist of the road. She'd connected on it briefly the night Chase mentioned Juan Gomez to her, but now she *was* positive Michael had been trying to tell her about Juan.

He'd said "Juan," and then his frantic gaze had shifted to the table. "There."

Erin closed her eyes and tried to remember the patio table.

Papers! She'd seen a set of papers lying on the table.

Had Michael been trying to tell her about the papers?

She turned toward Harland Jeffries, but the house loomed ahead of them, caught against the gloomy sky like a massive mausoleum. Could she do this? Could she go back to the place that had brought so many nightmares into her life?

She had to, for Michael's sake if nothing else. Michael deserved to have the people responsible for this brought to justice. He wouldn't have balked. Michael always found the truth. She had to do the same.

"We had such good times here, didn't we?" Congressman Jeffries reached for her hand and held it, the damp sweat from his palm causing her to shudder.

She couldn't speak. She tried to form the thoughts bottlenecking in her head in a crashing pileup. She could be wrong about all of it. The gun might be lost forever, thrown deep into the woods, or floating in a river somewhere. The papers could have been a bill the congressman was studying or some sort of contract he was working on.

"We're here," Jeffries said, his hand still caught in hers. He lifted a rifle up from the floorboard and strapped it over his shoulder. Then he pulled a handgun out from under his raincoat.

Erin closed her eyes and tried to draw another breath. All these months and now she was back here. She'd tried so hard to be strong, to build a case against Harland Jeffries so that she could prove her innocence. Would it finally end here tonight?

"You can't hide from me anymore, Erin. I brought you here because I thought this would be a fitting end for both of us."

"Not if Chase shows up." She turned to face the man who'd tormented her for so long. "The entire Capitol K-9 team will be looking for me."

"They won't find you in time, my dear. I've waited for this moment too long. By the time they arrive, you'll be dead. And I'll be gone. Gone away from everything I love."

Erin shivered, her body numb with a cold that wouldn't go away. How could she do this? She didn't want to die at this gloomy, sad place. She wanted to live and to love again.

She wanted to be with Chase again.

Then she thought of her beautiful, strong mother. Mom would want her to fight to the finish, to show courage in the face of tremendous odds. The only way she could come out of this whole was to face what she was afraid of most. And that wasn't Harland Jeffries or dying. Her worst fear stemmed from loving too much. She'd lost her mother. She'd lost Michael. What if she lost Chase?

She had to face that fear by staying alive to be with him.

God was with her. She had to believe that. Christ would give her strength.

So she took a deep breath.

It wasn't about the gun.

It was about those papers she'd briefly glimpsed on that table. And it was about finally facing her own horrible nightmares so she could bring Harland Jeffries to justice at last.

While the captain and several others walked with Leon Ridge as he tried to go back over his actions on that night, Chase and Valor combed the woods near the old barn over and over. The van they'd found was abandoned. Not a trace of anything, not even a clue from Erin.

What did he do now?

Chase mulled that over, but he wanted to get in there and get her out of this place. Things could turn ugly, even with a team hiding in the nearby woods around the vast property.

He checked in with the captain.

"We have to go in now," he said. "The less time we spend here, the better. If he doesn't have her inside that house, we have to start over."

Valor sat still with his ears lifted high as if he agreed with Chase's thoughts. They both needed to find Erin.

Lightning sizzled in a jagged line across the sky, followed by a boom of thunder that made Valor give him another glance. Full darkness settled around them, the air hot with a cloying dampness. Another round of storms would hit soon enough. Chase didn't intend to linger.

Captain McCord gave him the go-ahead to get closer in on the house. "Take Adam Donovan with you and we'll be nearby with Ridge. Do not go in without backup, you hear?"

"Yes, sir." Chase radioed Adam and soon they were stalking toward the back side of the large sloping yard around the Jeffries house.

Erin followed Jeffries into the house, her breath coming in fast, shallow gulps. The smell of lemon wax and sweet potpourri hit her nostrils, reminding her of how much time she'd spent here over the past few years.

To the right past the kitchen, the big comfortable den brought back memories of watching football games and movies, sometimes with Michael and his father and other friends. Sometimes alone with Michael.

She could almost hear Michael's laughter, could see him jump up when his team made a touchdown. Watch him throw popcorn when his team lost. Michael didn't like to lose.

But right now, she remembered his father's anger and the wild look in the congressman's eyes as he glared at her and his dying son, a few feet away from him on the big patio by the pool.

"Why did you bring me back here?" she asked, her voice echoing out over the silent house like a wail.

He clutched her arm, his hand as rigid and hard as a talon, the smell of his wet, sweaty clothes assaulting her. "Simple, my dear. You're my insurance policy while I search for something important. I decided if I can't get away then I will die here in the place I love. The place where my son died."

"Where have you been hiding?" If she could keep him talking, maybe he'd confess all to her. If she died with him, she'd at least die knowing the truth.

"Here and there, just like you," he retorted. "I just prefer hotels and country homes to running through the woods." He laughed and lifted his free hand in the air. "I've been back here several times. The matter of the gun—my gun—that Leon seemed to have misplaced forced me to take drastic, risky measures. Smart of him to confess so he could stay protected behind the jailhouse walls."

"But you sent lawyers to help him."

"I sent lawyers to delay him and to convince him to shut up. But that didn't work either. He has betrayed me. If I send anyone else, it will be to kill him."

Erin shuddered at that cold statement. So Leon had been willing to sit in prison rather than be out where this monster could find him. She couldn't blame him for that.

"And what about your other son?" she asked, wanting Jeffries to confess about Juan, too.

Harland Jeffries turned to stare down at her, his fingers digging into the sleeve of her hoodie. "I only had one son. Now shut up and move."

She shuffled in slow motion, but refused to look up the long hallway at the closed doors to the congressman's office.

He pushed her forward. "Toward the back and to the left. There's a stairway down to the basement that's hidden from sight."

Erin didn't ask why he was taking her to the basement. She knew this house just about as well as he did. Michael had shown her the hidden passages. One of them had led the authorities to the congressman's safe room, where they'd found strong evidence of his corruption. But there were other hidden closets and small rooms underneath this massive structure.

If only she could find something to prove the rest of his crimes. Or some way to make him confess so someone would know about it before it was too late.

They moved across the dark planked floors, each creak of the aged wood like a warning. The congressman's bodyguard touched a gloved hand to his phone flashlight, causing the shadows to scurry away.

"Leave us," the congressman told the big man. "I know my way around my own home. You need to guard the entryway."

The guard turned and walked back toward the front of the house.

"Everything looks the same," she said. "This house was always immaculate. You demanded that."

"Yes," he said in a conversational tone that indicated they might be going in to dinner. "I demanded the best from my staff, my constituents and my family. Michael disappointed me. Leon is a coward and Rosa only used me for her own gain. You let me down, too." He shook his head. "It's all such a shame, isn't it?"

"Yes," she retorted. "A terrible shame."

But she wasn't referring to the people he'd mentioned.

It was a shame that a powerful man had turned into a horrible, evil creature she didn't even know. It was a shame that Michael had to die because of this man's corruption and lies, and that she'd had to go into hiding for months now.

She thought of Rosa as they moved through the

kitchen. Poor Rosa, seduced by a man who'd had her killed in order to keep that power. Who'd killed his own son in order to keep the kind of power that made him think he was some sort of god.

Erin knew whom she could count on. But she also knew her time was running out.

You're his next victim.

Chase and Adam moved through the rain-soaked trees, their partners sniffing the ground and the air. When they reached a spot near the driveway, Chase heard footfalls moving away.

Valor alerted, his hackles rising. Adam's Doberman, Ace, growled low.

"Let me check it out."

Chase moved in front of Adam. He did a zigzag search through the trees, following Valor, his high-powered rifle at the ready.

"They must have brought her here in a car," he said when Adam returned without finding anyone. "But they must have hidden that vehicle. I think we alerted a foot guard."

Adam stilled Ace. "What now?"

"I need to get closer in," Chase whispered. "If Valor can pick up her scent, then we'll know she's somewhere inside that house."

"You go and I'll cover you," Adam said.

Chase nodded and moved through the tall shrubbery near the winding drive. "We've got to find Erin, boy."

Valor's ears perked up at the mention of her name.

Chase knew that feeling. His heart did the same thing.

When he heard a quick grunt and a thud behind him, he almost turned back, but Adam's voice in his ear alerted him to keep going. "One down," Adam said, his tone filled with victory. "Unconscious and cuffed to a tree."

Chase replied his acknowledgment and went on toward the looming mansion. When he reached the lush camellia bushes near the long columned porch, Valor alerted with a low growl.

Erin had to be in the house. But how was he going to get inside to find her?

She could hear her pulse in her ears, beating in a frenzied rhythm that had her dizzy with dread. Sweat beaded above her upper lip and moved like a sticky web down her backbone. She tried to inhale, but the cloying smell of the peach potpourri almost made her gag. She waited while the congressman opened the basement door.

"They took everything," he said in that same low, monotone voice. "All my important documents, my weapons, my laptops and anything they could find to implicate me for crimes I did not commit."

"I think you have that wrong," Erin said as he shoved her down the dark steps. "They have the proof they need to put you away for a very long time."

He tugged on a light, but it only flooded the big square room with a shadowy yellow gleam that showed off the cluttered shelves and creepy old furniture. The smell of something dank and musky replaced the scent of peaches from upstairs.

"They won't take me alive," he said. "I had to come back here one last time. Leon thinks he's so smart, playing games with me. But I'll make sure I take care of him tonight. And you'll be gone by then, too, dear Erin. Either with me or maybe even shot dead. A pity, but...you've caused me no small amount of inconvenience and aggravation."

"Inconvenience?" she shouted. "That's what you call me running for my life after I witnessed you killing Michael?"

He struck her, hitting her against her right cheek. She gasped and held a hand to her face. Warm, sticky blood colored her fingers.

"Shut up," he said on an angry growl.

Erin lifted her chin. "You won't get away with this."

"I've gotten away with much more," he retorted, the gun pressing against her ribs again.

Erin refused to panic. Chase would find her. She had to remember that. If anything happened—

She could feel the evil. She closed her eyes and wished she could blink them open and find herself safe with Chase, far away from here, and then she opened her eyes and decided she had to find a way out.

Congressman Jeffries had dismissed the one guard he'd allowed in with them, so she was alone with him. Now he grabbed her and shoved her toward a cabinet on a long wall of the basement, and then he hit a button on the wall. The cabinet moved to the left and a panel in the wall slid open to reveal a long narrow room lined with lighted glass cabinets. Empty glass cabinets.

The gun room. Erin had been down here once with Michael. He'd shown her some of the impressive weapons his father had collected over the years. One of those weapons had killed Michael. But that gun had probably never made it back to this room. She checked every shelf. Empty. Every drawer stood open and empty. Then she glanced behind her and saw the panel blinking near the door.

A security panel. These types of panels were all over the house. And…once when she'd been down here with Michael, he'd used the intercom to check with someone upstairs.

The intercom. Second button from the left? But she'd have to hold it down to speak into it. Or scream into it.

If she could activate the alarm system, that would at least make some noise. Would anyone hear?

Erin moved around the room, her mind whirling on how to find a way out. "I can't believe they'd take the weapons. They must have been looking for your gun." She glanced past the congressman and inched closer to the door. "Didn't you keep it in that fancy monogrammed box, the one back there on the last shelf?"

He pivoted and walked across the small space, giving her enough time to shift toward the partially closed door. She could take off upstairs or she could hit that button and hope someone would hear the alarm.

She was a foot away from the door when she felt his breath on her neck and the gun near her flesh. "Going somewhere, Erin?"

She turned to stare up at him, her right hand behind her, reaching, touching. "No. Okay, I thought about running, but… I'd never make it." She pretended to give in. "I'm afraid, Congressman. I don't want to die. What do you want from me? Why are we back here?"

Tears formed in his eyes, but he didn't try to drag her back to the other side of the room. "I want my son back, but we can't make that happen, can we?"

Erin backed up an inch and slid two fingers against the computer system that ran the whole house. Then she halted.

She needed to know the truth. Now. Before she died. "Why did you have to shoot Michael?"

Congressman Jeffries frowned, his eyes growing misty again. "I didn't mean to. He just made me so angry. Michael always had an exaggerated sense of justice, just like his mother. Had to prove everyone wrong, including me. He…kept harping at me about… Juan and Rosa. I paid her, you know. I paid her extra to help with expenses. But Rosa wanted more. I gave her gifts to keep her happy, but she expected me to care about *him*. She threatened to expose me, ruin me. Her demands became so unreasonable."

"He was your son," Erin said, moving around so she could see the security panel. "He needed a father."

"I couldn't claim that child," Jeffries said, each word cluttered with agitation. "She knew that. She agreed to that. But Michael brought papers for me to sign. He'd found out the truth and he wanted me to set up a trust fund for that…that annoying little boy."

Papers. Was that why he was back here?

"Where are those papers now?" she asked, hoping he'd forget everything but that. Hoping she could whirl and hit a button, any button on that panel, and then she'd run for her life. Again.

"I don't know," he said in a candid admission. "I thought maybe you might know, though. You need to tell me what you remember, Erin. Since my attempts to shut you up have failed, I decided to take matters into my own hands. I need those papers, and so here we are. I know you hid them somewhere. Did you and Leon conspire against me?"

"What are you talking about?" she shouted. "Why would I hide anything here in this horrible place?"

"Because you were always out to do me in," he said, his breath hissing like an electrical wire.

"I never did anything to you," she retorted, anger brimming over. "And I don't know what happened to those documents. Maybe Leon had someone take them."

"No, you're lying. You need to tell me what you did with the papers. You must have seen them lying there on the table that night."

"What does it matter now?" she asked, amazed at his lack of logic and reasoning. "Michael is dead and Leon is in custody. I only saw the papers once, on the patio table, and I've been running since then, so how could I have possibly hidden them? You've brought me back here for nothing, Congressman. They'll find me and then you'll have nothing left. Nothing."

He lunged toward her but stopped short. "Oh, but I have one thing everyone wants, my dear. You."

Erin kept talking, trying to stall him. "I'm not the one you want. You miss Michael, don't you?"

"He made me sign the papers," Jeffries shouted at her. "Told me he'd expose me himself if I didn't do it." He sighed, wiped at his eyes. "That brat stands to receive most of my fortune. Especially now that…my real son is dead."

So that explained it. Erin gulped a breath, wishing someone else could have heard this confession. "You killed Michael and forced me to run because you don't want Juan to have any of your money?" She shook her head and once again inched toward the control panel. "Rosa is dead. Michael is dead. Your staff is gone and your reputation is already ruined beyond repair. Leon is out there right now, searching for the gun and any bullet fragments that can prove he tried to kill me on your orders, and yet you've brought me here on a fool's mission because you're still worried about your money?"

Jeffries stomped toward her. "I won't let that little boy ruin what's left of my hard-earned fortune." He leaned close. "Leon isn't talking about that, but his silence won't save him. I know they have him out in the woods right now, trying to find the gun, but he'll be dead before he reaches that spot."

He grabbed Erin and shoved her back against the big steel door, causing her hip to hit hard. She winced at the pain and regained her footing before she turned to face him. "And what about me? You'll kill me just to prove a point? You think I have those papers? If I did, I would have turned them over to the authorities by now. It's over, Congressman. You've run out of options."

His chuckle sent a chill down her spine. "You'll be dead by the time they find me. Unless they let me take you with me, of course. Just until I get away from here. But if you tell me where those papers are hidden, I might be able to let you live."

She knew that was a lie. He'd make sure she never talked to anyone again.

"I don't know where the papers are," she said. "I remember seeing papers on the table, but—"

"Leon let it slip that you probably knew where the papers were hidden since they were lying there that night. He implied you'd hidden them here so someone would find them, so I'd be implicated in Michael's…accident."

Leon. Trying to save his hide. "Leon is lying to all of us," she retorted. "I haven't been back here since that night."

"How can I believe you?" he asked, stalking toward her. "You'll die if you don't help me."

"Not if I can stop you," she shouted. Then she whirled and hit the buttons on the security panel. When nothing happened, her heart sank and Erin took her last hopeful breath.

But then a green light danced across the console, silently announcing someone had entered the front door.

Her gaze crashed with Harland Jeffries's and he grabbed her and held her in front of him. "I think you're lying," he said on a slithering breath. "But it's too late for you now, Erin. It won't matter if you hide those papers here or anywhere else. You won't live to show them to anyone."

Chase made it to the front porch and tried the door. Then he reported back to Adam. "Door's open. I'm headed inside," he said. "Stand watch while I check around."

"Got it," Adam replied. "No sign of any more hostiles."

Chase slipped inside with Valor, his heart skipping a couple of beats. Darkness shrouded the mansion. Valor bristled and stood tall, his ears up, his nose in the air.

"Is she here, boy?" Chase whispered, praying they could find her in time. He hurried up the long, wide hallway, checking doors and rooms, all the while talking to Adam through the radio. Where had Jeffries taken her?

Adam reported back. "Chase, they found the gun hidden inside the barn floor and the crime-scene techs found the slug. It was near where Erin said, embedded in one of the barn planks. Looks like it's a match, but the techs will do a comparison in the lab. Ridge is sweating, though. He knows his freedom has gone down the drain."

"Roger that," Chase whispered. "Now we have to find Erin."

"I'm right behind you," Adam replied. "We all are. Found one guard hiding out in the garage."

Chase acknowledged that and kept searching. The team had always been behind him, even when he'd doubted everyone.

He went in, knowing he could count on the captain and everyone else to help him tonight.

When he didn't find anyone in the downstairs room, he started upstairs. But Valor tugged toward the back of the house.

And then, Chase heard a sound. A step against wood. A drawn-out echo of a door slowly opening. Maybe below?

The basement?

Waiting behind a door near the stairs, Chase silenced Valor and held his breath. When he heard footsteps hitting against boards, he checked his weapon and waited.

But he didn't have to wait long.

"Officer Zachary, I'm here with dear, sweet Erin. Won't you join us?"

Valor alerted and sent out a low growl. Somehow, Jeffries had heard them approaching.

Chase stared through the faint light and saw a shadowy figure standing near a wall toward the back of the house.

"Erin?" he called out. "Are you all right?"

"I'm here," she said. "I'm okay, but—"

"Shut up," the congressman said, advancing toward Chase. "I have a gun on her," he called to Chase. "I'll shoot her if you make one wrong move."

Lightning lanced like a spear through the sky, giving

Chase a visual. Valor growled and started barking. Chase couldn't shoot. He might hit Erin. And he couldn't release Valor. The congressman was using her as a shield.

"Let her go," Chase said, while the thunder and lightning clashed and opened a deluge of rain outside.

"Not just yet. I need something, and maybe my former aide Leon can help us since our dear Erin refuses to cooperate."

"What's that?" Chase asked, a hot wind moving over him from the open door. He switched on his radio and prayed the others would hear.

"A contract my son forced me to sign. Leon implied dear Erin had hidden those papers here to implicate me. Why don't you ask him about that? And soon."

"I'll see what I can do," Chase replied, sweat beading on his upper lip. "I need to radio to Ridge, okay?"

"Make sure that's all you radio. I'll kill her if one more person walks through that door. You know I will."

Chase believed the man. "Erin, hang on," he said.

"Just do it," the congressman shouted. "Before I lose my patience entirely."

The house went dark again, but one brief clash of lightning lit the sky long enough for Chase to advance a step or two. The hallway was empty now.

Chase made the call to Captain McCord. "He has Erin and he thinks she knows about some papers she saw that night. Ridge told him Erin might have hidden the papers here as proof against the congressman's claims. A contract that Michael had him sign. Proof, sir. Final proof. He brought her here to find the contract. He wants to talk to Ridge, or he'll kill Erin."

"We've moving in dark," the captain replied. "I'll talk to Ridge."

"Roger that." Chase ended the call and whirled back toward the kitchen. But Jeffries was now standing in front of the office, Erin in front of him.

"Call off your dedicated team," he shouted. "I've decided since you alerted too many people, I just need to get out of here. With Erin. You've ruined my plans, but I always have a plan B."

"Not this time," Chase called. He slowly leaned his rifle against the wall and brought out his handgun. "Leon Ridge showed my captain where he hid the murder weapon. And we found the slug that will match up to your gun. With Leon's testimony and Erin's, too, we'll send you away for a couple of lifetimes at least." He inched up the hall. "You will never make it out of here, Congressman."

"I said I'm leaving," the congressman called. "And I meant it."

He'd moved from room to room, zigzagging through the connected rooms and making it hard for Chase to get a bead on him. But each time Chase saw Jeffries, the man had Erin in a vise grip he used like a shield.

Chase held his gun trained on the shadowy figure. Valor lifted his head, a low growl emitting from between his bared teeth. "Don't make me shoot you, Jeffries."

"How about I just shoot you instead," the congressman called. Then he lifted the gun he held.

Chase heard a whish of sound and then fell to the floor, his gun clattering loudly as it hit the marble hallway. Stunned and writhing in pain, Chase searched for his weapon, his hand touching the hardwood floor. Valor started barking, but he went down in a whimper. He tried to get up but whimpered again and collapsed in a lump near Chase.

Then the man who'd disabled both of them came toward Chase like a figure out of a horror show and kicked Chase's gun across the hall, out of reach.

Erin screamed, but Jeffries now had an assault rifle aimed at Chase. "Shut up or I will blow him and that dog away."

Chase moaned and reached out a hand.

Erin's stomach roiled with all the force of the raging thunder in the heavens.

"What have you done?" she asked Jeffries, knowing everything he'd done. She realized the gun he'd held on her had been a Taser weapon. She could have gotten away, but it was too late now.

He grabbed her and shoved her back toward the basement stairs.

Erin screamed and struggled to turn around and take one last look at Chase. He tried to stand, but fell back to the floor, his hand reaching out toward her before the congressman shoved her around the dark corner and down the basement stairs.

"Erin?" Chase's weak call moved up the hallway.

"Chase, I'll be okay. I promise. I'll find a way."

"You should have kept running," Harland Jeffries whispered in her ear. With a cruel twist on her arm, he pushed her ahead of him, the steel of a gun pressing into her ribs.

"Chase," she said through a sob. "Chase… I'm so sorry."

"As well you should be," Jeffries said. "Now get down these stairs."

The congressman shoved her into the gloomy basement and slammed the door shut behind them and latched it, and Erin accepted that she might not ever see Chase again.

EIGHTEEN

Chase lay immobile for a few minutes, the effects of the Taser's electroshock slowly wearing away. Erin! He had to find Erin.

Hitting his radio, he called into the speaker, "Get in here! He's taken Erin."

He crawled toward the spot where the congressman had shoved his gun. Then he managed to stand, the vertigo making the room spin. Grabbing a door facing him, Chase lifted himself up and searched the dark hallway. Then he saw Valor.

"Up," he called, his voice weak. "Valor, go."

The dog whimpered and lifted his head. Had the congressman drugged him with a tranquilizer gun? Or had he used the Taser weapon on the canine?

When Chase heard boots hitting the porch, he headed to the front, but the door crashed open. Then the house filled with officers and canines.

Adam Donovan rushed to Chase. "Which way?"

"Basement," he said, pointing. "I'm fine. Go. Go!"

Adam and his K-9 partner, a Doberman named Ace, stomped off toward the back. McCord and several others broke apart, left and right, to sweep the first-floor level of the house.

"Valor's down," Chase said. "Either stunned or doped. What took so long?"

"We had some setbacks," John Forrester shouted. "Dogs got restless, so we did a search in the woods."

"He must have planted some kind of scent to mess with them," Adam Donovan added as he hurried back to them. "But we did find a couple more guards scrambling to get away."

"We'll take care of him, Chase," someone shouted. Isaac Black.

It looked as though the entire team had been in on this. Chase was grateful for that.

"I lost her, Captain," Chase said. "But I'm going after her."

"Whoa." McCord tried to hold his shoulder, but Chase wasn't about to sit this one out.

"He brought her in here, sir. I'm getting her out."

McCord studied him for a minute and then nodded. "Get your head straight and go. We'll spread out and catch up with you after we finish searching the house."

Chase hurried to check on Valor. But the big dog lifted his head, stood up and barked as if to say, "I'm okay." Then he sat back and finally curled onto the floor, his head still up.

"Stun gun," Adam called while he moved around. "We found it near Valor. He's up but not quite ready to go."

All of this happened in a matter of minutes, but to Chase it felt like hours. He checked his weapon and started updating while he hurried toward the basement.

"I think he took her down there to an exit door."

McCord followed. "We have Ridge in the patrol car."

"He decided not to wait to talk to Ridge," Chase said. "The man's deranged. He thinks Erin knows something about a contract he signed, and that she purposely planted it here for us to find."

McCord nodded. "Ridge knows all about it. He threw Erin under the bus on that one, hoping the congressman would bring her here and kill her. But he's singing now. Afraid we'd hand him over to Jeffries."

"Where are the papers?" Chase asked as they fanned out through the empty basement.

"Ridge had his helper take them that night. They're in a safe-deposit box at a local bank. We're sending someone to verify that right now."

Chase didn't bother answering. He was on his way to the basement door when his cell buzzed. His heart thumped a warning.

"Zachary."

"You need to listen to me, Officer Zachary."

Chase held up his hand to halt the others. "I'm listening."

"Good. I'm used to people doing my bidding, so you're wise to follow suit."

"If you hurt her—"

"Now, now. That's not listening. Threats won't work with me. As you can see, I always get my way. I decided I do want those papers."

Chase closed his eyes and took a calming breath, the rage burning through him giving him enough adrenaline to clear his mind. "We have someone retrieving the papers now. Let her go."

"I can't do that until I see those papers with my own eyes. I want to walk out of here with just a couple of things. My papers and… Miss Eagleton." A long sigh.

"I have your precious girl. But I need you to bring me my documents. Or you won't ever see her alive again."

Chase drew a hand to his forehead to steady himself. "Just give me Erin and I'll make sure the papers are destroyed."

"It's not that simple," Jeffries stated. "There are consequences and someone has to pay for that, too."

"Yes, well, how about *you* need to pay for that?"

McCord came up to Chase and shot him a warning glare. "Do I need to talk to him?"

Jeffries must have heard. "Tell Captain McCord I'm done with him. He let me down."

"I'll pass that on to the captain." Chase shook his head at McCord and tried to regroup. "Why do you need to take Erin out of here? We've put together a pretty good timeline on what happened that night. She didn't do anything wrong. She had to run for her life since Leon Ridge wanted her dead, too."

"Pretty good explanation, but not good enough to save my reputation," Jeffries shouted. "I'm ruined." Chase heard a shuffling noise and then he heard a small scream. "Ruined because Erin Eagleton had to show up unwanted. She ruined me. You all ruined me."

"Where are you taking her?"

"Why don't I let dear Erin tell you that?"

Chase waited, praying. "Erin?"

"I'm here," she said, her voice shaky. "I'll be okay. I know the truth now. Just get Leon out of there so he can tell the real story. We're in the woods—"

"She will not live!" Chase heard more shuffling. "If you don't get me what I need, I'll shoot her right now."

Chase mouthed *woods* to McCord. Then he grabbed the captain's sleeve and mouthed, *Check on Ridge.*

McCord went into action, motioning for the others to fan out and do another search. Then he motioned for Chase to buy more time while he got on his phone.

"Where are you planning to go?"

"Why are you wasting my time asking questions?" Jeffries shouted. "You can't stall the inevitable. Leon Ridge defied me and now he will pay for his betrayal. Erin defied me and she will pay. Even my own son betrayed me. After all I've done for this country and my state and those kids. All those poor, disillusioned children at All Our Kids foster home. I helped all of them over the years. All of them. Including your heroic Captain McCord."

"Except one," Chase said. "Congressman, there's still time to work something out. You have another son, remember?"

"No. No. That boy will never be a true Jeffries. Nothing will ever be the same, and someone has to pay. I want you to call off those dogs and that SWAT team your commander has already alerted."

Chase swallowed the bile forming in his throat. "Okay, all right. I'll bring you the papers. Just…don't take Erin with you. She can't hurt you anymore and you don't need to hurt her any longer."

"Someone has to pay," the congressman said again.

The phone went dead.

Chase pocketed his phone and described the conversation. "He has her somewhere on this property and he wants us to exchange the contract for Erin. He must have taken her through the basement exit. He's gone from irrational to delusional. He knows it's over."

McCord kept barking orders. "It might not be logical to us, but we have to do as he wants until we can corner him." He started issuing commands about perimeters and coordinates, but Chase wasn't listening.

"Zachary, don't be stupid," the captain called. "Wait!"

"With all due respect, sir, I waited long enough."

Then he ran up the stairs and started toward the back of the house. When he heard a *woof,* Chase bolted back around to where an officer was sitting with Valor. Valor came trotting toward him.

"No, boy, stay," he commanded. Valor stood firm, his dark eyes full of a resolve and determination that almost broke Chase. This canine had the heart of a warrior and the strength to overcome any obstacles.

"Let's go find her," Chase said, deciding he could be the same. Jeffries wanted the last shred of evidence, but that didn't matter now. He was guilty. And it could be proved in court.

He and Valor took off out the door, the storm scurrying after them in a slash of lightning and thunder that danced across the heavens.

Erin gritted her teeth against the biting rain. They tromped through a trail deep inside the forest behind the Jeffries estate. She'd tried to leave clues, but with little on her, and with the congressman holding her in front of him, it wasn't easy. She had no sense of direction or time or hope.

She had only a prayer.

Please, help us, Lord. Help all of us.

She didn't try to speak or persuade him. Harland Jeffries was too far gone for that. He was a desperate, deposed dictator who was used to having his way. He'd only pretended to be a dedicated policy maker and politician.

"It's your fault," he said to her, his words hissing

through the air. "Making me run like a common criminal." He shoved her forward, and Erin held on to her wet, drooping hoodie. "You should have minded your own business that night. I could have pinned this on Leon since he had already threatened me—about that Rosa woman."

Erin struggled to stay on her feet, her hands grasping for anything to hold her up. When her jacket fell forward, she noticed the weight of her notebook in her pocket.

And regained some of her hope.

If she could distract him, she could leave a trail.

"Why did Leon threaten you?"

Jeffries stumbled behind her just long enough for her to pull the soggy notebook out of her pocket. Hiding it against her stomach, she carefully flipped it open and started peeling off paper while she stomped and shifted to muffle the noise.

The rain aided her cause, so she kept talking. "I mean, you didn't care about Rosa. You didn't have anything to do with her death, right?"

He stopped and yanked her around. Erin barely had time to put one hand in her pocket. "You can't play games with me, Erin. You must know by now that this all started with that ungrateful woman. She wanted more money and when I wouldn't give it to her, she told me she'd just run off with Leon and that they'd tell the world the whole story."

Erin backed away, her hands in her pockets, shoved together over her notebook. "So if I hadn't shown up that night, you would have called Leon to the estate anyway and he'd be the one being accused. But you tried to pin this on me."

She let out a chuckle. "Too late, Congressman. Leon's confessed to everything and he's implicated you, too."

He let out a low wail of frustration and then straightened and pushed her forward.

"Yes, well, Leon will regret his bad decisions soon enough." He moved in a small circle, his dark form a shadow in the gray-black of the forest. "Michael heard Rosa and me arguing, so he kept digging and pushing me until it was just too much. He knew it, all of it. And he threatened to go to the authorities. My own son."

Erin realized he was heading back toward the front of the property. Why?

She had to keep him talking. "Michael was trying to do the right thing after he found out that Juan was his half brother." She placed one hand over the other in her deep pocket, tearing away at pages.

The congressman shoved at her again. "The right thing? This is Washington, DC, Erin. Nobody ever does the right thing."

Erin thought she saw a light's beam behind them on the path they'd just traveled. "Some of us still believe in doing what's right, Congressman Jeffries. We try to do what's best for everyone, not just ourselves."

He slammed against her and almost knocked her down. "Shut up! I have one last thing to take care of before you and I wait on that infernal contract."

Holding Erin in front of him, he lifted the rifle strap off his shoulder and stared through the weapon's scope. Erin screamed and closed her eyes. She heard the swish of a silencer. When she opened her eyes, the man beside her had a soft smile on his face.

Jeffries stared through the scope. "Goodbye, Leon, my old friend. Go to your precious Rosa now."

Had he shot Leon?

When his cell buzzed, Erin saw her chance to either run or drop pieces of papers everywhere. The man couldn't conceive that he was finished. Done.

But she couldn't risk being shot in the back. Not when she knew Chase was so close.

She waited, praying that Chase wasn't far behind them. And while she waited, she took slow, measured movements to make sure someone would know they'd been on this muddy, rocky path.

Because if they didn't come soon, she was about to run for her life once again.

NINETEEN

"So the chopper is bringing the papers from the safe-deposit box Leon told us about. We'll retrieve the papers, and Jeffries will get on the chopper after he sees the papers. We get Erin out of there and then we take out Jeffries." McCord shouted over the wind. "Zachary, you get out there and make the exchange and get Erin, but…let him go. We'll take him down."

Chase listened and nodded, but he wanted to keep moving. He couldn't be sure Erin and Jeffries were on this path. The dogs had followed the trail in spite of the wind and the rain. Now the rain had settled to a light drizzle but the paths were muddy, slippery and nasty. Hard to pick up a trail.

Captain McCord had called in one more favor with General Meyer. The chopper would set down on Jeffries's private landing area so Chase could make the exchange. Jeffries's precious papers for Erin. McCord had called Jeffries to let him know they had what he wanted.

The snipers were already surrounding the area, with an order to shoot to kill if necessary. Jeffries had caused enough problems. He was a wanted criminal and he'd covered his crimes for far too long. He'd killed his mistress and his son, and he'd tried to kill Erin, too. He had nowhere to hide.

So now they were spreading out through the woods in a net that would capture a madman. And save the woman Chase loved.

McCord came running up to Chase. "More news, son. Leon Ridge is dead. Shot with a silenced high-powered rifle."

"I thought we were guarding him," Chase replied, fear for Erin ramping up.

"We were. Had guards surrounding the car. He leveled him with a single kill shot right to the head. Shattered the side window into the patrol car."

Chase listened to the captain and then headed out again on the same path, ahead of the pack. The wind and rain slashed at him with a razor-sharp assault, but he kept moving.

He and Valor stomped through the mud, the canine stopping here and there to do a ground search. When Valor alerted a few yards ahead of the others, Chase held his flashlight down so he could study the roots and muddy dirt.

The light hit on something in the mud. A few shoe indentions and something else. Chase squatted and ran his gloves over the wet dirt. Paper. Little torn pieces of paper tossed just off the muddy trail. He lifted one jagged, tattered slip. Black ink smeared across the curled edges. The handwriting caught his eye.

Pages from Erin's journal.

"Good job, Valor," he said, rewarding his partner with a quick pat and a hug. "Let's get going."

They kept at it, Chase shining the light and Valor

sniffing out more pieces of the journal. Erin was leaving them a trail that told more than just her location.

The journal that she'd carried with her all of these months held her thoughts and her fears, but now it might help to save her life. All the more incentive for Chase and Valor to find her and bring her home.

Erin heard a chopper off in the distance. Exhausted, wet and cold, she saw the first rays of dawn and what looked like a clear sky. Had they really been out here most of the night? It did seem like an eternity since Jeffries had taken her off the path and through streams and hills to hide their scent. Every now and then, she thought she heard footsteps behind them. But maybe that was just the echo of her prayers.

"Why don't you give yourself up?" she asked Jeffries. She'd tried to figure out a way to run, but with the darkness and his threats to shoot to kill, she decided to wait until the last possible moment.

And first light.

If she knew Chase, he'd have every law officer within a hundred-mile radius stalking through these woods to get to her before Jeffries could kill her. That would give her the chance she needed.

"I can't give up, so I need you as insurance, dear Erin," the congressman said as they moved down toward an open meadow. "I have to get away for good this time, with the only papers that can prove Juan is mine. Your Officer Zachary is bringing my documents to me in exchange for your life."

Chase would do that for her. She loved him so much.

Erin wondered why Jeffries hadn't just gotten rid of the gun and the contract that night instead of asking Leon to wound him. "You trusted the wrong man to help you destroy the evidence," she said. "I guess you figured you could intimidate Leon into doing anything you wanted, but you were wrong."

Growing angry again, he grabbed her by the arm. "I trusted you, too, even when I told my son you didn't really love him."

"I obviously loved him more than you did," she retorted.

He slapped her and then dragged her down a cluster of rocks and saplings. Erin's arm burned in a twisted protest as her body hit against the jagged rocks and sharp twigs in a stabbing, grinding rag-doll descent. Gritting her teeth so she wouldn't cry out, Erin refused to show any more fear.

Then she saw the chopper blades swirling in the faint light of dawn. She had only a few minutes to make a run for it.

Chase and Valor topped the hill near the meadow as the sun's first piercing yellow rays crested the horizon to the east. He saw the chopper waiting on a level part of the big, open field. Searching the nearby wet woods, he rubbed at his eyes and repeated the silent prayer that had screamed through his thoughts for hours.

Help me to do my job to the best of my ability, Lord. Help me to save the woman I love.

Behind him in the dense woods, the entire Capitol K-9 team waited along with a SWAT team. McCord had warned Chase that Jeffries might force Erin up on that chopper and hold the pilot at gunpoint, but that was not going to happen.

When his cell buzzed, he ducked down to answer.

"Zachary, our shooters can't get a bead on Jeffries. He's making sure he has Erin too close for comfort."

"Roger that," Chase said. "Sir, please don't let anyone get trigger-happy. I have to get down there and pry Erin away. Valor will help with that, so I don't need anyone getting ahead of the game."

"Not a chance. We've worked too hard to keep this woman alive." Then a pause. "And… I owe you that much for doubting you."

Chase wasn't worried about doubts right now. "I think I can get to her. Valor loves Erin. He can take down the congressman and…she can run."

Erin had developed a knack for running, but Chase hoped to end that trend today. The next time she had to run, he wanted it to be straight into his arms.

"We'll provide backup on that," the captain said.

Chase closed his phone and waited. The timing had to be just right.

Erin cringed when she saw the black chopper waiting with whirling blades in the level center of the big meadow. Jeffries probably waited here for deer to cross the meadow during hunting season. She could almost imagine this angry, deranged man taking aim on a beautiful creature and bringing it down.

"It's time to move," he said, glancing around. "If your young man doesn't hurry, he'll find you dead and me gone."

"I thought you wanted the last of the evidence," she said, trying to stall him. "You have to meet Chase for the exchange. Your papers are on that helicopter, right? You'll be free soon. Don't you want that?"

"I do, but…it doesn't much matter now, does it?" He

gave her a glassy-eyed stare. "You just need to die, Erin. You can spend eternity with Michael, wherever he is."

Anger jarred Erin's adrenaline awake. Did this man think he could kill her in cold blood and then get away? Would he force her on to that helicopter?

He yanked her by her arm, sending a shattering pain throughout her shoulders and back. "Let's get this over with," he hissed in her ear, spittle at the corner of his mouth.

He shoved her out into the clearing and then brought his rifle up. Using her as a shield, he walked them toward the middle of the meadow. "Don't try to run. I'll maim you for life and make you wish I'd killed you."

Erin closed her eyes to that threat and thought about Chase and how he'd held her and comforted her, even on that first night when he'd found her. Even when he'd doubted her. Even when he hadn't quite forgiven her for leaving him behind.

She longed for that kind of unconditional love, and when the image of Christ came into her tired, scared mind, Erin found the last shreds of her strength. She did have that kind of love.

And if the worst happened, she'd take that love any day over the threats of a madman.

With that comforting thought front and center, she didn't struggle and she didn't try to run. Because she knew the truth and she believed with all of her heart that Chase would come for her.

"Hey!"

Chase called out over the row of the chopper, his heart swirling and twirling in a beat that moved much faster than those rotating blades.

Jeffries pivoted, Erin out in front of him, his wizened face hard with anger and the sheen of madness. Holding the rifle against Erin's back, he inclined his head.

Chase and Valor started across the meadow, Chase calculating how to grab Erin away so one of the snipers could bring down the congressman.

Jeffries saw Valor and shook his head. "Leave the dog behind, Zachary."

Chase stopped. "Stay," he commanded.

Valor looked confused, but the big dog stood still and then sat to wait, his eyes on Erin.

Chase was ten feet away from where Jeffries had pulled Erin underneath a mushrooming oak tree. Which made it hard for the snipers to get a good shot. The helicopter's blades caused the tree to shake and shimmy, but it was far enough away that they should be able to make the exchange.

"I'm here," Chase said, his gaze hitting on Erin. He pointed to the chopper. "Your papers are inside."

"I need proof," Jeffries said. "Let's walk to the helicopter, and you can show me."

Chase nodded. He'd do whatever it took to get Erin away from this deranged man.

Erin looked remarkably calm, considering she had an assault rifle pointed at her backbone—her eyes were as translucent and clear as the newborn sky. She gave him a quick, concise smile and then stood still by Jeffries.

"Did you bring the original contract?"

He nodded at Jeffries. "Yes"

They hurried to the helicopter, and Chase indicated to the officer inside to hand him the envelope.

Once that was done, Chase turned to Jeffries. "Here."

Jeffries shook his head. "Open it."

Chase moved closer, his every instinct telling him to run and grab Erin away from this monster. But he couldn't do that. Not yet.

When he got closer, the congressman pushed Erin forward. "Get the envelope, Erin. If you make one wrong move, I'll shoot both of you."

Erin nodded and gave Chase another quiet stare.

"Don't try anything," Jeffries called. "Give her the envelope and let her bring it to me."

Chase shook his head. "No. That wasn't part of the deal. I get her, and you get the envelope. Take it and get out of here."

"Do it my way, Officer," Jeffries called. "Or she will get a bullet to her back."

A static came through his earbud. "Can't get a good shot. Tree's blocking from this angle." Then another voice. "Repositioning."

Erin was a foot away. She reached out to take the envelope. "Just let me go, Chase. Let me go."

"Never." He handed her the package, their fingers brushing together like a whisper of a kiss. "Don't give up, Erin."

"Never," she repeated back to him.

And then she turned and shoved the envelope toward the congressman.

After that, the world shifted. The congressman pulled her with him toward the chopper. "We have to get away."

Chase called after them to stop. "Hand her over, Jeffries."

The congressman laughed and kept going. But the chopper pilot wasn't planning on giving him a ride. The blades whirled as the chopper lifted.

Chase was about to pull his own gun when he heard

an angry growl, and then something fast and furry leaped into the air and ran toward the chopper.

Valor.

Chase pulled out his gun and shouted, "Jeffries, let her go."

The congressman forced Erin toward the helicopter, his gun now turned on Chase. Chase ran toward the chopper, ready to shoot to kill, but Jeffries fired a round of haphazard volleys that whizzed in the air and tore through the ground all around Chase.

Erin screamed and tugged, trying to get away. Chase ran behind Valor, desperate to help Erin.

But before he could get there, Valor hurled himself at the congressman and sank his teeth into the man's leg. Harland Jeffries screamed and writhed, falling on the ground in agony, his rifle firing up into the early-morning sky.

Chase screamed again. "Erin, get out of there." Waving his hands at her, he kept calling, "Erin?"

She scrabbled away and started toward him, but Jeffries reached out a hand and caught her leg. Valor sank his teeth in and tore at the man's thigh, dragging him until he had to let go of Erin. She took off, running toward Chase.

The chopper lifted away and circled back, and then landed again and sat with blades whirling. Then the field swarmed with law-enforcement people. Captain McCord made it to Jeffries first and commanded Valor to release, his rifle trained on the weeping, writhing man at his feet.

"It's over," the captain said as he hauled Jeffries up. "You'll be serving in a different district from now on, but with a much longer term."

Chase saw Erin running toward him, Valor right by her side.

It was the most beautiful sight in the world.

He met her there in the dawn of a new morning and took her into his arms.

EPILOGUE

A crisp fall wind lifted out over the hills and valleys surrounding the brand-new barn Captain Gavin McCord had built on the ranch he'd purchased in Virginia. The captain had the barn to store equipment and hang out in, and a new house and a new facility nearby for the All Our Kids foster home. With General Meyer's help and funding from the Eagleton Foundation, not to mention donations coming in from all over the country, the new home would be renamed the Michael Jeffries Memorial Foster Home.

Chase sat with Erin inside the big open barn, his arm around her waist, his nose buried against her floral-scented hair. The whole team had been invited here to celebrate this new structure after they'd spent a lot of weekends helping the captain to build it.

But today was about much more than a new barn.

It was about a new beginning.

The barn was decorated with colorful fall flowers, and what Erin called garlands draped across the entryways and windows. Candles burned brightly in two tall glass holders, and the scent of new wood mixed with the sweet smells of the big cluster of bright orange, yellow and burgundy flowers centered at one end of the building.

Several rows of folding chairs parted in the middle to leave room for a center aisle. And soft music played by a quartet of fiddlers caused all of those waiting to stand and turn toward the back door.

Virginia Johnson came up the aisle first, carrying a simple bouquet of bright yellow flowers, her garnet-colored dress making her look less of a mousy woman and more of a stunner.

Chase smiled at Erin and saw approval and surprise in her pretty blue eyes.

The captain waited up by the makeshift altar with the local minister, looking more nervous than Chase had ever seen the man. And then a hush fell over the crowd gathered beneath the muted lights.

Cassie Danvers glided up the aisle in a lacy white dress that Erin had described as simple but elegant. Chase didn't know elegant from an elephant, but he had to agree Cassie looked nice.

He glanced from the smiling bride to the big man who'd stood by his side for six long months. Captain Mc-Cord looked happy. And in love.

"Can you believe this?" Erin whispered, her hand in his as they sat to watch Cassie and Gavin say their vows.

"Yes and no. I can't believe I'm sitting here with you."

She smiled and gave him a quick kiss. Then Chase listened to the sacred vows being said, his eyes on Erin. She teared up and tried to blink. But he couldn't resist reaching up to catch a single tear as it escaped down her cheek.

"I love you," he said.

"I love you back," she replied.

They'd said those words over and over, beginning with

the day they'd watched Harland Jeffries being carted off
in a paddy wagon. They'd held each other tight against
the world, including the fellow officers who had to take
their complete statements yet again and the relentless
reporters who wanted to interview them or write books
about them. They stood firm against Erin's father, when
he'd finally sat them down at his house and surprised
them by giving them his blessings.

And now, after seeing the captain and his bride so
happy together, Chase knew he wanted the same with
Erin.

After the ceremony was over, they all filed out of the
barn to a pretty gazebo where a white wedding cake decorated with what Erin called "eatable mums" sat centered
on a lace-covered table, waiting to be served up.

"Cake," Nicholas Cole said, pointing to the tiered con-
coction before he pointed to the other cake. "And K-9s."
His fiancée, Selena Barrows, giggled. They were still
planning their wedding, too.

They all laughed at the groom's cake, a chocolate sheet
cake with miniature dogs placed across the top in what
looked like a training yard. Big yellow letters stated Capitol K-9 to the Rescue.

"And barbecue," Isaac Black called out. "I'm starving."

"You're always starving," his bride-to-be, Daniella,
said.

Everyone was here. Lana Gomez and Adam Donovan, who were going to be married in a month or so.
Lana now had custody of little Juan. Veterinarian Jonas
Parker with Brooke Clark. They planned to marry and
adopt more children to go with Jonas's son, Felix. And
several others, including still-recovering Dylan Ralsey,

his gunshot wound slowly healing, and serious but dedicated John Forrester.

Even Fiona Fargo, the redheaded whiz who'd worked lots of long hours to help them crack the Jeffries case.

Chase watched Fiona now—her bright blue eyes matched her peacock-embossed dress and high-heeled sneakers. When Chris Torrance walked up and winked at Fiona, Chase shot Erin a grin.

"I guess we can thank Fiona and Chris for giving all of us the love bug. I think they were the first couple to fall in love."

Everyone started clapping. "Like we didn't see that one coming," Dylan called out.

After everyone congratulated the captain and Cassie with cups of apple cider, Selena announced, "Hey, now that the captain is finally hitched, the rest of us can plan our weddings, right?"

"Right," Nicholas said with a shrug. "Out of respect for you, Captain McCord, we've all been holding off. But…it's on now, buddy. It is so on."

Chase laughed and clapped with the rest of them.

It *was* so on.

So he took Erin out onto the dance floor and while the fiddlers played a slow waltz, he danced with her and held her close. Then the music stopped and before he lost his nerve, he got on one knee and looked up at her.

Erin put a hand to her mouth. "Chase, what are you doing?"

He took in her shiny navy blue full-skirted dress and the sapphire necklace she wore. "What do you think, beautiful? I want to ask you something."

She gasped and looked around while everyone laughed and smiled. "What?"

He pulled out a modest diamond solitaire ring. "Will you marry me, Erin?"

"Of course she will," Selena called out. "Tell him yes, Erin, already."

"Yes, yes." Erin smiled through her tears while he put the ring on her finger. Then he stood and kissed her.

"Double wedding," Selena shouted before she sailed into Nicholas's arms.

Soon everyone was hugging Erin and shaking Chase's hand.

Captain McCord came up and touched a hand on Chase's shoulder. "I'm happy for you, kid."

"Thank you, sir."

The captain didn't have to say anything else. They both knew how blessed they were.

Chase turned back to Erin, and together they took a stroll toward the autumn sunset gliding over a nearby valley.

"I miss Valor," she said. "He should hear our good news."

"He'll be at the wedding," Chase assured her. "He wants to be the best man."

"I think that's a perfect plan," Erin said. She tugged him close and kissed him. "It's nice to be running toward the sun, at last."

And then she took Chase with her as they did just that.

* * * * *

SPECIAL EXCERPT FROM

Love Inspired
SUSPENSE

*When her son witnesses a murder, Julia Bradford and
her children must go into witness protection with the
Amish. Can former police officer Abraham King keep
them safe at his Amish farm?*

Read on for a sneak preview of
Amish Safe House *by Debby Giusti,
the exciting continuation of the
Amish Witness Protection miniseries,
available February 2019 from Love Inspired Suspense!*

"I have your new identities." US marshal Jonathan Mast
sat across the table from Julia in the hotel where she and
her children had been holed up for the last five days.

The Luchadors wanted to kill William so he wouldn't
testify against their leader. As much as Julia didn't trust
law enforcement, she had to rely on the US Marshals and
their witness protection program to keep her family safe.
No wonder her nerves were stretched thin.

"We're ready to transport you and the children,"
Jonathan Mast continued. "We'll fly into Kansas City
tonight, then drive to Topeka and north to Yoder."

"What's in Kansas?"

Jonathan pulled out his phone and accessed a
photograph. He handed the cell to Julia. "Abraham King
will watch over you in Kansas."

Julia studied the picture. The man looked to be in his midthirties with a square face and deep-set eyes beneath dark brows. His nose appeared a bit off center, as if it had been broken. Lips pulled tight and no hint of a smile on his angular face.

"Mr. King doesn't look happy."

Jonathan shrugged. "Law enforcement photos are never flattering."

Her stomach tightened. "He's a cop?"

"Past tense. He left the force three years ago."

Once a cop, always a cop. Her ex had been a police officer. He'd protected others but failed to show that same sense of concern when it came to his own family. The marshal seemed oblivious to her unease.

"Abe is an old friend," Jonathan continued. "A widower from my police-force days who owns a farm and has a spare house on his property. He lives in a rural Amish community."

"Amish?"

"That's right."

"Bonnets and buggies?" she asked.

He smiled weakly. "You'll be off the grid, Mrs. Bradford. No one will look for you there."

Don't miss
Amish Safe House *by Debby Giusti,*
available February 2019 wherever
Love Inspired® Suspense books and ebooks are sold.

www.LoveInspired.com

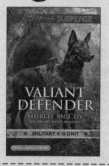

Love Inspired®

Save $1.00
on the purchase of ANY Love Inspired® book.

Available wherever books are sold, including most bookstores, supermarkets, drugstores and discount stores.

✂

Save $1.00
on the purchase of ANY Love Inspired® book.

Coupon valid until March 31, 2019.
Redeemable at participating retail outlets in the U.S. and Canada only.
Limit one coupon per customer.

52616176

Canadian Retailers: Harlequin Enterprises Limited will pay the face value of this coupon plus 10.25¢ if submitted by customer for this product only. Any other use constitutes fraud. Coupon is nonassignable. Void if taxed, prohibited or restricted by law. Consumer must pay any government taxes. Void if copied. Inmar Promotional Services ("IPS") customers submit coupons and proof of sales to Harlequin Enterprises Limited, P.O. Box 31000, Scarborough, ON M1R 0E7, Canada. Non-IPS retailer—for reimbursement submit coupons and proof of sales directly to Harlequin Enterprises Limited, Retail Marketing Department, 22 Adelaide St. West, 40th Floor, Toronto, Ontario M5H 4E3, Canada.

5 65373 00076 2 (8100)0 12404

U.S. Retailers: Harlequin Enterprises Limited will pay the face value of this coupon plus 8¢ if submitted by customer for this product only. Any other use constitutes fraud. Coupon is nonassignable. Void if taxed, prohibited or restricted by law. Consumer must pay any government taxes. Void if copied. For reimbursement submit coupons and proof of sales directly to Harlequin Enterprises, Ltd 482, NCH Marketing Services, P.O. Box 880001, El Paso, TX 88588-0001, U.S.A. Cash value 1/100 cents.

® and ™ are trademarks owned and used by the trademark owner and/or its licensee.

© 2019 Harlequin Enterprises Limited

LISCOUP08184